STEPHEN SOLOMITA

"Solomita really knows the city,
the heights and especially the gritty depths"
Los Angeles Times Book Review

"Our Find of the Year . . .
The tension Solomita creates is delicious."
Syracuse Post Standard

"Strikingly well-drawn . . .
Loaded with compassion for the tattered
humanity clinging to
the lower rungs of society.
His peeled-back views of crack houses,
rotting tenements and shelters
for the homeless
certainly seem authentic;
so do his feelings of sorrow and outrage."
The New York Times Book Review

"Solomita shines!"
Dayton Daily News

"Stanley Moodrow is one of the
more memorable cops
to come along in this or any other year."
Anniston Star

Other Avon Books by
Stephen Solomita

A TWIST OF THE KNIFE

FORCE OF NATURE

STEPHEN SOLOMITA

AVON BOOKS ◆ NEW YORK

AVON BOOKS
A division of
The Hearst Corporation
105 Madison Avenue
New York, New York 10016

Copyright © 1989 by Stephen Solomita
Published by arrangement with G.P. Putnam's Sons
Library of Congress Catalog Card Number: 89-30949
ISBN: 0-380-70949-X

First Avon Books Printing: September 1990

AVON TRADEMARK REG. U.S. PAT. OFF. AND IN OTHER COUNTRIES,
MARCA REGISTRADA, HECHO EN U.S.A.

Printed in the U.S.A.

RA   10 9 8 7 6 5 4 3 2 1

Special thanks to Jim Appello, Herb Goldstein, Mike Altman, Helmut Mendes and Bob Magrisso who gave me a close-up look at life as it's lived in the shelters, the welfare hotels and the subway tunnels.

For Ethan and Judy. Obviously.

This is a work of fiction. Despite the existence of a real New York City and a real NYPD. Example: the northern boundary of the real 7th Precinct in the real New York City is Houston Street. The northern boundary of the 7th Precinct in this novel is 14th Street. A word to the wiseguy.

POLICE DEPARTMENT: CITY OF NEW YORK

TAPE TRANSCRIPTION LABEL PD641-447 (4/85)

tape# 4377   case# MC201   loc 7th Pct

tape date 8/9/90   trans. date 8/9/90

transcribed by A. Pulliam

sig. *A Pulliam*

civ. emp. # 901-22-3345   badge # xxxxxxxx

pers: Det. Paul Kirkpatrick

   Det. Charles O'Neill

   ADA Leonora Higgins

   Angel Rodriguez

_____

_____

_____

_____

cross reference Major Cases 201

_____

_____

_____

DET. O'NEILL: (faint) one, two, three, four.

DET. KIRKPATRICK: (faint) Turn up the volume, asshole.

DET. O'NEILL: one, two, three, four.

L. HIGGINS: That's fine, Detective.

DET. O'NEILL: Date is August 9, 1987. Time is 9:35 A.M. Place is Bellevue Hospital, prison ward. Police personnel: Detective Charles O'Neill. Detective Paul Kirkpatrick. Assistant District Attorney Leonora Higgins. Angel Rodriguez, prisoner. Case number is MC201. Tape number is 4377. Okay, Miss Higgins. He's all yours.

L. HIGGINS: Mr. Rodriguez?

A. RODRIGUEZ: Yes?

L. HIGGINS: Mr. Rodriguez, do you understand that you have the right to have a lawyer present during this interview?

A. RODRIGUEZ: Cut the bullshit, lady. Just do the fucking thing, awright?

DET. KIRKPATRICK: Watch your mouth.

A. RODRIGUEZ: Fuck you, too, man.

DET. KIRKPATRICK: Okay, be a smartass, Angel. You got the upper hand right now, but in a couple weeks you're gonna be out on the street. Then your ass is mine.

L. HIGGINS: For Christ sake, Kirkpatrick, let's just get through the damn interview. Without the *macho*.

DET. KIRKPATRICK: (Pause. Laughter. Unintelligible.) Sorry, Miss Higgins. You go ahead and do your thing.

L. HIGGINS: Angel, I have to explain your rights before we can do the interview. And you have to answer out loud so the tape recorder can pick up your response. Even if you already know your rights. If you don't answer, which is also your right, you will have to remain in custody until or unless you can make bail. *Comprendo?*

A. RODRIGUEZ: Sure. The beautiful way you say it, even a spic like me could understand.

L. HIGGINS: I'm glad to hear that. Now, do you wish to have a lawyer present during this interview?

A. RODRIGUEZ: Ain't you a lawyer?

L. HIGGINS: Goddamn you, Rodriguez, if you don't get your act together in ten seconds, I'll walk out of here and let you rot. I mean right now. Do you understand that?

A. RODRIGUEZ: I understand that if I name the scumbag who blew away your policeman and that reporter on Delancey Street three days ago, you ain't gonna send me away for the hits you found on me.

L. HIGGINS: That's right, Angel. But in addition to the information (in fact, before I can ask you even one question about that night) you have to say the magic words. Now, do you wish to have an attorney, at no cost to yourself, to represent you while we conduct this interview?

A. RODRIGUEZ: No.

L. HIGGINS: Are you giving this information of your own free will?

A. RODRIGUEZ: Yes.

L. HIGGINS: Do you understand that the information you give here is an admission of guilt and in the event you refuse to testify against the man who committed these homicides, this interview could be used against you in a court of law?

A. RODRIGUEZ: Say what?

L. HIGGINS: It's simple, Angel. You're going to tell us who killed your pals on Delancey Street a few days ago. If we locate the man or men responsible, you're going to identify him in a court of law. If you change your mind, this tape we're making will be the same as a confession that, number one, you were at the scene to sell drugs. Number two, you were in possession of a substantial amount of a controlled substance. Number three, you are guilty of several C felonies, each punishable by a prison term, third offense, of fifteen years to life. Now, do you understand? Do you want a lawyer present during this interview?

A. RODRIGUEZ: No lawyer, lady. Shit, you gonna find out sooner or later who's doin' all the shootin' down there. Besides, I already talked to a lawyer and he says if I don't do this, I'm dead, so like I don't have no fucking choice. But I do got one question for you?

L. HIGGINS: Shoot.

A. RODRIGUEZ: Just for your fucking tape recorder, answer me this: if I agree to give you the name of the dude what blew them people away, you ain't gonna charge me with none of them crimes you named? That's the deal we made just for the fucking record?

L. HIGGINS: That's the deal. (pause) He's all yours.

DET. O'NEILL: Okay, Angel, why don't you start it up from just before you went down to the bridge. We'll ask questions as you go along.

A. RODRIGUEZ: I live in the projects on 4100 Columbia Street with my brother and his wife. On August 6, I got up for dinner about seven o'clock like always, then went out to do business. I was sellin' hits and the main place for hits is by the bridge on Columbia Street which is half a block from my house. The spot opens up after the car wash closes about 8:30.

L. HIGGINS: What are 'hits'?

A. RODRIGUEZ: Shit, lady. . . .

DET. O'NEILL: Just tell her, Angel.

A. RODRIGUEZ: Hits are like ups and downs, awright? (pause) Two pills, man, and they go up and down.

L. HIGGINS: What's in them?

A. RODRIGUEZ: How am I supposed to know that? I ain't no damn chemist and I don't know nothin' about what's in the hit. Alls I know is they get you colossal fucked up and people buy 'em. I'm a businessman. What else do I gotta know?

DET. KIRKPATRICK: Ain't you read the reports, Miss? It's in the goddamn reports.

(Unintelligible)

DET. O'NEILL: And our time ain't valuable?

L. HIGGINS: I apologize, Detective. I haven't studied Rodriguez' arrest reports. Our main concern, in this case, is homicide, not narcotics. But I should have studied the reports. I concede that. Somehow I never anticipated dealing with an unknown narcotic.

DET. O'NEILL: Unknown? Hits have been on the street for more than a year. The 'up' half is crank, Methedrine, and the 'down' half is Dilaudid, oxycodone, even codeine. Looks like the chemist's got supply troubles on the downside. Right now, hits sell for ten bucks and they're real popular with the white kids who drive in from the boonies. See, you can't shoot hits, so the kids don't have to feel like they're chickenshit about needles. By the way, hits are a narc's dream. Two controlled substances for the price of one. We catch 'em with hits, we charge 'em with two felonies.

L. HIGGINS: Very interesting. Hits? Who would have dreamed it. Angel, you can proceed.

A. RODRIGUEZ: First I meet my main man, Pincho Correa and we stroll down to the bridge. There's all businesses under the bridge during the day. There's even garbage men on the other side where they fix the trucks. But at night the white people go home and leave us to ourselves.

It's hot like a motherfucker that night, so we buy some beers at the *bodega* on the other side of Delancey Street, then dig in by the bridge to wait for the guinea to fall by with the hits. The delivery man's name is Little Ugly. That's so we can tell him from his muscle which we call Big Ugly. Both the dudes are Italians and they drop off every night around nine and pick up the left-overs and their piece of the action around two on weeknights, four on Friday and Saturday. This works out good for us two ways. One, we don't gotta carry money or hits with us during the day. Two, we got Italians protectin' us, so most times the bad boys leave us be. That's probly why I wasn't prepared for no action that night even though I shoulda seen what was comin' down.

Nine o'clock the man drives up in his midnight blue Seville and me and Pincho get inside. We're jus' goin' round the block so's we can count the hits. Sposed ta be four hundred in the sack, but it comes up short. Comes up three nine eight.

Now the Uglys is definitely bad people, but Pincho don't know no fear. Pincho say, "Yo, man, you short two hits."

Little Ugly say, "Be cool, brother. I got this Chinese bitch on East Broadway loves hits. Gets her pussy wet. Take it off the top."

Pincho don't say no more cause even if he got heart, he ain't crazy. Just seem more like they shoulda told us before we took the count.

Anyways they drop us off by the bridge and we go to work. There was already fifteen people waitin'. Dope been tight on the streets all this month and word with the junkies was hits could keep the pain away. We wasn't partial to no crowds and we cleaned up the junkies and asked 'em to move on.

Business got slow after that. It was so fucking hot the Puerto Ricans was spendin' their bread on cold beers. They didn't want no hits 'cause hits makes you sweat. That's the crank. Makes you sweat that real stinky sweat and nobody

wants to sweat even more than they're already
sweating when it's hot like that. Only real business we done was with the white kids. They come
rollin' up to the curb in they daddy's cars, open
the window, let the cold come pourin' out all over
me. Them little faggots didn't never sweat.

Around midnight, the two white bitches show
up, Marlene and Cindy. Young fine lookin'
bitches don't want nothin' more than a couple
hits and a big cock. Got feathers tied in their hair.
Little miniskirts. I'm sittin' on the curb and
Cindy walks right up until her cunt's starin' me
in the face. She say, "Angel, spare me a hit. I pay
you next week."

I say, "You stick around till we go home, I hold
out two hits and we party all night. Have a beer
while we waitin'."

She say, "Angel, I take you home tonight. Shit,
yeah. But lemme get started on my head, now.
That way I'll be ready when we get there."

What could I do? I put that hit in her mouth
like a priest layin' on the communion host. In
my mind, I was already tastin' them fine white
titties and probly that's why I wasn't ready when
the shit went down. I tell ya she was a fine lookin'
lady and she got her own apartment so I don't
gotta go back to my brother's house and do it in
the living room.

She takes a beer and she say she wanna party
hard all night. When she say 'hard,' she stops for
a second and smiles and I start prayin' them gui-
neas'll show up early. We ain't makin' no bread
anyway.

About 12:30 two white men come walkin' up
from the Drive. One I call Bennie. One I call Robert. This is the cop and the newspaper guy, but
to me they was just two more customers. They

got a six pack of Rolling Rock and we was out of
beers so when they offer, we take it and all sit
around drinkin'.

That cop, by the way, was super cool. He didn't
come on hard like you think a cop's gonna do.
But I tell you this for your fuckin' record: he do
his hits like everyone else. Right in front of me I
seen him down hits and I seen him break out into
sweats when the shit come on.

The other one, Robert, the reporter, look like a
little fag Jew writer from the first minute I seen
him. What kinda name is 'Robert,' anyway? Not
even Bob or Bobbie or nothin'. Only people I know
with names like 'Robert' is niggers and little
Jewboys and he definitely wasn't no nigger. Robert also did hits else we woulda caught onto him
right away. We didn' have no wholesale customers, if you take my meaning.

Fifteen minutes later this Chinaman name of
Ho Kong shows up with a friend I ain't seen before. I look at Pincho and he looks at me and he
shrugs. We calls the little chinaman Chung King
and all Chung King ever do is smile. Even the
first time when he showed with one of his boys
and Pincho told him in his face, "Don't never
bring no one, less we clear it first," all Chung
King do is crinkle up his fucking eyes even
smaller than they already are and smile. Nod his
head like a doll on the dashboard of my cousin's
Chevy. And damn if the next time he don't bring
somebody new. And the time after that. Couldn't
talk to him, so eventually we gave up. Never seen
no Chinese cop so what difference could it make?

Anyways, I got my back up against the stones
supportin' the bridge when Chungy drives up in
his old Buick looks about two blocks long. Roof's
torn. Bumper's pulled out. Rust every fuckin'
place. I was sittin' there with my arm touchin'

Cindy's arm, so far gone even this little shit is gettin' me hot. Robert and Bennie are standin' next to me, sippin' beers and waitin' for the hits to come on. Pincho takes Marlene's arm and walks her over to the Buick and tells Chungy go park the Buick around the corner and walk back. Chungy starts blowin' off in half Chinese and half English 'bout how he scared to walk around up here. Say the Puerto Ricans rob every Oriental north of Grand Street. Pincho just kicks the goddamn door and yells, "Park the bitch," and walks back to us.

"Man," Pincho say, "them gooks didn't make that good food they makes, they wouldn't have no use at all."

Wasn't all that funny, but we was high on the beers, so we start laughin'. Bennie say, "Yeah, but that sweet and sour shit is bad, bro. Got to keep them little yellow people cookin'."

Then I see this black dude walkin' over from his car. Big bad fucker. Not tall, right, but *mondo*. Kind of nigger make your balls crawl up into your asshole. His name's Kubla and I know his rep's as bad as his looks, but I also know he's been around the scene forever and he's aware that me and Pincho are connected to the Italians, so I'm not expectin' no problems. That's probly why I missed it cause I shoulda seen that he was wearin' a long coat, like a raincoat, on a night it was so hot my balls was in a lake. That coat don't make sense on the street and when it stops makin' sense on the street, a man is supposed to get ready to protect himself. I had my piece stashed about six feet away, behind one of the drainpipes comin' down from the bridge, but I swear I didn't make one move for it. I was concentratin' on Cindy. Tryin' to look down her blouse to where the sweat was runnin' into her

bra. The hit was coming on and she was rubbin'
her head against my neck, lickin' at my ear and
laughin' cause she knew I couldn' do nothin' till
the Italians showed up.

Then I see the dude flick back the coat and
there's like another arm hangin' under his right
arm and it starts comin' up at me and I sorta
know what it is, but I can't move. My mind starts
goin' oh shit, oh shit, oh shit and then there's a
big black hole, pointin' straight at me. Cindy
says, "Is that a gun?" with this tiny, little girl
voice. Like she really don't fucking know, man,
and I flip over behind her.

When it goes off it's so loud I swear it sounds
like I'm in the middle of a fuckin' H-bomb. Then
Cindy falls over across my chest. Her body is
soaked with blood and more blood is pouring out
her back. She keeps twitching. Lays on top of me
like a statue, then starts these little hard jerks. I
don't know I'm hit myself. I think my legs are
wet cause I pissed my pants. You always hope
you're gonna be tough when the thing goes down,
but what you are is shit-pants scared. Like a little kid at a horror movie.

(Unintelligible)

L. HIGGINS: Take it easy, Angel. Just relax.

A. RODRIGUEZ: I'm all right. (pause) I ain't been
through one night when it ain't happened all over
again.

L. HIGGINS: You mean in dreams?

A. RODRIGUEZ: Yeah, dreams. (pause) The first thing
was the black hole swung away from me. Pincho
was frozen, along with Marlene, watchin' it happen. Only Bennie was movin'. He was standin'
next to Marlene and he dropped to one knee, but
he wasn't fast enough and the shotgun went off
again. This time I saw the shell eject, flippin' over
like a high diver and Bennie slidin' on his back

into the stone on the bridge. Little drops of blood broke out on Marlene's skin, like she was in a sweat. Robert was screaming. Owwwwwwwwww-wwwwwwwwwwwww. Then the gun went off again and again, louder than you could ever believe, even in your dreams, and each time you wanna crawl down in a hole somewheres. You just wanna hide and there's no place to go.

Marlene goes down. Pincho goes down. He jumps in the air like he's shooting fucking baskets and comes down like a dog bouncing off a car. Then Robert stops screaming and it's so quiet I can hear the nigger's shoes as he comes across the pavement. I know for sure he's gonna check to see if I'm dead. He's gonna check and then he's gonna put that black hole up in my face. . . . But he steps over me and goes to the trunk of this stripped-out Pontiac against the bridge and takes the stash from up under the fender where Pincho hid it. Then he walks to his car and drives up Pitt toward Houston Street. Then he's gone.

Two minutes later the streets were filled with people and the cops came through the crowd with their sirens screaming. When they saw I was alive, they went crazy. One cop starts kissin' my fucking mouth and punchin' me in my chest. I didn't know what the fuck was going on. I said, "Man, don't I have no rights."

Then this black cop said, "That ain't his blood on his face. That's the woman's blood. Let's get him on the stretcher." But when they picked me up, my leg hurt so bad I passed out.

(Pause)

L. HIGGINS: That's it?

A. RODRIGUEZ: I don't remember nothing after I passed out on the stretcher.

L. HIGGINS: Yeah? Well, the joke wasn't half bad, but you forgot the punchline.

A. RODRIGUEZ: What is she sayin', man?

DET. O'NEILL: Who did it, asshole? You didn't say who the fuck did it.

A. RODRIGUEZ: Kubla done it, man. Levander. (Pause.) Levander Greenwood.

L. HIGGINS: Are you sure, Angel?

A. RODRIGUEZ: We grew up in the same project. We was like brothers.

1

The Investigator's Daily Activity Report is one of the most creative aspects of police work in New York City. Long ago, when newly-appointed Detective Jim Tilley was still a boy, the NYPD was rocked by an enormous scandal which culminated in the creation of a special investigative body, the Knapp Commission. Crooked cops dominated the news headlines for months as a relentless prosecutor tore through the department, and, once the furor died down, the politicians responded by creating a system of paperwork that, theoretically, forces every cop to account for every minute of his or her working life. Patrolmen, for instance, carry a memo book at all times and are expected to make an entry for each job-related incident on a tour. This memo book is read and signed by the patrol sergeant as he makes his rounds, often several times in the course of a shift.

The principle is the same for the city's detectives, even if the supervision is more sloppy. Detectives are expected to prepare Investigative Daily Activity Reports (universally referred to as "Dailies") and turn them in to the precinct whip, usually a lieutenant of detectives, every week or so.

Theoretically, a Daily accounts for every minute of a tour, but most detectives keep them as vague as possible unless they (the detectives) do something worth bragging about. In any event, it is considered absolutely essential that the Daily not include anything of

13

a detective's complex relationship with the ugliest aspects of urban life. One may, in good taste, mention crowd control at a suicide scene, but it is bad form to describe the sound of rubber-soled shoes on small pieces of bone.

For sheer creativity, the Dailies created by Detective Sergeant Stanley Moodrow, a thirty-five-year veteran of the NYPD, were considered the finest in the job. They were invariably obscene, involving complex interviews with the hookers who work Delancey Street or Third Avenue. Interviews that never took place. He would describe their bodies, the clothes they wore (or didn't wear) and their determined efforts to seduce him, sliding out of halters and spandex mini-skirts while he struggled to maintain his sexual integrity. Invariably, they were confidential informants, with properly assigned code names like Mimi or Babette or the queen of the Lower East Side, Cecil the Armenian Hooker. And, also invariably, their information shed light on Moodrow's current case.

Stanley Moodrow may or may not have been the only detective who *totally* fabricated his Dailies, but it was his opinion that they were never read, in any event. "Look," he explained to his new partner, Jim Tilley, "all the Dailies are collected at the beginning of every month and put in storage. What really matters is that there's paper in the file with words on it so the whip doesn't feel compelled to cover his own ass by going to the integrity officer with an empty file. Don't forget, the whip probably doesn't write a true report either and if anyone needs information about a particular collar, they go to the complaint and the follow-ups, not the Dailies. The Dailies are nothing but a politician's fantasy of a police department that runs like a prison. It's really a fucking joke."

Tilley nodded solemnly, just as if his opinion of Stanley Moodrow didn't vacillate between aging department dinosaur and self-destructive maniac. Moodrow was the cop who, all by himself, had captured the American Red Army, the terrorist group responsible for the bombing of Herald Square. And then survived the outrage of the department when every reporter in the city knew (though few dared to say it) that he had deliberately held back information and planned to execute the whole bunch personally. His clear lack of contrition had made him a legend in the job, a hero to most and a warning to others. But even cops who always stayed on the right side of the Patrol Guide were willing to concede that Stanley Moodrow probably had the biggest pair of balls in the NYPD.

Jim Tilley's own Daily, meticulously detailing every minute of their tour, had been typed and shoved into a manila envelope before he went to bed. Not that there was anything much to put in it after a single day as Stanley Moodrow's first partner in more than twenty years. But cover your ass is the most fundamental law of self-preservation in the job and Tilley was determined to distance himself from Moodrow by adhering to the letter of NYPD procedural law. Unfortunately, his conscientious attitude had left him with nothing to do except try to read his partner's mind. Which, he concluded after a moment's concentration, was like trying to guess what's inside a refrigerator without opening the door.

If he'd been offered a choice, of course, the young detective would have picked a more conservative man to be his partner, but fate is fate and Jim Tilley's had begun in the Nine Nine, an obscure Brooklyn precinct. In a three-month period, nearly every narc in the house had been arrested for drug-related scams. There had been so many cops involved that each shift had had its own gangs and its own methods. Naturally, the game was generally played by seizing contraband without making an arrest, then reselling to a middle-level dealer in some other borough. But there was one bunch who ripped off dealers set up by their informants, then turned around and fronted the drugs to the same snitches. And there was straight extortion, too, genuine strong-arm, give-me-the-money-or-I'll-blow-your-brains-out scenarios.

The final blow had come in mid-April when, after a raft of police brutality complaints, a gruesome story had come to light. Two black men (both convicted murderers) had been beaten to death on the way to the precinct by four coups, three white and one Hispanic, then buried in the basement of an abandoned building near the Hunt's Point market in the Bronx. Naturally, with that many co-conspirators, somebody, trying to save his own butt, dropped a dime on his brothers. Unfortunately for Jim Tilley, the same rat called the media first and the reporters dug up the bodies and took pictures before the cops could close off the scene.

NYPD Policy Directive B/17–233 came down exactly four days later, proclaiming that nobody, not the oldest veteran, nor the most decorated cop in the department, could walk without a partner, and all cops were to be rotated from precinct to precinct every three years. When the cop unions announced their intention to bring suit against the city, the Mayor backed down on the last part and allowed fifteen-year men to be exempt from transfer. But the partnering bit, though totally unrelated to the corruption it was designed to prevent, stuck, and eighty-seven days later Jim Tilley had a partner.

Curiously, though he continued to scribble furiously, Moodrow was also engaged in the process of sizing up his new partner. Tilley's face was so openly Irish, with its heavy cheekbones and tough-guy jaw belying innocent blue eyes, that it took Moodrow back to his earliest days in the job, a time when the Irish still dominated the department. Moodrow hadn't had a partner since Bartholemew Klug, who'd retired in 1964, and he was more than a little anxious about Tilley's willingness to learn. Of course, Moodrow could have chosen a veteran, but no veteran would have allowed Stanley Moodrow the freedom to be the kind of cop he had always been.

They were sitting in the kitchen of Moodrow's apartment on the Lower East Side of Manhattan, a room Tilley would get to know very well. Though he didn't seem to mind the rattle of the ancient air conditioner in the window, Stanley Moodrow hated the noise and the chaos of the 7th Precinct, the endless complaints of criminals brought to justice as well as the angry voices of cops trying to shout them down. To some extent, his status as Captain Allen Epstein's backdoor into the strange mixture of classes and cultures that made up the Lower East Side stemmed as much from Moodrow's desire to avoid the house as from a need always to walk the line between law enforcement (as he understood it) and standard operating procedure.

Finally, just to break the tension, Tilley crossed the room and refilled his coffee cup. He wasn't used to being dismissed, not after a ring career that had run through forty-five amateur and nine professional fights before an opponent's head had put a thick scar above his right eye, a scar that poured blood even in sparring. That butt had driven him out of the ring and into Fordham University where the NYPD recruited him by promising a gold shield, the coveted badge of the detective, after only two years on patrol. He'd graduated in the top five percent of his class at the Police Academy, dominating the other recruits in every aspect of hand-to-had combat and at one-ninety, a mere fifteen pounds above his fighting weight, he sometimes felt he was ready to jump back in the ring whenever a street punk challenged him. That attitude had served him well in Fort Greene, Brooklyn, where he'd spent two years on patrol, but it would not, he was beginning to realize, make any impression on Stanley Moodrow.

His black coffee fortified with two teaspoons of sugar, Tilley returned to his seat at the table and stared at his preoccupied partner. Moodrow's face, as big as his features were small, had all the expression of a spanish melon, but it matched his enormous, square body perfectly. Tilley estimated Moodrow's weight at two-sixty plus and his height at six feet five inches with little, if any, fat hanging over his belt. Moodrow's gut was rounded, all right, but not like he'd stuffed a pillow beneath his shirt; more like a bowling ball.

Twenty minutes later, the bell for the outside door went off and Moodrow, without comment, buzzed his guests inside. "It's Kirkpatrick and O'Neill," he predicted while they waited for their company to arrive, "also known as the Murphy Twins. The only way you could tell them apart is that O'Neill wears scuffed black shoes and Kirkpatrick wears scuffed brown shoes."

As usual, he was right on target. Though they were not related, Kirkpatrick and O'Neill were both tall and broad-shouldered, with red faces and redder noses, enormous guts and no ass. Their belt buckles were down in their crotches and covered by their bellies. After shaking hands with Jim Tilley, they carefully ignored him, while Moodrow, back in his seat and still writing furiously, carefully avoided *them*. The farce went on for about ten minutes. Until O'Neill couldn't take it anymore.

"Hey, Moodrow," he said, "tell us what kinda bullshit ya puttin' in ya Daily."

"You should only wish it was bullshit," Moodrow answered without looking up.

Kirkpatrick was so excited, his jowls quivered. "I suppose ya spent the night with one of ya hookers? Gathering information." The two of them laughed the same phlegmy laugh, a liquid sound ugly enough to send ordinary humans running. But Moodrow ignored the comment and the laugh, scribbling even faster until he reached the end of the line. Then he scrawled his signature across the bottom of the page and raised his eyes to look at Kirkpatrick and O'Neill.

"Good morning, Sergeant," O'Neill said, bowing his head slightly. "Think you could give us a few minutes of ya precious time? I know you're busy with the Great American Novel." He gestured toward Moodrow's Daily Report. "But what we got's important. You do remember about Levander Greenwood, don't ya? The scumbag who offed all them people by the bridge? Including a cop. We come to beg for ya help in solvin' this important case."

Moodrow looked at Tilley as if they were alone in the room. "You know what he's talking about?"

Tilley nodded, careful not to show his excitement. The papers were calling it the Delancey Street Massacre: four civilians, a reporter and an undercover cop. All taken out within two blocks of the 7th Precinct. Under normal conditions, a rookie wouldn't get within sniffing distance of an investigation this important and Tilley suddenly woke up to the potential benefits of being Stanley Moodrow's partner.

"Levander Greenwood," Moodrow continued, "is an old-timer in the neighborhood. Grew up in the projects and started in the drug business when he was eight. Running heroin for the Baruch Noblemen."

This was a common method used by street level drug dealers to stay out of jail. Juveniles, if caught with narcotics, seldom do serious time. As a street patrolman, Tilley had busted more than one kid (how sophisticated could a ten-year-old be—they just walked up and handed it to whoever the dealer pointed out) and had testified at a number of juvenile hearings. Guaranteed, the first few busts are an automatic probation.

"Now he's thirty," Moodrow continued. "With twenty-two years experience. He's done nearly six years hard and been in court two dozen times. I don't think he wants to go back inside."

O'Neill nodded solemnly. Suddenly, they were four cops talking shop. "That's my make, too. He's not coming in on his own and if we corner the scumbag, he's gonna shoot first." He looked directly at Tilley, probing for weakness. "No warning, y'understand? Ya come around a corner and the motherfucker's liable to be there waiting. Even if he could walk away."

"Well, one thing," Tilley couldn't resist getting in his two cents, "if he wants to stay out of jail so bad, how come he did those people right out in the open? How did he think he could get away with it? Is he stupid?"

"He is stupid," Moodrow said. "But he's also crazy and, from what I hear, does crack full time. He used to be a small-time pimp and a rip-off artist, turning out the runaways coming through the Port Authority bus terminal and taking off middle-class kids from Jersey and Long Island." He turned to Kirkpatrick, nodded at the folder under the detective's arm. "You got a picture?"

Kirkpatrick's thick fingers flipped the pages for a moment, then he passed a standard mug shot to Moodrow who passed it to Tilley. Levander Greenwood stood just over five feet eight inches tall and looked like he weighed two-forty. His neck was wider than his head and his shoulders damn near ran out of the photo. The young cop, staring intently at what he considered the path to promotion, recalled his days as a fighter. He'd fought a number of small men in the ring. The announcers invariably referred to them as "fireplugs." They were usually slow and clumsy, easy to tie-up, but in a narrow corridor without gloves, without rules. . . . Jim Tilley made a mental decision to get a backup piece and carry it. "Is this guy as strong as he looks?"

"This guy is a fuckin' nightmare." O'Neill turned to his partner. "Am I right?"

Kirkpatrick pinned Tilley with small, glittering,

black eyes. Tilley was a novelty, both as a rookie and as Moodrow's partner, and the Murphys were having a good time trying to frighten him. "The only decent thing about a squeal like this is we most likely get to kill the asshole in the end. He's probably stronger than Moodrow. He don't feel no pain in a fight. At least not so you could tell. He'll kill you without thinking twice. Plus, he's been wanted for another murder for nearly six months, so wherever he's got his hole, he's had plenty of time to make it safe." He rubbed his chin, causing his jowls to do a little dance.

"We got Greenwood's name from one of the victims," O'Neill offered. "Little spic name of Angel Rodriguez. He had a bunch of hits and we traded it for the name. Imagine that shit? I gotta give this spic a favor to get him to tell me the name of the scumbag that shot him. You'd expect he'd wanta tell me."

"I think he was glad to talk," Kirkpatrick said. "He just hada save face. That's why the hits. We didn't have no probable cause and the dope wasn't nowhere near the spic, so what's to lose? Anyways, he told us the nigger's been takin' off dealers right and left. Greenwood's a complete outlaw, now, and the Italians got a major contract on him. Only thing is nobody's too anxious to collect. Word on the street is the mighty Kubla Khan got a sawed-off twelve gauge he carries under his coat. Which, by the way, if a guy's wearin' a coat in this weather, he probly does have something underneath. Naturally, Rodriguez don't know where Greenwood's holed up, but he thinks maybe Brooklyn."

"Did you take the name back to the rest of his victims?" Moodrow asked.

"Sure. You think we're stupid. He's the one. No question about it." Kirkpatrick stood up and went over to the stove. At first Tilley thought he was after another cup of coffee, but Kirkpatrick ignored the coffee pot and began to rummage in the cabinets. "How come ya never offer, Moodrow? Ya come to my house, I always offer, but you never offer." He returned to the table with a bottle of bourbon in his hand, poured a shot into his coffee and passed it to his partner. Tilley was shocked at first, surprised that they were stupid enough to do this in front of a stranger. Later he found out that thirty-year men fear only two things—retirement and a bullet. "When we said the name Greenwood, they froze up. Each one dreamin' his own fucking revenge. Like they see themselves in an alley blazin' away, but I guarantee they're gonna recuperate in their apartments until Greenwood's outta the picture."

"Which leaves us," Moodrow said.

"Right. Unless the scumbag does something incredibly stupid, like take a walk in an Italian neighborhood, there's no one down here that's got the balls to do it for us."

Moodrow stood up and stretched, towering over the table. "So what do you want?" he asked. "What's the play here?"

O'Neill stated the case for both of them. "Y'understand this is coming from Captain Epstein. I mean if ya don't believe me, he'll tell ya himself."

"Whatta you think? You think I want out? When was the last time you saw me want out? Besides, I already spoke to Epstein."

"Now you hurt his feelings," Kirkpatrick quipped. "And you know how sensitive he is. That's what happens when ya dick falls off from fuckin' so many whores. You get sensitive."

O'Neill threw his partner a wink and a wet, phlegmy laugh. "We been to see Greenwood's mother and the ex-wife. They won't give us the time of day. Ditto the sister and acquaintances. We don't have no way to work it up from the bottom."

"I take it he doesn't run with any of the dealers now?"

"The fucking guy's been rippin' off people who used to be his best pals. There ain't nobody close to him anymore. You got all them hookers tell ya everything that happens on the street. Shouldn't take more'n two or three blow-jobs to find the bastard."

"And what are you gonna do?" Moodrow asked.

O'Neill smiled and shrugged. "We're gonna do all the things you think you're too good to do. We're gonna tie it into a five borough task force to keep the politicians happy. Establish a hot line and a reward. Would you believe his fucking Honor's goin' to the writer's funeral? Anyways, we'll get Greenwood's picture in the media and distribute it to the precincts. The papers are bound ta give his mug a big splash since he took out one of their own and most likely we'll get the bastard quick. But if we don't, Epstein's gotta cover his ass which makes you the toilet paper."

"No problem," Moodrow said, a sudden smile brightening his face. "Actually, I been looking forward to a little action. So I can break in my new partner."

2

Once Kirkpatrick and O'Neill were safely out of the
way, Moodrow put the bourbon back on the shelf and
poured himself another cup of coffee while his partner
went through Greenwood's M.O. file. M.O. *(modus op-
erandi)* files are kept in every precinct and contain information from a variety of sources on individual
criminals known to be living or operating within the
precinct, along with their associates and crime pat-
terns. This is in addition to major crime files which
include the same information under broader categories
such as arson, robbery, narcotics, etcetera. With these
basic tools, a detective can approach an investigation
from either end. He can begin with the crime and work
toward the perpetrator or start with the criminal and
widen an investigation to include associations with
other criminals in the same field. The final backup, of
course, is the precinct computer (operated by civilians)
which not only ties the whole city together, but is
capable of tapping the warehouse of information controlled by the FBI.

Being a native of the 7th, Greenwood's file was ex-
ceptionally thick, the oldest pages already yellowing,
the newest handwritten. The story it told was common enough. In trouble with the police since he was
ten years old, he'd been examined by a dozen social
welfare agencies. Some pronounced him severely dis-
turbed, some pronounced him normal, but in either
event, he and his problems were thrown back into the

hands of his family. His first four arrests got him probation, then six months in Rikers juvenile followed by two more probations. When he was eighteen, he'd done two years hard in Attica, come back smart enough to stay out of police hands for nearly two years (four arrests with no convictions) then got snatched at the scene of a particularly brutal rip-off by two alert patrolmen. Not that Levander went down easy. He broke one cop's leg and bit halfway through the other one's finger before a second set of uniforms, responding to a 10–13, filled his mouth, nose and eyes with Mace, then broke their nightsticks over his head. For this sin (and for all the sins of his past life) Greenwood drew a dime, of which he did six. According to his sheet, he went back to his old trade, the separation of children from their parents' money, almost as soon as he was released.

Greenwich Village, which is west of the Lower East Side and much more affluent, has been attracting rebellious youth since the turn of the century. On weekends, the streets are full of suburban children in daddy's sedan cruising for girls and drugs. The Village, itself, now that the uniforms have sealed off Washington Square Park, is too commercial and too hectic for most of the street dealers, but the scene on the Lower East Side, where the condos give way to housing projects and tenements, is wide open, with marijuana salesmen out on the street soliciting the kids as they drive up First Avenue. The dealers, small-timers selling ten dollar bags, stare into the open windows of the cars and press their fingers to their lips as if they were hitting on a joint. If the occupants respond, there follows a quick exchange of envelope for cash.

According to his file, Levander used this relationship to work his own scam. He'd approach the cars as they sat waiting for the lights on 11th Street, sell the occupants a small amount of pot, then ask them if they were interested in a little coke. Naturally, coke being a much more dangerous drug to handle, he couldn't carry it on him, but if they just drove a few blocks . . .

If they were afraid, he'd promise that they wouldn't have to leave the car or hand the money over in advance. Just drive him to a certain apartment building and wait a few minutes until he came out. Once he had them parked among the burnt-out tenements on 4th Street, he would pull a gun, usually an automatic, smash the driver across the face by way of opening negotiations, then grab whatever cash and jewelry he could find. On several occasions, after taking the keys to the ignition, he dragged young women, screaming, into abandoned tenements.

Most of this was "alleged," of course, much of it coming from snitches, because the kids, realizing they had no hope of recovering their money, saw no sense in compounding their problems by having to tell their parents they were on the Lower East Side trying to buy cocaine. Better to take the beating and keep the cops out of it, which is what cheap rip-off artists like Greenwood counted on. Despite the violence, despite the stitches in the emergency room, it's almost impossible to motivate cops without a signed complaint.

In the first week of January, for reasons unknown, this pattern changed abruptly. Greenwood gunned down a middle-aged biker named Bill Ryder and made off with several ounces of newly manufactured methamphetamine. The eyewitness, the dead man's common law wife, Sue-Ann Dosantos, had positively fingered him and wasn't backing off.

After adding murder to assault and rape, the department assigned Detective Paul Kirkpatrick to find him and put him away, for parole violation if nothing else could be proven. Unfortunately, this was after he changed his style, when he was no longer working openly on the street.

Then the bodies began to pile up. Two in February,

another in March, another in April. All dealers. Even where there were no witnesses, word on the street, from several different sources, kept coming up Levander Greenwood, aka Kubla Khan.

"Any surprises in there, Detective Tilley?"

"Huh?"

"You've been buried in that file for half an hour. I thought you might like to share your thoughts. Impress me with the depths of your insight." Without asking, Moodrow filled both cups with coffee, then pushed the sugar bowl across the table.

"You want Greenwood's exact address?" Tilley asked.

"I want your analysis. Tell me how you'd play this if you were on your own." He sat down and folded his hands on the table as if preparing to wait indefinitely for his partner to get serious.

"I think Greenwood's gotta be working with at least one partner."

"Why?" Moodrow leaned forward eagerly.

"Let's take the first rip-off. The biker. Greenwood took three ounces of amphetamine. He can't use that much personally. It'd last for years. But if he's selling it locally, he'd have to be visible. It's one thing to make an unannounced visit to a bar at three o'clock in the morning, another thing to meet one buyer after another when half of them are gonna head for a telephone as soon as the deal's finished.

"Of course, he might be taking his action into another part of town, into South Jamaica or the Bronx, but then they'll catch him from the other end. After they set up the task force and get his face in the newspapers, every rat in the city'll come forward. Whoever turns Greenwood's gonna be owed a hell of a favor. Not to mention that the reporter's magazine has a $20,000 reward out. Put that together with the automatic twenty-five grand on any cop killing and you got quite a nice bundle.

"With no takers, right? No, I don't think they're gonna find anything. I think Greenwood's probably dealing with one partner. Someone smart enough to let him do the killing." Tilley stopped for a moment, trying to work it through. "The way Greenwood's going, someone's most likely gonna kill him. That would leave the silent partner in the clear. Think about it, Moodrow. You put this sick fucker on the street, let him do his thing, split the profit and walk away after someone chills him. Not the dumbest scam we've ever come across."

Moodrow nodded. "Let's suppose there is a partner. Just like you say. A dealer of some kind who takes whatever Greenwood comes up with and sells it on the street. Or even wholesale, if there's enough of it. What's this guy's biggest problem?"

"The partner's biggest problem has to be Greenwood, himself. First of all, the man is unstable; a certified psychopath who went off the deep end six months ago and hasn't hit bottom yet. Shit, this guy walked up to a crowd of people two blocks from a precinct house and started blasting away with a .12 gauge shotgun. Imagine what he might do if he thought his partner was cheating him? Whoever's using him must be pretty bad in his own right." He paused for a moment, looking for Moodrow to make a comment, but Moodrow continued to sip his coffee. "By the way, do you know if any of his shit is hitting the streets again?"

Moodrow shrugged. "I'm gonna try to find out, but I don't have much expectation of running him down that way. The amount he's taking isn't enough to make much of an impression if it's put back into circulation. But I'm gonna put out the word that I'm looking for any trace of the mighty Kubla Khan and when my little rats come back to me, I'm gonna turn you onto the ones who're willing to meet you."

"Let's start with Cecil the Armenian Hooker." Actually, despite the weak joke, Tilley was surprised. Most detectives guard informants like they were made of gold.

"You ain't ready for Cecil," Moodrow pronounced solemnly. "Cecil would eat your little ass for breakfast. We'll start with Greenwood's mother. She lives in the Vladek Houses off South Street."

"Greenwood's mother is a snitch?"

"Greenwood's mother is a citizen. But they're allowed to help, too."

"She must be some sweetheart to have raised a monster like Greenwood."

Moodrow shrugged into his jacket. "She's all right. She works as a practical nurse at Mt. Sinai."

"And she lives in the project? How can that be?"

"What's the matter with it?"

"I thought you had to be poor to live in the projects."

"How much you think she makes?"

"Too much for low income housing."

Moodrow started to open the door, then stopped and turned to face his partner. "She makes fifteen thousand a year, gross. Maybe, after taxes, she's got eleven. If she ever lost her apartment, she'd be sleeping in the fucking bus terminal."

"That doesn't mean we can't threaten her with it."

"If she knows anything, she'll tell me without any of that." He gave Tilley a worried look. "You can't put everyone in the same bag, Jimmy. She's a citizen. She's one of the people we're supposed to help."

"Does that mean she's under the personal protection of Don Moodrow?"

"That's exactly right." Moodrow's face registered his surprise. "My personal protection. If there ain't no good guys, why be a sheriff?"

"Hey, a job's a job. You might as well say, 'Why be an accountant?'"

Moodrow's face went blank. His small features

seemed to shrink back into his skull. For ten seconds, he fixed Tilley with his hardest stare. Then he pushed himself away from the table and stood up. "Let's get to work."

3

Virtually all of New York City's vast network of public housing was built during the liberal post-WWII era of Mayor Robert Wagner. Not that it was easily done, despite the prevailing New Deal mentality. The overwhelming question, even then, was whether or not "we" had an obligation to do anything at all for "them" and the prediction, as these red and yellow brick buildings went up, was universally bleak: substandard from the first, it was solemnly declared, they would soon fall into disrepair—"instant slum" and "breeding grounds for crime" were the phrases most often heard.

Tilley was born in 1962, just as the construction was getting into high gear and if he'd ever heard this depressing forecast (though he certainly heard plenty about "us" and "them"), he didn't remember it. For Jim Tilley, New York's projects were a fact of life, a given. Moodrow, on the other hand, had listened to the forecasts patiently, then was surprised at the city's simple, effective solution—the creation of a special police force to serve the nearly five hundred thousand citizens living in the projects. Now each set of public houses has its own miniature police force, cops who come back to the same group of buildings day after day, until they (or the better ones, at least) can tell the good guys from the bad guys.

But, crime or no crime, the irony is still clear, because it's New York's alternative housing, the tenements built early in the century to house the vast labor

31

force emigrating from eastern and southern Europe, that have fallen into disrepair. For all the poverty closed off by those narrow, yellow hallways, the projects, including the Vladek Houses where Mrs. Louise Greenwood lived, represent the housing of choice for most of New York's poor. The absolute proof of that assertion can be found in the ten-year waiting list for available apartments, even for apartments in the Vladek Houses which, an exception to the general rule, were completed in 1940 as part of the cure for the Great Depression.

The Vladek Houses, however, are only a small part of the network of subsidized projects blanketing the waterfront area of the Lower East Side, and as he and his partner drove toward Louise Greenwood's, Moodrow ticked off the names as they drove south from 14th Street: the Baruch Houses, the Lillian Wald Houses, the Jacob Riis Houses, the Seward Park complex. "Nearly thirty thousand people, Jimmy, who need help to pay the rent. This neighborhood was never good. It was always dirt poor. First Irish, then Jewish and East European. Now it's mostly Puerto Rican and Chinese with a few leftover whites and a gang of punk artists and yuppies north of Houston Street. And dope, of course. Probably the most dope of any place below 96th Street. You know how in black neighborhoods, it's hard to tell the good kids from the bad ones? Well, we got punks down here with green hair knocking down half a million dollars a year making sculpture out of garbage. We also got punks who manufacture speed. Some of the guys out there with rings in their noses write for *Rolling Stone* magazine. You fuck with them, you find yourself on page one. But others, looking just exactly the same, like to pimp young runaways. Think you can tell 'em apart? The 7th ain't a regular precinct. We got more than a hundred thousand Puerto Ricans living here. We got nine different kinds of ethnic whites above Houston Street. We got

Chinese by the Brooklyn Bridge. We got Hasidic Jews on Grand Street. We even got junior executives in co-ops. It might be a pot, but most of the time, it don't melt. It fucking boils."

Moodrow parked the Plymouth next to what was left of the nearly demolished Gouverneur Hospital and the two cops stepped out into the noontime heat. There are no air conditioners in city houses and the pathways and small parks dotting the Vladek Houses were crowded with residents seeking the nonexistent breeze. Moodrow and Tilley walked from their car to the headquarters of Public Service Area #41, without looking too closely at the gangs of kids openly smoking joints. The two cops were about to check in with the housing cops, a courtesy that, if overlooked, would come back to haunt them if they should need a favor sometime in the future.

Naturally, the desk sergeant, an ancient warrior named Handlesman, knew Moodrow and welcomed him, "How're the whores treatin' ya these days, Moodrow? You got AIDS yet?"

"Yeah, from sharing a needle with your sister. This is my new partner, Jimmy Tilley. Guess what we're here for?"

Brian Handlesman threw the young detective a close look, wondering how anyone could be so unlucky. Handlesman was extremely fat, even by the beefy standards of the NYPD, and he kept shifting his weight on the armless metal chair behind the small desk at the entranceway to PSA #41 headquarters. "I bet you're here about Levander Greenwood. Am I right?" He laughed. "We got a bulletin today. In fact, we been gettin' bulletins once a month for the last six months." He gestured to a corkboard in the hallway leading to the back rooms. A mug shot of Greenwood glared from the case.

"That's our boy," Moodrow admitted. "Any word?"

Handlesman shrugged his shoulders. "I think you're

wastin' your time. His mama got a restraining order nearly a year ago. He ain't allowed within a hundred yards of the Vladek Houses. Last time he was here, he absconded with the fuckin' rent money."

"Were you here when Greenwood was a child?" Tilley asked. "Did you know him?"

"Shit, kid, I testified at his first juvie hearing. Long fuckin' time ago. I told the hearing officer, Kill the little bastard. *Now*. Don't let this kid grow up. They got mad as . . . What's ya name again?"

"Jim."

"They had one of these fag social workers there. Judy Cohen. Judy the Jew, I used ta call her. I swear ta fuckin' Christ, Jim, every time one of these little animals stabbed someone, this bitch was up there tryin' ta protect him. Tryin' ta protect Levander Greenwood. I hada sit there and listen' ta her fuckin' defame me to the judge for over an hour.

"I mean, I been in these projects almost thirty-five years and I say Levander Greenwood was the meanest kid I ever seen. No shit. Even when he was stumbling along in diapers, he couldn't be near the other kids. As he grew up, he got fuckin' worse. Would ya believe that? He got fuckin' *worse.*"

The fat cop hesitated, as if waiting for Moodrow or Tilley to dispute his claim. He stared at each; noted their silence. "One day, about fifteen years ago, we came up on him smokin' a joint in a basement hallway where he wasn't supposed ta be in the first place. Now we don't wanna bust nobody for smokin' a lousy fuckin' joint. We know that's the kind of bust gets a brick dropped on ya head, but the kids're supposed ta play the fuckin' game. When they see us comin', they're supposed ta run away. Greenwood just stands there lookin' at me and my partner, Joe Jefferson, who was colored, by the way, darin' us to make a move on him.

"Now Joe was a mean son of a bitch and everybody

in the projects knew it. The kind of big, black ugly nigger hates all other niggers cause they 'bring down the race.' He walks straight up ta Greenwood and slaps the joint out of his mouth. Damn if Greenwood don't uppercut him right in the balls. I mean the fuckin' kid is only fifteen years old. Weighs about a hundred-twenty pounds.

"Naturally, I figure I gotta disabuse the kid from his violent tendencies. I mean Joe's rollin' around on the ground, fa Christ sake. So I go up to him, smilin', and ask, 'Why'd ya do that for?' Then I jab my nightstick into his gut while the stupid nigger's tryin' ta come up with an answer. Doubled the little fuck over.

"Joe's yellin', 'Kill em; kill em; kill em' and I know we're all alone down the basement, so I decide ta teach the asshole a lesson he won't forget. I drag his fuckin' black ass over to one of the steam valves. It was winter and the heat was goin' full blast.

" 'Now I'm gonna show ya somethin'. They all say ya too stupid ta learn, Levander fuckin' Greenwood, but this time ya gettin' a lesson you ain't never gonna forget. You're gonna remember this every time ya try ta comb ya hair.'

"Naturally I didn't wanna actually go through with it. I thought the kid'd break down and cry or some-thin', but he don't even blink. He don't even try ta pull back his hand.

"So what could I do? What could I fuckin' do? I hada do it, right? I open the valve and the steam comes pourin' out, but Greenwood don't make a sound. Then I put his hand in it and he still don't say nothin'. Blank face like a fuckin' jigaboo Indian. Finally, I got dis-gusted. I just threw him down and took my partner out of there. I mean with a kid like that you ain't got no fuckin' choice. You gotta kill him. Right?

"We ended up puttin' a buzzer in the mother's apart-ment. Rings on the wall behind me. Figure if he comes knockin', I'm gonna go huntin'. I got a special place on my wall reserved fa that nigger's head."

Racism exists in the NYPD, as it does in every other aspect of American life, white or black, but Tilley had never before heard it expressed so violently, or so blatantly. Here was a cop, a hairbag finishing up his career behind a desk, admitting to the torture of a fifteen-year-old child as if torture was a police function described in the Patrol Guide.

The young detective looked over at Moodrow, but the big cop's face was expressionless.

"You and a hundred other guys," Moodrow said evenly. "When did you put the buzzer in?"

"A year ago. When the restraining order went into effect. I don't expect we'll see him around here again. His mother don't have enough money to make the risk worthwhile."

Moodrow shrugged. "We're going up anyway, take a shot. You think the old lady's home?"

"Do I look like a fuckin' doorman?"

4

The interior of Louise Greenwood's building was depressingly familiar to the two cops. Minuscule lobby (there probably wouldn't be any lobby at all if the city could have found another place for the mailboxes), narrow hallways, fresh graffiti scrawled across yellow tile walls announcing the existence of the most macho ENRIQUE 193. The architect, no doubt encouraged by politicians spending the taxpayers' money, had clearly acknowledged no motivation greater than mere utility. Still, the floors were clean, the outer door locked and the stairs smelled of disinfectant instead of urine. Someone was making an effort.

Moodrow and Tilley, already sweating, trudged up the stairs to the third floor and knocked on the metal-covered door of apartment 3D. A few seconds later, after the peephole was drawn back and the cops were subjected to close scrutiny, a clear, unmistakably angry woman's voice called out, "Who is it?"

"Police. Sergeant Moodrow." Moodrow held his badge to the peephole, then motioned for his partner to do the same.

"What do you want?"

"C'mon, Marlee, open the goddamn door."

"That tone of voice will get you exactly nothing, Moodrow." Nevertheless, the sharp, metallic sound of opening locks filled the next few seconds and the door swung in. "If you're here about my brother, you can turn around and walk down the stairs." She was tall

37

and heavily built, a round face all huge, black eyes,
maybe thirty-five years old, wearing a New York Mar-
athon t-shirt and gray warm-up pants cut just below
the knee. She gave Tilley a withering look guaranteed
to boil the blood of any cop. "What's this, Moodrow?"
she asked. "You get a dog?"

Moodrow reached out to put a restraining hand on
Tilley's arm. "Marlee, if you don't get control of your
tongue, I'm gonna tell your mother on you."

A brief smile flickered across her face, then her features froze once again. "Don't bullshit me, Moodrow.
Where was your bullshit when we needed it?" She
paused, got no answer and rushed on. "Do us both a
favor. Turn around and go back down the stairs."

"You're Miss Redmond? Mrs. Redmond?" Tilley finally managed to get a word in. He wasn't nearly as
much of a Rambo as most of the younger breed, but
he still couldn't believe that Moodrow would take her
shit.

"Do I know you?"

"Detective Tilley, Ma'am." He kept his voice neutral, but he was so angry his fingers were trembling.
"You work for the Transit Authority?" He didn't wait
for a reply. "What do you take home? Ballpark figure.
Twenty-five thousand? Figure in the o.t. and your
mama's salary, it probably comes to near forty thousand for the household. That about right? What's the
cutoff for the projects? Isn't it around twenty-two? I
hope you haven't been lying on your financial form."

Everything stopped. The question was so unexpected that, for a moment, even Moodrow had nothing
to say. Then his face clouded and Tilley thought
Moodrow was actually going to come after him. The
idea didn't frighten him; he was ready to fight anyone,
though he would have preferred Marlee.

"Who is it, Marlee?" A middle-aged woman, leaning
on a cane, stepped out of the kitchen and began walking toward the front door.

"It's a couple of pigs who want to know how much money we make."

"Now why would they want to know that?" Louise Greenwood was short and gray-haired. Her eyes, behind thick glasses, peered at the two detectives until they recognized Moodrow. "Oh, it's Sergeant Moodrow. Why didn't you say who it was, Marlee? Come in Sergeant. Who's your friend?" She turned abruptly and began to walk toward the small living room, obviously expecting the two cops to follow.

The apartment was spotless. The walls, bare except for a painting of the crucified Jesus on black velvet, looked freshly scrubbed. The living room set, a couch and two chairs, was covered with heavy plastic and the end tables gleamed with polish. Even the fibers on the rug stood straight up, as if they'd been combed by hand. "Just take a seat anywhere. Do you want coffee?"

"No thanks, Mrs. Greenwood." Moodrow lowered himself into one of the stuffed chairs, then leaned back confidently. "This is my new partner, Jim Tilley."

"Will you have coffee, Officer Tilley?"

"No thanks," he said contritely. He felt like an utter asshole, like he had on that unforgettable afternoon when Sister Dennis caught him looking up Patricia McNeill's dress. The woman was not an enemy.

"What's all this about money, Sergeant Moodrow?" If the mention of money was upsetting to her, she didn't show it. Her look was questioning, curious.

"They want to know about Levander, Mama," Marlee cut in. "The baby, here," she pointed to Tilley, "thinks he can scare us with questions about how much money we make. He's gonna have us thrown out of the project if we don't cooperate."

"I didn't say that," Tilley protested.

"What you gonna do now, boy? You gonna run away from it? What other reason could you have to ask about our income? Don't bullshit me." She was still standing up, though the rest of them were seated, and her

attitude was so aggressive it absolved Tilley of his guilt
as surely as ten Hail Marys, five Our Fathers and a
perfect Act of Contrition.

"Maybe I didn't know there was a human being," he
gestured to Mrs. Greenwood, "standing behind the animal."

Suddenly Mrs. Greenwood broke into laughter. Not
the breathy tinkle of an elderly woman, but a deep
whooping belly laugh that had Moodrow giggling back,
an odd high sound that leaked out between closed lips
as if the humor of the situation was something only
he understood.

"Well," Mrs. Greenwood said at last, "isn't it wonderful how the children get along?" She paused momentarily, then went on. "Actually, I expected you'd
be stopping by."

"That means you already know." Moodrow was suddenly all business. His eyes locked on those of Louise
Greenwood and they didn't move until he was ready
to leave.

"Yes. Mrs. Perez told me that her boy heard it at
school from the members of some street gang. Now
I'm not saying that I knew it was true, Sergeant, but I
was not surprised. You know all the troubles we've
had in this home since my husband died. Better to
count your blessings. That's why I thank the Lord for
Marlee."

The daughter flinched as though she'd been struck.
"You don't have to talk to these people, Mama. They
got no right coming here. Knocking down people's
doors." Her teeth were clenched, nostrils flared; so angry her voice hissed.

"They're here because I invited them." Louise
turned to face her daughter. "I have something I want
from Sergeant Moodrow," she said evenly. "I know
those other policemen would lie to me. They'd promise, but they wouldn't mean it." She turned back to
Moodrow. "They feel that promises to black people

don't have to be kept. They're different from other promises."

"What do they want, Mrs. Greenwood?" Moodrow asked gently.

"They want to kill my child." Her voice cracked and out of the corner of his eye, Moodrow saw Marlee's hands float up, palms extended, like she was cradling an infant.

"Do you think that's true, Sergeant Moodrow?" Louise Greenwood continued.

"I would have to say it is." He didn't flinch from it.

"And you, Sergeant Moodrow. Do you want to kill Levander?"

Moodrow didn't respond immediately. Tilley, watching intently, wondered if he was trying to make up a lie or just at a loss for the right words. Then Moodrow surprised his partner by saying, "Yeah, I do. He killed a cop."

"And you came here because you want me to help you?"

Moodrow didn't answer and Louise Greenwood struggled to her feet, accepting her daughter's arm. Tilley expected to be invited out the door, but the two women went to the closet and took out a small metal box. "I have to show you about this, Sergeant. So you'll know why," said Louise. Marlee set a glass table in front of Moodrow and Mrs. Greenwood took a seat behind it. Tilley was completely ignored.

"I know what my son is, Sergeant. I've known about it for a long time. He was two years old when my husband passed away. Marlee was six. Up till that time, he seemed like a normal child. He walked real early and he understood every word you said to him. When I read to him at night, he never took his eyes off the book.

"But after my husband died, I started losing control. I was just a country girl from South Carolina. A little colored girl right off the farm. I tried to work at first, but I wasn't qualified for city work. I spoke like, 'yes-suh ma'am, us workin' real hawd fo y'all.' I probably could have gotten work as a domestic servant and I would have taken even that, if I had my own mama near me to look after the children. There wasn't any day care back then and the kind of baby sitters I could afford to hire would as likely kill the children as look after them.

"So I did what a whole lot of other black mothers without husbands did. I went on welfare and the case-worker helped move me from a house on Wales Avenue in the Bronx to this project. There were projects going up all over the city then, and I thought the kids would get better schooling in Manhattan. By that time, Levander was five and I put him in preschool even though I knew in my heart he wasn't going to be able to be with the other children. He was already hard to control. Marlee was four years older and she was afraid of him. He had a terrible temper, but he was cruel and mean beyond that. When I would punish him, he'd stand there with a half-smile and eyes like black glass. Eyes that you couldn't see into at all. Any fool knows that being scared is the worst part of the punishment for most children. What do you do with a child that has no fear?

"Then the teacher at the school started sending back reports that Levander was fighting with the other kids. And he wouldn't stay at his desk. And he threw things at the teacher. And he spit on the principal. I could see what was coming. The teachers were almost all white women in those days and the school adminis-tration was all white, too. I just couldn't talk to them about what to do, so I went to my caseworker, Judy Cohen, and I told her all about the situation. I said, 'I know my son, Levander, has a problem and I want to get help for him, but I don't know what to do.' At that time, I was also trying to get into a training program to become a practical nurse and Judy was helping me.

"She knew about Levander, of course, from home visits, and the letters from his teacher, Miss Hauptmann, came as no shock to her. She said the first thing was to put in a request through the school for a psychiatric evaluation which she did. I have a copy of it right here."

She began to ruffle through a thick stack of documents and Tilley had a premonition that they were in for a very long afternoon if Moodrow didn't cut her short. Once again he wondered if Moodrow expected to get any information out of her. Maybe he was only being polite. Listening out of respect. In any event, he took the paper she offered and read it slowly.

"You see the date, Sergeant? April 18, 1963. Levander was five years old. I waited two months to hear from them, then Judy called the principal, Dr. Rudoso, to find out what was happening, but Dr. Rudoso said the school system wasn't an insane asylum and that, anyway, Levander would receive more benefit from a prison cell than a psychiatrist's couch. Then he said something about women social workers and they should stick to giving away the city and stay out of Department of Education business."

As Mrs. Greenwood went on, her voice began to drop and she seemed to shrink on the overstuffed chair, to sink into the cushions despite the stiff plastic slipcovers. At one point, her daughter took her hand and began to caress the backs of her fingers. "Judy took everything he had to say. Then she reminded him that he was obliged to either approve or reject the application. That he could not sit on it forever. That if he didn't act, she would take it to the Commissioner. Judy was tough that way. She knew what she wanted and she would never give up until she got it.

"A week later we received a letter in the mail with an appointment for Levander to go see Dr. Smithley at the Bushwick Psychiatric Center. Here's the letter. It's signed by Dr. Rudoso.

"Levander and I kept the appointment. It was one of the hardest days I ever had with him. He seemed to know he was being tested and there was a lot of waiting with other patients in a small room between tests. I had to hold onto him every minute, but I felt so good when I went to bed that night, Sergeant, because I thought at last something was going to be done.

"About a month went by and nothing happened. I called the Center several times and was told the test results were being evaluated. By this time it was summer vacation and Dr. Smithley said they would forward all the information to the school administration. I wouldn't have to come back again. I asked what did he intend to do to help Levander and he said it was up to PS22 and he was hired by the school to do the evaluation, so he couldn't talk about it without their permission."

"Mrs. Greenwood, you don't have to tell me this," Moodrow finally broke in. "I know how hard you tried."

"You don't know shit," Marlee said, stepping forward. "When you *try* to do something you're supposed to at least have a chance. What chance did my mama have? No chance at all. When Levander went back to start first grade that white pig Rudoso got even with Judy and my mama by putting Levander in a special education class. You know how to spell 'special education'? R E T A R D."

Mrs. Greenwood put her arm around her daughter's waist. "They didn't tell me about it. I thought he was with the rest of the students. Of course, when I did find out, I went to see Dr. Rudoso. I said, 'Dr. Rudoso, I don't think Levander is retarded, but even if he is, he still has a problem with his temper. When he gets angry, he loses control and he hurts the other children. How will these classes help him?'

"Two years later, Dr. Rudoso was replaced by Simon Hooks, a black man, and I thought I would get some help, but when I went to him he told me my son was 'incorrigible.' He said he was hired to bring discipline to the school, to end the reign of the juvenile delinquents. He said he was going to show the brats who was running the school system.

"Levander was eight years old, Sergeant. Eight years old and they showed him who was running the school system by putting him in PS607 on Henry Street. Do you remember the old 'six hundred' schools?"

"Yeah, I know about them. I remember them real well."

"Then you recall they took all the 'problem' children from the regular schools and put them together in these 'six hundred' schools. They didn't teach them anything. They just kept them caged until three o'clock in the afternoon. By the time Levander was ten, he was gone. He started living on the street, running with street gangs. Come home and take money from my pocketbook. When he was about twelve, he hurt one little boy real bad. Hit him with a stick in his ear and made him deaf. Then the policemen started coming around. They said my son was a menace. They asked me why I didn't do anything about him and I explained that I did try. I tried from when he was still a baby, but I couldn't do it by myself and nobody would help me.

"Now here." She passed several pages across to Moodrow. "My caseworker, Judy Cohen, finally got a psychologist from Social Services to examine Levander. That's a copy of his report that I just gave you. It says right there that Levander needs help. It says that Levander is likely to act out. It says that he will hurt people unless someone helps him."

"Know what they did to help my brother, Moodrow?" Marlee's voice was sharp with contempt. "The pigs talked us into sending him to the state school on Staten Island. Willowbrook. The pigs didn't tell us they were going to drug him until he pissed all over himself. Until he didn't even know who we were. The pigs didn't tell us nothin' and it took us nine months to get him out of there."

"How many requests could I make?" Mrs. Greenwood asked quietly. "I could understand it if they didn't know about Levander, but I started telling them when he was five years old." She stopped abruptly, then took a deep breath. "If I had money, the doctors would have jumped all over themselves trying to help Levander with his problem, but I was poor. I was a poor black woman without a husband. Sergeant Moodrow, I don't want you to kill my son. I want you to try not to kill Levander. If you promise, I'll help you find him."

Moodrow straightened up immediately. The idea of a deal, information for a promise, was a lot easier than handling a straight plea for mercy. "I can't make a promise for all the cops in the city. I'm not Superman."

"Just make it for yourself. If you're there and if he lets you, you won't kill him. I know you'll keep to it, if you promise me."

"And how many other people will he hurt? Do you think because he's in jail, he won't be able to hurt anyone?"

She stared at Moodrow, collecting her thoughts. By that time, she was barely whispering. But she was still determined. She had made the decision to save her child and she wouldn't give up until Moodrow walked out of the apartment. "It just doesn't seem right to me. They should have helped him when he was a little boy, but they let him grow up wild. They knew about it and they allowed it to happen. Now they want to shoot him down. If he's alive, he *could* be saved. It's possible. Jesus *could* save him. If he dies, he'll be in hell forever." Her voice dropped off momentarily. Then she picked it up again. "I don't want them to kill my child."

This time Moodrow didn't allow any gaps, but when he spoke his voice had a strange urgency. "Yeah, sure. I won't kill him. All right? I promise that I won't commit a homicide, namely premeditated murder, on Levander Greenwood. But I'm not saying I'll take any risks for him and I'm not speaking for anyone but myself."

"He don't mean it, Mama. He's just another damn liar. . . ."

"Shut up, Marlee," Moodrow snapped. He didn't bother to look at her. "I'm even saying I'll try to fix it so he has a chance to surrender. I don't know if I can do it, but I'll try. Understand that when we go to take Levander, there'll probably be a lot of other cops there and I won't be in charge. Not even close, but I'll try to set it up so he can surrender. Also, if he gets in touch with you and he wants to give up, talk to me first and I'll take him into the stationhouse. Understand? First. Nobody else. Now what's this earthshaking information?"

Louise Greenwood smiled then. Satisfied with the results of her efforts. At no time did she try to include Tilley in the deal, which was just as well. With a man like Levander Greenwood, Tilley reasoned, if you hesitate at a crucial moment, you might as well put your own gun in your own mouth and pull the trigger.

"I said I'd help you, Sergeant. I didn't say I knew where he was." She continued to smile. "But I do know he's been to see Rose. He's been to see his wife and his children."

"Mama," Marlee said angrily, "Rosey's gonna be furious when she hears about this."

"Rose told me to mention it, Marlee. She said if Sergeant Moodrow came by I was to say she wanted to see him as soon as possible."

"So you sold me information that you were told to give me for nothing?" Moodrow, despite the challenge, spoke evenly.

"I don't recall Rose putting a price on it," Louise Greenwood countered.

"And if I walked out without promising, you wouldn't have said that Rose was looking for me?"

She dealt with his logic by ignoring it. "Levander was there last week. He's very hard with her."

"When was the last time you heard from him?"

"We haven't seen him in over a year. There's nothing here for him, now. And I don't know anyone who knows him. I work full time and most nights I go down to the church and help out. That's not exactly Levander's style."

"Does he visit Rose often?"

"Ask her that question yourself, Sergeant. I spoke to her while you argued with Marlee at the door. I told her you'd be over to see her."

5

The contrast between the project where Louise Greenwood lived with her daughter, Marlee, and the tenement that housed Rose Carillo was sharp and clear, even from out on the street. In an effort to avoid the expense of repointing the brick, the landlord had painted the building a dark, heavy red, a red the color of arterial blood. Now it was flaking so badly the five-story tenement looked like it had psoriasis. Shards of thick black paint projected from the wooden window-frames like razor blades. The frames themselves were obviously swollen and the lintels above them broken off. Several apartments on the second and third floors were empty, their windows covered with sheets of unpainted plywood. Scorch marks on the brick announced the occurrence of one of the most dreaded events in a New Yorker's life—a burn-out.

As they walked quickly up the front steps, Jim Tilley threw his partner a disgusted look. The whole scene—the heat, the filth, the raw poverty, offended him. The lobby was no better than the exterior. The door lock was missing, the mailboxes wide open, the ammonia reek of urine so sharp it pinched his nostrils. On the way up the stairs, his foot crunched hard on some object. Instinctively, he jerked his leg away and glanced down, expecting to find an old chicken bone, perhaps a piece of broken glass. Instead, he found a two inch water bug, its body crushed, its antennae still frantically tasting the world.

The inevitable question, popping off in his head like grease spattering on a grill, was "how can people live like this?" Despite a year in the poverty of Fort Greene, he found himself asking it whenever he entered a slum like this one. First he would ask the question, then imagine himself at the head of an army of tenants, all armed with tools, restoring the building to a glory it never had . . . in spite of the fact that he knew the tenants had no money and the landlord, who dreamed only of the day he could tear the place down, build condos and retire to Bermuda, was as unlikely to supply the necessary capital as Jim Tilley was to go to heaven.

"Look, Jim." Moodrow stopped him on the third floor landing. "Let me do the talking this time, all right? I know Rose Carillo and you won't get anything out of her with threats."

Unused to apologizing, Tilley replied in a whisper. "Listen, I feel sorry for the old lady, right? But how could I know from Marlee what her mother would be like?"

"What you need to do," Moodrow turned to face him, "you need to relax until you get so you do know. Most of the folks in the 7th hate the scumbags as much as we do, but they don't trust us worth a shit, either. And the reason they don't trust us is most cops never learn to tell the citizens from the criminals. For most cops it's all from the 'darkie' side of the force. If that's as far as you can see into this world, you won't never amount to anything as a cop. Not really." He slowly scratched the thin strip of hair over his right ear, a habit he had when he needed time to think. "Ya know, one of the reasons I picked you out was your evaluations. They said you were 'eager' for action. I like that word. Eager. I didn't wanna get stuck with a twenty-five-year-old hairbag. I wanted you ta have balls, okay? But not basketballs. Like you don't bounce 'em up and down on concrete. Ya gotta have balls with brains.

"Anyway, I want you to take a step back with Rose. She's tough as nails and if she don't want to tell us something, we'll never get it by threatening her." His expression was earnest, almost worried, as if he were responsible for his partner's big mouth.

Looking into his small, black eyes, Tilley swallowed hard. "Don't worry about it. I may be a slow learner, but I'm not retarded."

"Sounds like you're describing Levander Greenwood."

"C'mon, man."

Moodrow just laughed. "Don't worry about it, Jimmy." He waited for a response, but Tilley couldn't think of anything to say. Then Moodrow put a hand on his partner's shoulder, a hand that weighed about ten pounds. "One thing you need to understand, though. No matter what I say to Louise Greenwood or to Rose, my first aim is to get Levander Greenwood off the street. If there was no other way, I'd use your method. I wouldn't hesitate."

Tilley shrugged, then brought his attention back to Rose Carillo. He didn't know what to expect from Greenwood's ex-wife. The name sounded Italian, but she was from West Virginia somewhere and had been married to a black man. All the images contradicted themselves and left him utterly unprepared for the model-perfect white beauty who opened the door. She was small and quick, perhaps a little too bony in the shoulders, with a sharp nose and sharper chin, full lips and deep creases in her cheeks when she smiled. Her hair was raven-black and so glossy it shimmered as if freshly oiled. It fell over her shoulders, in front, to the tops of her breasts.

"Hello, Moodrow." Her dark eyes flicked from Tilley to Moodrow to the landing and the stairs. Only then did she step back to let the two cops in. "Why don't you go on down to the living room and get com-

fortable? I'll be there in a second. You want something
to drink?"

"What have you got?" Moodrow asked.

"I have scotch and Jim Beam and Coors. And I got
vodka in the freezer I could mix with just a trace of
cranberry extract. Get ripped and dissolve your kid-
neystones, all at the same time."

"I'll take the bourbon. Neat, okay?"

"How 'bout your friend?"

"Oh yeah, sorry. This is Jim Tilley. He's my new
partner."

"Yeah? For real? You really have a partner?"

"Why not?"

She came back, looking bemused, and gave the
young cop a closer inspection. "Well, good luck, Jim
Tilley. What'll you have to drink?"

"Do you have something without alcohol?" He
could feel the heat of her body across the room, despite
her neutral expression and a matter-of-fact voice with
just the trace of a southern question mark at the end
of each sentence.

"With two kids?" Her smile was natural, easy. "Orange juice. Milk. Those're the big two. And cranberry-
grape for when Lee's feeling adventurous."

He smiled, then found his lips were glued to it.
"Orange juice. I'm feeling kind of tame at the moment."

All at once, the front door slammed open and the
sound of shouting filled the hallway, followed by running feet and two light-brown children, obviously
brother and sister. When they saw the cops sitting in
their living room, they skidded to a halt and their eyes
grew big. They knew that men in suits usually meant
serious trouble and they turned to look at their mother
questioningly.

"You know Sergeant Moodrow, don't you?" She
waited a second for their memories to click in. "So,
what do you say?"

"Hello, Sergeant Moodrow." They looked to be about a year apart, the oldest, the boy, around seven. As they stared up at the two cops, suspicion (not awe or even curiosity) was evident in their gaze. No surprise in a neighborhood that sucks out innocence like a junkie sucks the sugar out of a candy bar.

"And this is Detective Tilley. He's Sergeant Moodrow's partner." She nodded at Tilley. "The boy's Lee and the girl's Jeanette."

"Hello, kids," Tilley said lamely.

Nothing. A blank stare. Four large, dark eyes boring into his. At first it was funny, then annoying. Then he just wanted to backhand them into another room. Fortunately, Rose, returning with the drinks, bailed him out. "I want you kids to go upstairs and stay with Estelle for a while."

"How long?" Jeanette demanded. "I'm hungry."

"You just go do it, missy. I'll be along when I'm through talking to these gentlemen. Estelle's expecting you, but if you see anyone else, you're not to mention that policemen came to this house."

They turned and left without speaking. As Jim Tilley watched their backs retreat down the hallway, he suddenly guessed the reason for their hostility. The two cops were the bringers of bad tidings. No good would come from their visit.

"Moodrow, can I speak in front of your friend? No offense, Detective Tilley."

"You can speak about anything, but our secret sex life," Moodrow returned cheerfully.

"I'm serious, Moodrow." She turned away from the closed door at the end of the hallway to meet his eyes. "You, I trust. But I don't know your friend."

Moodrow sat up in his chair, surprised to be getting down to business so quickly. "Tilley's my partner. For better or for worse. And, by the way, if you're gonna ask me serious questions, next time don't start the conversation off with three ounces of bourbon."

She smiled. When Moodrow was in a good mood, he was hard to resist. "Maybe you're right," she said. "I'll just pour the rest down the sink."

Moodrow's eyes opened wide. He grabbed the glass and held it away from her, like a parent teasing a child with a toy. "This is not the way to ask a favor," he said flatly. He drained the half inch in the bottom of the glass, then handed it to her. "Why don't you do that again, before we get down to work."

As soon as she disappeared, Tilley turned to his partner. "Do you know what you're risking when you drink on duty with a civilian? There are headhunters that'd eat you alive for that."

"I'm not risking a fucking thing," Moodrow replied. "I've been a cop for thirty-five years. What can they do? Make me retire? But you, you're being smart. You don't know Rose from shit and you got your whole career ahead of you. No good reason why you should take a chance. By the way, I really like this woman. You ever see that John Wayne movie? *True Grit?* Where he says about this kid, 'By God, she reminds me of me?'"

Rose Carillo came back into the room, cutting off any response. Enveloped by Moodrow's praise, her beauty struck Tilley again, as if it was something she pushed ahead of her whenever she entered a room. She was wearing a plain, white skirt and a white blouse, both made of some artificial fabric. A uniform, as it turned out, required by her doctor employer. The dress was old, the material soft; she had no slip underneath and the folds of the dress had more or less molded themselves to her legs. As she walked toward them, a glass of bourbon in one hand, orange juice in the other, Tilley had a hard time pulling his eyes from the point where legs and belly came together. He wondered, at the time, if she noticed it. Later he found out she could see him coming a mile away.

"What was I doing when you first met me, Moodrow? How long ago was it?" Her voice was much quieter.

"I think it was just before Lee was born," Moodrow replied, sipping his drink. "You were living with your mother-in-law in the projects. I was after Levander for ripping off some kids."

"So you don't really know what I did before that?"

"Actually, I don't."

"Wanna hear it? My life story?'

"Do I have to?"

"Yeah, you gotta." She crossed her left leg over her right, absentmindedly tugging the hem of her skirt down over her knee. "I grew up in Augusta, West Virginia, with my parents and one of my father's brothers. It was a small railroad depot for the coal miners and we were the only Italians in the town. My mother never learned English and my father spoke only enough to describe carburetors that needed rebuilding and batteries that needed to be replaced. He beat me, my father, for all of my life. He beat me and my mother, beat us without anger, and he did it in front of his younger brother, carefully explaining why this was a necessary part of the care and treatment of women.

"My mother died when I was twelve years old and I got my period a week later. For a long time I thought the two events were related. My father, who always drank wine, took to whiskey and staying in the bars until they closed. His brother, Uncle Dominick, did his drinking at home. He began, secretly, to touch my breasts while I was working in the kitchen or cleaning his room.

" 'Rosey, you come inna here and clean up dissa spill. You Uncle Dominick make a big mess.'

"First my breasts, then lower, then naked on the bed; sweating over me, grunting, slobbering." Her eyes never left Moodrow's; her voice was even, as though she was describing a case history in a psychology class.

"I left home at fifteen. Stole three hundred dollars

from a sock in my father's drawer and got on a bus for New York. There's no way to explain what it feels like to be a fifteen-year-old girl arriving at the Port Authority bus terminal. It seemed like there were more people in that building than in the whole state of West Virginia. Suddenly the toughness dissolves and the real questions—shelter, clothing, food, income—pour in.

"I drifted among the homeward-bound commuters and the alkies from the welfare hotels and the rip-off artists and the pimps, like a stick drifting down a river. I had done it. I'd gotten all the way to New York City and I had no idea what to do next. Believe it or not, with two hundred and fifty dollars in my purse, I was thinking of going to a hotel. In New York, two fifty would last about a day and a half."

She flipped her head back, then ran long, thin fingers through her hair. "I was half-way through the main lobby at the terminal when a black kid, about my age, grabbed my purse and took off. Two steps later, before I could react, he was grabbed by another, older, kid. A man, really. That was Levander. He slapped the guy who took my purse the way you cuff a dog that won't obey, then came back over to me.

"Naturally, I was grateful. I never suspected this was a scam Levander repeated as often as he felt he could get into the terminal without being arrested. Most times, the girl took the purse and went on her way, but once in a while someone came through with no idea where she was going or what she would do when she got there. A baby, really, like myself, who'd been beaten by her father and fucked by her uncle so many times she ran into the arms of the first man who'd both beat and fuck her. Such a girl, Moodrow, no matter where she comes to ground, finds Levander Greenwood waiting for her.

"He took me home for the night. Fed sweet and sour pork to a little country girl who'd never eaten a dish more exotic than a Pizza Hut pizza. Fed cocaine and reefer and a pharmaceutical lude to a girl who never even touched the wine passed at her father's table.

"Two weeks later I was on the street. I worked Long Island City most of the time. The johns there always grab you as soon as you get in the car, to see that you're not a transvestite. It's all car sex. There's no hotels." She paused to gather up the empty glasses as if her confession were no more unusual than an old friend reminiscing on the days of her youth. Moodrow was sitting back in his chair, the glass of bourbon cradled in his lap, like he, too, had all the time in the world. "It took me a long while to realize that I was a prisoner. At first I was high all the time. High on dope mostly, though we smoked joints as casually as you'd smoke a cigarette and carried little pill boxes filled with Seconal and black beauties. Ups and downs, whichever way you needed to go. I thought it was heaven and as for the sex . . . we got off by despising the pitiful johns, so fucked up they bought the flesh of women who felt absolutely nothing for them.

"I think I probably could have gone on like that for a good ten years if Levander hadn't decided to make me his permanent woman. He never explained why he did it; he never said, for instance, that he loved me or he was jealous of other men. One day, he simply announced that I was to live with him and not to sleep with anyone else. Ever. Three months after that he told me that we were going to be married and I was standing next to him, while a Baptist minister in a storefront church in Brownsville mumbled some bullshit about 'do you take this man' when I first realized that, as far as Levander Greenwood was concerned, I was a prisoner for life.

"But, fuck it, baby. I was still high all the time. So high that somehow, even though we rarely had sex, Levander managed to knock me up without my seeing it coming. I didn't realize anything was wrong until my stomach was near the size of a watermelon. Lev-

ander was pleased as punch. He bragged to all his
friends about what a great father he was going to be
and just to prove his point, he cut me off from all
drugs for the last month of my pregnancy.

"By the time Lee arrived, somehow healthy, in spite
of my losing twenty pounds in two weeks, I knew I
had to leave. I knew I was a human being in spite of
my life up until that point. When they put Lee on my
belly, I looked down at his curly wet hair and his
closed eyes and my heart fell out of my chest. There's
no way to explain that feeling to someone who's never
felt it or to explain what it feels like to watch your
child being beaten by a crazed animal named Levander
Greenwood.

"You see, I made the mistake of telling Levander
that I wanted to leave. Lee was about three months
old and I was already pregnant with Jeanette. I should
have known better. I'd been beaten by him and seen
him beat other women many times, but I had some
fantasy of living in the neighborhood. I was only eighteen, and despite three years of Levander, still naive in
the ways of predation. Levander not only gave me a
good 'whippin,' he took away all my money. I was
given only enough to perform specific tasks and was
expected to produce receipts.

"Then he went after Lee. He said that I loved the
'little rat' more than him. He complained that Lee
cried too much. How could he not cry when the man
who beat him nearly everyday started screaming at
him? I was frantic. Sometimes I put myself between
them. Sometimes I jumped on Levander's back. But
the result was always the same. The result was the
sharp crack of his palm on Lee's face. Or his fists on
my ribs."

Slowly, without making a great show of it and with
no embarrassment whatsoever, she pulled the bottom
of her blouse from her skirt and lifted it to reveal a

row of greenish-purple bruises that ran from her lower ribs to her armpit.

"When Jeanette was a year old, Judge Sidney Weinstein dealt Levander five to ten for manslaughter. A plea bargain, by the way. Down from second degree murder. Believe it or not, I thought I was free. The day they convicted him, I went to the welfare offices near City Hall and spoke to Adrienne Epstein from 'Battered Women.' She got me into a residential treatment program on Staten Island where I stayed with fifty women who'd all been through the same thing. By the way, that was the most depressing part of the deal, admitting that what happened to me was common. That my suffering wasn't special.

"I stayed there for six months, then I came back to this apartment. I had never lived alone before, never had to take care of myself, but I discovered that I thrived on freedom. I found my way into the office of a doctor friend of Adrienne's and learned the Latin words, the names of the instruments, how to wheedle money out of patients who pleaded poverty, even how to type. The kids went to day care in the mornings and to Granny Louise and Auntie Marlee in the evenings when I worked late. I had no desire for sex or even for a relationship. My idea of fulfillment was getting my high school diploma. Of starting classes at Manhattan Community College. Of taking one lousy, three-credit anthropology course that turned out to be about as exciting as locking myself in a closet for six hours a week.

"Paradise, right? To be suddenly given a life after twenty years of dreaming . . . if you've never been there, you'll never know. Anyway, six years later Levander Greenwood came out of prison. He was calling himself Kubla Khan, then, after the character in the poem and two days after they let him out, he showed up to reclaim his kingdom.

"I fought." Her voice dropped now, deepened as she

came to the point. Moodrow was sitting upright, his shoulders hunched forward as if protecting her. Or claiming her. "Naturally, I fought. The thought of letting him abuse my children panicked me. I was not the same woman anymore. I had the police take him out of the house and he came back and beat me up. I went to court and got an order barring him from coming within one hundred yards of me or my children and he came back and beat me. I had him arrested and they tried to violate his parole. He was inside for a month and the judge told him if he harassed me, he'd do another three years.

"Two days after his release, I found him in the apartment after I picked up the kids. He'd jimmied the window gate and busted open the window to get inside. He explained himself very clearly. 'See what I'm gonna do is teach you about fuckin' with me.' He took Jeanette by the hand and dragged her into the bathroom. By this time, both the children were crying and I was begging him not to hurt them, but he just laughed and explained how he'd been too easy with us. Now he was going to show us the 'hard edge of his will' in such a way that we wouldn't ever doubt him again.

"He filled the tub with hot water; it was midsummer and the landlord was sending it up scalding hot. Levander sat on the edge of the tub and let the steam boil around his face. I remember sunlight pouring through the leaded glass window and lighting up the beads of sweat on his neck. From somewhere in the distance, I heard my own voice. I was still pleading and Levander was still ignoring me. When he put Jeanette's hand in the water I thought I would go mad.

"He held her hand under the water for a long time. I couldn't count it. A second seemed like an hour, like there was no time at all, then somehow it was over. He told me, 'Put these kids to bed, then come in your room. I'll be waitin' for you. And don't you ever disrespect me again or else the little bitch'll think this was her Saturday night bath.'

"Aren't I entitled to a life? Doesn't the Constitution say I have a right to have a life? Don't my children have a right to their lives? Do we have to run and hide? Where do you run when you never have an extra dime? When you have to work fifty hours a week to pay the rent? But I'm still entitled to a life. It's my right."

She paused, her eyes riveted to Moodrow's. Her face was strained, now, her eyes narrow. "How many murders is he wanted for? I saw his face on the news tonight and the newsman was talking about a dead cop. When you take him, you can do anything you want and nobody will give a shit about it."

Moodrow reached out, as if to cover her mouth, but she was quicker. She laid her hand on his and gently pushed it down. "Kill him, Moodrow. It's your job to protect the innocent, and even if I'm a whore and a junkie, the children will never be free as long as he's alive. Never.

"I've already tried the 'right' way. I went to the cops and I went to the judge and they couldn't protect me. What's next?" She got up abruptly, walked to a cabinet lying against the wall and took out a small, automatic pistol. "I could shoot him, Moodrow. I've dreamed it a thousand times. But if I do, the cops—maybe you, eh?—will have to arrest me. The district attorney will have to move for an indictment. Maybe I'll get lucky. Battered women are 'in' these days. Maybe I'll find a good lawyer who'll represent me for the publicity and a good jury to find me innocent. And then, after two years of hell, my children, if the state lets me keep them, can grow up knowing I blew their father away, a little added burden for two zebras coming up in New York. No, you're the one, Moodrow. You have to see that it gets done. You have to protect us."

She stopped cold then and the room filled with tension. Moodrow stood up, as if he was in a hurry to get somewhere, then realized he had no place to go and sat back down. He was smart enough to keep his mouth shut, but Tilley couldn't resist stepping in. Not that he wasn't moved by what she'd said. The urge to protect her was as powerful as the physical attraction a few moments earlier. It's just that the answer seemed so obvious. "You know if he's taken alive, he's gonna get convicted of first degree murder? You know that, right? That's for killing a cop. He'll have to do forty years, minimum."

She turned to him for the first time and when she spoke, her voice was patient, gentle. "I'll never be safe as long as he's alive," she said. "He'll never stop trying to get out and if he gets out he'll come back to me. I'll never go through a day knowing we're safe. And there's something else I haven't told you yet. When Levander came by last week, he brought a man with him. I doubt very much if he was a friend."

Like slapstick comedians doing a double-take, Moodrow and Tilley sat bolt upright in their chairs. The whole visit had been full of surprises, but this was the most unexpected of all. It put her request on a whole other level and all three of them knew it.

"If I give you the name, you'll go after him and Levander will hear about it. He'll know I gave it to you and he'll come back. Well, I won't be here, Moodrow. I'm going to stay with a friend in Washington Heights, but I can't live there forever. I have to work. I have to go about the business of earning my life. I have to know that when the smoke clears, I'll be free forever."

"You got a lot of nerve, Rosie. You're asking me to commit a murder. Asking me in front of a witness."

"You told me you trusted him," she replied evenly. "And I wanted someone else to hear you promise."

"I haven't promised."

"Yet. My bags are already packed." She smiled.

"Why bullshit, Moodrow? Huh? Why bullshit? Levander isn't the most popular fellow on the Lower East Side these days. The man he was with had to be some kind of a partner. He stood by the window the whole time Levander was here. Watched Levander beat me up without blinking an eye. For a change, Levander didn't want sex. He wanted money and I didn't have enough. Levander's smoking crack, now, and he's insane."

Her assessment of the investigation was virtually identical to that of the two cops. Levander's partner would be the map to the hidden treasure.

"How do you want me to do it? You want me to do it in front of witnesses? You think a cop can't be indicted? Maybe I should kill the two hundred other cops that'll probably be there when we take him, so no one can testify against me."

Suddenly, Rose Carillo showed her anger for the first time. The muscles in her cheeks balled up and Tilley caught a glimpse of her determination. It was so close to that of Louise Greenwood, it shocked him. "Don't fuck me around, Moodrow. You try to arrange it so that you'll take him alone. That's how you wanna do it anyway. If it doesn't work, then it doesn't. I'll have to hope you can keep him in a cage, but if it does work, I'll have a life for the first time. The kind of life that *you* take for granted." She stopped then. Stopped to catch her breath, then sat back in her chair. "What's the story, Moodrow? You in or out?"

A huge, wolfish smile. An angry smile, palms turned up. "I'm in, Rosie. Naturally, I'm in."

6

Moodrow left Rose Carillo's apartment at a dead run, Jim Tilley trailing behind. Moodrow was obviously angry, but there was something else beyond that. By his own standards, Moodrow had compromised himself by promising both to keep Greenwood alive and to kill him. According to "Moodrow's Law," each woman was entitled to the fulfillment of the deal he'd made with her. Add to this his agreeing to commit a homicide (whether he meant it or not) in front of a rookie detective he'd known for twenty-four hours and you have the picture of Don Moodrow pounding down the stairs (waterbugs be damned) and into the street. Rose had named Levander's associate, then given Moodrow her new address in Washington Heights. If her ex-husband was looking for her, she wanted to know about it.

The name she gave them, Peter Katjcic, belonged to a white biker, a founding member of a dealing gang called Satan's Gentlemen. Unlike more notorious outlaw gangs that specialized in greasy, denim cutaways, the Gentlemen wore leather jumpsuits when the weather was cool enough, leather pants and matching armless jackets over white, silk shirts when it was hot. Their motorcycles, far from the stripped down behemoths favored by outlaw bikers, were loaded with every conceivable accessory. Wide cowlings in front held twin stereo speakers, dual headlights, tachometers, air vents (on a motorcycle!) and enough amber lights for a glitter-crazed cowboy in a customized ten-wheeler. Not that the backs of the bikes had been neglected. A truck mounted above fiberglass saddlebags supported two more stereo speakers, dual antennas and chrome racks. Every inch was encrusted with red lights and trimmed with chrome strips that accented more chrome in the dual exhausts, sweeping engine guards, shock absorbers and spoke wheels. These motorcycles, of course, were always spotless, as were their riders. The whole effort was to stand apart from their outlaw brothers, the same outlaws with whom they traded homebrewed methamphetamine (called crank) on an almost daily basis.

Tilley knew none of this, of course, as he trotted behind Moodrow. It was enough just to keep up with him. Moodrow didn't speak a word until the two of them were in the car (Moodrow on the driver's side) and started moving. Then he finally muttered, "Okay, basketballs, you're gonna get your chance now."

"You talking to me?" Tilley may have resented the calculating, controlled Moodrow, but he was nevertheless infinitely preferable to the maniac who swept onto Avenue C, tires screaming. Moodrow had the red bubble cupped to the roof of the Plymouth and he jerked the sedan around the buses and the parked trucks as if somehow Katjcic knew they were coming. They roared onto 4th Street, barely cleared a double-parked car (a Spanish kid loading a stereo into the trunk crossed himself as the Plymouth tore by) and turned abruptly into a vacant lot next to a long-ago burnt-out tenement. Behind the building, in a locked, fenced, impromptu parking lot, Satan's Gentlemen kept their motorcycles. In spite of the shadows in the courtyard, they glowed as if every square inch of paint, each spoke, even the black leather seats had been polished and repolished a moment before the two cops arrived.

"What the fuck is this?" Jim Tilley might as well have tried to communicate by smoke signals for all the impression his question made on Moodrow, who nosed the Plymouth forward until it was touching the gate, feathered the gas pedal until the lock gave, then coasted to a stop in the backyard. Tilley could feel the eyes behind the boarded-up windows. If he had been at a drive-in with his high school sweetheart, this is where he would have made his move.

"That's the entrance to the club." Moodrow pointed to a black, windowless door set five or six steps below ground level. "The first person comes out of that door, you hit him. Don't wait. Don't let 'em think even for one second that you're weighing your decision." He walked back to the trunk of the car, opened it, took out two aluminum baseball bats and handed one to Tilley. "Hit him with this."

"You're crazy, Moodrow. You're out of your fucking mind. I'm not gonna jump through your hoops. No way."

Moodrow looked into his partner's eyes for a moment, then nearly smiled. "You better do it, Jimmy. Cause if you don't, we're gonna get our asses kicked. Guaranteed." He crossed to the row of parked motorcycles. The bat, raised high above his head, looked as small as a nightstick in the hand of an ordinary policeman and he brought it down with enough force to completely justify Tilley's sense of being the sacrifice in a horror movie. It crashed into the cowling of a huge Kawasaki, cracking the plastic, smashing the dual headlights and the side mirror, making that singing sound aluminum bats make when they strike a baseball, like a tuning fork gone berserk. Then he turned to his partner with a relieved grin on his face.

"You're blowing your lines again. You were supposed to say, 'You rang, sir?' "

Piiiinnnnnggggg. Piiiinnnnnggggg. Ten times on the first of eight or nine bikes parked in the lot, until the door opened and Satan's Gentlemen appeared at the bottom of the steps, about six feet away from Jim Tilley.

To his everlasting credit, Tilley didn't pursue the question of violence any further than the absolute conviction that their aim was to break his bones. He took one step forward and swung the bat at the lead head, giving it his best power-hitting first-baseman homerun swing. The head ducked back into the doorway, as he'd hoped, and the bat crashed into the edge of the brick framing the steps, sending a shower of brick dust into the face of the man he'd swung at.

Before he could raise the bat again, Satan's Gentlemen withdrew into their headquarters. Up to this point, they'd been clearly out-crazied. Now that they knew they couldn't bluff or subdue Moodrow and Tilley without getting their own heads split open, they had to acknowledge a second problem—if they attacked Moodrow and Tilley, what jury would believe that *they*, the cops, had deliberately challenged the whole gang? As Tilley read it, there didn't seem to be a hell of an upside for Satan's Gentlemen anywhere in the encounter and he suspected they were inside considering this fact.

Meanwhile, Moodrow was methodically destroying motorcycles. The unbreakable aluminum bat, though it was twisted and bent, rang out with each blow and the sheet metal and fiberglass dented and cracked and split. He was on his third bike, when a voice, shouting so as to be heard above the sounds of destruction, threatened them from the second floor window.

"Stop it, ya motherfucker. Stop it or I'm gonna blow your eyeballs outta ya fuckin' head." There was no face behind the voice. Just the command.

"You gonna kill me, asshole?" Moodrow didn't pause. "You ain't got the balls." He whipped the bat sidearm into the windshield of an enormous red Yamaha, sending pieces of clear plastic sailing across the yard. "If you were gonna shoot me you woulda done it when I busted you four years ago. Or at least when you got outta the joint." Very deliberately, like a bear trying to pray, he dropped to his knee and began to jam the bat handle into the polished spokes.

"Well, what the fuck do ya want? What the fuck are ya doin' this for, Moodrow?"

Moodrow, obviously winded, turned toward the house for the first time. He looked over at Tilley and said, "It's good to be recognized. It makes you feel warm all over." To the voice behind the window, he said, "Peter Katjcic. I wanna talk to him."

"Why didn't ya just say that? Are ya fuckin' crazy? You got a fuckin' disease?"

Moodrow wheeled around, whipping the bat into the chain drive of an especially ostentatious Yamaha. This one had chrome fenders and a blood-dripping swastika painted over a nude, chained blonde on the gas tank. "Peter Katjcic, Gunther." He was working harder now, the muscles on his neck and shoulders humping up beneath the skin.

"Do ya see Katjcic's bike here, Moodrow? Didja even look for his fuckin' bike?"

Piiiiinnnnnggggg.

"I can't make him here if he's not here. What do I look like, the Blessed fuckin' Virgin?"

Piiiiinnnnnggggg. Crash. A beautiful shot. Downward at a slight angle, clearing the handlebars and smashing the complex of instruments along with the stereo and the CB. Suddenly Tilley felt much better. He knew the men in that house were armed. He knew they were capable of tremendous violence. But they were not the outlaws of twenty years ago who would fight out of principle. They were dealers, money-men, and they would think twice before giving two cops a reason to enter and search their place of business. Besides, all of a sudden Jim Tilley didn't give a shit. He kept thinking about Levander Greenwood jamming Jeanette's hand into a steaming tub. Of Louise Greenwood sitting in a welfare office, begging for help. Of shotgunned bodies alongside the Williamsburg Bridge.

It was too crazy to sort out, but the result was simple: he just didn't give a shit.

"Fa Christ sake, Moodrow, that's my fuckin' bike."

Piiiiinnnnnggggg.

"I'll kill ya. I swear it."

It was steaming hot and the sweat was pouring down the side of Moodrow's face; his pants were plastered to his thighs and his unbuttoned jacket showed black under the arms. He laid the bat on the ground, then ripped the already broken trunk from the back of Gunther's bike and hurled it at the window. The plywood, long exposed to the weather, gave way and crashed backward into the room. "Peter Katjcic, Gunther. If he's not in there, you come down and take me to him."

No answer. Moodrow took up the bat. "I'm getting tired of this shit," he whispered. "I'm too fucking old. I shoulda let you do it."

"Wanna switch?"

Gunther, his voice filled with equal measures of anger and frustration, broke in before Moodrow had a chance to reply. "Lemme come down and talk to ya? Awright? Gimme two minutes with my people and I'll be out." He showed his face in the window just to prove his good intentions. Now Tilley understood the "Gunther" bit. He was blue-eyed and blonde, his wavy hair parted nearly in the center, with a long scar on one cheek. Like many of the outlaw gangs, the Gentlemen were organized on racial lines. Though they despised Jews and other mongrels, they saved their real hatred for the blacks and the Puerto Ricans with whom they constantly did business.

Five minutes later, the door opened and Gunther, looking like he stepped off a Nazi Youth poster, came out. Tilley was surprised to see him alone, but he seemed at ease as he walked directly to Moodrow.

"Why the fuck are you doin' this ta me?" he said, waving his arms. "Why the fuck?" He was a big man, almost as tall as Moodrow, but when Moodrow stepped forward until their noses were about to touch, Gunther took an involuntary step backward.

"You're my snitch," Moodrow said quietly. "You forget that? You're supposed to keep me informed of what goes down in the neighborhood. Meanwhile, Peter Katjcic's doing business with Levander Greenwood who you fucking well know I personally wanna see and you don't even call me. You're making me look like an asshole in front of my new partner. I don't like that."

"What ya did here today was bullshit, Moodrow. Just for the fuckin' record. There wasn't no reason for it. We wanna get Greenwood off the streets as much as you do."

"Then why didn't you get in touch with me as soon as you heard Levander killed that cop? I put out for you. I kept your faggoty ass out of jail when your P.O. wanted to violate your parole and I expect you to pay me back. If you don't, I'm gonna collect the debt by coming down here every fucking day until I drive your ass out of the Lower East Side. And I'm gonna tell the world why I'm doing it. Now, let's go find Katjcic. I wanna talk to him."

Gunther threw his motorcycle a last, stricken look, then led the way through the lot, across 4th Street and into a sixteen-family white brick tenement, this one still occupied. Moodrow, one hand on Gunther's elbow to insure a slow pace, kept up a running commentary. "This is my partner, Gunther. This is Detective Tilley. I'm turning him onto my rats. You know, like the little animal with the pointy nose and the tiny, black eyes. Like you. But don't worry, I won't tell him your real name is Bernard Pushky, not Gunther Bauer. I won't tell him you come from Bayside instead of Bavaria. And most of all I won't tell him you got that scar in a schoolyard fight with a Negro.

As long as you remember to jump for him the same as me, I won't say nothing about it."

Gunther, the Aryan, took it all without flinching, though his eyes blazed with anger. He was not the sort of man who was accustomed to taking shit, despite his deal. On the other hand, he had violated the terms of the agreement by keeping the news of Levander Greenwood from Moodrow. And he had done it in order to turn a profit. If Moodrow let it slide, without punishing the transgression, he would lose face. The motorcycles might be repaired, but the message would linger. In a real sense, Gunther was as tied to Stanley Moodrow as Rose Carillo was to Levander Greenwood.

Perhaps Bernard "Gunther" Pushky didn't see it quite this way (how many prostitutes ever reach the understanding of Rose Carillo?), but he led the two cops along a corridor on the main floor and pushed into apartment 1C without knocking. The apartment consisted of a single large room dominated by an old, open, convertible sofa. The man lying on the mattress was somewhat smaller than Gunther, but still large. He was propped up on pillows, one side of his face enormously swollen. Bandages covered the back of his head and the shaven skull underneath them announced the presence of stitches. Moodrow and Tilley looked at each other and shrugged, already disappointed.

"Greenwood do this?" Moodrow asked.

Katjcic gave the pair his hardest look; his eyes moving deliberately from Tilley's to Moodrow's; his feelings for them more than obvious.

"He asked you a question, asshole," Tilley said, his voice as full of fury as the look in Katjcic's eyes. It surprised even him.

"You don't know?" Katjcic finally responded.

"Just say if it's true or not?" Tilley shouted. "Did Levander Greenwood beat the shit out of you or not?" He allowed himself the luxury of a smirk, then said to

Moodrow, much more quietly. "It don't look like he put up much resistance."

"You better talk to this guy," Moodrow advised Katjcic. "He's not an old man, like me."

"Why'd you bring these fuckers here?" Katjcic asked Gunther.

Gunther shifted his weight uneasily. "I called," he answered defensively. "I explained what he was doin' and ya said to bring the scumbags across."

"Scumbags? Scumbags?" It was perfect. Tilley was standing about two feet from Gunther. He slid his right shoulder back about six inches then shot a completely unexpected right hand into Gunther's chest. It crashed into his ribs about two inches below the left nipple and the outlaw dropped to the floor in a dead faint. "Listen, Katjcic," Tilley said, careful to keep the hiss in his voice, "If you don't stop the bullshit, I'm gonna launch an experiment to see if I can't split open them bruises on your face. Probly do it with a few short jabs." He hesitated for a second, then stepped forward. "Think I'm bluffing?"

"All right," Katjcic said, though the hatred in his eyes glowed even more brightly. "Greenwood did it. I figured you already knew that."

"Why should we know it?" Moodrow snapped.

Katjcic laughed, then wrapped his arms around his ribcage, trying to hold back the pain. "Kubla Khan is a snitch, man. Kubla Khan is a little mousey goes 'squeak, squeak, squeak' in the piggy's ear. And the piggy tells him who's heavy and where and when they're heavy. And the piggy tells him when to hide. And who's looking. Yessir, the piggy and the mouse."

He fell back against the pictures and allowed his eyes to close momentarily. He was stoned on heroin to ease the pain, which was just as well, because he looked halfway to dead. Moodrow knelt by the side of the bed and put his hand on Katjcic's arm. "Who, Katjcic? Who does Greenwood snitch for? Gimme the name." He was so eager, he nearly drooled.

"How do I know?" Katjcic responded. For the first time, his lips curled into a smile. "Maybe it's you."

7

"You shouldn't have done that to those motorcycles," Jim Tilley said for the third time. He pulled at a bottle of Heineken and eyed his partner narrowly. "You can't destroy private property."

"It looked to me like you were having fun," Moodrow said quietly. "I'm sorry if I got the wrong impression."

Tilley shook his head in disgust. "It's not a question of enjoying it or hating it. It's a question of being a cop and wanting to stay a cop. I know about you. Everyone on the job knows about you."

Moodrow turned and signaled to the barmaid for another beer. They were sitting in a booth in the Killarney Harp, on Houston Street, and the smell of the steam table was making him hungry. He would eat as soon as his partner left. In the meantime, though he was off the clock, he had work to do.

"So what do they say about me?"

"They say you think you own the law. They say you're still living in the old days. When cops were like God."

Moodrow laughed. "Like God, huh?" He paused to accept the beer offered by the barmaid, pulling on it eagerly. The sweat had dried on his body, but his suit was still damp and plastered to every fold and crevice of his body. He was very uncomfortable, but a few more beers would make it better. They always did. "So you're gonna tell me you never went outside the Patrol Guide? I don't buy it."

Tilley blushed, a sudden rush of color brightening pale Irish cheeks. "Even if I did make some mistakes, that doesn't mean I have to *keep on* making mistakes. If Gunther Baumann gets hold of a lawyer, we'll be written up. At the least. Maybe it doesn't matter to you. Maybe what you said before is right—all they can do is make you retire."

"You married, Tilley?" Moodrow suddenly changed the subject, a technique common to interrogations, but not altogether appropriate to barroom conversations.

"You know I'm not. You read my file."

"I mean, do you live with someone? An old lady. Without benefit of clergy." Moodrow stopped long enough to drain his glass. The beer was refrigerator cold, but the thirst he'd built up during his workout wouldn't go away. "It ain't that uncommon right? I been known to do it myself, on occasion."

"I live uptown. In Yorkville. With my mother." Tilley glared at his partner. The mother bit always embarrassed him. Next, Moodrow would be asking him if he was some kind of a fag.

"Is your mom sick?" Moodrow ignored the signal coming from his partner.

"Look, we got a four-bedroom apartment up there. Rent-controlled. My father took it five years before he died and we been there ever since. I mean, we're paying less than *five hundred* a month for it. Where am I supposed to go? If I left that apartment, I wouldn't be able to afford Manhattan. I'd probably end up on Long Island."

Moodrow motioned to one of the barmaids, a Spanish girl named Cheena, for two more bottles of beer, then abruptly came back to the original topic of conversation. "Okay, you're ambitious. I don't have no problem with that. But if you wanted to work your way up in the job, you should have stayed away from the detectives. You should have stayed on patrol. Then you could have got promoted by studying for the exams. Sergeant, lieutenant, captain. You pass, they gotta move you up. In the detectives you get promoted for the busts you make and the influence you got in the big house. And this bust, Jim Tilley, is a big one. You take Levander Greenwood outta the brass's hair and they'll kiss your ass from here to City Hall."

Moodrow paused, but Tilley had no answer to his partner's questions. He was asking himself why he *hadn't* stayed on patrol. His experience at Fordham had demonstrated the strength of his memory. Promotional exams in the NYPD were all memory, rehashings of the Patrol Guide. Without meaning to, Jim Tilley reached into his jacket pocket and touched his gold shield, the symbol of the New York detective. In some ways, even the lowest detective has more status than the commissioner. Like a Green Beret standing next to a senator.

"So what'd ya do?" Moodrow asked, his voice still matter-of-fact.

"What did I do when?"

"C'mon. In Fort Greene. You said a minute ago that you pulled some shit when you were on patrol. Tell me what you did."

Tilley couldn't help but grin. "You're a nosy son of a bitch," he announced.

"I'm a cop. It's my job."

"And how about you? What have you done?"

Moodrow giggled, the high-pitched sound trickling out over the table. "If I start with that, we'll be here till next week. Levander will die of old age before we get through."

"That's another thing," Tilley insisted, pulling himself up. "I don't know what made you promise those two women, but if you're really planning to execute Levander Greenwood, you better find another partner. That shit went out fifteen years ago. The headhunters watch too close these days. Not to mention the newspapers."

"You think we're gonna be alone when we take Greenwood?" Moodrow asked innocently. "There's gonna be a fucking army, for Christ sake."

"Why don't I believe you?" Tilley grinned. His emotions had been on a roller coaster all afternoon. First the bizarre stories of Louise Greenwood and Rose Carillo, then the heart-pounding insanity of Satan's Gentlemen, now the air-conditioned bar and his third ice-cold beer. It was like the parties he'd thrown after big victories in the amateurs, when he still hoped to make the Olympic team.

"Tell you what, Jimmy. When the time comes to take Mr. Greenwood, you can call the shots: who gets involved; how we go in; what we do with him. How's that?"

"What we do with him, Moodrow, is put him in cuffs and take him to jail."

"Fine with me." Moodrow spread his hands as if he had no objection to standard operating procedure. "Now tell me about Fort Greene."

Tilley's grin spread to cover the lower part of his face. Then he leaned forward. "There was one scumbag in the Two One Four. Name was Daniel Roberts. Called himself Chubs. Liked to get drunk, snort a little coke and spend the weekend beating on his wife and kids. Heavy dumpings, Moodrow. Broken bones. Lost teeth. Faces always swollen and that wet purple color that looks like it's about to explode. You'd take the bastard away and the next night he'd be back. The courts don't give a shit what you do to your family if you're black or Puerto Rican and you got a job. But even when the courts ordered him to stay away, I think his old lady used to invite him back if he had any money. Sometimes these violent guys can talk very sweet and innocent.

"I didn't make a real decision to get him. Patrolmen

are always moving from one call to another. Like you said, we never get to follow through on anything. We show up at a crime, secure the scene, interview the witnesses, then turn whatever we got over to the detectives. But every time I saw the bastard, I used to get mad and one night, I remember it was freezing cold and near Christmas, I sort of let my feelings catch up to even. I came across him arguing with another man, a nickel-and-dime pot dealer. Chubs was drunk and rowdy, as usual.

"I slid my nightstick out of my belt and walked over. The dealer, who was facing me, turned and began to walk the other way. He knew the argument would give me probable cause for a frisk and he was obviously dirty. Chubs, on the other hand, was too drunk to realize how fragile his situation was.

" 'What you want, pig?'

"I still wasn't sure what I was going to do, but I knew I couldn't just let it end there. I started out by calling him a subhuman piece of shit. I was almost whispering. I told him he should be in a cage instead of on the street. There was all kinds of hesitation in his eyes. Not that he was afraid. He was too drunk to be afraid. He just couldn't figure out what I was after.

"So I showed him what I was after by spitting flat in his face and he finally took a swing at me. There was no chance that he was going to hit me. It was a set-up all the way. I stepped off to the left, waited until he stumbled forward, then swung the nightstick with both hands like it was a baseball bat.

"The only thing that saved me from a departmental investigation was that he did have a knife in his pocket along with a small vial of cocaine. And I didn't kill him. I just fixed it so he wouldn't eat solids for six months and required seven operations to reconstruct his lower face."

* * *

By the time Captain Allen Epstein made his way to the Killarney Harp, Moodrow was on his second plate of corned beef and cabbage and Detective Jim Tilley was having a celebratory dinner with his mother in a German restaurant in Yorkville. The empty beer bottles had been collected and replaced with coffee and Moodrow had visited the men's room to wash his face with cold water.

"You mind if I sit?" Epstein asked, jerking Moodrow's attention away from his plate.

"You gotta ask? What's the matter with you?"

"Same old shit, Stanley. With three lieutenants in the precinct who already passed the captain's exam, you can't expect no peace. They're like vultures, for Christ sake. Like kids waiting around for Grandpa to kick off. Come to me with those shit-eating grins. 'Just a suggestion, Captain.' I look in the mirror and I think I'm a hundred years old." He stopped long enough to order a Miller's from a passing waitress, then launched back into it. "I'm looking at property in Florida. Me and Alma. Not that I'm going without a fight, but I wanna be ready. It's my nature, for Christ sake. So how'd you make out with young Jim Tilley?"

"It's like I figured. He's ambitious and he thinks he has to do things by the book. But he can't get rid of that macho prizefighter bit, either. Kid's living in two worlds. He's not street-wise, but he is street-hard and he's got a fucking brain. That's the important part. He's too smart to get lost in the bullshit. I just gotta find a way to make him realize it. I gotta make him understand that he cares about the civilians. That there ain't no point, if you don't."

Quickly, Moodrow outlined the day's events, including Katjcic's assertion that Greenwood's partner was a cop. He'd deliberately held back that piece of news, knowing the effect it would have on his friend. Allen Epstein had spent his working life trying to protect the 7th Precinct from outsiders and now the headhunters would descend in droves, drawn like flies to the blood of a corrupt cop.

"I can't say I haven't considered it," Epstein admitted, "but it still hurts. The dope is what does it. Too much money out there. You going to the task force with it?"

"I really don't think we can do that. We might be pumping information right back to Greenwood."

Moodrow sat back and sipped his coffee, considering the options. Word of a scandal in the 7th would effectively end Allen Epstein's career. As would any extensive delay in the apprehension of Levander Greenwood. And without Allen Epstein to cover his back, Moodrow's own career had the life expectancy of a butterfly in a blizzard.

"How long you think we have before the brass comes down on us?" Moodrow asked.

"They're already checking in. I got a call from the commissioner asking me to give the case my 'personal' attention. Then the chief called, then a deputy mayor. It's gonna be a fun investigation."

"Actually," Moodrow said, sincerely, "I'm looking forward to it."

"I wish my goddamn ulcer could say the same," Epstein returned. "The sad part is I remember when I used to jump into cases like this. I was eager. Now all I wanna do is make the precinct quota for summonses and go home. Which I can never even do that 'cause the goddamn portables won't give out tickets unless the sergeant points at the car and says, 'Write.' "

Moodrow had heard all this before. Heard it many times over the years. It was irrelevant to him; he had never been part of the bureaucracy of the job. But he knew he could trust Epstein and that, for all the bullshit, Epstein wanted Greenwood as badly as Moodrow did.

"So what're you gonna do, Captain?"

Epstein sat up straight. "Any patrolman doesn't

make his quota is gonna get vacation time in February. I'll have the bastards working traffic on the Williamsburg Bridge in a snow storm. I don't . . ."

"For Christ sake, man. I'm not talking about tickets. I'm talking about Greenwood."

"Greenwood?"

"Yeah, Greenwood. The guy who killed a cop and a journalist. Remember?"

"I think I'll go to the D.A.'s office. See if we can keep the cop thing under wraps without going too far outside of regulations. What about you? What're you gonna do tonight?"

Moodrow tossed his napkin onto his plate and stood up. "I'm gonna go to work. What else would I be doing?"

But Allen Epstein's beeper went off before Moodrow could get the check, and the obligatory telephone call transmitted news of gunshots fired, of cops killed and wounded, of an urgent summons to a deathbed in a private room at Bellevue Hospital.

Even as they left the bar, Epstein was composing two statements: one for the press and one for the brass.

POLICE DEPARTMENT: CITY OF NEW YORK

TAPE TRANSCRIPTION LABEL PD641-447 (4/85)

tape# 4401   case# MC201   loc 7th Pct

tape date 8/10/90   trans. date 8/11/90

transcribed by Benjamin Wright

sig. _Benwryl_

civ. emp. # 4381-99-766   badge # xxxxxxxx

pers: DA Samuel Weiser

Captain Allen Epstein

Det. Paul Kirkpatrick

Det. Charles O'Neill

Det. S. Moodrow

Dr. Marvin Jackson

Ptlmn. Franklyn Peters

cross reference 7th Pct Homicide 7-675

EPSTEIN: one, two, three . . .

WEISER: For shit sake, Epstein. He's going out again. Get the doctor. What's his name? Jackson? Tell him I want his ass in here until we finish with Peters' statement.

O'NEILL: Take it easy. Take it easy. Hey, Franklyn, can you hold onto it? Just a couple more minutes.

JACKSON: What's wrong?

WEISER: For Christ sake, the guy's practically out of it.

JACKSON: What'd you expect? Mr. Peters is heavily sedated. I'm surprised he's stayed awake this long.

WEISER: Can't you give him something to keep him up? We need five minutes to get a statement.

JACKSON: No way. He's still bleeding internally. I want him quiet.

WEISER: Are you fucking kidding me? You just told me he's gonna die. Now you want him 'quiet'? He's gonna be quiet for a long time, Doctor.

EPSTEIN: C'mon, Simon. It's not the doctor's fault.

WEISER: I want a dying declaration, Allen. I want an i.d. that'll stand up. I want when we catch this piece of shit, he'll get so many life sentences, even the fucking bleeding hearts won't be able to get him out. I want he should die in jail. Now, for shit sake, Doc, does he have a chance or doesn't he?

JACKSON: He has no chance.

WEISER: Then wake him up for ten minutes. Let him at least get even with the animal that did this to him.

JACKSON: I can't.

WEISER: Bullshit!

JACKSON: I want to help you, Mr. Weiser, but I can't deliberately administer a medication that might hasten a patient's death.

WEISER: Bullshit!

JACKSON: Bullshit? You forget that you prosecuted a doctor from this hospital for giving a morphine overdose to a ninety-four-year-old man with advanced Alzheimer's? You forget all the speeches you made about prosecutions for euthanasia? You forget the Sunday morning TV interviews? Hey, pal, read my lips: fuck you.

MOODROW: Wait a second. Hold it. He's coming around. You hear me, Franklyn?

PETERS: Yeah. I hear you.

MOODROW: Do you know who I am?

PETERS: Moodrow, tell the doctor to give me something for the pain. My guts're on fire.

JACKSON: I can give him more morphine.

WEISER: You wanna put him asleep? He just woke up and you wanna put him back asleep? I feel like I'm talking to a goddamn Martian. Hey, schmuck, read my lips: fuck you, too. Is the tape running, Epstein? Is the fucking tape at least running?

EPSTEIN: It's running. Go ahead and get the statement.

MOODROW: Franklyn, you know how bad you're wounded, right?

PETERS: Yeah.

MOODROW: I gotta tell you it don't look good for you. The doctor says you ain't gonna make it.

PETERS: I figured that.

MOODROW: We want your statement, Franklyn. It's a dying declaration. You understand what I'm saying? It's admissible if I tell you beforehand that you're gonna die.

WEISER: He's falling asleep.

MOODROW: For shit sake, Weiser. I just told the poor bastard he's not gonna make it. Can't you give him a second to think about it? Hey, Franklyn, can you talk? Help us get this guy.

PETERS: It was Levander Greenwood.

MOODROW: Are you sure?

PETERS: His picture's been all over the precinct for the last week. Plus I knew him from the street. Everybody figured taking him would get them out of uniform. Get them a gold shield.

MOODROW: Then you're identifying the man who shot you as Levander Greenwood.

PETERS: Yes.

MOODROW: Did Levander Greenwood also shoot Officer Cruz?

PETERS: Yes.

MOODROW: Do you think you could tell us what happened this afternoon?

O'NEILL: Jesus Christ, he's folding up.

JACKSON: He's in pain.

WEISER: Don't put him to sleep. We just need a couple of minutes more.

PETERS: I'm all right.

MOODROW: Tell us what happened, Franklyn. From when you got the call.

PETERS: Me and Cruz were in 7 Adam. About four hours into our watch, Central ordered us and 7 Henry to switch over to channel 3. That's Special Ops. There was a detective on the mike I didn't know. Identified himself as Carero, something like that. He ordered us to proceed to an apartment building at 887 Henry Street. 7 Henry was ordered to cover the front and back entrances. We were ordered to secure the third floor landing. The perpetrator . . .

WEISER: What the fuck happened?

MOODROW: I think he fell asleep.

PETERS: (unintelligible)

MOODROW: Can you speak a little louder, Franklyn?

PETERS: Carero said the perpetrator was in apartment 4C. Levander Greenwood. Wanted for murder. We all knew who he was.

O'NEILL: Christ, he's coughin' blood.

MOODROW: Just keep on talking, Franklyn. The doctor's right here.

PETERS: We were ordered to secure the third floor landing. . . . Did I say that?

MOODROW: Don't worry about it. Just keep talking.

PETERS: Nobody was allowed to go up and if anyone came down, they had to stay down. Carero said the task force would have a SWAT team ready in fifteen minutes. Just keep him bottled up for fifteen minutes.

The only thing was he had the wrong apartment. As we proceeded up to the third floor, I heard a noise behind me and he was standing there in a doorway. I had my gun in my hand, pointing up at the ceiling, but I didn't get close to bringing it down. Greenwood opened up with a twelve gauge without giving us any warning. You understand? He didn't say, 'drop it' or 'freeze.' It was an execution.

I thought getting shot wouldn't hurt. My brother was shot in Vietnam and he said he didn't feel anything at first. But this hurt like hell. My gut was torn open and it was like someone poured kerosene inside there and lit it. I could feel my organs trying to slide out and I kept pushing them back in. Cruz didn't say a word. He laid on top of me and his blood ran down in my face. I know I was screaming and trying to kick my partner away, but he was so heavy. I thought the whole world was lying on top of me.

JACKSON: He's asleep.

EPSTEIN: We get enough, Simon? Can we let his wife in now?

WEISER: Yeah. We got it.

EPSTEIN: Wait a second.

WEISER: What? What's wrong?

EPSTEIN: I forgot to label the tape.

WEISER: So do it now.

EPSTEIN: Date is August 10. Case number: MC201. Place is Bellevue Hospital, Intensive Care Unit #4. Witness is Patrolman Franklyn Peters, shield number 1677. Present: Simon Weiser, District Attorney; Allen Epstein, Captain, 7th Precinct; Detectives James Kirkpatrick, Charles O'Neill and Stanley Moodrow, 7th Precinct; Doctor . . . What's your name, Doc?

JACKSON: Jackson.

EPSTEIN: Doctor Jackson. This is a dying declaration.

8

The next day, Saturday, was, theoretically, Jim Tilley's day off. Unfortunately, just like in the movies, real detectives work whatever hours the job demands. A detective might, for instance, spend a month sitting through a series of eight-hour stakeouts, his life as regular as any clock-puncher's, then suddenly be assigned to a case (like Levander Greenwood's) where the public demands an immediate arrest. Then all bets are off and he works fourteen-hour days until his family can't (or won't, more likely) recognize him.

This is only one of a number of ways in which cops are the victims of the criminals they pursue. Even worse is the tendency of most cops to carry the job home. In spite of the inevitable macho barroom attitude, certain memories repeat themselves, like the words of familiar songs, for days or even weeks before they're finally buried deep enough to display themselves only in nightmares. As he pulled on his running shoes, Jim Tilley remembered clearly the first time it happened to him. He had dreamed of it only moments before.

The incident had taken place about three o'clock on a warm October afternoon. A drunk had stepped in front of a bus on Myrtle Avenue just as the driver turned his head to check the side mirror before pulling into traffic. The bus wasn't going very fast when it hit the man, but it picked him up anyway. Picked him up and tossed him through the rear window of a double-parked Buick.

Tilley saw the whole thing coming, saw the drunk stagger toward the curb, the bus driver's head swivel to the right, the enormous steering wheel starting to spin. He yelled for the man (his name turned out to be Sam Watson) to stop, but his voice only blended with the boozy haze surrounding all those reflexes which keep human beings from stepping in front of buses.

Mr. Watson's throat was cut to the bone by the window glass and he was spurting blood on the occupants of the Buick, an elderly black lady and her two grandchildren. For a moment the scene froze that way, the only movement being the pulsing jets of blood spraying the passengers of the car. Then the old lady jumped out into the street and began to scream at the bus driver. She called him an "ignorant, nappy-haired homeboy," said he was "common" and "trash." Meanwhile, the driver's eyes never left Sam Watson's body. Tilley thought the poor bastard was in shock, but when he pulled him away and told him to wait in the bus, the driver turned and shook his head, disgustedly.

"Fucking asshole." He pointed over at the dead man. "You believe that fucking asshole? This is my third accident. They're gonna fry me for this. Man, I got kids."

"Common trash. You hear me, homeboy?" the woman shouted as he disappeared into the bus. The two kids wouldn't stop crying. They were young, maybe six or seven, and they held hands and bawled as they waited for Granny to regain enough composure to comfort them.

Tilley couldn't shake the memory for weeks. Not the ugliness or even the blood. He had seen death coming and been unable to defeat it. Whenever he closed his eyes, it was there again. Sam Watson lurching toward the curb, the bus pulling away, the enormous force of the impact despite the slow speed, the dark, emaciated body flying through the air like an enormous dart, piercing the glass. For about ten seconds Sam Watson's legs stuck straight up in the air, then slowly fell to the top of the Buick's trunk. The blood, dark in the shadows, covered the inside of the windows. In his dreams it drenched the two kids and the old woman.

"What am I gonna do about this car?" the old woman asked him as he took down her name for the report. "You don't suppose Mr. Trash over there is gonna clean up his mess?"

Tilley was on the job three months when Sam Watson bought it and for the first couple of days he couldn't sleep at all. It was like someone had painted the scene on the back of his eyelids so that whenever he tried to close them, the bus started moving all over again. Then it got better. By the third night he was so exhausted he went out the minute he hit the pillow and didn't dream until nearly daybreak. By the seventh day it was only an occasional flash and now, finally, an instant of panic when he saw a pedestrian walk too close to a moving bus.

Louise Greenwood and Marlee came home with Jim Tilley just as Sam Watson had done, along with Rose Carillo and her two children. The only difference was that now he recognized the scenario and he knew it'd work itself out if he gave it enough time. That's why, at 5 AM on Saturday morning, he'd abandoned any hope of a night's sleep. He jumped into his shorts and a PAL t-shirt, laced up well-worn Nikes and trotted to the walkway over the East River Drive. A series of thunderstorms had passed through the city around 2 AM, flashing enough thunder and lightning to jolt him out of the trance he'd been substituting for sleep. A Canadian front trailed behind the storms and by the time he reached Carl Schurz Park, the temperature was twenty-five degrees cooler than it had been when he'd gone to sleep and a fresh breeze was blowing down the

East River. He hit the bricks eagerly. There are aches
and pains, Tilley was convinced, for which running
was the only cure.

He knew it wasn't any one thing bothering him here.
True, it was the first time he had worked into the interior of a crime, into the bowels. He had known criminal and victim, quick arrests and questioning
detectives, but hadn't understood that violent crime
never occurs in a vacuum, that it spreads back through
families, back through communities. Beyond that,
Moodrow had him thoroughly frightened. There was
no way to know what he would do next. Prime example: Did the scene at Katjcic's come about as a result of Rose Carillo's sob story? Or was Moodrow
pissed off because his snitch had cheated on him?
Moodrow told his partner (he laughed while he did)
that he had no intention of keeping his promise to
Rose Carillo and Tilley found himself believing that
no cop would be so suicidal as to agree to commit
murder in front of a witness, partner or not. Yet, as
Moodrow made the explanation, his eyes were as blank
and unyielding as the eyes of a dead fish in a storefront
window.

And suppose Moodrow did kill Greenwood? Where
would Tilley be if he failed to report Moodrow's promise to, for instance, Captain Epstein? What if, in going
back over Moodrow's record, the headhunters got wise
to their game of Kill the Motorcycle? It was one thing
for the Captain to sic Moodrow on the underbelly of
the Lower East Side when the only career to be destroyed was Moodrow's. Now there was Tilley's career
as well. The name of the game in the NYPD, a game
shared by all civil servants, is "Cover Your Ass."

In between his considerations of Stanley Moodrow
and his potential for career-threatening behavior, Rose
Carillo's features floated like a ghost in a cheap black-
and-white movie. And not the helpless woman who
described Greenwood's brutal attacks, but the laugh-

ing girl who'd teased Moodrow about his drink. Tilley
couldn't believe she didn't know how beautiful she
was. All women know the value of that commodity,
know how to package and sell it. Or so he assumed.

One thing was certain. The fifteen-year-old girl
who'd walked through the Port Authority bus terminal was not the Rose Carillo who'd calmly told of her
struggle to be rid of Levander Greenwood. She'd said
it was the birth of her son that gave her the strength
to fight. Imagine the irony, then, of that fight leading
directly to the abuse of the children she wanted to
protect.

The sun rose on Tilley's left, turning the sky over
the houses on Roosevelt Island a flaming orange. It
burned, a soft, luminous copper, in ten million panes
of midtown skyline. The sky in the west, behind the
buildings, was still dark and the air, cleaned by the
rain, was so clear the massive towers stood out like
volcanoes in some piece of Spielberg movie trickery.
Tilley recalled taking a cousin out to Boulevard East
in Weehawken, to the spot where Aaron Burr had
killed Alexander Hamilton, and looking east over the
Hudson River to where the aircraft carrier *Intrepid* was
berthed. He remarked that the *Intrepid* looked like a
rowboat. Less than that, a gray dot against the massive
skyline of Manhattan.

There are times when the city simply shrinks you
down to size. When somehow you can step outside it
long enough to feel its power. The sunrise burning in
the windows slowed the runners, though they didn't
speak to each other. Anyone who runs the Drive sees
this sight sooner or later and almost everyone slows
down long enough to acknowledge it. In the shadow
of Roosevelt Island, the East River reflected an ice-blue
sky and looked clean enough to drink. The tide in New
York Harbor was pulling rapidly south across the face
of Queens and Brooklyn and an oil barge, headed north

for depots in the Bronx, was having trouble making headway.

Tilley started running again, more slowly this time. Louise Greenwood's image floated up, pleading with the school principal. Psychology had been his first major at Fordham. After a few courses, he'd switched to Political Science, but he'd learned enough to believe there was no hope for the Levander Greenwoods of this world. The criminal psychopath is beyond the reach of modern medicine and responds only to drug therapy, which, as Marlee remembered, renders the person dead-in-life, as if the government had decided to take a mental life because it didn't have the guts to take a physical life.

Now Louise Greenwood clung to the idea of Jesus reaching out a hand to 'save' her child. If only Moodrow would spare Levander Greenwood's physical body, the Lord would spare his soul. Still, her assumption (that the police were prepared to kill her son on sight) was outdated. In the 50s, before Escobar and Miranda, when the police were immune to any punishment but that of the department, cop killers were never brought in. Tilley had this scoop from his ex-cop uncles, now retired to beer and the barroom. They delivered the information at every family gathering along with their estimates of how far the department (and the city and America) had fallen from the pinnacle of its majesty. A pinnacle reached, not incidentally, during their tenure and which they referred to as B. M.: Before Miranda.

Tilley suspected that Moodrow knew this when he made his promise to Mrs. Greenwood. As he'd predicted, there would probably be a hundred cops present when Greenwood was taken, not to mention photographers, journalists and the American Civil Liberties Union. It's one thing to take out an anonymous perp in a burnt-out tenement in Brooklyn, quite another to publicly execute Levander Greenwood.

Which meant, Tilley hoped, that unless Greenwood decided to fight it out, Rose Carillo would probably not get her wish. Nonetheless, the murder of a policeman (first-degree murder) is a special crime in New York State and carries with it a mandatory life sentence. Realistically speaking, "life" means something less than an actual lifetime, but cop killers in New York cannot expect to spend less than thirty years in prison. Add to this Greenwood's half-dozen other murders and he would undoubtedly receive one of those unimaginable three-hundred-year sentences given out by New York judges in cases where reporters outnumber spectators.

Her fear that Levander would escape was even less realistic. Not that it wasn't possible, but the chance of being killed in traffic does not keep one out of automobiles. Perhaps, though, the mouse walking by the caged cat still trembles with terror. Maybe certain fears cannot be erased. Seeing her once again, her eyes fixed on Moodrow's, Tilley realized that Levander's life, even in prison, was the last remaining bar on her own cage. That without him, she would be free. Then he remembered the children.

All the while he continued to run effortlessly, as if he could dissipate the agitation in his mind through the automatic rhythms of running. Instead of coming back up the drive, he crossed over the traffic onto 64th Street and ran west toward Central Park before heading back uptown. He had the women tucked into safe places, having worked through to the resolution of the Greenwood case. Moodrow, on the other hand, continued to trouble him. Not that the resolution of his conflict with the big cop wasn't equally simple. Tilley knew he couldn't hope to control Moodrow, but he could report him. Or request a new partner without specifying a reason.

Fifth Avenue, across from the Park, was still in shadow as he made his way past 79th Street. In spite of the early hour and the weekend, the limos and radio cars were lined up in front of the canopies, ready to transport high-power executives to their offices. A lone cop, a uniform driving a motor scooter, was standing alongside a double-parked Lincoln with a DIAL 4311 sign in the front window. The driver, a turbaned Sikh with a jet black beard, was complaining loudly. "Why you do this to me? This is Saturday and whole city is quiet? Why are you writing me this ticket? Forty dollars. You hear this? I work whole day I only make forty dollars."

The cop went about his business as if he was writing up an empty vehicle. Tilley, approaching and curious, slowed down enough to attract the cop's attention, and the uniform threw him a challenging look.

"Detective Tilley," Tilley said confidently. "Everything under control?"

"Yeah. Sure. Fuckin' scumbags think they can park wherever they want."

Tilley shrugged and picked up the pace. There were detectives, he knew, who approached their jobs the way that cop wrote tickets on a Saturday morning. Make the quota, then go home. It's all time-in on the pension. That magical, twenty year, half-pay, yellow brick road that keeps cops in line.

Is that what he wanted? When Moodrow and he were alone in the backyard with the biker motorcycles, they were completely in sync. Again, with Peter Katjcic lying in that filthy bed, he had no doubts at all. Only later, when he made that lame explanation of his promise to Rose Carillo, did Moodrow start to scare him again.

Tilley slowed down at Park and 85th. Like all serious runners, he walked the last few blocks to give his legs a chance to cool down. One thing seemed certain, his partnership with Stanley Moodrow was leapfrogging him over the mediocrity in the job. Big cases win the attention of the administrators at One Police Plaza

as well as the eyes of the media. And Levander Greenwood was as big as they got, a genuine maniac busily
engaged in the eradication of his fellow citizens. His
face was on page four of the *Daily News* every day.

Most rookie detectives fortunate enough to be assigned to such a case would sit at the bottom of a task
force, maybe answering the hot line published in the
papers. Moodrow and Tilley were like parasites on
Levander Greenwood's underbelly, chewing their way
inside. Suddenly he found himself imagining the final
scene: Greenwood trapped in a room, the reporters
asking questions, the cameras turning. Was he so
frightened of Moodrow that he wanted to play the
rookie detective to some asshole from Levittown?

He was hooked. And it only took six miles to realize
it. Six miles to run out the emotional kinks of the last
twenty-four hours. Still, he felt much better. He was
satisfied with a resolution to protect himself even as
he slid deeper into the muck, and he wasn't at all surprised to find Moodrow waiting for him when he got
home.

9

They were together in the kitchen—Susanna Tilley, Jim Tilley's mother, and Stanley Moodrow, his partner. Mugs of steaming-hot coffee sat on the table in front of them. Tilley supposed he should have been shocked (or at least surprised) to find them conspiring like old neighbors watching a soap opera, but somehow it seemed as natural as the progression of scenes in a movie he'd already watched. Or that moment at the top of the first hill on a roller coaster, when the clank-clank-clank of the chain hoist stops and the carnival, spread out below you, freezes solid.

"This is a great apartment," Moodrow said, just as if they hadn't gone over the same ground less than twenty-four hours earlier. "What have you got here. Five rooms?"

"Seven, actually," Susanna Tilley answered. "Four bedrooms."

"How'd you get it? I thought these places disappeared ten years ago."

"We got this place right after Pete and I married. That was thirty years ago. It was a tenement then. Now people would kill to get it."

"Thirty years rent control," Moodrow observed. "You must have it for next to nothing."

"Four-fifty a month."

"I got the same thing, but not so big. I took my apartment on 5th Street near Avenue B when I got home from Korea. One bedroom. I pay three-fifty, but the landlord's letting the building go down. Probably wants to convert it."

Talking about housing (or the lack of it) is New York's favorite pastime, but Tilley, though he knew his partner was only making polite conversation, was too pissed at finding Moodrow so comfortable to be more than civil. "What's the scoop, Moodrow. What'd you come up here for?"

"I tried to reach you last night, but there was no answer." Moodrow handed his partner a copy of the *Daily News*. The front page photo showed two attendants loading a closed bodybag into an E.M.S. ambulance. The headline read COP KILLER HITS AGAIN. The incident had taken place just before the *News* went to press and the story was fairly sketchy, but the basics, two dead cops, another in critical condition and the name Levander Greenwood, came through well enough. Tilley tossed the paper back to Moodrow and poured himself a cup of coffee.

"Were they set up?" he asked.

"I don't know. It seems like it could be, but I can't figure out why."

"Should I go inside?" Susanna Tilley asked. She pushed back her chair and started to get up.

"Suit yourself," Moodrow shrugged. "But if you wanna stay, it don't bother me."

"Good," she said. Avoiding her son's sharp glance, she dropped back into her chair.

"The paper doesn't say what the cops were doing there," Tilley said. "Gotta be a tip, right?"

"Exactly. Someone dropped a dime and these were the first cops on the scene. The rat said Greenwood was holed up in 4D, but the word from the survivor is he and his partner were ambushed from an apartment on the second floor. Then the moron covering the front entrance Rambo'd his way up the stairs and got caught from behind. Didn't even stop to call it in. When the task force showed up ten minutes later, they found the fourth cop still covering the back of the building."

"That's it? There was nobody in the apartment? Who was he there to see?"

"Apartment 4D was a burn-out. Abandoned. There was a mattress on the floor. A woman's underwear on top of that. Clean underwear. Could be he was holed up there, but most likely he was out for a piece of ass." He stopped suddenly and looked over toward Susanna Tilley. "Sorry, Susanna. Sometimes I get carried away."

"That's all right, Stanley."

Moodrow looked over at his partner, pudgy-cherub expression firmly in place. "The task force knocked on every door. It's a heavy crack building on a known crack block. The owner hasn't paid the taxes in four years and as far as the city is concerned, the building is empty. In fact, there were signs of occupancy in every room, but except for a trio of homeless seniors on the third floor, the tenants had all abandoned ship. Hear me? Maybe twenty-five people in the building. They had to step over the bodies, but nobody bothered to drop a dime. Left the one cop bleeding to death."

Susanna Tilley, somewhat unnerved, got up and went to the refrigerator. Without asking, she poured out three glasses of orange juice and began to crack eggs into a bowl.

"So how does it fit in with us?" Tilley asked.

"I doesn't, really. The task force'll search the building. Probably got thirty cops in there now, all waving tweezers and magnifying glasses. Think they're gonna find Greenwood's address in the dirt?" He leaned back in his chair, accepting the juice Susanna Tilley put in front of him. "The kids on the street are starting to make Greenwood into a hero. Kubla the Invincible. I'm talking about the ones that have a chance. The sixteen-year-olds trying to decide between dope and work. We don't take the bastard soon, he'll have disciples."

"That's why you came here? To lecture me? You could have done this over the phone."

"Actually, I came here to talk to you about Rose Carillo. I want you to go up to see her."

Tilley's heart jumped in his chest. But, at the same time, he shifted his weight in response to a more basic sensation. "Something wrong?" he asked as innocently as he could.

"We gotta move her out of there. Or at least warn her if she won't leave. Word's already on the street that Greenwood knows she talked to us about Katjcic."

"What if she doesn't have any place to go?"

Susanna interrupted before Moodrow could answer. "That's what Stanley and I were talking about before you got back."

Tilley threw Moodrow a look that would have melted asbestos. Then his mother finished the message. She said, "We have so much room here. Don't you think she could stay with us until her husband is out of the way? Stanley says it shouldn't be more than a week or so."

"Stanley should have asked me first," Tilley returned evenly.

"He didn't say a word, Jimmy. It was my idea completely."

She looked so shocked that Tilley started laughing. There was no doubt in his mind that Moodrow had come there to set this up. No doubt whatsoever. Still, the image of Rose Carillo sitting in his living room, a glass of vodka in her hand, didn't offend him at all. He wasn't even surprised to find himself so eager.

Finally, Moodrow broke the silence. "Hey, if it's inconvenient, we could always think of something else. It's just that we gotta get her out of there if there's anyone who knows where she is. I guarantee he's gonna kill her if he gets the chance. That's the word on the street. He's bragging that he's gonna chill her out before he gets it himself. Anyway, there's no harm if you go up and talk to her. See if she's got some place to go. I'm gonna stay on the backs of a few people who claim they're close to Greenwood. Most likely bull-shit, but I don't feel like sitting home."

Susanna Tilley dropped a bowl of scrambled eggs into a hot frying pan and the sharp crack of the eggs hitting the butter jolted their attention.

"I hope you're not making breakfast for me," Mood-row protested.

Susanna didn't bother looking up. "Don't worry. I only made enough for me and Jimmy. You weren't hungry, were you?"

"No, no."

"Sure? You could have Jimmy's eggs if you want."

"I couldn't take his eggs. . . ."

She executed a quick turn and dropped a plate in front of him. "Shut up and eat, Stanley." Then she went back to the stove and filled two more plates.

Moodrow watched her retreat, his eyes glued to her backside. Tilley kicked him under the table, not even knowing what he meant by it, and Moodrow turned calmly back to his partner. Automatic respect for a friend's mother may be dying out, but in Moodrow's time, it was as unquestioned as patriotism. Tilley knew he had no right to interfere (it wasn't the first time he'd seen a man stare at her), but watching it made him itch, especially considering his own quick fantasy of Rose Carillo's lips on his.

"You should come to my house tomorrow early," he said. "Eight o'clock. We're gonna talk out Katjcic's tip with Epstein and someone from the D.A.'s office. These are people I trust, Jimmy. Other than them, let's keep it entirely quiet."

In the course of his run, Tilley had considered every aspect of the Greenwood case except Katjcic's asser-tion that another cop was behind it. If it was true that some cop, probably a detective from the 7th, was run-ning Levander, the man was responsible for the deaths of ten people, including four cops. That didn't seem possible, but Katjcic had been very convincing and neither one of them thought he was lying. Not that he (or they) couldn't be wrong.

"Eight o'clock's a little early for a Sunday, isn't it?"

"What could I do? Epstein's driving out to Riverhead to visit his grandchildren. He wants to get an early start."

"Figures. We gonna be there all day? Do we get the afternoon off at least?"

"Yeah, your mom told me you were going out." He shrugged without looking at Tilley. "But I don't know. Epstein'll pull Greenwood's entire package and photocopy it tonight so nobody should know it left the precinct. Tomorrow, after he leaves, we'll go over it with the D.A.'s man. I don't remember any hint that Greenwood's a snitch, but we'll make a list of the cops that busted him and work up any likely candidates. If that don't work, we can pull the files of every narc in the precinct, one at a time, and see if there's any mention of Greenwood."

"Fine, but when do we finish tomorrow? I mean if the assistant D.A.'s running the show, just tell me. I'll understand."

Moodrow glanced up, clearly annoyed, and Tilley threw him his best Irish altar boy look.

"You know what scares me?" Moodrow abruptly changed the subject. His voice was very low, his eyes riveted to the tabletop. "If we call in the headhunters at Internal Affairs they'll tear the precinct apart. The captain won't take it. Me neither. We'll be retired in six months."

"What's Internal Affairs?" Susanna's voice shocked both of them.

"Internal Affairs are the cops that put other cops in jail," he responded. "When they decide to run through a precinct, nobody's immune. They find one cop who's on the take and use him as a wedge to batter the whole force. Or they take a thief or a dealer and have him offer bribes to arresting officers. That's when cops stop caring about the people they're supposed to protect. When they get frightened, they always react by trying to avoid contact with the public as much as possible. They expect to be set up by the headhunters and they don't trust anyone."

10

Rose Carillo was staying in an apartment on 174th Street near Audubon Avenue, a mixed neighborhood called Washington Heights which sits just above Harlem at the northern end of Manhattan. The island is only half a mile wide at that point and buildings on its western edge rise from bluffs high above the Hudson, offering spectacular views of the George Washington Bridge and the New Jersey palisades. The apartments along this edge, especially on Cabrini Boulevard and Haven Avenue, are solid and middle-class, rentals going co-op with most of the former tenants showing their faith in the neighborhood by purchasing their apartments. Hard to believe that two blocks away, from Broadway to the East River, a Puerto Rican/Dominican *barrio* provides the marketplace for hundreds of crack dealers serving the Jersey trade.

The housing in the Heights is more solid than the tenements on the Lower East Side. The neighborhood began much later in New York's history and the Jewish immigrants who built it up were a step further from Ellis Island. But Washington Heights lacks the hip veneer of the Lower East Side. It lacks the art galleries and the Indian restaurants on 6th Street; the flaming punks and the Krishna devotees dancing in Tompkins Square Park. Except for the students at Yeshiva University which sits, defiantly, on both sides of a few blocks of Amsterdam Avenue and which is heavily protected by private security, the only white people left in Washington Heights stay west of Broadway.

That's not where Tilley was going, of course, west of Broadway. He was headed for cocaine heaven: ten or fifteen square blocks that defied the strenuous efforts of local residents to improve the Washington Heights area. Rose Carillo's building was only four blocks from the George Washington Bridge, a golden highway for the privileged children of northern New Jersey who drove their own TransAms or their daddys' BMW's slowly down Audubon Avenue, criss-crossed all through the 170s, and cut back down St. Nicholas. The dealers checked them out, approached them every bit as boldly as the pot dealers on First Avenue in the Village. Except here the dealers sold rock cocaine in little plastic vials: tiny pellets of passing ecstasy.

Moodrow had left the car with Tilley, since it was expected that Tilley would be coming back with Rose and her children, but driving a black Plymouth onto 174th Street was equivalent to waving a badge at the locals. There was no possibility of remaining anonymous.

But, what cannot be cured.... Tilly put on his brown cop suit, his scuffed brown shoes, a white on white shirt and a solid brown tie and drove up the East River to 179th Street. There were derelict cars, burnt-out rusting hulks, on every corner, another sign of neglect in this out-of-the-way corner of Manhattan. They would not have been tolerated in any part of the city frequented by tourists, and their presence made the inevitable hunt for parking space (even illegal parking space) that much more absurd.

All of which presented Tilley with another problem altogether. Several years ago, the city had purchased thousands of these black four-door Plymouths and handed them out to the various city agencies. Because of their high visibility, they had become the target of choice for teenage vandals out to make a rep. Tilley didn't relish coming out with Rose and her children to find a car with four slashed tires. If he parked six blocks away and the locals noticed him walking into the sunset, it would be like waving the proverbial red flag in front of the bull.

He circled her block twice, looking for a safe spot before he gave up and double-parked in front of her building. There was a narrow stairway leading down to an alley between hers and a neighboring structure and the knot of people gathered at the head of those stairs took off at a dead run the minute Tilley stepped out of the car. They looked like a stand of zebra flushed by a lion.

By the time he came around the car, only one man remained, hands on his hips, defiant. Tilley gathered he was an entrepreneur put temporarily out of business by the cop's appearance on the scene and he obviously had no fear of being arrested, probably because he was only the lookout. The drugs must have been somewhere in that alley and were surely gone by now. Still, he was mightily pissed. It was Saturday, trade was just beginning to build and this was his place of business. He could not pack up his bags and move, like the peddlers along Fifth Avenue. Most likely, he and his partners had fought to obtain this spot. Their regulars knew where to find them, as did their suppliers. The last thing they needed was Jim Tilley to spoil the best day of the week.

Nevertheless, Tilley was there and the man reacted with a hard stare that only got him into more trouble. Tilley walked straight toward the sentry (the man didn't run, though he looked like he was about to explode) and stopped about two feet away, just close enough to make the man nervous.

"I'm not blocking you in, am I?" The Plymouth was parked alongside a rusted-out derelict with all four tires gone. It had been there so long, the kids had smashed the roof down until it rested on the seatbacks. The hood was missing and thin black wires hung over the empty fenderwells.

"Whaaaa?"

Tilley's question caught the man entirely off-guard and when Tilley flashed his best "two buddies in a barroom" smile, it only added to the confusion. "Am I blocking your car? See? Over there? I double-parked and I was afraid you might want to get out."

"Thass no my car." He was much smaller than Tilley and slender, wearing a half-dozen gold chains and paper-thin leather pants over the pointiest shoes Tilley had ever seen. Even his bandanna was silk and carefully pressed. Most likely, if he broke into a sweat, he'd take the damn thing off.

"That's too bad. I was really hoping it was your car. You know why?"

"Why?" What could he say? His basic mistake, of course, was in not leaving as soon as Tilley got out of the car.

"Because I gotta leave my car and go up in this building. I'm a police officer and I gotta talk to someone. I ain't gonna be up there long. Maybe fifteen minutes. But supposing the guy who owns this car wants to get out and sees me blocking his way? Not knowing that my car belongs to a police officer in the performance of his duty, he might get mad and do something bad to it." Tilley stopped abruptly and waited, his eyes locked on those of the smaller man.

"How is someone gonna fuck with tha' piece of shi' car? How come you don' esplain to me wha' the fuck you wan' with me?"

A medallion, solid gold of course, dangled from one of his chains. The name Enrique was engraved on the front. Tilley reached out and gave it a little tug. "Do you support your local police, Enrique?"

Enrique hesitated a moment and then said, "Yeah."

"You got a lot of money on you, Enrique?" There was just the possibility that he was the banker, the man the dopers paid before they went down the alley to collect their little vials.

"You going to rip me off?" Enrique was incredulous.

"I want you to do me a favor. I want you to stay out here for the next fifteen minutes and make sure that if the man who owns this other car turns up and gets mad, you'll tell him the car belongs to a police officer in the performance of his duty. Remember: 'Police officer in the performance of his duty.' "

Enrique thought about it for a moment, then flashed a big, gold-toothed smile. "Sure, man. I watch your car for you. But if the dude come tryin' to get his car out. Like if it's a mergency and he got to go out right now, what 'partment I should tell him you're in?"

Tilley smiled back. "Hopefully, yours."

Rose Carillo's uptown residence was every bit as decrepit as her downtown apartment. As he pushed past the broken door locks in the lobby, it occurred to Tilley, that if this hell was all you had to run to when you were in trouble, your life must be very marginal. The intercom system with its rows of buzzers had been gutted and lay strewn about the tile floor, most likely an act of robbery on the part of one doper looking for another doper's stash. The mailboxes hung wide open, an invitation to junkies who steal Social Security and welfare checks, then fence them for ten cents on the dollar. The tenants of buildings like this (and there are tens of thousands of them scattered about the five boroughs) know enough to gather by the mailboxes before the postman arrives, to take the check from his hand and, protected by the company of fellow tenants, melt back behind locked doors or trot off to the supermarket where the check can be turned into cash and the cash hidden in a shoe or an undergarment.

By the time he got to the third floor and Rose Carillo's apartment, Tilley was lost. He felt like an alien stumbling on a new civilization. One he was entirely unprepared for and from which he could expect nothing positive. The only hope was to get out and the sooner he got his job over with, the better. He was as brave as Sir Lancelot on the street, but inside, with the hallways so narrow his shoulders almost brushed the walls. . . . He pushed on the bell and held it.

Nothing. Not a sound. He pushed on it again, this time with his ear to the door, listening for a buzz to indicate the damn thing was working. Absolute quiet. Then he heard a noise on the floor above him, the sound of a door closing, and his hand went behind his back, searching for the handle of his .38.

But there was nothing more coming from upstairs, either, and with a tremendous effort, he calmed himself down. He'd been in places like this before, many, many times. But the narrow hallways, the sharp turns in the stairs, the bare plaster walls and concrete floors which echo every sound always made him jumpy. Add the stench of cooking and urine, of cat vomit and dead rats in the walls and Jim Tilley felt like he was about to be attacked.

All of this translated itself as an intense desire to be inside the apartment, to be on the other side of the door with the door triple-locked. He knocked very hard, three times, just like in the movies, but there was still no response. Did he have the right address? Did she *give* Moodrow the right address? Again he reached out, now more annoyed than nervous, but this time the door suddenly swung inward and he found himself facing the barrel of a small automatic pistol.

As it turned out, the pistol was .32 caliber, one of those cheap handguns as likely to jam as to fire, but at that moment, it filled his entire field of vision. He could have been looking into a narrow hallway or into the main lobby of the Waldorf Astoria. All Tilley could see was a round, black hole.

Then the hole dropped down, the darkness dissolved

and Rose Carillo, her features tight with rage, floated into focus. "What the fuck are you doing here?"

It took him ten seconds to respond. Ten seconds to convince his chest to start moving again. Seven-year-old Lee was standing in a doorway leading to the kitchen, still holding the knob of the front door. His eyes were wild with terror, but he'd had the courage to whip that door open. Even though he expected to find the father who tormented him behind it.

Which meant the move had been carefully planned and if Levander Greenwood had been on the other side of the door instead of Jim Tilley, he would most likely be dead. Of course, there was no guarantee that Levander would knock before he made his entrance, but the point was well-taken. She must have been scared shitless or she never would have made her child part of an execution.

"Why didn't you look through the fucking peephole, you stupid bitch?" Despite his understanding, Tilley was livid. Or terrified. Or both. "You could have killed me."

"People shoot through peepholes," she explained. "They hear the rattle when you move the eyepiece and they shoot straight through it. Why didn't you call before you came?"

"The phone don't work, that's why. You couldn't even live in a place with a phone that works and now you wanna shoot a cop."

She looked past him with practiced eyes, searched the other doorways on the floor, the shadows by the stairwell. "You better come in."

He didn't hesitate. Her fear was contagious, as if she was expecting Levander at any moment. Tilley waited until the door was locked, then took his .38 from its holster at the small of his back and shifted it to the front, jamming it down inside his waistband. When he turned to face her, she was still holding the .32 automatic.

"Is that gun registered?" he asked.

She raised her eyes to his questioningly. They were almost perfectly round and nearly black. "Moodrow . . ."

"Fuck Moodrow. Moodrow isn't here. You didn't try to shoot Moodrow."

"Look, I'm sorry about what happened. I heard from downtown that Levander knows where I am. Or at least some people think he does."

"How is that possible? How many people did you tell?"

"It's not only that. Levander smokes crack. He's been doing it steady for about a year. You must have seen what this building is when you walked into it. I know he comes up here to cop."

"So why did you stay here?"

"Where am I gonna go?" She suddenly called her children to her and sat down between them on the couch. They pressed up against her, staring at Tilley with large, accusing eyes.

"Why didn't you go to the shelter? There's a shelter for battered women."

"Haven't you figured it out yet? Levander will kill anyone who gets between him and what he wants. Or he'll try. He'll walk through the door with that shotgun and keep firing until he's got me or he's dead. I think I might have a chance with the gun. If I surprise him . . ." Suddenly she started crying, huge, consuming sobs that had her children frantic. Tilley assumed they were blaming him, but they seemed to be paralyzed without her instructions. She hugged them against her chest and rocked back and forth.

He waited until it was over before he spoke. It didn't take very long. When she finally raised her eyes to face him, he said, "Rose, give me the gun." It lay on the floor between her feet. He could have grabbed it, but he wanted her to hand it over. He wanted to make sure the fear hadn't driven her insane before he invited her to his home. "I can't let you keep the gun."

At first she looked incredulous, then panicky. "We have to have it."

"Is it registered?"

"Don't be an asshole. How could it be registered?"

"If I leave you here with that gun and you use it to kill someone, it makes me an accessory to murder. I don't want to take the chance." His voice, calm and determined, surprised him. The adrenaline rush was over and the man who remained was very sure of himself. "Give me the gun," he repeated.

She reached down and took it in her hand, her fingers curling around the butt, then swiftly reversed it and passed it over. "Now you're responsible," she said. "You've taken it out of my hands."

Tilley suspected that she was relieved. Certainly, she seemed more relaxed. She leaned back against the couch and took her children's hands in her own. "I want you to go into the kitchen and pour Detective Tilley a glass of orange juice. Put in a couple of ice cubes and bring it out here." They ran off and she looked back at him. "I have some vodka out here in case you want to finish it up."

"You know, you can't take him with this." He held up the little .32 for her inspection. "He's too crazy and too well armed. You'd probably only make him mad."

"What should I do? Go back to my daddy and his brother? It's you cops that made Levander Greenwood happen. You should have put him away a long time ago, but you didn't. Now he's out there committing murders and you're up here disarming me. Doesn't seem fair, does it?"

The kids came back with the juice. Naturally they tried to hand it to their mother who redirected them to Tilley's chair. He took the glass, added two fingers of Smirnoff and began to explain what Moodrow had in mind for them. Without telling her that a cop was involved with Levander, he let her understand that they could get a policeman assigned to her for protection, but for the same reason she couldn't go to a shelter, they couldn't guarantee her security. Moodrow had a different and a better idea, one that was completely safe. Tilley described his apartment, its size and how far it was from the Lower East Side, adding that he lived there alone except for his mother.

"You live with your mother?" At first he thought she was making fun of him, but then she said, "Damn, I wish I had a mother to go to." Whispered it, really; wistful as a young girl dreaming of spring. Then she clapped her hands and the two children jumped off the couch. "Lee. Jeanette. We're moving again. We're going to a place where we'll all be safe. All three of us."

"Weren't we safe here?" Jeanette asked seriously. "We had the door locked."

Her brother stared up at the cop defiantly. Every time he came around it meant trouble for them.

"What are you gonna do, Lee?" Tilley asked. "You gonna stand there or you gonna help your mother get ready? I promise you're going to a place where you won't have to yank open any doors, all right?"

"Who are you?" he demanded, ignoring Tilley's suggestion entirely.

"You can call me 'Mr. Tilley.' "

Jeanette giggled loudly. "What kind of name is that? Mr. Tilley. It sounds silly. Silly Tilley."

Out of the mouths of babes.

11

Ten minutes later Rose Carillo had her family's possessions crammed into three large suitcases and they
were on their way. Tilley eyeballed every doorway,
half-hoping Levander would emerge, like a bear from
a cave, but the building was quiet, as tenements usually are when cops are present. Enrique was still manning his station when they came outside and he waved
eagerly. Whatever nightmare Tilley represented, it
wasn't about to haunt *his* dreams. Tilley flipped him
a *"Gracias,* Enrique," and the Hispanic kid flashed a
brilliant smile. *"Vaya con Dios, Señor Policía,"* he
called.

Though she knew she wasn't returning, Rose kept
her face turned away from Enrique's, hurrying her children along. The way they followed her instructions
amazed Tilley. In the house, when she told them to
pack, they'd complied without a murmur of protest
and now, on the street, they scurried obediently into
the backseat of the Plymouth while Rose loaded the
suitcases into the trunk.

The Drive was slow as usual, due to permanent construction in the underpass below Gracie Mansion, but
it was early Saturday afternoon and the summertime
weekend rush for the beaches and the mountains was
in full swing, so most of the traffic was going the other
way. Even here, on the Drive, in the most anonymous
of anonymous situations, Rose kept looking around,
examining the faces in the cars that surrounded them.

And it was not the look of a panicked woman, but that of a grazing antelope, as natural as that sudden graceful leap at the first hint of danger. She was so beautiful. Tilley's mind kept wandering back to her lips and her throat. The bones of her shoulders seemed as soft and delicate as those of a bird. He couldn't accept the idea that she could be exploited. In his experience, women like her inevitably made men (or him, at least) afraid. But Rose was more than afraid; she was permanently scarred by fear and for the first time, Tilley got a glimpse of the man he was hunting. But it wasn't a man he envisioned. It was a force of nature, a phenomenon unrelated to humanity or even to life itself. Tilley could see him, just as Rose had suggested, coming through the door of his apartment, shotgun in hand. There would be no more chance of reasoning with him than with a bolt of lightning.

Of course, that couldn't happen. Tilley had complete confidence in Moodrow's integrity. With only the two of them knowing, there was no way for Greenwood to make the connection. Still, he was glad to pull up in front of his building. He flipped down the sun visor so the restricted parking permit taped to it could be read by the traffic department (who would probably ticket it anyway) and while Rose hustled the kids out of the car, he pulled the bags from the trunk and led the way into the lobby of the building. He was so intent on getting inside (and so pleased to be there) that he ignored everything else until he heard a familiar voice.

"That you, Jim?" It was Mr. Strauss from 1B. He'd been in the building even longer than the Tilleys and for a while, when Tilley was in grade school, had played the part of "daddy" to a fatherless boy. At least he was the man Jim Tilley could talk to when he needed to talk to a man. Now, he was staring at Tilley, not only puzzled, but accusing as well.

"Yep, it's me, Josef. You were maybe expecting a burglar?"

It wasn't much of a joke and Tilley didn't get a hint of a return smile. Josef was looking past him at Rose and her two children. Later on he told a neighbor that he couldn't understand what the two little *schwartzers* were doing with Rose. He guessed she must be some kind of social worker. That she was the mother of the children and had, presumably, copulated with a black man in order to conceive them was so outside the realm of his understanding, it never even occurred to him.

When Tilley finally realized what was bothering his neighbor, he was angry at first, then embarrassed for Rose. She, on the other hand, seemed unaware of his scrutiny. She was gazing at the lobby like she was Dorothy entering the wonderful city of Oz. As they walked up the stairs, children in tow, she suddenly took his hands and held them up. For a second Tilley thought she was going to cry again, but she simply said, "Thank you" and kissed his cheek. He read the kiss neither as promissory nor as reward. Just relief.

Susanna was waiting in the small foyer when Tilley opened the door. She and Rose looked at each other closely for a moment. The children never stirred, never made the slightest attempt to leave Rose's side. Finally, Susanna introduced herself. "I'm Susanna Tilley."

"I'm Rose Carillo." She smiled a smile that didn't seem terribly sure of itself, then turned to the children. "This is Lee and this is Jeanette."

"Hello, Mrs. Tilley," Jeanette said.

Mrs. Tilley? Jim Tilley really wasn't surprised to hear it, but the tension was thick enough to spread on a sandwich. And straight lines are straight lines. "What do you mean Mrs. Tilley? What happened to Silly Tilley?"

"You're Silly Tilley," Jeanette replied with perfect

logic. "Two people can't have the same name." She pointed to his mother. "She's Mrs. Tilley."

"I'd rather be Susanna," his mother replied.

"All right," Rose said eagerly. "Susanna." Rose just assumed she would be called by her first name. She began to walk slowly into the living room, looking around her as she went. "I can't remember the last time I felt safe. I think maybe not since before my mother died. Maybe never." She turned toward Tilley. "I trust Moodrow completely," she said. "You know what I'm saying? Moodrow would never screw it up. I don't know you, Tilley, so I'm asking you. Please don't tell anyone that we're here. Don't trust anyone."

He looked at her for a minute, then turned to his mother. All of a sudden, he was very pissed off at the little conspiracies going on around him. He hadn't been in charge of anything since he pulled on his t-shirt and went out for a run. Now it was time for a little payback. "Well," he said evenly, "I've still got a lot of work to do today. I'll take off and let you all get to know each other. Rose, make yourself at home. I'm sure we'll have Levander in a couple of days."

Susanna Tilley looked surprised, then shocked and then stricken. She hadn't foreseen being left alone with three strangers (one of whom was an admitted prostitute and drug addict) when she made the offer to Moodrow. "Do you have to go?"

"Oh yeah," Tilley replied. He even threw in a little New Yawk, just to make sure she understood. "Wit guys dis bad we gotta work all kinda hours. Ya never get no rest wit guys like dese."

When Moodrow left his partner's apartment, he took a cab down the Drive to Houston Street. He had every intention of working, but, no matter how hard he tried to place his attention on the Greenwood case, his thoughts kept returning to Jim Tilley and to his own precarious position in the job. He recalled chasing a

perp two weeks before, a very ordinary runner, the sort
Moodrow would have brought down without any trouble a few years ago. Yet, this time, he didn't make a
single block before the pain in his chest brought him
up short. It wasn't his heart, the doctor at Beth Israel
explained, but it was a warning.

"Go slow," the doctor, a young resident, had advised
breezily. "You're not as young as you used to be. You
have to learn to relax."

But Moodrow *was* relaxed. He had no wife, no girlfriend, no family. Not even a dog or a cat. His family,
such as it was, was the NYPD and he did not relish
the end of that relationship, although he knew it was
coming. Even if they didn't fire him, they would put
him behind a desk somewhere and that would be the
end. He would have to turn in his papers. For a second,
he imagined the new captain, a half-smile on his face,
accepting the proffered badge, saying, "We're sure
gonna miss you around here."

The image was enough to depress him and he turned
his thoughts to his new partner, Jim Tilley. The kid
was clearly sharp and willing. Moodrow would not
have to worry about his back. On the other hand, Tilley was also ambitious and, as Moodrow well knew,
the best way to promotion is to play it conservatively.
Which is exactly what Moodrow had never been able
to do. Not that he had any regrets; his career had been
an adventure all the way, both in relation to the criminals he pursued and the department which dogged his
every step. If it hadn't been for Allen Epstein, who
both protected and exploited the big cop, Moodrow
would have been gone fifteen years before. And he
knew it.

Some men are obsessed with children as the key to
personal immortality. Moodrow had never been married and, as far as he knew, had never fathered a child.
His immortality revolved around leaving someone behind him, a cop, who would protect the 7th the way

he protected it. And, of course, Jim Tilley was the most likely candidate.

No one, not Higgins nor Epstein, knew how carefully he'd chosen his young partner. The college education intrigued Moodrow, but, by itself, would not have been enough to make him Moodrow's choice. It was the boxing that had swung Moodrow over. Moodrow coached the young boxers at the Boys Club on Houston Street twice a week. He knew enough about the fight game to pass for a half-assed trainer and he had seen Jim Tilley fight. The kid was good. Too slow to make it in the three-round amateurs, but strong as a bull and seemingly impervious to pain. As a pro, he'd inevitably caught up with his opponent by the fifth round. By the eighth round, they'd lost the will to fight and were looking for an excuse to fall down and stay there, which young Jim Tilley, with his absolutely devastating short-armed left hook, was glad to provide.

From Moodrow's point of view, matching Tilley with Rose had been a brilliant idea. Moodrow knew of a dozen places where Rose would be more than safe, but if Tilley fell for Rose, it might bring him to live on the Lower East Side. Moodrow considered it essential that a good cop live in the precinct he served. The rest of the police force considered it proof of a well-developed psychosis. After all, what sane cop wants to carry the job around twenty-four hours a day? Don't shit where you eat was the most common rationale for the majority of cops who lived outside of New York City altogether.

Even lost in his ruminations, Moodrow managed to work. Stopping in at the various stores, the boutiques and the bodegas, he passed along a copy of Levander Greenwood's mug shot with the stern warning that they not try to apprehend Greenwood by themselves. The managers in the boutiques, of course, were completely ignorant of Levander's existence, while the Hispanics behind the counters of the small grocery stores knew him without seeing his photograph. Still, all denied knowledge of his present whereabouts.

"You kill him, man," one store owner said, his helpers echoing the sentiment. "Shoot him like a dog in the street, before he kills anyone else."

"I'll do that," Moodrow replied. Whatever they wanted. He would promise it in return for the phone call that gave him Levander Greenwood.

His promise to Rose, on the other hand, presented him with more serious problems. Contrary to his reputation, only once had he been prepared to kill a man without regret. Actually two men and three women. But that had been personal. Levander Greenwood had to be taken off the street, but an arrest would keep him behind bars until he was far too old to cause any more damage. Still, despite that reality, he had made promises to Rose and to Louise Greenwood. Conflicting promises. Clearly, only one could be kept. Unless, of course, the task force got to Greenwood first. Then it would be out of his hands.

His route took him south, across Houston, to the center of the dope scene on the Lower East Side. As he turned up Rivington he spotted a kid he knew, one of the new breed of crack dealers who never carried drugs on his person. Didn't even use them. He was wearing the obligatory gold chain (which not only announced the affluence of the wearer, but his ability to keep it as well) along with a sparkling new leisure suit.

"Hey, Cool," Moodrow shouted, walking toward the dealer, who didn't move a muscle. "I wanna talk to ya for a minute."

"What you want, cop?"

"I want Levander Greenwood."

"You think I know where he is? That fucker hit one of my boys for sixty vials two days ago. The boy is lucky Kubla didn't kill him."

"Listen up, Cool. I don't give a fuck what you know. If we don't get that scumbag in a day or two, nobody's gonna do business on the Lower East Side. You remember Operation Pressure Point? We'll put that shit back in the neighborhood and keep it here till you have to pawn that gold you're wearing for cigarette money."

"I'm legit," Cool protested. "I don't do no dope. I'm in real estate."

"I don't give a fuck if you're in your sister's asshole. If Greenwood ain't found, everybody pays. I pay because the papers and the brass are up my ass. You pay because we scare all your customers away, and maybe kick your ass for the fun of it."

Cool was not accustomed to direct assaults by policemen, but he understood the reality surrounding the murders of cops. The police grab anything they can see and keep shaking until the killer drops out.

"Man, you askin' a lot. Greenwood's a ghost, man. He comes out at night, then disappears. Like into *nowhere*. The nigger just vanishes. But I *will* keep an eye out for him. If he shows up I'll send one of my boys over with the particulars. Levander a crack freak now. A fool like that don't belong on the street no way."

"One more favor," Moodrow finished. "Put the word out among all your people. If we don't have Greenwood, we're gonna put two hundred uniforms on the street. Plus the detectives are gonna hit the apartments. Clean out the abandoned buildings."

Moodrow walked away without another word. There was nothing more to say. He suddenly felt a rush of pleasure. Putting one foot in front of the other was all he really knew. He had no doubt that Levander would be taken. It was just a matter of time.

Remembering the children, Tilley unlocked the door and came in as quietly as he could. It was after 11 PM and, as expected, his mother was in bed. Only Rose was awake. She was lying on the couch in front of the TV, wearing gym shorts and a white cotton halter with a sweater thrown across her shoulders. As Jim Tilley walked into the room, her smile nearly blew him away. It was impossibly young.

"Your apartment is so beautiful. How in God's name did you manage to find it?"

Quickly, he explained the history of his digs; of his father, a firefighter who'd died when a roof collapsed in a tenement on 143rd Street, and his plans for an immediate increase in the Irish population of Yorkville. He'd told the story hundreds of times and had it down pat. "When he first did it, his neighbors told him he was crazy to pay so much rent. Now, if the building went condo, it'd be worth three quarters of a million."

Then he told her the rent and she said, "That's what I pay for that hole on the Lower East Side. Where's the justice, right? I've been on the waiting list for the projects for six years. I can't even find anyone to tell me where I am on the list. 'Please don't call us, Ms. Carillo. You'll be notified when your turn comes.'"

She sat up and stretched and Tilley's gaze immediately dropped to her breasts. When he looked back up she was staring into his eyes. Yet there was neither amusement nor condemnation in her glance.

"You get along all right with my mother?" Tilley asked, trying to ease over his lecherous stare.

"I think she's a good woman. I mean I think she won't throw us out. That's the only thing that worries me. If we got thrown out, we wouldn't have any place to go."

"My mother's a pretty strong woman," he said. "But we share the apartment. We split all the bills down the middle, including the rent, which means nobody gets 'thrown out' unless we both want them gone. Me and Moodrow are committed to you. No matter what, you aren't leaving until Levander's caught. Unless you want to leave."

"Uh-uh," she said. "I think I'll hang around." She hesitated for a moment, but Tilley could see she wanted to say something else and he waited patiently.

What she finally said, however, nearly blew him out of the chair. She said, "You're really a pretty man."

"What?"

"Especially that scar over your eye. Your mother says you used to be a fighter. She said you were very good before you got hurt."

"I might have been good. There's no way to know. I never had a fight so close I had to see what was in my heart. And besides, you're not too bad yourself." Was this possible? Suddenly it occurred to him that he might actually get laid here and the idea began to make itself visible. As casually as he could, he took his shirt out of his pants and laid it loosely in his lap.

"Sometimes when I think about it, I feel like I'm still a virgin."

"How do you figure that?" As an ex-prostitute and mother of two, Tilley didn't see how she'd qualify for innocence.

"I'm twenty-five years old and I've never been with a man because I loved him. Or even liked him. I've never had sex with a man because sex feels good or because I wanted him to feel good. It's always been a transaction. A deal. Sex for money. Or drugs. Or a place to stay. Or to protect my children. Don't you think that makes me a virgin?"

"No." He smiled when he said it. "It makes you a victim, though."

The distinction didn't seem to bother her. "That's why I waited until after you told me you wouldn't throw me out." She tossed her hair back from her forehead, an unconscious gesture as sexy as a full scale striptease. "You know, after I came off the drugs, when Lee was born, for a long time I didn't even think about sex. I didn't want to use my body as trade bait and I didn't know there was any other use for it. But after a couple of years, I began to wake up and there were a number of times I was really tempted. Of course, Lee and Jeanette acted as a natural filter and most men, white or black, fled at the sight of them, but still, men asked me out often enough; patients where I worked or other students at the school. But there was always Levander and the thought of what he would do to them if he found out. I mean I didn't just want to have sex. I had to care about the man I was with, but if I cared and I saw him again, Levander would find out. And he would kill him. Or cripple him.

"What do you do about that? I figured it was better not to get started and for the last five years my sex life's consisted entirely of being raped by my ex-husband. Sounds like fun, right?" She took a deep breath, then smiled. "Without him I'd be free. Shit, I'm already free. I'm free in my heart and in my mind. You know, when I first went to the shelter, they put me in these group therapy sessions. There were a dozen women most of the time and all they talked about was what they would do to avoid falling into the same situation again. But I had no fear of that. I know I'll never fall under a man's domination again. If I survive Levander, it'll be like the knight surviving the dragon. After that, there are no more dangers." Tilley's apartment got afternoon sun and it was still pretty warm. Rose dropped the sweater and ran her hands over her arms. "I feel so safe here. I feel like nothing can happen." She grinned. "And you're so pretty. Such a pretty man."

Tilley thought briefly of her motivation. Gratitude. Protection. Perhaps an insurance policy. But he wanted her so badly, he really didn't care why she was coming on to him. For a moment, he flashed back to Fort Greene, to come-ons to the single women who asked him for directions. Half the cops in the job (including the married ones) had women stashed in the various precincts. But he would never have tried it with Rose, not in his own apartment like this. She wanted *him*, though, that was the thing. Such a pretty man. He wondered if she was the kind of woman to get him into bed and then go to the department complaining of sexual harassment. No, Moodrow trusted Rose completely. She wanted *him*. And he was so hot.

"You know my mother and I have an arrangement about not bringing our lovers into the house."

"We already talked about it."

Tilley came out of the chair in a hurry and Rose shrank back on the couch. He supposed she'd seen that anger before and the look in her eyes checked his annoyance. "I wish the two of you would stop fucking with my head. And goddamn Moodrow, too. It's not the way I've lived my life."

"I don't like it either, but I couldn't take a chance that she'd find out and ask me to leave. I have to protect my family."

Neither one of them said anything for a minute. That's the problem with talking your way into bed, but the ordinary course of seduction, the dinners and the movies and the drinks were closed to them. Sitting there, ready to fly across the room, Tilley realized that he'd wanted her from the first time he'd seen her; had found her stunningly beautiful and brave in a way he couldn't begin to understand.

"I want you to pick me up and carry me into the bedroom," she said. "Isn't that the right way for a virgin? To be carried across the threshold?"

She weighed less than nothing, but when her arms went around his neck and she buried her face in his throat, his knees buckled. He stumbled into the room and they fell across the bed. Her laughter rang out as she swung herself up to sit across his chest.

"Now let's say a quick prayer, Jimmy. One quick prayer."

"What are we praying for?"

She slid her halter up to her throat and pressed her breasts into his face. "Repeat after me," she said. "Please, Lord, don't let the kids wake up."

12

Tilley didn't sleep at all that night. He and Rose made wet, sloppy love for a long time and when, near dawn, they finally dropped back onto the sheets, it was more from exhaustion than from any lack of desire. Nevertheless, Rose popped off before Tilley could reassure her with the usual bullshit about how wonderful it was. She stretched, curled her back into his chest, closed her eyes and began to snore lightly. At first he thought she was making a joke about men and how they pass out after sex, but when he nudged her, she rolled onto her back and the snore deepened. She was straight out unconscious.

So he spent the rest of the night thinking about her. Thinking and looking. It seemed like every ten minutes he had to pull back the sheet and stare at her body. She was fairly short, maybe five-two, but she was strong at the same time (despite the delicate bones in her wrists and ankles) with the muscles of her forearms and her thighs pressing firmly against translucent, ivory skin. Tilley had been with a lot of women, even with a few upcoming movie stars when he was fighting and there was the possibility of a championship somewhere in his future. They had beautiful bodies and faces like angels, but none of them had ever affected him as strongly as Rose. Perhaps because she'd been so vulnerable for so long. Or because she was so strong and so determined, despite the physical reality of Levander Greenwood's fists. Despite the heroin, the pills, the cocaine. And even despite the reality of blow-jobs in the backseats of automobiles. Of strange men thrusting their hands into her crotch. "Just wanna make sure you're a little girl and not a little boy. Don't take it personal, honey."

By five o'clock, he was up and running. The one good summer day had passed in the night, replaced by a drizzly warm front that reeked of humidity. The difference in the weather mirrored the difference in his body. His legs felt like rubber bands, his Nikes like lead weights. His swollen head wobbled on a neck that felt as strong as an overcooked noodle reheated in a microwave. It was a wonderful run.

Back inside, with everyone sleeping, he showered, dressed and headed downtown for Moodrow's. New York is one of the busiest places on earth, but even here, there are moments when the city pauses for a deep breath. Tilley came down Second Avenue, catching every light, including the long one by the 59th Street Bridge. Even the cabbies and the bus drivers had forgotten their vows of eternal hatred and cruised without benefit of the upraised finger. Maybe in the suburbs or out in the country, families were putting on their Sunday best and getting ready for church, but in Manhattan, the citizens were in bed with the Sunday papers and would remain there until noon, at least.

It was a quarter to eight when he arrived at Moodrow's and the building was deserted. He pushed open Moodrow's door, as usual, and stepped dreamily inside. His mind was still reviewing Rose's body (he couldn't get the salty odor of her breasts out of his nostrils) and the last thing he expected was the tall black woman, telephone in hand, who cried out in surprise as he stepped into the living room.

Naturally, Tilley panicked. It was like being in a dream. Even though the furniture was identical to Moodrow's and the building was Moodrow's building, he didn't have the slightest doubt that somehow he'd

entered the wrong apartment. His first thought was to
prevent a panic and he started to mumble something
about being a police officer when she smiled and said,
"You're Jim Tilley, right? You'd better be." She held
out her hand. "I'm Leonora Higgins. I'm representing the
district attorney. Moodrow's down on Delancey Street
picking up blintzes and sour cream. The captain's gonna
be a little late. You want coffee?"

Tilley nodded his head and sat down at the kitchen
table. Leonora Higgins was a very good-looking
woman, maybe thirty-five years old. She gave off an
air of self-confidence as neat and tailored as the navy
blue suit and white silk blouse she chose to wear on a
muggy Sunday morning. She poured out coffee, passed
him the milk and sugar, dug out a small paper napkin
with such graceful assurance, he was suddenly convinced this wasn't the first time she'd been in Moodrow's apartment. In the short time he'd known his
partner, Moodrow had never spoken about any woman
(except the snitch-prostitutes that screwed their way
through his Dailies), but if this was his woman, he'd
done all right for himself.

"Have you known Moodrow for a long time?" Tilley
asked innocently.

"Not long, but it's been intense. If you know what
I mean."

Tilley raised his eyebrows in mock horror. "You
telling me this never stops? The test never ends?"

To his surprise, she took the question seriously.
"Not that I know exactly what happens out there between you two, but I'd say Moodrow doesn't change
much from day to day. There's a story circulating
about an illegal motorcycle wrecking yard on 4th
Street. But then Moodrow always did like to stay
busy." She grinned deliberately, obviously teasing him.
"You know the district attorney is committed to civil
rights for *all* New Yorkers. Even criminals."

Tilley sipped his coffee and tried to make the question as casual as he could. "But no one's gonna do anything anyway? That's what you're saying?"

"Your partner's very good at walking the edge, but then again, he's got plenty of time." She grinned again. "That's all he does."

"What are you saying?"

"I'm saying Moodrow doesn't drink. I'm saying he doesn't gamble. There's no drugs. No steady girlfriend. No church. No politics. Not even inside-the-department politics. Moodrow's only got one hangup and that's justice. He's addicted to it and he doesn't give a damn about regulations or rights or what a bunch of politicians wrote two hundred years ago. Each time it's a different problem. Each time he solves it or tries to, at any rate. He's a very practical man, once he makes up his mind to do something."

Tilley held up his hand. "This is not a summation, counselor. And I'm not the jury, either." She grinned apologetically and he went on. "What I'd like to know is what makes you such an expert on Stanley Moodrow. You don't look like his type. Don't get insulted. I mean *you* could do better, not him. So the point is why you care at all." He wasn't trying to challenge her, just curious, and she understood.

"I used to be an FBI agent and he and I and Captain Epstein were on a big case together."

As soon as she said "FBI agent" the whole story clicked into place. The "case," of course, had involved The American Red Army, and the story (which was universally believed) was that Moodrow had originally planned to execute all five of the terrorists and had been shot by an FBI agent because a bullet was the only way she could convince him not to go through with it. That agent had been a black woman and her name was Leonora Higgins.

"I followed him for a long time before the arrests were made and I got to know him. He's a very rare type. You don't meet many people who live their lives

according to moral principles." She reached across the
table and touched the back of Tilley's hand. "You'd
expect a man like him to be innocent, somehow. Vulnerable, that's a better word for it. But we don't worry
about him, not as long as he remains a cop. Moodrow's
been bullshitting the department for thirty-five years.
The captain is worried about *you*. He asked me to try
to speak to you alone. To ask you how things are going." She hesitated momentarily, then finished it. "See
if you want out."

Tilley thought of Rose sitting in his apartment uptown; of Levander Greenwood holed-up in some basement, sitting on a couch, maybe, with a crack pipe on
the table and a shotgun across his legs. Without a
sound, he walked around the table and kissed Ms. Higgins on the cheek. "If you and Epstein are as close to
Moodrow as you say, Lenny, it's just gonna be one big
happy family." He stepped away from her. "Funny
thing is the son of a bitch gives me such a hard time,
I don't feel I should have to take it from anyone else.
Like I already did my penance, ya know?"

She looked at him for a second, trying to read his
smile, then tossed her hands in the air. "I was going
to tell you that if you wanted to stay with Moodrow,
you were going to have to let yourself be a little crazy,
but I see you've managed to accomplish that without
my assistance."

"Most likely that's why Moodrow picked me in the
first place."

They passed a few more minutes with general bullshit about the job and the D.A.'s office, then he asked
her if she knew anything about a cocaine possession
case involving a boy named Marvin Morgan. He explained that Marvin was a friend of a friend and that
he'd been swept up in a larger raid. Now Morgan's rel-
atives didn't trust the legal aid lawyer and wanted to
know how strong the case was.

He expected to be put off (no A.D.A. likes to feel

pressure from a cop), but Higgins was familiar with the prosecution and perfectly willing to talk, explaining that Morgan was part of a much larger operation and, yes, he was guilty as hell. Only his clean record and his efforts to gain an education stood between him and a stretch upstate.

"Tell him to take the plea, Jimmy. If he does, I'll get him before a judge next week and he'll be on the street again. If he goes to trial and he loses, he'll draw three years minimum."

Tilley was nodding his agreement when Moodrow and Epstein showed up. He was anxious to finish this business and get back uptown, to retrieve what was left of his Sunday, but the smell of hot blintzes was too strong and they spent the following half hour with their faces stuck in Moodrow's chipped plates and coffee mugs, shoveling cheese-filled pancakes smothered with sour cream into their mouths.

Nobody said a word, not even small talk, until they were finished and the dishes were piled in the sink. Then Captain Epstein took a handful of manila envelopes from his briefcase and dumped them on the table.

"We got Greenwood's file here plus files on all the narcs in the precinct. I've been through them quick and I don't see any obvious connection."

"What about the last cop that busted him?" Higgins asked. "The time he got sent upstate."

"He's retired," Moodrow volunteered. "That was Donaldson."

"Retired and dead," Epstein said. "His heart stopped on a Boca Raton golf course about two months ago."

Tilley glanced over at Moodrow, knowing how he felt about retirement, but his face was impassive and Epstein continued with his briefing. "Nobody knows these files have been copied. Nobody but the four of us and I'm determined to keep it that way. Leonora's only here because we need to cover our asses. We got a corrupt cop out there and we, meaning Tilley, Mood-row and myself, don't wanna be accused of a coverup if it should come out some other way before we make the bust. You're listening, I hope? Nobody says anything about a corrupt cop until I give the word. *Capisch?*"

He passed the folders over to Moodrow who tossed them on top of a bureau. The move seemed casual enough, but Tilley knew he'd be spending his Sunday going through them syllable by syllable.

"May I say something about the witness you're protecting?" Leonora asked. "Rose Carillo and her children?" Epstein nodded and she went on. "If you want, I can register her and the kids in a witness protection program. That way, there won't be any questions later on."

"Forget it." Tilley was shocked to hear his own voice.

Epstein looked up in surprise. The young cop was low man on the totem pole and Epstein could have shot him down easily enough. Instead, he asked, "Why do you have a problem with the program?"

"For the same reason we're keeping word about a corrupt cop among ourselves. You register them, put it all down on paper in some filing cabinet, you don't know who's gonna have access. It's possible that whoever's running Greenwood reads his file everyday. We already know Greenwood blames his wife for giving us information. Face it, the fewer people know where Rose Carillo's hiding, the fewer people can give her away."

Tilley spoke as forcefully as he could and when he'd finished, there was a brief silence, broken, again, by Leonora Higgins. "You can do what you want," she explained, "but if some lawyer gets ahold of this witness and turns her around, there's going to be hell to pay."

"How so?" Epstein asked.

"Say she claims she's being held against her will, maybe as bait for her ex-husband. Or supposing he should somehow find her in spite of where she's hiding. Suppose he should hurt her or her children. How will you explain the lack of paperwork? At the very least, you should get a notarized statement from her, indicating her cooperation."

"That's bullshit." Moodrow spoke up for the first time. "Jimmy's right. The fewer people who know, the fewer fuckups there'll be. Rose will never make trouble for us."

"Look, it's no skin off my nose," Higgins declared. "I'm only a lawyer. What do I know?"

"Not much." Moodrow smiled when he said it. "But you're getting better. Look, Leonora, Rose Carillo gave us information when we didn't have any way to persuade her. It wasn't a trade, understand? Now I have to protect her."

"It's Jimmy who's going to be hurt, if the shit hits the fan."

"So be it," Tilley said and realized that he already thought of Rose as a lover. As a *regular* lover and he didn't want her moving any further from his bed than absolutely necessary.

"Ease off, already," Epstein said firmly. "What we say here in this room protects all of us. If one goes, we all go. I'm saying that in my judgment and in my capacity as precinct commander, the public will be better protected if we keep Rose Carillo and the possible existence of a rogue cop out of the files. After all, the whole point of Higgins' presence is to let us bypass epartment regulations. We're supposed to report this to Internal Affairs, but we're not doing it. And we're not registering Rose Carillo, either. Now let's get on to other things." He paused, waiting until their brains made the jump, then planted his thought. "Peter Katjcic says a cop's running Levander Greenwood. I

say, 'So what?' Why should we believe an asshole like
Peter Katjcic? How do we know it isn't bullshit?"

"The only thing I believe, is that Katjcic wasn't lying." Moodrow stood up and began to gather the plates
and the silverware. As he spoke, he wiped the table
clean, then handed Tilley half the folders Epstein had
brought. All of a sudden, Tilley's Sunday afternoon began to retreat into the distance. "*He* thinks Greenwood's tied in with a cop. Yesterday I heard it again.
Twice. There's always a lotta rumors on the street, but
this one seems to be coming from Greenwood himself.
I hear that he shows up at parties or in the social clubs
after hours. Stays a few minutes looking for crack, buys
a few hundred vials at a time, then retreats to his
cave."

"Maybe he's preparing a defense," Leonora suggested.

"Just like you're preparing a prosecution?" Tilley
needled her and she grinned back. In that moment,
they were friends.

"Touché, Officer Tilley."

"Anyway the cop thing makes sense," Tilley continued. "Right from the beginning we thought he must
have a partner selling the dope he rips off. A narc
would fit the pattern perfectly. Someone who could
set up the original robbery, then hand over the contraband to another snitch. That's why the rats haven't
put us onto Levander. The dealers who sell what he
rips off never see him."

"I agree. I have to admit it," Epstein said. "Not only
that, but I got a bad feeling that when Greenwood goes
down he's gonna take half the fucking precinct with
him. You ready for retirement, Stanley? You got a fish-
ing pole?"

Moodrow shook his head. "I'm gonna wait until after I see whether he gets taken alive or not. If he dies,
everything's different."

"From your mouth to God's ears," Epstein implored.

"In thirty-six years I never wanted a man as bad as this. Any idea who could be running him?"

"Have to be someone in the precinct," Moodrow responded. "The rip-offs are going down right here. If he was borough-wide or inter-borough, they'd be hitting all over the city. I spoke to O'Neill over the phone and that's not what he's getting. In fact, except for us, the city's been pretty quiet the last couple of weeks. Meanwhile the shitheads're lining up at the telephones to give us Levander's address. Fifteen different tips in the last two days. Imagine knocking on all those doors? Never knowing if this time the shotgun's waiting on the other side? Anyway, I'm throwing you out, Captain. You, too, Leonora. Now that our asses are good and covered, me and James are gonna go through these folders, see if there's anything here."

13

There was nothing there, of course, but Moodrow and Tilley didn't know it until the afternoon was long gone. Epstein had been very thorough. He'd gone outside the precinct to include narcs from inter-precinct, borough-wide and city-wide task forces—any cop who'd worked closely enough with the 7th to have accumulated a file. Add to this the files of men who'd transferred out or retired and the two cops were forced to wade through forty-two thick folders. By the time they were finished, all they knew was that none of them had ever been directly involved with Levander Greenwood, but since it's understood that all detectives have snitches whose names are never put to paper, this simple fact meant nothing. Moodrow, however, pronounced himself satisfied. If none were implicated, none were exonerated either and they could continue the present line of their investigation without the nagging fear that they'd missed something.

"I'm gonna let you go," Moodrow finally tossed the folders into a drawer. It was nearly six o'clock and the kitchen table was littered with McDonald's wrappers and empty cans of Coke. "How's Rose taking the change?"

"I'd say she's overjoyed to be somewhere safe." Tilley kept his voice as matter-of-fact as possible, but Moodrow threw him a sharp look anyway.

"I hope she's not too much trouble for you. I mean

136

with the kids and everything. That kind of invasion can wear thin in a hurry, so if you can't take it anymore, just let me know and I'll find someplace else for her."

"I'll keep it in mind."

Actually, the chances of Jim Tilley sending Rose any further than the next room were slim to none. He'd been itching for her all day and the sensation only grew stronger as he drove uptown. He had some daydream of walking into the apartment and carrying her off to the bedroom, but he came home to Lee and Jeanette playing noisily (and confidently) in the living room while Rose and Susanna prepared a family dinner, the first in that house in months. It wasn't what Tilley wanted, but even this scene out of some TV sitcom didn't take place until he'd been interrogated by still another neighbor.

As Tilley entered the building, Irving Blaustein, all eighty-five years of him, sat on a chair in the lobby, apparently waiting for him to come home. Tilley had known Blaustein for most of his life. A refugee from a deteriorating Jewish neighborhood in Brownsville, Brooklyn, Blaustein had moved into the building when Tilley was four years old. Irving, long retired, had made his living as a union organizer in the garment center and rumors of mob connections had followed him into retirement. Even now, more than twenty years later, some of his neighbors professed to be afraid of him. Curious that they'd turned to him in time of need.

"Jimmy, Jimmy," he said, his voice raspy from seventy years of unfiltered Chesterfields. "You could come here a minute, please? Talk to Irving?"

His presence in the lobby was a shock. He lived on the fourth floor and was very thin and somewhat arthritic. Still, Tilley didn't manage to put it together until after Blaustein spelled it out.

"Irv," he said innocently, "what's up? You come out to see me?"

"Jimmy, I want you should personally know that this is very embarrassing to me. This is not a thing I would dream up all by myself, but some of the neighbors came to me. They think because I was with the union, I know how to talk to people, so they ask me to wait here for you to come home. They wanna find out about the situation. You know . . . about the little *yams* in your apartment. They're only babies, I know, but the people here, they find a roach in the kitchen, they think the Russians are at the door. You gotta make allowances for such ignorance. For them, two little babies mean the coloreds are taking over the building. They see dope dealers in every apartment. Junkies climbing through the windows. It's their nature to be frightened. Me, I worked all my life with the niggers and I know how to get along, but the others . . ."

"Get to the point, Irv." The word *yam* was a corruption of an Italian word which meant eggplant.

"Your neighbors just wanna know that the kids ain't stayin' permanently. Maybe they're like sick and you and the pretty lady are takin' care of 'em." He waved his hands apologetically. "Ah, Jimmy. This ain't my style. I tol' them Jimmy wouldn't fuck us. Jimmy wouldn't dirty his own house. How long they gonna be here, Jimmy?"

Tilley had been raised and educated as a Roman Catholic and one of the most basic assumptions of that religion is that any sin can be forgiven. When he was a child, first trying to grasp this principle, he conjured images of murderers on their knees before black-robed priests. His own failures, on the other hand, had always been smaller; unexpected moments when he could make the cowardly choice without fear of witnesses. He knew how Rose felt about her children; he could feel the strength of her commitment to their well-being and her contempt for the white world that rejected all three of them, but what he said was, "Hey, what're you worried about, Irv? They'll be with us for a few days. It's a police matter, so I'm not at liberty to go over the details, but you got nothing to worry about."

"Oh yeah, yeah," he answered. "I heard you made detective. Congratulations." He stared into Tilley's eyes for a moment, perhaps remembering the days when he would have simply told the cop to get rid of them, then began to shuffle toward the stairs. There was no elevator in the building and the journey back to his apartment would be a long one. Despite an urge to kick the old man down the stairs, Tilley followed behind him, step by step, in case he should slip. When they got to his door, Blaustein turned and grabbed Tilley's arm with one bony claw. "You're a good boy, Jimmy. So many bad ones in the world, but you're a good boy."

When Tilley came down the hallway into the living room of his apartment, Lee and Jeanette were playing tug-of-war with a coloring book. Instead of a greeting, they checked him out closely, then went back to their game. Rose came out of the kitchen, a huge smile across her face. Tilley wanted to hug her, but didn't quite have the nerve to do it in front of the children. Instead he took her hand and said, "Well, we didn't get him today either. Maybe tomorrow."

But they didn't get him on Monday. Or any other day that week. Levander Greenwood had disappeared as completely as if he'd left the country, and the speculation among members of the task force was that someone had killed him and buried his body in one of the abandoned tenements. Considering their special information about his relationship with a police officer, neither Moodrow nor Tilley was prepared to reject that theory. Nevertheless, acting in concert with the task force, both agreed that a show of solidarity was more important than the line they were pursuing and they decided to make good on Moodrow's threat to put heat on the entire neighborhood, to force the underworld of the Lower East Side to give up its most infamous member.

This is a common practice in New York's various ghettos and *barrios* and the procedure is very simple: without any regard for Constitutional principles, the cops arrest everyone who comes within two hundred yards of any known drug location until their actual target is behind bars. This is done in order to encourage the businessmen engaged in the drug trade to sacrifice the man for the sake of the dollar. The dealers understand, of course, that even though the arrests have no chance of standing up in court, a massive police presence inevitably negates the possibility of a positive cash flow and they're usually more than willing to cooperate, if they can.

On the other hand, the method does have one serious flaw: it almost always sweeps up the citizens with the dirtbags. Which is why it's *only* used in the hunt for cop killers and why it's very rarely applied to mixed or white neighborhoods. The Lower East Side, on the other hand, is the most integrated neighborhood in Manhattan, with a number of relatively famous artists and writers as long-term residents. It would not do to have these people standing about in crowds waving police brutality banners (which they are liable to do even without provocation) and so the task force planned the operation much more carefully than they ordinarily would. Instead of wholesale street busts, they made lists of known dealing apartments and they started with the ones they were most sure of, the residences of their own informants.

The rationale was the snitches were *supposed* to supply cops with information and their failure to hand over Greenwood entitled the cops to dump their side of the bargain. Consequently, the task force members printed the names and addresses and tossed them into a hat along with the addresses of drug houses run by noninformants. Then Epstein took the hat into his office and drew up a master list. That way, no one could be absolutely sure which snitch belonged to which cop or even if an individual was a snitch. Finally, they broke off into three groups of ten and went through the doors with sledgehammers.

The odd thing was that no one fought back. The cops were brutal in a way that was new to Tilley, brutal without emotion, sometimes striking out before they even identified themselves. Apartments were torn apart while children stared in terror. The cops made piles in the centers of the rooms, piles of everything that wasn't drugs so they wouldn't have to check the same items twice. Inevitably, they found drugs on somebody and they arrested everyone in the apartment unless there were children. Then they let the mother slide.

The hit on a Henry Street shooting gallery the following Tuesday was a perfect example of the technique. Shooting galleries are at the bottom of the heroin industry and, for the most part, drugs are not even sold there. They offer only a safe place to shoot up and nod out and are often run by families who don't use drugs, families desperate for money. The task force hit this particular house about 2:30 PM. The detectives on the squad had been taking turns smashing the doors open and Moodrow crashed through the lock on this one, forcing the door inward with a single blow of the sledgehammer. A Spanish man, middle-aged, came to the door with a faint smile on his face and Kirkpatrick stepped forward and punched him in the mouth. The junkies sitting against the wall tried to force what they hadn't injected into their noses. One kid, sweat pouring down his face, frantically jammed a full needle into the soft flesh on the inside of his elbow. Naturally, he missed the vein and his arm swelled up like a balloon.

There were four detectives on Moodrow and Tilley's team, wearing sweatshirts and sneakers, and six patrolmen in black SWAT Team uniforms carrying shotguns. While the detectives slapped bags of dope out of the hands of thoroughly panicked junkies, the uniforms went from room to room, shotguns proffered, and collected the family of the man who operated the gallery. Then the apartment was systematically torn to pieces. They ran through every inch, ripped it apart and left what was now garbage piled in the center of the rooms. Finally, they arrested everyone except the woman who lived there and her four small children. The amazing thing is that no one complained. Not one sound from anyone. The message the cops were sending and which the junkies received was simple—cops were dead and until Levander Greenwood could be made to pay, everyone would pay.

By the fourth day, however, word had spread and the dealers were taking long vacations in the Bronx. On Thursday the task force hit six empty apartments and they decided to, at least temporarily, abandon the strategy. Instead, Epstein put half the precinct on the streets. There were a hundred cops walking patrol and dozens of cars criss-crossing the avenues. All had orders to harass no one, but the dealers (and especially their middle-class customers) kept as far out of sight as possible. From the detectives' point of view, the investigation had settled into the pattern cops hate most. All they could do was sit and wait.

Tilley's life uptown had also settled into something like a routine. Now that Blaustein had spread the word, his neighbors smiled at Susanna as she came and went. The bit about "a police matter" gave her an excuse to withhold the details from the gossipers and Rose showed no desire to leave the apartment until Greenwood was safely in custody. She was secure, she was comfortable and every night, after Susanna and the children were asleep, she came to Tilley's bed.

They fucked hard and quickly, with a violence Tilley had never experienced before and even though he had the feeling he was being used, a machine to bleed the edge off all those years of frustration, he was so hot for her it didn't matter. Sometimes, in the middle of a conversation about the kids or Moodrow (whom she'd known for years), they'd jump into it as if someone had thrown a switch. She'd be sitting across from him on the bed, naked, her legs crossed in front of her and he'd reach for her with more intensity then he'd reached for his lover on the night after a big victory in the ring. Rose Carillo was the most beautiful woman he'd ever known and in spite of sessions that stretched until dawn, there wasn't a time, as he watched her walk down the hallway to her own room, when he didn't ache to pull her back into his bed.

Surprisingly, she didn't talk much about Greenwood or the nightmare of her childhood. What Tilley finally got from her, after four or five nights of the usual lover's bullshit, was totally unexpected. Rose was grateful, insisting that only a slave can fully understand freedom. She swore that the girl who shot dope and whored for Levander Greenwood, who snuck out of some preposterous redneck town in West Virginia only to find imprisonment in the promised land, no longer existed. And with no past to carry on her back, the new woman, Rose Carillo, could become anything. The future was limitless.

Always assuming, of course, that Levander Greenwood disappeared permanently from her life. And her fear of him was as apparent as her love for her children. All of Rose Carillo's plans involved a life with her children, a life of what most consider drudgery; of getting up in the morning, of cooking breakfast then rushing off to drop the kids at school before going to work. That life (or, possibly, *any* life) would be denied to her as long as Greenwood stayed free and, to a certain extent, as long as he was alive. Rose told him that Greenwood had escaped custody three different times. Twice from juvenile facilities where escape is almost as simple as walking out the door, but once from a corrections department bus transporting inmates from the courts back to Rikers Island. A dozen of those buses make the trip everyday, moving hundreds of prisoners, yet there have been only six successful escape attempts. Levander had accomplished his by having a friend sideswipe the bus with a stolen oil delivery truck. After the bus flipped, Levander forced himself through a very small opening in the steel mesh covering the windows, an opening so small he'd arrived home with long, deep cuts from his chest to his hips, courtesy of the jagged steel.

He was apprehended on the following day, but the point was made and Rose was convinced that sooner or later, assuming he got his inevitable life sentence, Levander would escape and the scenario she concocted seemed almost plausible. Once they become institutionalized, most lifers are transferred to medium security or even minimum security facilities. Occasionally, a savvy con only pretends to be that ultra-safe lobotomized trustee in order to be in a situation where the administration pronounces him harmless. To a man facing fifty or sixty years in prison, ten years between the planning and the execution of an escape is not a very long time.

"I want to raise my children on the Lower East Side," she explained. "You think I didn't see the way your neighbor looked at us when we came through the door that first day?"

"You mean Strauss?"

"I see that look everyday," she said gently. "And if I'm getting it in New York, imagine what it would be like in Boise? The Lower East Side is the only place I know where my kids won't be rejected before they have a chance to show what they are. I'm sure there're other neighborhoods in other big cities, but I don't know them. The only place I know where there are so many freaks that me and the kids look like ordinary citizens is the Lower East Side and that's where I want to live. And I can't live there knowing that any knock on the door might be Levander coming home to collect his property."

Her answer brought up a question that had been bothering Tilley for days. "That morning, when I came through the door and you were holding the gun. If it was him, Rose, would you have pulled the trigger?"

Her mouth curled into a sudden, disbelieving smile. Of all the asshole questions Tilley had asked in his life, that was the stupidest. If Levander Greenwood had been on the other side of that door, she would have blown his eyeballs right through the back of his fucking head.

14

As the task force moved from location to location, Stanley Moodrow watched his partner closely. Raids like these were essentially bully operations. The surprise, the savagery, the overwhelming manpower were all designed to eliminate the possibility of resistance. The objects of the attacks, the junkies and the pushers, were reduced to helplessness by the level of force used against them. In most cases, they were terrified and if truth be told, many cops derive a great deal of pleasure from their enemy's fear. Moodrow had long ago defined his aim as a cop—to separate the criminals from the citizens and it was his opinion that cops who indulged their sadism rarely kept that primary aim in focus.

Thus, for Moodrow, frightening already half-dead junkies was a joyless task. But he didn't run from it. Not every aspect of police work was pleasurable, but what had to be done had to be done. If you were going to be effective, you took the good with the bad.

Of course, it was easy for Moodrow, thirty-five years into the job, to be philosophical. It was Jim Tilley's first experience at rendering unendurable the already miserable lives of New York's addicts. Initially, the young cop had been apprehensive, his service revolver, barrel to the ceiling, held tight against the side of his head. But at the end of the first day, as he began to understand that Levander Greenwood was not hiding behind those doors, his attitude eased considerably, even as other members of the team gleefully smashed plates and furniture, as they cracked jokes while ripping into the soft bellies of teddy bears: "You don't got no dope in here, do ya, *mamacita?*" Then a smirk as they slapped the faces of any brazen enough to challenge their authority.

Tilley's expression, Moodrow noted, grew more and more grim as the days went by. He stopped talking, became almost a hermit within their midst, yet he continued to do his job professionally, staying as close to Moodrow as possible.

"You having a good time, Jimmy?" Moodrow asked as the team finished destroying the last apartment on the day's list.

"I'd rather direct traffic at a Jets' game in a snowstorm," Tilley observed. "Does this crap really do any good?"

"Yeah, I'd have to say it does. If Greenwood's operating anywhere near here, someone'll give him up. Money talks, bullshit walks. And as far as the dopers are concerned, Levander Greenwood is just so much bullshit."

Tilley shook his head in disgust. "What the fuck we're doing here . . ." He pointed to the mess, to the figures huddled against the wall. "These assholes enjoy it. I thought detectives were professional. This is stupid."

They were silent for a few moments, watching the faces of a Cuban family whose furniture was being systematically rendered into kindling. In his inexperience, Tilley expected rage, but, no surprise to Moodrow, the expressions were blank. Only the eyes demonstrated an ultimate resignation, as if the victims, too, believed they deserved this treatment. The family would have to leave the apartment, at least temporarily, for fear that the team would come back and do something worse. That could easily mean a homeless shelter and the separation of the father from his family.

"So what'd you think, Jimmy? You thought maybe it was gonna be like Agatha Christie? Charlie Chan, maybe? I got some hot news for you, it's more like Paul Bunyan than Sherlock Holmes."

Tilley grinned ruefully. "I think I shoulda stayed in college."

"Listen," Moodrow wrapped one enormously powerful hand around his partner's arm. "I almost never stay with these assholes. Y'understand? Once in a while in cases like this, but usually I'm far away from the bullshit. That's what I'm saying could happen for you. I got ways I haven't even shown you a piece of. Just be patient. You're gonna get it all."

An hour later, as Tilley made his way uptown, Moodrow walked along Avenue B, his eyes searching those of his neighbors. If he was satisfied with his partner's performance, he was anything but happy with the status of their search for Levander Greenwood. He tried, unsuccessfully, to conjure up an image of Greenwood's place of refuge. Like a burrowing animal, Greenwood continued to emerge in search of prey, then disappear as soon as he'd fed. Since every incident had taken place on the Lower East Side, Greenwood had to be somewhere close by. The small scale of his thefts (which bore no relation to the scale of his violence) precluded the possibility of any motivation more complicated than desperation.

As he strolled along, Moodrow was greeted by many of the shopkeepers, most of whom were quick to inquire about the Greenwood case. At first, he thought they were being critical, but then he realized that, from their point of view, the massive police presence brought on by Greenwood's crimes made their lives that much easier. The criminals, the junkies, the crack addicts, were staying off the streets and that made le-

gitimate customers feel more at ease. For once, it was
a pleasure to walk the streets of the Lower East Side.

Moodrow was not heading home. It was after eight
o'clock and he stopped to pick up a ham sandwich, a
six-pack of beer and a bag of potato chips, then continued walking west on 11th Street, searching faces as if
Levander Greenwood might appear at any moment.
Now that his official police day was over, he could
begin the work he expected would finally bring him to
Levander Greenwood. He walked past Avenue A and
First Avenue, leaving most of the tenements behind.
There were brownstones here, mixed in with the
cheaper housing, and the process of gentrification, this
far from the projects on Avenue D, was almost complete. Along Second Avenue, one trendy restaurant after another begged for the credit cards of the newly
affluent. Boutiques sat side by side with antique and
art galleries. Moodrow ignored it all, plodding on until
he reached a five story brownstone across from St.
Mark's Church between Second and Third.

The building had an entrance, below street level, for
what should have been the apartment opening out to
the garden in the rear. In fact, it consisted of a single,
small room with a bathroom (toilet and sink) off to
one side. The walkway from the street to the door, a
series of granite steps, twisted back on itself and the
doorway, without a light of course, was deep in the
shadows.

This was Stanley Moodrow's office. Far more pro-
ductive than his desk in the 7th, the apartment was
known to each of the dozens of informants he had built
up in his thirty-five years on the job. He had put the
word out; he wanted Levander Greenwood. Now, he
hoped, the telephone would begin to ring and the underworld of the Lower East Side would drop by to visit.
As he popped open a can of beer and bit into his sandwich, he thought briefly of Rose Carillo and then of
an old love, Rita Melengic. He had seen Rita die, seen

that flame go out of his life forever and he would not let it happen to Rose, even if he had to tear the Lower East Side apart brick by brick.

Three hours later, half asleep on a battered sofa, he was startled by the ringing of an old rotary telephone. It was his third call of the evening. The first two had given him the same piece of news: no one was claiming credit for Greenwood's death. Levander would never let the cop running him get close enough to make an attempt, but he could have gotten it on the street from any one of a hundred people anxious for revenge. But then, of course, the shooter would be putting out the word in every bar on the Lower East Side. No cowboy could resist the temptation to display that scalp.

"Yeah?" Moodrow's voice was thick with sleep.

"Are you still spending your nights in that hole? When are you going to reform?"

For a moment, he couldn't place the woman's voice. It was familiar, all right, but he was so locked into his hunt for Greenwood, he kept trying to place it with those who might call with messages about his quarry.

"Stanley, if you don't say my name right this minute, you're going to spend a very lonely night."

"Just like all the rest of them."

"Don't be bitter, dear. Do I have to give you a hint?"

"No, Tamara, you don't. How's life on Wall Street? Does it beat working on your back?"

"And my knees and my stomach?"

"That, too."

"Well, to be absolutely honest with you, it's more stressful, but the benefits are a lot better. I've got hospitalization now that covers gonorrhea. You looking for company tonight?"

Moodrow smiled for the first time in hours. "Yeah. Please."

"Should I bring a pizza?"

"Just bring a slice."

As Moodrow tried, unsuccessfully, to push the litter into a corner with a worn broom, its handle long ago broken on a recalcitrant visitor, he considered the phenomenon of Tamara Whitefoot. She had literally worked her way through school as a call girl, pushing ten thousand dollars a year of her income into college and postgraduate tuition. She wasn't attractive enough to command the five-hundred-dollar client, but had more than enough class to avoid the streets. Her plan was to complete her education without piling up fifty thousand dollars in educational loans. Instead of years of struggle to repay the banks, she would have a serious portfolio.

The only blot in this carefully worked-out scenario was the potential for getting busted. As a business major, Tamara knew that virtually every big brokerage house investigated the backgrounds of prospective executives. When Stanley Moodrow had walked in on her that afternoon and pulled Johnny Palmer out of the saddle, she had seen her career go straight down the toilet. Of course, she had no way of knowing that Mister Palmer, who presented himself as a plumbing supply executive, was a con artist who specialized in removing old ladies from their life savings. To her, he was just another horny male with a hundred dollars.

She begged Moodrow not to arrest her, though she was sure he would have to use her to establish the time and place of the bust. As she made her plea, Moodrow looked on incredulously.

"Forget about it," he finally said. "I never arrested a whore in my life. Not for fucking. And I don't think I'm gonna start now." He gave Johnny Palmer, who was small, skinny and very shriveled, a shake. "As for Mr. Palmer, I don't expect he'll mind too bad if I say I took him on the street." He passed the stunned Tamara Whitefoot a business card. It had no name on it, just a telephone number. "You give me a call the next couple of days. Maybe you could help me sometime."

Surprisingly, Tamara called two days later, then took

the trip to Moodrow's 11th Street office. As it turned out, she worked a little too far up the prostitution ladder to know much about the street, but she had been as intrigued with Moodrow's odd relationship with the NYPD as he was with her educational ambitions.

That was fifteen years ago, five years before Tamara Whitefoot took her MBA and went to work for Bache Halsey in the financial district. Curiously, as an entry level executive, even with a portfolio, she had found the attitudes of her superiors, male and female, every bit as objectionable as the johns she'd left behind, and after three years of paying her dues, had opened up her own office and worked her portfolio into seven figures. With that kind of money, she could have bought Chippendale's chorus line, but every few months something in her reached for a link to the past and that link was Stanley Moodrow.

Though Moodrow had been pushing dirt around for twenty minutes, by the time the bell rang, the apartment was as messy as when he'd started. Moodrow tossed the broom into the corner and went to the door.

"Hi, Stanley. How's it hangin'?"

"Fuck, I don't think it's hanging at all."

Tamara Whitefoot, thirty-eight and a long time gym freak, had the carefully honed body of a teenager. She wore a black mini, cut high enough to show the softly rounded edge of her pink, cotton panties. In keeping with her Indian name and background, a supple white vest barely covered her breasts. Her cheeks were brightly rouged, her eyes burdened with enormous lashes and electric blue eye shadow. "Here's ya pizza, sir," she said, jaws working a wad of gum. "That'll be ten dollas and fifty cents. Without a tip."

Moodrow took a step backward, regarding the pizza box dubiously. "Wait a second, lady, I didn't order no whole pizza. I only asked for a slice."

Tamara stepped into the room, closing the door behind her. "Maybe that's why the box is empty," she said.

PROPERTY: NYPD

B3445-FF   MAJOR CASES PATROLMAN REPORT FORM

date _8/29_   (hand) ~~steno~~

case# _MC 201_   loc _7th Pct_

stenographer _none_

sig. _____

civ. emp. # _____

patrolman _Patricia Kelly_

sig. _Patricia Kelly_

shield # _19413_   pct. _7th_

cross reference _7th Pct - Homicide_

Approximately fourteen hundred hours. Routine foot patrol with partner, Martin Samuels, on Allen Street. Heard gunshots from the west, approximately one block distance. Called in report of shots fired. Requested backup.

Ran one block to Eldridge Street where I observed several civilians exiting from partially abandoned building at 2113 Eldridge Street. Civilians broke up and ran in different directions as we approached, but male Hispanic, approximately thirty years of age, indicated that gunshots had been fired on the fifth floor.

We proceeded into the building and up the stairway. There were no sounds and all doors were closed. Took approximately six minutes to arrive on fifth floor landing where we observed door to 5B slightly ajar. Smell of gunpowder very strong in the hallway.

We knocked on the door and identified ourselves as police. No response. Acting on belief that a felony had been committed within the premises, we then pushed the door open. I observed a black male infant, approximately nine months of age, lying on the carpet in the hallway. Infant had apparent shotgun-type wound to the abdomen and was motionless. Extreme loss of blood was evident and infant appeared to be dead.

Entered main room of dwelling. Observed male and female blacks, both approximately twenty years old. Male black had apparent shotgun-type wound to the face and appeared to be dead. Female black had suffered shotgun-type wound to both legs, but was conscious.

We proceeded into the bedroom and noted open window to fire escape. Bedroom was empty. We continued to search the closets and bathroom until the apartment was secured. I called Central for an ambulance and the patrol supervisor. My partner, Martin Samuels, placed a tourniquet on the upper thighs of female black. Examination showed child and male black to be apparently dead.

Observed numerous evidence of contraband use within premises, including envelopes filled with white powder, scale, syringes, candle, spoons with bottom burned black. Advised female black of her Miranda rights then asked her to identify herself. Female black identified herself as Yvonne Carson. I asked her if she wanted to talk to us and she said, "Levander Greenwood did this to me. Levander Greenwood killed my family."

Ambulance arrived approximately fourteen hundred twenty hours. Patrol supervisor arrived approximately fourteen hundred twenty-five hours. Relieved by Sergeant Grassi and ordered to secure the crime scene which I did.

15

Moodrow and Tilley were uptown when they caught the squeal over the Special Ops channel on the radio. They were sharing this channel with two unrelated task forces, but even so, it was far quieter than the endless static, punctuated by dull cop voices, from Central on channel two. Their vehicle was designated as Green 5, the last of the vehicles involved in Operation Greenwood and the message came from task force headquarters in the 7th Precinct building.

"Base to Green 5. Base to Green 5, K."

At first they ignored the request to respond. In truth, they didn't even hear it. Then it was repeated twice more, followed by, "You out there, Moodrow? Please. For just once don't make us have to look for you." Moodrow's tendency to be away from (or even to ignore) radio messages was legendary and a constant source of friction between him and the Murphys.

"Green 5, K." The radio mike literally disappeared in Moodrow's fist, like a jelly bean in the hand of a child.

"Hey, I got 'em." Then a scrabble of overlapping voices before Kirkpatrick came on. "Hey, Moodrow." No dispatcher, he actually waited for an answer, then repeated: "Hey, Moodrow."

"Yes, dear," Moodrow said.

"Our boy finally come outta his cave. Twenty-one thirteen Eldridge, fifth floor. Two dead, one survivor."

Moodrow sat straight up in his seat. With the mike

156

closed, he said, "I think this is it, Jimmy. I think the motherfucker just made his one mistake." Then he opened the mike and asked, "What'd he get?"

"What'd he get? You mean Greenwood?"

"No, I mean your fucking grandmother."

"You can't use them words on the radio, Moodrow. You're gonna get us in trouble with the FCC."

"Please," Moodrow said after a pause.

"Now that's better. That's the magic word. Levander got drugs. Like always."

Moodrow took a deep breath, then he said, very quietly, "If you were any stupider, you'd be dead. I'm trying to find out what kind of drugs."

"Heroin. We don't know how much."

"You said twenty-one thirteen Eldridge?"

"Right. Two one one three."

"Muchos gracias, subhuman. Ten-four." He slid the mike back into its holder, then turned to his partner. "Let's go with the lights. I wanna be down there in ten minutes."

Ten minutes? They were on West 95th Street and couldn't have made the Lower East Side in ten minutes with anything slower than a helicopter. The roads in Central Park were closed to traffic, as they are all summer long, and Tilley headed down Columbus, hoping to skirt the worst of the midtown traffic before he tried to cross the Island. Instead, they ran into an ocean of steaming metal which began at 74th Street and extended south as far as they could see. Moodrow, disbelieving, flipped the channel on the radio, contacted Central and was told that a Jersey Transit bus had overturned in the east tube of the Lincoln Tunnel and caught fire. The tunnel was closed in both directions and Jersey-bound traffic had flooded the west side of midtown Manhattan.

So there was no choice but to go east along with everyone else. The flashing red bubble on the top of the car was, of course, impressing no one. Not that

there was anywhere for the traffic to go. When streets
are curb-to-curb metal, all you can do is wait. Of
course, they would have made slightly better progress
if they went with the siren. It's absolutely unnerving
to sit, motionless, in front of a screaming siren, but it
would be a clear violation of department guidelines to
run with the siren in a nonemergency situation. Besides which, Tilley didn't really see the reason for
Moodrow's haste, and when Moodrow asked him to go
up on the sidewalk, Tilley balked.

"Look, Moodrow, I'm not gonna kill somebody just
so we can go look at a bloodstained apartment. I seen
them before and advise we get there *after* the M. E.
carts the bodies off to the morgue."

Moodrow laughed. In spite of his haste, he seemed
very happy about something. "Think for a minute,
Jimmy. I mean you don't know all the details, but you
should be able to see something different this time.
Then you'll know why we gotta hurry."

They were on 65th Street, heading for the Central
Park transverse. Tilley was prepared to go straight
across Manhattan to the East River Drive and the
trucks and taxis were making room for them. Then a
city bus pulled away from the curb, forcing Tilley to
brake sharply before it stopped for the red light on
Central Park West. Moodrow jumped out of the car,
went to the driver's window and banged on it hard,
waving his badge like a flag on the fourth of July.

"Gimme your goddamn driver's license," he yelled.
The bus driver seemed about to faint. Moodrow, with
his massive head and his rumpled woolly jacket,
looked like a carnivorous buffalo and each time he
slapped his palm against the window, the bus rocked
on its suspension. "Before the fucking light changes,
asshole," he demanded.

From behind the wheel, Tilley could just see the
driver's face and it was hanging damn near to the middle of his chest. He was very, very sorry he'd cut off a

cop. Most likely, the heat and the traffic had gotten to him and he just didn't give a shit until after it was too late. In any event, he handed over his license and Moodrow carried it back to the car.

"Let's go," Moodrow said as soon as he was inside. Never one to argue, Tilley pulled around the bus and crossed Central Park West against the light. In the rearview mirror, he could make out the bus driver pounding his steering wheel in frustration. It would take half a day to get a duplicate at the MVB on Worth Street; four hours of dealing with the most hated bureaucracy in New York City.

The move relaxed Moodrow immensely, and once through the park, they began to make better time. "Listen," Tilley said. "This 'difference' you talked about. That's because it's heroin, right?" From the little information they had, that's the only thing that could have been different. Though he'd moved freely from one drug dealer to another (not surprising if a cop, with access to every corner of the marketplace, was running him), Levander had concentrated mainly on cocaine dealers. It was common knowledge that Levander was a terminal crack addict, so the pattern came as no surprise.

"That's exactly right," Moodrow responded.

"You know what brand?"

"I think so, but I have to make sure. That's why I wanna get down there in a hurry. If it's what I think it is, we'll catch it coming back out on the street. If we're fast enough."

Moodrow was referring to a marketing device commonly used by larger heroin-dealing gangs. Ten dollar bags were now stamped with a trade name so the user could identify the source. The names, Blue Thunder, Red Dragon, Smiley D, were not very imaginative and the scrollwork surrounding the name on the glassine envelopes was equally crude. Yet the names were used week after week and whenever any especially powerful dope hit the streets, the brand name would spread quickly among the junkies. A dime bag is a dime bag, but the purity of the drug inside varies enormously.

"So what's your guess? What do you think it is?"

"It's Blue Thunder. Ninety-nine percent sure. Eldridge Street is all Blue Thunder."

"But isn't that the problem?"

"What? Spell it out." They were on the Drive by now and moving quickly downtown. In the lighter traffic, other vehicles were making an effort to get out of the way and Tilley was doing about forty-five miles an hour which is all FDR Drive, with its massive potholes and roller coaster dips, will allow.

"Moodrow, if *all* of Eldridge Street is selling Blue Thunder, not to mention the other fifteen places scattered around the neighborhood, how is it gonna help that one more dealer is handling it on the street?"

"If it's Blue Thunder I think I might be able to shut it off. For a while."

The statement sat with them like the atmosphere after a loud fart. Nobody wanted to be the first to breathe it in.

"You really think you can do this?" Tilley finally asked.

Moodrow looked at his partner strangely for a moment, then said, "I know the wop who runs Blue Thunder on the Lower East Side. I went to high school with him."

"This guy is your friend?"

Moodrow broke into a nervous giggle. "That's the one problem. I hated him from the first day I met him. He was a vicious bastard, so mean I took him for an ordinary bully. I thought he'd run if I stamped my foot, but I was wrong. We fought from when we were freshmen until after we graduated, without anyone coming out a clear winner. I see him on the street and I still wanna hit him. He's a mob scumbag who feeds on

human misery. A real threat to everything and everyone in that neighborhood."

"You mean Don Moodrow's neighborhood?" As the
hours passed, they were becoming more and more
committed to each other. It was a fact, not a decision.
Now Tilley could tease Moodrow without worrying
about his reaction, and though Moodrow's testing of
his partner never really stopped, he no longer looked
like he expected Tilley to fail. On those few occasions
when Tilley put his foot down (as he had when Moodrow asked him to pull onto the sidewalk), Moodrow
respected it.

"What makes you think they won't repackage?"

"If they do, they do. But I think Greenwood's too
desperate for that and, naturally, he believes there's
twenty other people out there with the same product.
Nobody has any idea that I could do this thing. By the
way, if I *can* do it, it's gotta stay between the two of
us. Understand?"

"Not even Higgins and the captain?"

"The two of us," he repeated, his eyes glued to the
road ahead. "Until we decide what we're to do with
cousin Levander."

16

The crime scene at 2113 Eldridge was as gruesome as Tilley had expected. Even though Emergency Services had taken the survivor off to Bellevue and a half dozen detectives were covering the apartment in fingerprint dust while another squad plucked fragments of tissue from the rug with tweezers, the medical examiner had not yet arrived, so the two bodies, the man's and the infant's, lay exactly as they'd fallen, one in the hallway and one on the living room floor. Shotgun wounds are messy. They leave pieces of human beings in unexpected places and Tilley could not find a way to get down the hallway without squishing through a soaked, bloody carpet.

Moodrow, oblivious, plodded along, his black brogans crunching matter-of-factly on fragments of bone. He was looking for someone he could "trust," another detective whose judgment he respected. That definitely wasn't O'Neill or Kirkpatrick, who nodded when he came in, then turned back to their work. The reason for their curt greeting was evident as Moodrow and Tilley continued into the living room where Chief of Detectives Franklyn Goobe stood along with Leonora Higgins and Captain Epstein around the chalk-outlined body of the dead adult. As soon as Moodrow saw them, he started to turn around, but he wasn't nearly quick enough.

"Just a second, Stanley," a clearly harassed Epstein called.

"I hope this isn't gonna take forever," Moodrow said. His face was set and serious. "I really gotta stay on top of what I'm doing."

Franklyn Goobe was an impressive individual, one of those men who receives instant respect on the basis of his appearance alone. His enemies in the job called him the "Lion Man" because of his large face and mane of snow white hair. Hair which was teased and blow-dried every day. Despite the vanity, however, Goobe, a third generation New York cop, was grudgingly admired by the department for his relentless pursuit of anyone who attacked a cop.

"Sergeant Moodrow," he cried, offering his hand. "It's been a long time, hasn't it?"

"Yeah, nearly forever," Moodrow returned, dodging the technicians as he moved into the center of the room. For once, standing toe-to-toe with Franklyn Goobe, Moodrow didn't physically dominate the scene. Epstein and Higgins, wisely silent, literally stepped away from the two of them.

"You seem to be in a hurry," Goobe observed affably.

"I am."

"I expect that's because you're on your way to arrest Mr. Greenwood. Am I right?" His smile lit up the room. "Do I win the million dollars?"

Moodrow sighed impatiently. He was addressing the chief of detectives, one of the most powerful men in the New York Police Department. It was rumored that Goobe had personal files on a number of local politicians and acted as point man for the P.C. Men like Goobe are pissed off even when everything goes right. That Levander Greenwood, with his record (which was reproduced nearly every day in the tabloids), should be on the street weeks after murdering police officers, was definitely *not* right. It was not remotely acceptable. Though Moodrow and Tilley didn't know it at the time, the police commissioner had also been present.

He had kicked the Murphys' butts from one end of the apartment to the other. Now it was Moodrow's turn.

"No," Moodrow said. "I don't see anything before a few days. Maybe a week."

"A week." The Chief's eyebrows rose in surprise. "What do you think, Ms. Higgins? Do you think it's because we haven't been holding up our end? Have we denied Sergeant Moodrow a search warrant or refused to authorize a wiretap? How have we failed him?"

"Sergeant Moodrow hasn't requested anything like that, sir," Higgins said brightly.

The added "sir," delivered in a forthright military manner, almost brought a smile to Franklyn Goobe's mouth. But not quite. "I already know that, really. I know that Sergeant Moodrow hasn't been asking for anything because I've been going through the Sergeant's Investigative Daily Activity Reports for a clue as to what he *has* been doing."

As soon as Goobe said the word "Daily," the whole room stopped dead. It was a doubletake worthy of a silent comedy. Not sure of what was happening, Tilley looked to Moodrow and saw the red blush as it crept up Moodrow's neck and over his ears.

"Yes," Goobe continued. "They're very interesting, but somewhat confusing. Take this one dated 8/24." He paused, looked up at Moodrow with innocent eyes. "You don't mind my asking you about this? I'm trying to keep up with the investigation, especially now that it's going long-term."

Moodrow, his eyes locked with Goobe's, shrugged in resignation. "I knew I was gonna have a bad day. This morning, when I tried to pee, my dick fell off."

"That usually is an accurate indicator," Goobe nodded. He held up Moodrow's report, peered at it for a moment, then took out his glasses and put them on. "Let's see. Have I got the pages right?" He shuffled through them for a moment and when he began to read, the apartment was as still as the dead bodies waiting for the medical examiner. Strangely, of all the cops in that room, Jim Tilley was the only one who seemed to think Moodrow's reprimand out of place. The simple fact of death, of carnage, of blood-spattered walls, of an infant's body growing cold on a hallway rug meant no more to the rest of them than typewriters and desks to a vice president reaming out a junior executive.

0200 hours. The Mansion coffee shop on 86th & York. I am meeting, by appointment, with sometimes transvestite informant, codename Samantha Bankhead, and have been offered information concerning a gang of drug dealers selling to a homosexual clientele on the west side docks. Informant wishes to sell information, declares self desperate for money to finance revolutionary business venture: Rectal Bikini Waxing.

"Have you seen those new swimsuits we're expected to wear this summer?" Ms. Bankhead tells me. "Have you seen what those bastard designers have done to us? They think they own us, for shit sake. Believe me, Moodrow, when that string goes between those cheeks, there's nothing back there at *all*. We might as well be naked."

Informant then approaches close enough to whisper. "Do you know what electrolysis costs today? Thousands! And not only that, it takes dozens of visits and sometimes the damn hair grows back anyway. I can bikini wax a tush until it's like glass for under fifty dollars. For seventy-five I can do the legs and the chest as well. Three waxes carry you right through the season. And I'm talkin' clean, Moodrow. I'm talkin' 'slippery when wet.' "

All during interview, informant continually searches faces of others in restaurant. When asked, she declares herself fearful of others stealing her idea. "I'm not as young as I look," informant insists, "and

I don't relish the idea of dying broke. I *know* you can't get by on your looks forever. Youth, alas, is not eternal, but it might be for sale. That's why I've got to press ahead." She wrings her hands pathetically. "That's why I'll even sell out my friends. I'm that desperate. And that sure."

Waiter approaches and we order coffee, mine black and Ms. Bankhead's "as sweet as you can stand." Then informant, sensing skepticism, presses on, gripping my hand to reinforce her conviction. "Don't think it stops there," she declares. "Seasonal rectal bikini waxing is only the beginning. Do you know what buttock hair does to silk?" I had to admit that I didn't. "It's pure *el destructo*. Likewise for dainty synthetics and pantyhose. And as for lace . . . the look alone is enough to melt the wax in my tray. Once the trade realizes how much they're getting for their money, they'll use my services the way women bikini wax all year round to look good in lingerie. Don't forget, we may not be able to fuck like we did in the old days, but that doesn't mean we don't want to be attractive. And it doesn't mean that when we dance together, if dancing is as far as we dare go, we don't want to give our suitors a nice smooth squeeze to carry home with them. Moodrow, it's a winner."

Finally, I ask informant if she wants to sell me information or get me to buy stock. I explain that I don't care if she uses the money to plug her grandmother's asshole as long as there's something in it for me.

"How does an *ounce* of cocaine every week sound to you? In the summertime, two ounces! People buy whole grams at one time!"

"You're kidding."

Informant looks at me with astonishment. "My integrity is my currency. Without it I am nothing." Then she sits back in her chair. "This will be my slogan: ELECTROLYSIS IS FOREVER. WAXING IS FOR NOW. Or do you like, NOW! WHILE HE STILL CARES?''

"How much, Samantha?"

"Forty thousand to open the doors."

"Forty large for a gram coke dealer? I'd have to say that's a real bargain. But, see, since I don't work that precinct, you gotta go over my head for help. In fact, you gotta go all the way to the top for that kinda money. Tomorrow morning, nine o'clock sharp, you call the chief of detectives' office at One Police Plaza and ask for Franklyn Goobe. Tell him just what you told me. He could be your first customer."

Pin-drop time. Not a sound from the audience of detectives. Nobody doing any work, either. Epstein looked stricken, but Higgins was proud. From her position behind Goobe, she winked at Tilley and grinned.

"I must admit, Sergeant," Goobe finally continued, "even though I've leafed through hundreds of Dailies, I've never come across one in which the actual words were reported in such detail. You must have recorded it and then used the tape to make up your report. My congratulations, then, on your enterprise, even though, to my knowledge, Ms. Bankhead didn't follow up on your suggestion."

"C'mon," Moodrow said irritably. "Why don't you just tell me what the fuck you want."

Goobe's eyes narrowed and all the "politician" disappeared from his face. "I want Greenwood, you fat asshole. I want him and you spend your time writing bullshit reports when you should be working. Maybe you think you're the Rodney Dangerfield of the NYPD, but this ain't the time for jokes. Until you take Greenwood, I want to know exactly what you do with the time you spend on the job. Every goddamn minute. If you think *I'm* joking, I'll send these fucking reports to a board of inquiry in ten minutes. I'll have you out of the department before you manage to die on the job."

So saying, he stepped across the body of the dead man and stalked out of the apartment, followed by Epstein and the two suits assigned to guard his body. Moodrow swayed slightly as Goobe passed him, as if he was ready to launch himself onto the district attorney. Even after Leonora placed a calming hand on his arm, he said nothing. Naturally, with the two bigshots out of the room, the other cops, as they went back to work, felt it incumbent upon themselves both to invent and to verbalize such phrases as "Oh, Samantha, would you wax my rectum, I'm going to the prom tonight" every three or four seconds.

Not surprisingly, Tilley felt instinctively protective and was actively considering punching the brains out of one particularly obnoxious detective when Moodrow, his face as blank as a pane of glass, addressed Higgins as if they were the only ones in the room.

"How bad is the survivor?" he asked.

"Might lose a leg, but they don't think she'll die."

"Was she any help?"

"Only that she's sure it was Greenwood."

"She didn't say what he got?"

"Heroin," Leonora replied. She opened a manila envelope and slid its contents, four glassine envelopes filled with white powder, onto the palm of her hand. Each had the words Blue Thunder stamped on the front.

Moodrow's eyes lit up when he saw them and Tilley instantly recalled Leonora's analysis of Moodrow's addiction to "justice." Apparently, he even put it before his pride.

"How much he get, Leonora? Did he get enough?"

"She said around thirty bundles. Ten bundles in a bag. She wasn't a hundred percent sure, but not less than two hundred fifty bags. Is that enough?"

"That's plenty."

17

The trip from 2113 Eldridge across the Bowery to
what's left of the neighborhood called "Little Italy" is
not a very long one. The Italian ghetto of the early
1900s and the once-Jewish Lower East Side were both
victimized by the flight of second-generation Ameri-
cans from the inner cities to the suburbs which characterized the decades following World War II. They
were replaced, both Italian and Jew, at first by the
Puerto Ricans, who arrived as full citizens, then in the
80s by a new wave of Asian immigrants, who pushed
the borders of Chinatown across Canal Street so that
most of the newer shops have signs in both Chinese
and English.

Still, a few of the old Jews remain and Sammy's, a
Jewish restaurant featuring garlic-soaked Roumanian
pastrami (which Moodrow placed before sex as a sen-
sory experience) draws diners from every borough, especially on Saturday evenings after *shabbas*. The food
is straight out of the Yiddish culture that once dominated Allen and Essex Streets where another joint,
Bernstein's, a restaurant featuring (believe it or not)
kosher Chinese cuisine and deli, is full nearly all the
time.

On the other side of the Bowery, Little Italy took a
different path. Long-established as a cultural landmark, Little Italy and its coven of restaurants reach,
not to second and third generation Italians living in

169

the borough, but uptown, for the tourists and the business crowd.

There are very few Italians on Mulberry Street these days, even fewer than there are Jews on the Lower East Side, but one element of the culture does remain. The social clubs, originally organized to give men from the same town or region a chance to keep the old country alive, still dot Grand and Mulberry Streets. In the earliest days of Italian immigration, they were headquarters for the emerging underside of the Italian community, the criminal caste, called the "mob" or *cosa nostra* or the *mafia* or whatever buzzword the reporters think will sell newspapers. Today, in spite of the sing-song Chinese voices heard along Elizabeth Street, they exist to fulfill the same function.

"Prohibition changed these assholes from thugs into millionaires," Moodrow explained. They were walking west along Hester Street. Their destination, the Favara Athletic Club, at 677 Mulberry Street, was only four blocks from the crime scene, too short a distance to justify moving the car. Still, in deference to the summer heat, they took their time. The sun, nearly straight up in the sky, beat down on them unmercifully, pasting their trousers to their thighs, their shirts to their backs. Moodrow, oblivious as always, alternately briefed and lectured his partner on the Lower East Side drug trade and the mobsters who ran it.

"And the same fucking thing is happening all over again. You've got prohibition against drugs and the money is too big to resist. These kids on the streets, they might live in public housing, but they walk out on the street wearing a thousand dollars in gold around their necks. Eighteen years old. Cruising the city in red BMWs.

"Young kid, ten, twelve years old. He sees a chance to make that kinda money, you think he's gonna be a bicycle messenger? You think he's gonna go down to the garment center and push a hand truck? Uh-uh.

Maybe the smart ones'll work their way into one of
the city colleges, but that don't help the ordinary kids.
For them, if they got any balls, they're gonna fight for
a piece of those millions and some of 'em are gonna
make it. They're gonna buy their way outta the
slums."

They started across Forsyth and a narrow concrete
park, dotted with benches, that runs from Canal Street
up to Houston. Its official name, Sara Roosevelt Park-
way, belies its status as a hangout for the dopers who
get off in the dozen shooting galleries located within
a block of the park. Naturally, as soon as they stepped
into the gutter, junkies began to scatter. Not quickly,
of course; heroin addicts don't do much of anything
quickly. But they did get themselves out of the way.
All except for one luckless individual who was stoned
to within an eyeblink of an overdose. He was standing
directly under a frying sun, swaying like a snake attempting a handstand. Moodrow was headed right for
him and Tilley expected a monumental collision, but
Moodrow stopped in front of the junkie (who still took
no notice) and gestured with his chin.

"Behold the fearsome dope fiend. Real aggressive,
ain't he? Poor fuck just wants to get high. Give him
his dope and he's as harmless as a human can get.
Don't give him his dope, make him go out and buy his
dope at black market prices and you end up with
scumbags like Levander Greenwood." He stepped
around the man, wiped his face with the back of his
sleeve and continued walking. "I was born in '33, in
the heart of the Depression. Nobody had anything except the mob guys. Jewish or Italian. They made it big
during prohibition. Turned them from punks running
crap games into millionaires. But they still lived in the
neighborhood and all the kids wanted to be just like
'em.

"Imagine. There's Uncle Emilio works two days a
week carrying bricks for a scab contractor. His family

eats pasta with lard. Then there's Uncle Dominick who goes to work in a Buick. His kids eat veal. Eat steak. His kids make their First Communions in white suits and dresses, then hold a party so all the neighborhood brats, the ones with nothing, can take a look at Dominick's fucking success."

They were walking north along the Bowery by this time, trying to catch a little shade from the buildings along the west side. Moodrow, when he lectured, had a tendency to go on forever. Tilley, on the other hand, was less than patient. He said, "You're too young to reminisce. And your timing's for shit, too. How about a punch line for this joke."

"The punch line is one of those kids who watched the gangsters strut and decided to join 'em is Dominick Favara. Called 'Little Bullets' because he made his bones with a .22 instead of a .45 which was the gun everybody wanted after the war. You get the connection between the Favara Athletic Club and Dominick Favara, right? Favara is a small city in Sicily and when Dominick's old man came through, the clerk on Ellis Island didn't wanna bother with his name, just wrote Tommaso Favara on the entry card and that was it. Now Dominick uses the name to prove his Sicilian purity.

"I told ya that I went to high school with Dominick. He was one of the kids who idolized the wiseguys. They called them 'soldiers' back then. All he ever wanted was to get into the mob. To grab a piece of that power. And he did it. He went to work for Tony Licata who had a little gang. Him, his three brothers and a couple of neighborhood kids. Tony Licata was a lieutenant in the Carini family which, back then, did shylocking, books, numbers and prostitution. The mob had a lot of extra money after the war, capital left over from prohibition which they didn't have no way to invest. No way that would bring the kinda return they made on bootleg hooch.

"Dominick Favara was one of the first to see the way of the future. He made a connection with a factory in Marseilles that was producing a new drug, a variation of morphine called heroin, then took control of the dope business on the Lower East Side in the 50s. The Puerto Ricans were pouring into these tenements about then." He gestured to the buildings which surrounded them. "Dope was a very hard sell when the Jews were here, but the Puerto Ricans ate it up. I guarantee that there are five thousand dope addicts within a mile of Eldridge Street and another ten thousand who do it occasionally. *Mucho dinero.*"

Moodrow pulled up short and turned into a small Chinese grocery at the corner of Bowery and Grand. They were near the Manhattan Bridge, in the heart of a small district devoted to restaurant fixtures and wholesale lighting. Double-storefront windows featured gleaming cabinets or dozens of chandeliers, all carefully lit to capture maximum glitter.

"I want to get a Coke. I'm frying."

Tilley followed his partner into the store (and the air conditioning) without a protest. "One thing's got me confused," he said. "You're not saying this guy Favara controls all the heroin on the Lower East Side? I don't buy that."

Moodrow eyed Tilley approvingly, opening the ice cold bottle of classic Coke he pulled from an ancient, horizontal cooler. "Once upon a time, he had it all to himself. For about fifteen years, starting around 1955, there wasn't anyone on the Lower East Side but 'Little Bullets' Favara. He paid tribute, of course. Paid the bigger bosses through the nose, but he kept his territory pure. Then a new generation of kids came out of those projects. At first, they worked for the Favara clan. They were the ones who put their asses out on the street. They retailed, but they didn't use the drug themselves. Instead, they saved their pennies and bought in such large quantities, they forced Favara further and further from the action. Instead of selling them ounces (or even bundles, for that matter) like in the 60s, he sold them kilos.

"Then they started traveling. They went to Jersey or up to Boston where their money was appreciated and there wasn't a fucking thing Dominick could do about it. He started a war, of course, but he was lucky to get away with his life. These kids weren't afraid of death. They didn't have homes in Westchester. Instead of spending the last twenty years wearing silk under-wear, most of the kids had already done time and if they could survive prison, they weren't about to run away from some guinea in a white Cadillac.

"After the first bloodbath, Dominick got realistic. Competition was here to stay, but there was a lot of money to be made. Everybody was using drugs and even though Dominick's piece of the market was shrinking, he found a way to maximize profits. He took a shithead gang with no real leadership and no capital called the 'Wald Assassins,' after the Lillian Wald housing project where they lived, armed the shit out of them and gave them the retail end of his operation. He set them up as employees and he protected them from the other gangs. He took Eldridge Street, by the Seward Park Houses, and made it into the showroom for his newest brainstorm: brand name dope. He stamped his trademark, Blue Thunder, on every bag of heroin he sold. He was better connected, so he could afford to make his smack a little more pure, give just a pinch more product in every bag.

"Word got out and the fucking customers came from all over the city. We didn't know what to make of it in the 7th. It was like fucking lemmings. All these broken-down, runny-nosed junkies staggering along Eldridge Street which had never been known as a drug neighborhood. By the time the competition caught on, 'Little Bullets' had a big piece of the market and he's held on to it ever since. Blue Thunder belongs to him and him alone."

By this time they were standing in front of the Favara Athletic Club. Despite the name, it bore no resemblance to Jack LaLanne's. A storefront, its display window had been completely bricked up except for a three-foot square pane of glass so dirty it had yellowed like plastic. Behind the filth, on a dust-covered ledge, with heavy drapes closing off the scene inside, a small sign announced the Favara Athletic Club. The faded letters, once clearly gold, surrounded the 1947 team photo of the Favara Soccer Club, champions of all Italy.

There was a door just to the left of the window. A flimsy wooden door that by its very vulnerability, advertised the character of the people inside. Moodrow and Tilley both knew, without having to say it, that spotters in the tenement windows were already on the phone, announcing their presence to the demons within.

"Moodrow," Tilley asked, "you know we're walking into hell? Understand what I'm saying? I'm not used to entering hell without my .38 in my hand. What makes you think Dominick Favara's gonna help you? If you hated him all the time you knew him, why should he be interested in the good of the community?"

"I gotta trade him," Moodrow announced. "The asshole's a fucking businessman and I gotta convince him I got something worth the lost business."

"Like what?"

He shrugged, smiled. "Whatta you think I got?"

Tilley lowered his voice, looking around before he whispered. "You gonna let him off the hook on something else?"

Moodrow giggled. His eyes lit up. "This kinda scum don't get busted by precinct detectives, Jimmy. You gotta have joint task forces for perpetrators like Dominick Favara. Court-ordered wiretaps. Voice-operated remote transmitters. Witness protection programs. I read where it took four million dollars to get John Gotti in a courtroom and he beat every charge. Uh-uh, Jimmy. Dominick Favara's got more lawyers than I got years on the force. I gotta find some other way I can persuade him."

Suddenly Tilley thought he understood. It was obvious. "You're gonna give him the guy who comes up with the dope. After you find out who's running Greenwood, you're gonna give the guy to Favara."

"Close," he said. "See, if Favara cuts off the supply of Blue Thunder, he could find out for himself. In fact, if we're not quick, Favara might beat us to it. So what I'm gonna do is *offer* whoever I find with Dominick's dope to Dominick's tender care. But what I'm gonna *give* Dominick is *me*."

18

The door, when Moodrow turned the knob and gave it a tentative push, was unlocked, one more proof that the occupants sensed their own invulnerability, and the two cops stepped across the threshold into a scene carved out of a 30s gangster movie. The outer room was all wood, from the wide pine floors to the faded paneling to the narrow slat ceiling. Perhaps, every few weeks, a porter dragged a dustcloth over the small formica tables and a broom across the floor, but no one had taken soap and water to the filth for decades and every inch of the Favara Athletic Club was dark with grime.

The room itself was large, a twenty-foot-wide storefront that ran back about thirty feet to a doorway leading into the back rooms. Small tables, replete with wizened old men in tweed caps (the club was refrigerator cold, courtesy of a huge air conditioner which dripped water onto the warped floorboards), dotted the room. A cappuccino machine, its once gleaming copper and brass fixtures as faded as the photos of FDR on the back wall, sat atop a small bar.

All and all, it seemed like an urban version of a western ghost town. Tilley expected to come across old newspapers; rusted irons; an abandoned washing machine. Even the club members, who froze as soon as the cops stepped inside, could have been manufactured out of plaster and plastic and arranged by a contemporary artist. All except for one man. Enormous, bigger than Moodrow and twenty-five years younger, he stood in front of the door to the back room. Dressed in a pale blue silk jacket and ivory linen pants, black handmade shoes as soft as butter, he was wearing a month of Moodrow and Tilley's combined wages on his back and he stood out from the general atmosphere of the Favara Athletic Club like a peacock in a hog pen. Then he spoke:

"Youze forgot ta knock," he said mildly. "That ain't polite." The bulge of the gun hidden beneath his jacket was so pronounced that Moodrow knew he was deliberately displaying it. And that he had a permit to carry it.

"Yeah, Matty, but I'm a policeman," Moodrow replied. He pronounced it poe-lease-man. "And I got special dispensation from the Pope. That means I don't gotta knock. You wanna see?" He hauled his WWII dogtags out from under his shirt and held them out toward the apparition in the blue jacket. "The Pope sent me these along with a freedom from probable cause certificate. I didn't bring the certificate. You got a permit for that gun?"

"Sure I do." Smiling a smile as warm as frozen liver, he dragged a cheap St. Christopher's medal from under his own shirt. "From the fuckin' Cardinal," he declared. "Come wit its own Freedom from Permit permit. Ya know, youze ain't got no search warrant and youze is trespassing on private property. This here is a private club."

Tilley was standing slightly behind Moodrow and, as usual, he didn't know how to react. Moodrow had a perverse instinct for putting himself into situations that defied ordinary police procedure. They were there, basically, to ask a favor. It probably wouldn't pay to force the issue, in spite of the fact that Tilley *knew* he could off this motherfucker inside of thirty seconds. His knuckles itched with it. Musclemen are the worst fighters of all—slow, clumsy and quick to tire. If Tilley took him, however, they would almost certainly come under attack from the old men scattered about the room. Neither of the two cops was laboring under the delusion the old men, despite their age and small size, had come into the Favara Athletic Club to play gin rummy. On top of this, it was clear that Dominick Favara was not in the room. If they forced their way into the back and Favara wasn't there either, they'd probably never find him.

"Tell me something, Matty," Moodrow finally asked, "how much you weigh now?"

The gangster sucked it in. "Two seventy-five. How 'bout you, Moodrow?"

"Two sixty. And it's gettin' soft as shit."

"Whatta youze benchin'?"

"Three thirty."

"Y'ova the hill, Porky. I benched four twenty-five last mont'."

"At the Favara Athletic Club?"

"Very fuckin' funny. It just so happens I belong to the Vertical Club on 61st Street. The dues is maw than ya pension."

He glanced around the room and, as if he'd thrown a switch, the old men huddled around the tables looked up and laughed softly. When he returned his attention to Moodrow, they fell back into immobility.

"You shouldn't make fun, Matty. One day you're gonna get old, too. If your buddies don't put a round between your eyes. I wanna see Dominick Favara."

"Who?" Once again the acolytes announced their appreciation with a low chuckle.

"Dominick Favara. Also known as Little Bullets. Emperor of Blue Thunder."

"Blue Thunder? I thought that was some kinda Air Force crew. Ya know, like they do flyin' shows and shit like that."

"Listen, fuckhead. . . ." Almost involuntarily, Tilley took a step toward the gangster. He was wearing a

charcoal Izod shirt with oversize sleeves and his arms
were so tight the veins crawled over his flesh like blue
snakes. Instead of reacting with his fists, however, the
gangster stepped back and let his hand slide up toward
his armpit.

"Moodrow, keep this crazy fuck away from me.
Youze got no cause ta be in this domicile. If youze
make trouble, we're gonna defend ourselves."

Moodrow put out a hand to restrain his partner.
"Jimmy don't know the neighborhood too good," he
said evenly. "He don't understand that you're a cultural landmark. He thinks you're a regular scumbag
like the rest of the fuckin' mob."

Not a sound. Matty, despite his seven hundred dollar sports coat, was out of wisecracks and he clearly
had to make a decision. Unfortunately, as decision-
making was beyond his talents, when he spoke his
voice was unsteady. "Dominick ain't here."

"Really?" Moodrow said evenly.

"No foolin'. He ain't here."

"That means if I go out in the back and smash the
shit outta that silver Mercedes with the license plates
say 'LilBull,' he won't be pissed about it?"

"Why couldn't his car be here and him be gone? Did
youze think about that?"

The game could have gone on forever, except that
the back door opened and a small, serious man stepped
through. He was extremely thin, with a sparse black
beard and a matching yarmulke. His suit, a dark blue
pinstripe, more suitable for January than August, was
dusty and wrinkled. "My name is Morris Teitlebaum.
I'm Dominick Favara's attorney. One of his attorneys.
Would you please tell me what your business is and
why you've entered private property without permission or a warrant?"

Moodrow was taken aback. The presence of a lawyer
eliminated the possibility of threat as a tool. "Tell

Dominick that Stanley Moodrow would like to speak
with him on a matter that benefits both of us. Please."

"Mr. Favara is not here."

"Fuck that shit!" Moodrow's roar filled the room.
Even Matty lost his smirk. "He's the fucking client.
You're the fucking lawyer. You don't decide. Go tell
him Stanley Moodrow is here and see what he says."

Morris Teitlebaum disappeared without a murmur,
despite the obvious fact that he wasn't intimidated by
Moodrow's outburst. Lawyers regard cops as slightly
above Great Danes (but well below German Shep-
herds) in intelligence. And less of a threat than either.
Cops, in turn, when referring to lawyers, invoke the
one virtue which they (the cops) have in abundance:
courage. Every cop dreams of being in a locked, sound-
proofed room with some lawyer who made him look
like a fool on the witness stand.

The wait seemed endless. Minutes went by, but the
door remained closed. Finally, Moodrow asked Matty
what was happening and the bodyguard inched back
to cover the doorway. "Dominick don't see so many
people these days. He's kinda semi-retired. Just like
you'd be if ya had a fuckin' brain in ya head."

Moodrow regarded him narrowly. "Favara's my age.
Fifty-five. I heard of wiseguys running the show when
they're eighty."

Matty shrugged his shoulders (a heavy motion that
resembled a worker hoisting a side of beef) and started
to whistle. They were waiting and that was it.

Finally, after Tilley had become convinced that
Dominick Favara was hotfooting out the back door
while they cooled their heels in the front parlor, Morris Teitlebaum reappeared and motioned them inside.

The room they entered was about one-third the size
of the front room and light years removed from the
dirt and grime outside. The rear of the Favara Athletic
Club was a hospital room, replete with beeping mon-
itors and a white uniformed nurse. Against the back

wall, a single hospital bed, adjusted so the patient was nearly upright, held what appeared to be an old, shrunken man. This was Dominick Favara. His body was so thin his black eyes, enormous in a sharp face all bones and transparent flesh, bulged insanely. Thin plastic tubes ran from bags of fluid hanging from aluminum stands, one to his wrist and another to a large vein on his neck. Two other men, besides the nurse and Morris Teitlebaum, sat on chairs near the edge of the bed. All through the conversation, they kept their backs to Dominick Favara and their eyes on the two cops. Though they laughed on cue, their attention never wavered. Like prizefighters, they didn't even blink.

"Dominick," Moodrow began. Then his voice trailed off. "I didn't know about your sickness."

"Whatsa matter, Stanley? Ya see yaself? You and me, we're the same fuckin' age. Whatta ya think? Just 'cause the average lifespan is seventy-two, you got another fifteen years? A year ago I get a pain in my leg. A little pain, but it don't go way. Naturally, I see a Jew doctor and he takes me to Sloan-Kettering Hospital where they put pieces of me under a microscope. Thirty-two thousand dollars and this little faggot comes to my bed and he says, 'You got bone cancer. We gotta take the leg.' I'm not happy, but I ain't surprised, neither. I say, 'Sure. Take the fuckin' leg. I'm too young. I don't wanna die yet.' But what happens is the cancer comes back in my lungs, then my kidneys. Now I go on a machine ta clean my piss and my Jew doctor says I got between ten minutes and six months. Ya feel sorry fa me, Stanley?"

Moodrow ignored him. "I gotta ask you for something, Dominick. Greenwood ripped you off today. Took your dope."

"Don't say a word." The little lawyer actually jumped at Moodrow and began to push him out of the room. "This is insane that you should come in this room with such a statement."

"Morris." Favara's voice was husky, but surprisingly strong, as if the very habit of authority was enough to power him, despite his weakness. "Take a hike, Morris."

"For God sake, Dominick, don't say anything I can't defend."

"Listen, Morris, me and Stanley go back to high school. I hated his asshole guts from the first day I met him, but I know he ain't so stupid he should come here with the idea he's gonna arrest me. He's just a precinct flatfoot." Suddenly, he dropped back against the pillow and his mouth twisted with pain. The nurse ran to his assistance and began to prepare an injection. Morris Teitlebaum, without a sign of sympathy, left the room.

The drug took effect within seconds. Favara's eyes reopened and he smiled a ghastly smile. He couldn't have weighed more than eighty pounds. "There are things," he said confidentially, "which even a Jew lawyer shouldn't hear. Like ain't it strange that what I sold all my life to the spics and the niggers should be goin' in my own arm? The doctor gives me morphine, but after a couple weeks it don't do shit. Then I switch to my own dope and it makes the pain better. The nurse says I should put it right in the intravenous. Let it drip continual, but ya know somethin', Stanley? I like the rush. Does that make me a junkie?"

Moodrow looked at him evenly. He obviously felt no compassion and no need to pretend that he did. "So who's taking over when you kick, Dominick? Who's the new king of Blue Thunder?"

Favara laughed. An ugly, rattling sound that made even his bodyguards wince. "Youze was always a kidda. Even back in high school when I hadda kick your ass a few times, yiz had a sense a humor." Then the smile faded from his lips. "I ain't got much energy these days, Stanley. Tell me what the fuck ya want and then get out."

Moodrow pulled no punches. "I want you to keep Blue Thunder off the streets for a week. You already know Greenwood took your dope, but he won't be the one to put it back on the market. Somebody else is running Greenwood and the only way to find him is to pick up the dealer when he tries to put your dope into circulation. You know the heat's been going down in the neighborhood over the last few weeks? You want it should continue indefinitely? We'll never close it down until we get Levander Greenwood."

"Ya threatenin' me, Stanley? That what ya doin'?"

"I'm talking reality. I need your help, Dominick. I can't take him without you." Moodrow made the statement simply, then hesitated for a moment before he continued. "You do what I said and I'll give you the name of whoever tries to sell your dope. After I find out where Greenwood's holed up, I'll give you the name."

Dominick Favara fell back against the pillow and signalled the nurse over. Her name tag—Ms. M. Favara—explained her presence in the room despite the sensitive nature of the discussion. Without asking, she filled a glass with juice from a thermal carafe and held it while he drank. Then she handed him a green, plastic oxygen mask and switched on a canister that stood at the head of the bed. For the next several minutes, while the patient sucked greedily at the pure oxygen hissing out of the tank, everyone waited. Then he passed the mask back to his nurse and smiled at them. "Soon comes the tubes. Tubes for the lungs. Tubes for the stomach. Make me look even prettier than I already am." He smiled, as if he was talking about some distant relative, and folded his hands across his stomach.

"We known each other fa how many years, Stanley? Forty-five years now and you never before come ta me

fa my counsel or my help? Why cannot I remembâ
when youze invited me ta ya house fa coffee or fa dinner? What was you afraid I would do?"

The two bodyguards, along with the nurse, began tc
chuckle. Moodrow looked confused and embarrassed.
Tilley had never seen his partner caught off guard before and he didn't quite understand what was bothering him. Or what Favara and company were laughing
at. Then Favara held up his hand. "Don't say nuttin'.
Don't talk. Youze figured America was a paradise.
Youze figured youze would be a policeman and find
justice. I couldn't tell yiz how my feelings was hurt,
but I neva tried ta push myself on youze. I said ta myself, 'Dominick, be patient, one day Stanley will come
to you.' "

Favara stopped, his efforts at speech producing only
a breathless wheeze, but his bodyguards continued to
laugh loudly. Even the nurse, probably a granddaugh-
ter, stared at the cops with open contempt. Then Tilley understood what the old man was doing. He was
playing out the wedding scene from *The Godfather*.
Where the undertaker, Amerigo Bonasero, goes to Don
Corleone for vengeance.

"Well it looks like you were right, Dominick,"
Moodrow admitted. "Cause here I am."

"Yes, yes, but do youze come ta me with respect?
Do youze come ta me fa justice? No, youze say 'I give
you the man's name. I pay you with the man's name.'
What did I ever do that you should treat me so badly?"

Suddenly, Moodrow did a double-take, apparently realizing the import of Dominick's speeches. His face
broke into a quick smile, then immediately composed
itself. "Tell me what you want from me?" he finally
asked.

"If youze came ta me in the beginning, in the name
of friendship, this Greenwood animal would already be
in ya hands. Do yiz know this to be true?"

It wasn't true. Virtually every dealer on the Lower

East Side had been trying for Greenwood. Apparently, nobody had even gotten close. Moodrow, however, nodded his head, then bowed it contritely. "Dominick," he whispered, "please, be my friend."

This time the audience literally roared with laughter. In spite of their vigilance, the two bodyguards shook until tears ran down their faces. In their eyes, the humiliation of this supercop, this hero of the neighborhood, was worth any price.

Favara's bones, his knees and elbows, little pyramids beneath the sheets, trembled with pleasure. "Youze didn't say my right name, Stanley."

Moodrow hesitated for a moment, then raised his head until he met the mobster's eyes. "Don Favara," he said. "Please do me this favor."

Slowly, wincing back the pain, Favara's hand crept from beneath the sheets. His wrist and fingers were skeletal, the skin and nails yellow with nicotine, and he shook with the effort of extending his hand toward Moodrow's face. Everything else in the room had stopped and only Favara's quick, labored breathing compromised the sudden vacuum. "To show your love," he explained.

Moodrow once again hesitated. If Tilley hadn't heard Moodrow's prediction before they'd entered the Favara Athletic Club, he would have accepted his partner's portrayal of a man torn by doubt and hatred without question. Slowly, Moodrow bent forward, his head moving in short, tight jerks, and touched the hand to his lips, then waited while Favara withdrew it.

"Youze understand," Favara said, "that I ain't sayin' I got anything ta do with this 'Blue Thunder' shit ya talkin' about. But what I am sayin' is if youze should see any 'Blue Thunder' on the street this week, it won't be mine."

19

Instead of returning to the car, the two cops walked up Mulberry to Houston Street, then turned east a couple of blocks to a hole-in-the-wall workingman's bar with the name Cappolino's hanging over the door. In spite of the Italian name, the bartender, the barmaid and the four customers clustered together at one end of the long, pitted bar were all speaking Spanish when Moodrow and Tilley stepped inside. The bartender, a small, wiry man with a strawberry birthmark covering the left side of his face, calmly strolled the length of the bar and greeted Moodrow. Enormous quantities of drugs are dealt in the hundreds of bars on the Lower East Side, most of it by independents who use the barrooms for offices. Nonetheless, the owners of these bars (especially the trendy neon-lit emporiums catering to the uptown trade) are fully aware that alcohol is only one of many drugs consumed on the premises and that, in some cases, the ready availability of cocaine is the *only* attraction they have.

Except at Cappolino's. One of the last of a vanishing breed, it was a bar dedicated to the consumption of alcohol. It was not a place to be seen; just a place to drink.

Moodrow introduced the bartender as Paco Assante and the barmaid as his wife, Carmen. The customers, fully aware Moodrow and Tilley were cops, ignored them completely. Two wore hardhats and all were covered with dust, the sweat stains under their arms caked with dirt. They drank their shots and sipped their beers as if they were in a different universe.

"What could I get you, Sergeant?" Paco asked. His wife, seated at a table with the *National Enquirer* in her lap, looked up and blew a kiss at the two cops. Like nearly every one of the small business owners in the neighborhood, they knew Stanley Moodrow and saw him as an ally; an ally, as Tilley was beginning to understand, even if their affairs ran against the current of standard police procedure.

"Caulfield's Wild Turkey. A double. No ice. Jimmy? You drinking?"

"Yeah, why not. You got a Schaefer, Paco?"

Paco turned his head away when Moodrow ordered the cheap bourbon. He looked like he was going to puke. "Don't drink that shit, Sergeant. Have something decent. I ain't gonna make you pay, am I?"

Moodrow just shook his head and waited while Paco dragged a bottle of Schaefer from the refrigerator under the bar and passed it (without a glass) over to Jim Tilley.

"Thanks, Paco. C'mon." Moodrow, snatching both his glass and the bottle of bourbon, led his partner to a wooden booth tucked in a corner and collapsed heavily on the bench. To Tilley's utter amazement, when Moodrow drained the glass, his hand shook hard enough to spill some of the liquor onto his fingers.

"What's with you, Moodrow? You have a hard time kissing ass? I thought you were putting on a show back there."

"Did you see that guy? How could he be alive like that? He weighed about twenty pounds. Nobody could be alive like that. When we were kids he was one of the hardest guys in the neighborhood. I'm talking about the Lower East Side just after the War. Scratch the dope and it wasn't that much different than it is today. Favara'd fight anybody, anytime. Fight just for the fuck of it. Now he weighs twenty pounds and they gotta wash his piss."

Tilley sipped at his beer and shrugged his shoulders knowingly. "For Christ sake, Moodrow, it's an act of God."

"Which one?" He straightened up in his seat, the empty glass still in his hand. "Was it the gentle Jesus? Or the one that made the flood? Maybe the one that used Job to play party games with the devil. Or Allah with his flaming fucking sword."

For a minute, Tilley couldn't think of anything to say. Moodrow was really shook up, which didn't make the slightest sense considering the nature of their business. "Look, man, an hour ago we were standing in a room with two dead bodies, including a baby, and you didn't say a word about it. Then you see one asshole with cancer and you start talking about God. I don't get the point."

"That's different. You could fight Levander Greenwood. You could be faster and smarter. You could even get lucky and duck at the right time. Shit, he could fall down the fucking stairs ten minutes from now and it would at least be the end of his killing. I don't like these tubes. I don't like little things that get in your body and make you weigh twenty pounds. I survived thirty fucking years on the job, but I ain't gonna survive some little bug you can't even see. It ain't right."

"You're talking like you already got the disease." Tilley said it slowly, one word at a time. He was terrified of some revelation. Every minute he spent with Moodrow, his respect for his partner increased. In the 7th Precinct, Moodrow was God-like, an irresistible force spreading itself over the community. God ain't supposed to get sick.

"No, I'm all right." Moodrow dismissed the idea with a wave of his hand. "But I'm not gonna be around for the neighborhood much longer. Epstein's getting pushed out. There's a Lieutenant Ruiz. Luis Ruiz. He's forty and he passed the captain's exam two years ago. Luis does everything right: he's smart; he's ambitious; he's articulate; he's Puerto Rican. This is the way the department wants it. This is the image. Plus he's been waiting a long time and he's good enough." Moodrow paused to take a breath and fill his glass, sipping at it before he resumed. "Levander Greenwood's gonna be the straw that breaks the captain's back. Even if there's only one cop running Greenwood, the press'll be all over the precinct. Shit, Levander's already a fucking media star. When they find out he's tied to a corrupt cop, he's gonna make the six o'clock news in Topeka."

The bit about Ruiz surprised Tilley. He hadn't been in the 7th long enough to be aware of the politics, but he'd seen Ruiz confer with Moodrow on several occasions and there had never been any animosity between them. Nevertheless, he sensed some bitterness in Moodrow's voice.

"When the captain goes, I go with him," Moodrow continued. "Ruiz is a good guy. I'll even give you that he's a good cop and he understands the precinct ten times better than Camillo and Anderson who also want the job. But Ruiz won't stick his neck out for me. Why should he? I'm too much of a risk for a very short-term proposition. No, Ruiz'll transfer me to a fucking desk somewheres. Sure as shit, Jimmy. The department ain't run my way these days. Now it's the attack of the Long Island Rambos. Live in Valley Stream and think they know about cops from watching Dirty Harry with that jerk-off bazooka he carries. They wanna make task forces that cover the whole borough. Tactical units so they could transfer out every two weeks and carry a shotgun in the trunk of the car."

What he said was partially true. A majority of New York cops live outside the city (or on Staten Island, which is the same thing) and most white cops (Tilley included) grew up in blue-collar, middle-class neighborhoods. To a certain extent, Tilley was prepared for his submersion in the lower depths by his years in the ring, but there's no way he could really know Fort Greene or the Lower East Side as if he'd grown up there. On the other hand, affirmative action programs have gone a long way toward bringing minorities into the city's civil service and there's a new wave of young blacks and Puerto Ricans who are intimately familiar with the territory.

"So what are you saying, Moodrow, that hasn't been said a hundred times before?"

"Look, any other neighborhood—Bed-Stuy, Brownsville, East Harlem—there's kids grow up there who become cops. But they don't stay there, Jimmy. They save their pennies and buy houses in the suburbs. If that's the American dream, it's fine with me, but there's gotta be someone to speak up for the neighborhoods." He poured himself another drink (his third) and threw Tilley his cherub-innocent face. "I figure I got time to train you to take my place. But just barely."

"What're you, fuckin' nuts?" Tilley rose halfway out of his seat.

"Take it easy. Take it easy." Moodrow grabbed his partner by the shirt and literally held him down. The son of a bitch, Tilley noted, was as strong as a gorilla. "I shouldn't have said anything. I always did have a big fucking mouth. After a while, you'll want to." Moodrow drained the glass of bourbon as if it was water. "All right, take down this address. Come tonight about one o'clock. I'll show you the rest of it."

He gave Tilley the address on 11th Street, at the northern end of the precinct, between Second and Third, right where the Lower East Side gives way to much ritzier Greenwich Village.

"Say, Moodrow?" Tilley couldn't resist the parting question, though he was sure he knew the answer. "Where does Ruiz live?"

Moodrow looked up at Tilley, then down at his glass, then back at him. "Westchester."

An hour later Tilley was in his living room, Jeanette on his lap. He was reading her a story while Susanna entertained Lee on the other side of the room. They were working with an ancient computer, one of those tiny Ataris sold by the thousands one Christmas when American parents decided, *en masse,* that the destinies of their children revolved around the ownership of a personal computer. It was the middle-class equivalent of Operation Head Start, though it was less effective. In fact, most of these computers found their way onto closet shelves in suburban basements as soon as the children became bored with the video game package sold with the unit. This Atari, a relic, had filtered down to Lee Greenwood via a sympathetic volunteer at the day care center where Rose sent the kids when grandma wasn't available. Susanna Tilley had been a programmer before she went to the data processing department at Salomon Brothers and she was showing Lee how to make the computer draw Mighty Mouse on the screen of their television. Lee was only marginally interested, though he loved Mighty Mouse. He understood how to do it, but lacked the patience to put his knowledge into practice. On the other hand, he worshipped Susanna and he would sit there and fake it long enough to learn the process, at least until his own mother finished making dinner.

Lee had still not accepted Tilley's presence in his life, but there was no way Tilley and Rose could keep their feelings private. Though the two of them were still too shy (she of her children and he of his mother) to hug or kiss in public, both children knew something was going on. Lee dealt with it by attaching himself to Susanna. Jeanette, on the other hand, had apparently decided to seduce the seducer. Whenever Tilley entered the apartment, solemn as a miniature butler,

she took him by the hand, led him to the green armchair in the living room, perched on his lap and demanded a story. One story—that was her deal.

She kept her supply in a little cabinet near the
kitchen. As soon as she knew he was coming in, she
would walk to this cabinet, carefully choose a book
and then look up at him, the beginning of a smile on
her face. The plots of these stories were almost identical. A giant (or a monster or a demon) terrorizes the
poor humans. This giant is as merciless as he is fero-
cious, often preferring the flesh of children to that of
adults. At first the situation looks hopeless and Jeanette, totally absorbed, grips Tilley's arm fiercely, but
then, unexpectedly, a hero arrives. Tall, young and,
inevitably, white, he fights and kills the giant. Kills
him dead.

As Tilley sat down to a meal with his new family,
Moodrow wandered south, across Houston and Delancey, into the underbelly of the Lower East Side, past
Stanton, Rivington and Broome, the heart of the dope
scene, to Grand Street with its discount dry goods emporiums. There were plenty of shoppers still active
here, Puerto Ricans and Asians as well as the Jews
who still lived along this street. The kids were out in
force, bare-chested against the heat and browned by
the sun, their sharp voices breaking with adolescence.
The girls, quieter, gathered around ghetto blasters (kept
mercifully low this close to a commercial district), and
thrust their suddenly-discovered sexuality at prospective boyfriends.

Old women, their heads wrapped in scarves, trailed
dresses that ran to the tops of hi-top black leather
shoes, the same leather shoes the punks along Avenue
B snapped up the minute they were displayed in the
windows of second-hand clothing stores. Junkies,
wearing long-sleeved shirts to cover the scars on their
veins, scurried along, eyes darting from car to truck to

store, looking for anything unguarded. Sixteen-year-old kid dealers, on their way to the small park behind the Seward Park Houses, displayed gold chains around their necks, the way their consorts displayed their charms in gym shorts that fell two inches short of covering their buttocks.

As Moodrow walked east, toward the river, the shops gave way to large apartment buildings, to restaurants, supermarkets, drugstores. The housing here was mostly middle-income, though desperate slums, many abandoned and awaiting demolition, provided retail outlets for the crack, the dope, the weed that kept the other side of the neighborhood afloat.

Moodrow could not stop thinking of it as *his* neighborhood. He had fought the job as well as the criminals for so long, that leaving it would be the equivalent of entering another lifetime. Which might have been all right, if he could have conjured up another life worth having. Lacking that, he had, by his own lights, to settle for Jim Tilley.

"You Moodrow there. You Moodrow. Please. Here."

Moodrow turned to find a young, white woman, thin, in her twenties, staring up at him. "Yeah?" It took him a few seconds to pull himself back to the present. "Do I know you?"

"Please. You are Moodrow, yes?"

Moodrow couldn't help but smile. "I am Moodrow, yes." The woman's eyes were so dark and serious, he half-expected her to genuflect and kiss his ring.

"I am Lisa Epanomitis. I am Greek, but Jewish friend I have, Sarah Eskenazi, says you are man to see for helping me."

Sarah Eskenazi was a cousin of Alma Epstein, the captain's wife, and her recommendation was enough to make him listen. It was too hot to stand in the sun and Moodrow led the woman into a small Israeli cafe where he ordered a beer for himself and ice tea for her.

"Why don't you just get started," Moodrow said gently.

"I have boyfriend. Niko Makresias. Since I come to this country. He is not such a good boy sometimes and the police have put him in Rikers Island jail for having cocaine. Now he has problems."

"So why don't he make bail and get out?"

"They give him ten thousand dollars bail. Where is he getting ten thousand dollars? He is immigrant. He is poor."

"Wait a second." Moodrow took a long pull on his beer. "This is a white guy, right?"

"Of course."

"Why do I think I'm getting hustled here?"

"I do not know what is hustled."

"Tell me something, Miss Epanomitis, how much coke did your boyfriend have when the police picked him up?"

"One kilo."

"A fucking kilo? Are you crazy?" The woman cringed, but Moodrow, unimpressed, pushed harder. "Let's dump the innocent immigrant bit. A kilo of coke is gonna get him sent upstate for at least a couple of years. After which he's gonna be deported. Which I don't give two shits to prevent."

The woman looked up for the first time and Moodrow saw that, even if she wasn't the little match girl, she was still afraid for her man.

"Listen," she said more strongly. "Niko is stupid, not bad. You understand this? In jail, he cannot take care of himself and the blacks, they try to make him into a woman. He fights. Niko is not a coward, but there are so many and he cannot fight everyday. He asks for protection and they put him in a cell twenty-four hours a day and even there he is not safe. The blacks say they will set his cell on fire with him inside. I think Niko will kill himself if he does not get away from them."

"Enough, already. You think you're telling me something new here? What makes you think I can help him?"

"This is what I learned from Mrs. Eskenazi. That I should speak to the Detective Moodrow who would help me."

"You live around here?"

"In Astoria."

"That's what I figured. Why should I help you?"

Lisa Epanomitis looked back down to the floor. "I have only one thing to offer. I will give it to you if you help my Niko."

Moodrow stared at her, expecting a gold chain or some other piece of jewelry as payment for his services. When he finally understood that she was referring to her body, he nearly fell off the chair laughing. "What I could probably do is as follows. I know the warden in protective custody where I presume your boyfriend now lives. I could get him transferred to the Tombs in Manhattan which has no dormitories and better guards. It's safer, but it still ain't the Plaza. Niko's gonna be inside for a long time. That kinda weight carries mandatory time. It's an A-1 felony which is a minimum of three years and a maximum of life. You tell Niko to get his hands on a shank and stick it in the face of the first con tries to grab his butt. In the long run, if they got him spotted for a punk, that's the only way he's gonna come out of it with his asshole intact. And you can keep your body. I owe Sarah Eskenazi a favor, so if you hustled her, good for you. Either way, I'm even up."

Susanna Tilley went to her weekly bridge game at 8:30. The kids went to sleep at nine o'clock. Rose and Tilley went to bed at 9:30.

Thinking about it later, it was Tilley's belief that keeping the affair hidden (in spite of knowing that everyone else knew exactly what they were doing, in-

cluding Sergeant Stanley Moodrow) increased the
intensity of those first few weeks. He knew that, inevitably, as soon as she came into the room, he wanted
her. And no matter how many times they made love
(made love? they fucked like two hogs in a swamp),
the touch of her body set him on fire.

It had never happened to him before. Even the acci-
dental touch of her breasts on his arm as she sat cross-
legged on the bed, telling him of her plans for the
future, complaining about her children or her finances,
evaluating professors and fellow students, made him
instantly hard. He wanted to ingest her. He wanted to
take her flesh into his body, to become her flesh burning his skin away like acid burning the rust off tar-
nished metal.

In spite of the heat on this particular night, Tilley
turned off the air conditioner, then waited, just strok-
ing her gently, until the sweat poured from her dense
black hair to run swiftly along the vein at the center
of her throat. He sucked at it, sucked at her throat,
then down over her breasts and belly as if he could
suck out her soul.

But that was the one thing Tilley could never touch.
Rose had long ago embraced the belief that no man (or
woman, for that matter) could save her. Or even that
a man could protect her. Only Moodrow. Moodrow
was the hero who would deliver her and the children
from the evil giant. After which, she would never need
anyone again. It was that simple. Tilley never mentioned Louise Greenwood's request that Moodrow keep
her son alive and, though Rose spoke to her mother-
in-law nearly everyday, Mrs. Greenwood apparently
never mentioned it either.

Not that Rose was obsessed with her ex-husband's
death. Most of their conversations, when she wasn't
thanking him or Susanna for giving her refuge, revolved around the future. Rose had decided to become
an accountant; further, to become an accountant and

work for the city. Like most of those engaged in civil service, she was aware of the coming revolution in New York City politics. The black and Puerto Rican minorities are not minorities anymore. The old Irish-Italian-Jewish coalition, which has run the city for decades, is being challenged on every front and the changing of the guard is nowhere more apparent than in the city's underbelly, in the bureaucracy which makes New York possible.

Rose was acutely aware of her children's color. Though she never bothered moralizing on the failures of white society, she had no illusion that she would be accepted by corporate America. Or that the coming political revolution would extend to the giant companies which occupy the postcard skyscrapers. "If I pass the exam," she explained, "I'll be a C.P.A. It's the only profession that doesn't require graduate school. The city pays about fifty percent less than private industry for accountants, so there's plenty of demand. It's nearly impossible to get fired if you work for the city and nobody gives a shit about your private life."

"So when you're a big shot," Tilley teased, "I suppose you'll finally move out of that slum."

"Jim, you must be kidding. I've got a five room apartment I pay two hundred and thirty dollars a month for. As long as there's rent control in New York, I'll never leave." Then she told him the story of how she had gotten the apartment in the first place. "Somehow, about ten years ago, Levander got close to a real estate speculator, an Armenian named Burt Artujian. This Armenian would do virtually anything for money and Levander fit right into his plans. Artujian bought rent-controlled buildings, buildings that other landlords were ready to walk away from, with the intention of turning them co-op. Naturally, he had to get the tenants out first. What better way than to have Levander move in?

"We lived in six different buildings in two years.

Levander terrorized tenants, especially the old ones who had the lowest rents. He was still working for Artujian when the judge finally sent him away. Naturally, the Armenian tried to have me evicted, but a judge in the housing court, instead of throwing me out, forced Artujian to give me a lease. Then Artujian was arrested for tax evasion and the city seized the building. That's when the services stopped. No more super. No more plumbers. No more electricians. We're trying to buy the building and turn it into a co-op. I mean the present tenants."

"You include yourself in that 'we'?"

Suddenly she was angry. "Fuck that," she declared. "That motherfucker isn't gonna keep me out of my home forever. I have a right to my home."

Tilley had heard this speech before, had actually provoked it deliberately and he started to laugh. Not surprisingly, Rose punched him in the chest, a half-way decent shot, but it was the sight of her body as the sheet slipped off her shoulders that took his breath away.

"Don't make fun of me, Jimmy."

"Why? You going somewhere?"

She sat back up and her features relaxed. "You'll never know what it's like. You can't. You're a man and you've got all those muscles. So many muscles. They even grow between your ears."

Touché. Sooner or later you reach the point where you know how to press each other's buttons. Is this a sign of progress? Tilley's greatest fear, whenever he was around people whose opinions he respected, was to be thought stupid. An ex-pug. Scarred, but amusing, not, however, to be taken seriously. That fear had underlined most of his early suspicions about Moodrow and Rose had found this fear very quickly. Just as he'd discovered her obsession with personal freedom.

At 12:15, he got dressed and headed over to Moodrow's. They were through with their fight by that time.

Had made love, then snuck into the shower together, something they didn't ordinarily do for fear one of the children would awaken and come looking for mom. He kissed Rose goodbye in the doorway to her room, snapped the hall light off and left the house.

Outside, he double-locked the apartment, turned toward the stairway and tripped over a large paper shopping bag. The bag was filled with bananas and there was a note pinned to the outside. It read, "Food for the monkeys."

A few moments later, standing near the outer door, he scanned the names printed next to the apartment buzzers. Irish. Italian. German. One Ukrainian. One Pole. They, like his mother and himself, had been there for ages.

20

The address Moodrow gave Tilley, his "office" on 11th Street, was so lost in its own melodramatic shadows that once inside, Tilley couldn't help asking Moodrow if he was a cop or a spy.

"The people I see down here ain't Russians, but they are spies." Moodrow opened a small refrigerator and offered Tilley a bottle of beer. "This apartment is owned by a friend of my old man's, Arthur Flashman. He was in the garment business when he was young. In fucking hangers, believe it or not. Made his fortune and moved into this brownstone. Arthur's a cop buff. Loves the force so much he has a whore come in every Wednesday to put him in handcuffs. At least he used to. Now he's almost eighty. I talked him into giving me this room about twenty years ago. No rent. Just detailed stories of murders and rapes. I haven't laid eyes on the guy in the last five years, but this is the place I do my business. I got more than fifty regular snitches and they all know to find me here. We'll have a lotta visitors tonight."

He wasn't kidding. Fifteen minutes after Tilley arrived, the phone rang (the phone, four ancient armchairs, a cigarette-scarred endtable and the refrigerator made up the total furnishings) and Moodrow announced a terse, "Okay" after listening for about thirty seconds. Five minutes later, the bell rang and two women, one obviously a hooker, the other in white slacks and a matching jacket, pushed into the center

of the room. The hooker, a platinum blonde in an
electric-blue, spandex miniskirt, sat heavily in a chair.
She crossed her legs, shoved a wad of Juicy Fruit gum
into her mouth and looked away indifferently.

"Who's your friend, Moodrow?" The second woman,
tall and willowy, ran her hand through her dark hair
and gestured over at Tilley.

"This is my partner. I already told you about him,
Cecil. His name's Tilley." Moodrow's voice was cold,
the voice of a businessman come to the bargaining table. "Jimmy, this is Cecil. Cecil runs a string of girls
working Third Avenue. We do each other favors. The
lady on the chair is Lucille."

Though they exchanged cold glances, nobody said a
word. Tilley was acutely aware of the fact that information is the real barometer of success in the job. Even
if he wasn't too thrilled with Moodrow's plans for his
future, Tilley couldn't help but feel that his partner
was passing on the efforts of an entire career.

Moodrow broke the silence. "Blue Thunder. You
know what that is?"

"Sure." Cecil answered without hesitation. "Eldridge Street smack."

"Any of your girls use it? Your customers? Your protection?"

"Probably. Junkies get their dope where they can."

"You hear about any Blue Thunder, you let me know
who's holding it. Big time, Cecil. If I found out you
knew and you didn't tell me, I'd remember it forever."

Tilley found out later that Moodrow was usually a
bargainer and not a threatener. In any event, Cecil took
a deep breath and turned her face away from his. She
met Lucille's eyes and they must have exchanged some
kind of message, because she turned back to Moodrow
and began to challenge him purposefully. "Everybody
knows Levander Greenwood pulled that rip-off. He's
the only one crazy enough."

"Greenwood won't put it back on the street. It'll be somebody else. Somebody I gotta find in one piece."

Cecil cocked her head and smiled. "You think it's coming back into the Lower East Side?"

"I dunno. I hope so."

"You want me to look real hard for this dope?"

"Yeah."

"I got a problem. I gotta get someone off the street." She finally sat down and relaxed. "Gimme a beer."

Moodrow obliged. Though he had no glasses (not even a paper napkin to wipe the top of the can), neither Cecil nor Lucille seemed offended. They drank for a moment, then Cecil made a gesture toward her purse. "Would it be okay to do a couple of lines?"

Moodrow looked at Tilley and blushed. "You're gonna make my partner think I'm a fucking dope fiend."

Lucille spoke for the first time. Her voice was flat, matter-of-fact. "Moodrow don't use cocaine," she said. "We was talking about for us. But maybe we should forget about it." She threw her partner another significant look. They were questioning the level of Tilley's involvement.

"Why don't you tell me what you're looking for?" Moodrow's voice was surprisingly gentle.

Once again Cecil smiled. "I need protection from my protection." She paused for effect and Moodrow waved her to keep going. "My girls and me don't have a pimp. We pay a straight two thousand dollars a week to a group of Puerto Rican gentlemen for the privilege of operating in their territory. Now the Ricans are getting themselves run off by a pack of Dominicans from Chelsea." She stopped to light a cigarette, her mouth curling up in contempt. "Sounds like an ethnic comedy, right? Meanwhile the Ricans can't take care of me, so I'm negotiating with this Dominican named Elio, who's mostly into cocaine and not whores. Then just when I think I got a deal, Elio says I gotta send my girls up when he and his boys wanna party. Some of the girls like to party. Fuck for money or fuck for dope, it's all the same to them. But not as a matter of principle. So I said, 'No' and he said he'd run me off Third Avenue."

"And what'd you say to that?" Moodrow asked.

"I told the asshole I had friends in low places and walked the fuck out."

The words, spoken at breakneck speed, rattled through the room. Then she stopped dead, as if Moodrow should know what she wanted.

"These Puerto Rican boys work out of a social club down by Avenue B?" Moodrow finally asked.

"Yeah. The Barcalounger."

"You mean the Barcelona?"

"Well, we got our own name. They took a big bust six months ago and they haven't come back from it."

"And the Dominicans?"

"If they got a name, I don't know it. But they're all supposed to be from Santiago, which is in the north. They have connections in Peru for the paste. It's easy to run from Peru into the Dominican Republic. Elio brags about it. He's all ego. That's why he thinks my women are his property. Shit, if I can't protect them from Elio, I can't be no use to them at all."

Moodrow tossed the can of beer into an open garbage bag, already half full of empty cans. "I'm expecting a lot of company tonight, Cecil. Think you might get to the point."

Cecil took a deep breath and launched into it. "They process the paste into coke and smuggle it by speedboat from some place in the Dominican jungle. It lands on the east coast—a different point every trip. Then they bring it to a house on 27th Street and cut it up for distribution. I know they're gonna meet a boat two days from now. They move in the neighborhood of ten kilos a trip."

"You got intentions of testifying?" Moodrow said softly.

"Forget it."

"I take it you're under the opinion that if you take Elio off the street, it'll give the Ricans a chance to recover. Then you go back to them for protection. That right?"

"That's exactly it."

"I can pass it along to the dicks working Chelsea and they'll probably put the house under observation, if they don't know about it already. But there's no way they can get warrants unless you testify."

"What if I know the car? It's a van, actually."

"You got the license plate? Year and model?"

"Yeah. And I also know the scumbag'll be driving it himself."

"You said 'ten kilos'?"

"Ten kilos."

"Write down the year, make and model and the license plate. I'll do what I can. And Cecil, I want whoever's holding Blue Thunder. No bullshit. That's the road to Greenwood and that means better business for everyone."

Cecil and Lucille left without another word being spoken. Not even "so long" or "see ya later." The business of business is, apparently, business. Then Tilley found out how wrong he'd been about the two of them. Cecil and Lucille were lovers, partners and absolute equals in the administration of their affairs. Neither of them were prostitutes. Lucille's bizarre dress, her platinum hair and rhinestone halter scooped low over ample breasts were simply part of the bohemian scene on the Lower East Side. The scene the media refers to as "punk." In the late-night druggie bars, the clientele was uniformly hip and it was Jim Tilley, in his Izod shirt and summerweight pants who was the freak.

Moodrow, of course, had known them too long to be impressed with their relationship or their appearance. They were just two more criminals, two entrepreneurs with enough connections to offer a special service to the whores in their territory. Yes, the prostitutes would still have to kick money back to the partners, but they would not have to fear the brutality of a pimp trying to squeeze the last dime out of their pussies. And they could quit the life whenever they wanted to.

Of course, aside from getting their message out on the street, Cecil's mention of the vehicle, especially of the license plate, caught both their attentions. Ordinarily, cops need a warrant to search a car or a truck. Unless, the Supreme Court ruled four or five years ago, the driver or the vehicle is cited for a violation of the traffic code. *Any* violation. A frayed driver's license, depending on the defense lawyer, is good enough, as are dirty license plates or a broken headlight.

It was after this ruling came down that certain police officers, in their zeal for aggressive law enforcement, began to carry small, hard objects, like blackjacks, the purpose of which was to crack a headlight or a taillight and thus validate the magical phrase "probable cause."

And ten kilos is a lot of coke for a New York City detective. Especially if it doesn't come as a result of twenty men working for six months. Task forces are tough on budgets. In Moodrow's estimation, ten kilos would be good for a commendation, even a promotion. Waiting for the next phone call, he and Tilley decided that Cecil's tip was reliable enough for Moodrow to pass it personally to a friend of his in Midtown South, a cop named Patterson. Tilley's job was to call it in, complete with time and license plate, to the same detective. An informant dropping a dime for reasons unknown. Patterson would record the phone call, as good detectives are prone to do, and it would give him and his backup a legitimate reason to be in the neighborhood when the van arrived.

The scheme wasn't foolproof by any means. A good lawyer, a Barry Slotnick, for instance, would make mincemeat out of the conveniently-broken headlight, but Cecil's nemesis, Elio, would sit in the cell until he made bail. If he made bail. And the loss of ten kilos of cocaine would probably be sufficient to curtail the gang's dreams of expansion, at least long enough for Cecil's original protection to recover.

The rest of the evening passed in similar fashion. First a phone call, then a visit, kept as brief as possible, while Moodrow spread the word about Blue Thunder. Occasionally, they received tidbits of information, though nothing so promising as Cecil's revelations.

In the course of the night, Tilley discovered that there were two kinds of soldiers in Moodrow's information network. Most of them were "rats" in the best B movie tradition; furtive, ashamed of themselves, afraid of Moodrow and of Tilley and of their reputation. In each of these cases, Tilley found himself playing the "bad" cop. He fixed them with his hardest look, the one he'd used when staring into the eyes of an opponent while the referee mumbled something about "clean breaks." He gave it to them from the moment they entered until Moodrow dismissed them with a contemptuous wave of his hand. If they wanted to be afraid of him, that was fine.

There were a few, though, who sauntered in, as proud as Cecil or Lucille. This breed didn't inform out of fear. They did it for money, or to get even, or to put a competitor out of business. In a way, they had a right to flaunt their bravery. They were playing a dangerous game. They had to reveal their own affairs in order to convince Moodrow of the validity of their information, which marked them. And because they informed for profit, he was not obliged to protect them if they were busted.

* * *

It was seven o'clock before Tilley headed uptown.
He was taking the car home regularly by then, because, living in the precinct, Moodrow really didn't
have much use for it. The freedom from mass transit
made things easier, but he was dead tired by the time
he parked in front of his building, even though he knew
he was coming home to a house full of energy. It was
one thing when he was only sharing the place with
Susanna. Hell, she was already enroute to work. In the
presence of guests, he would be forced to smile when
all he wanted was oblivion.

Jeanette and Rose greeted him at the door. Rose's
look, as she appraised the condition of his eyes, told
him that she understood how he felt. Jeanette's look,
on the other hand, revealed greater expectations and
they did one more story before Jim Tilley got into bed.
The last thing he remembered before he dropped off
was Rose asking the children to keep it quiet.

They must have complied, because when he woke
up, it was after four. Which was fine, because the task
force was out there doing all the legwork and Moodrow wouldn't need him before seven or eight. He
stumbled out of bed, groggy and a little disoriented.
For a second he flashed back to waking after late tours
in Fort Greene, then he remembered that he'd been
dreaming of Lucille, Cecil's partner. The previous
night, despite Moodrow's assertion that she was gay,
she'd sat facing him, then crossed and recrossed her
legs twenty times in the course of the interview. Each
time flashing the crotch of her metallic silver panties.
Tilley had always been a "morning" man and Lucille's
image was, in its proper course, replaced by the randy
notion that Rose was in the next room and just maybe
the kids were asleep or maybe they were visiting or
maybe they'd been kidnapped by space aliens and carried off to Jupiter.

He shrugged into his robe, a black velvet bathrobe
with red piping along the pockets, and went out to

look. They were there, of course, sitting on the rug in
the living room. The sun was pouring through a southern window, illuminating thick, green drapes and cast-
ing a rectangle of color over the three of them as they
huddled over a well-developed game of Monopoly. Lee
was complaining about the expense of a turn's stay on
Pennsylvania Avenue, which Jeanette owned. His argument ran along the lines of "she always gets the
greens." Rose put her arm around Lee and began to
explain the bit about losing being part of life. Lee had
been evading this reality for a long time, so he'd heard
the lecture before. Still, the soft voices, the three of
them framed in afternoon light, the touch of Rose's
arm on her son's flesh . . . it hurt him to watch it. Hurt
him because he was forced to acknowledge his love for
Rose and because he felt he might never enter the co-
coon that held her family together.

"Hi, guys," he said cheerfully, as men are prone to
do on such occasions. But he didn't wait for a response. Though he got a chorus of greetings, he kept
on going down the hall into the bathroom where he
spent the next half hour making his body socially acceptable. It was while he was standing in front of the
mirror, admiring the finished product, that the phone
rang. Rose must have picked it up, because she called
Moodrow's name through the door and asked him if
he wanted to call back. Instead of answering, Tilley
opened the door, checked for the children, then gave
her a quick peck on the lips.

"I'll get it," he said, striding back down the hall. "I'll
take it in the kitchen."

Tilley was still horny as hell when he picked up the
receiver, but he knew that Moodrow would not be calling unless it was important. Tilley was hoping Moodrow had heard from one of his people when he barked,
"Yeah, what's up?"

"Where are you now?" Moodrow responded. His
voice was unusually quiet.

"Mars. Where do ya think I am?"

"I mean, are you where Rose can see you?"

Tilley's heart dropped down into his gut. "Yeah."

"Well, keep your face together when I tell you this. Levander paid a visit to his mom's last night. I want you to get down to the projects right away."

Tilley smiled and kept the smile plastered to his face. "Anything else?"

"Nobody's dead, though Marlee looks half way to it. I want you to come down here and listen to what they have to say."

"Half an hour. At the site."

After they hung up, Rose came out of the bedroom. The stricken look on her face gave away the fact of her eavesdropping on the extension. "I did this," she said. "It's because I ran away."

"Rose, please . . ." Tilley reached out for her, but she slid away from his hands and slapped him hard. Slapped him contemptuously.

"You and the great Moodrow. Will you wait until he kills us all before you shoot him?" The kids had come down the hallway and were standing, one against either hip. The clan had come together, as distrustful as the first time they'd laid eyes on Detective Tilley.

"I said I could keep you safe and I did," Tilley said, stepping away from them. "I can't make miracles."

"You should have put him away ten years ago."

"Ten years ago I was in high school."

She tossed her hair back over her shoulder. "Nobody's ever responsible," she said. "How can that be? How can no one ever be responsible? You go help your partner do justice, Jim Tilley. Do justice for me and my children. Do justice for those dead cops. Do justice for Marlee and Louise. Do it, Tilley. Do it for yourself."

21

When the bell rang, Moodrow stood up and walked through the living room, pushing the debris aside with his feet. He'd been waiting patiently for more than an hour, having chased out the forensics squad as soon as he'd arrived. There was no doubt of the identity of this particular perpetrator, and no need for further evidence.

"I'm sorry it took me so long. There's a crane down across FDR Drive . . ." Jim Tilley stopped dead, his head swiveling as his eyes took in the devastation. "Holy shit," he whispered. "This guy is fucking crazy."

Louise Greenwood's apartment had been torn apart with a viciousness that went far beyond the needs of a simple search. Every piece of furniture was slashed and broken. Every dish had been swept from the kitchen shelves. The covers had been ripped from the mattresses, exposing yellowed foam rubber and scattering loose springs over the carpet. Even the heavy bureaus had been smashed with such force the dowels had pulled loose and pieces of wood were strewn throughout the bedrooms.

Moodrow was smart enough to allow the scene to have its own effect. He waited until Tilley had been through the wreckage, room by room, before he spoke. "You suppose Levander thought it was Mother's Day?" He wasn't smiling.

"What?" Tilley was standing near a linen closet by the bathroom. Levander had systematically torn every towel and every sheet before tossing them into the bathtub. "You think this is funny?"

Moodrow spread his hands apart and shrugged. "How is it different? Just because you know the people involved? Because you're sleeping with Rose?"

"This guy has gotta be stopped."

"You just figured that out, right?"

Tilley looked at his partner and shook his head. There was no percentage trying to be reasonable with Stanley Moodrow. "What happened here? Is it any use to us?" he asked, instead.

"I don't know yet. Louise is at Beekman Hospital with Marlee. They'll be home in a half hour, as soon as Marlee finishes straightening out the hospital staff. They wanna admit her overnight, to protect themselves, because concussions go bad without any warning. Like I said, Marlee's straightening them out. When Louise brings her home, we'll get the details. Meanwhile, I got a call from Cecil this morning. Guess what?"

Once again, Tilley felt it rushing up at him. Felt out of control. "You gonna tell me? You cockteasing bastard?"

"Blue Thunder's back on the street. And I'm not a bastard. In fact, my father was a saint."

Tilley ignored the jibe. "Cecil say who's got it?" The adrenaline was running so hard, he felt ready to go fifteen with Mike Tyson, fighting on the inside.

"One of her girls bought it from a friend who got it somewhere else. Cecil's running down the friend. She don't think it'll be a problem."

"How long?"

By way of an answer, Moodrow took a plastic beeper from his pocket and held it up. Beepers are not part of a cop's equipment. Portable two-ways are more their style. The presence of a beeper obviously meant that the first step, both to Levander and the rogue cop running him, was imminent.

* * *

At 7:10, the door opened and Marlee Greenwood, supported by a black man and followed by Louise Greenwood, came through the door. Marlee had been badly beaten. Her face was swollen, her eyes cut and bruised. One ear and part of the left side of her head was covered with thick bandages, the kind they put over stitched-up wounds. Sitting on what was left of the sofa, Tilley wondered what her reaction would be when she walked through the door to find them. Someone, probably the beat cops on the scene, had gotten her version at the hospital, but the task force considered the Greenwoods to be Moodrow and Tilley's problem, so they were the first detectives Louise Greenwood had seen.

As expected, Marlee was less than thrilled to see them, but she was too weak to do more than protest. Her mother introduced the two cops to the man who accompanied them. His name was Roger Peterson and he was the pastor of the Gethsemane Baptist Church on Montgomery Street, the church where Louise Greenwood spent most of her evenings. With his help, Mrs. Greenwood laid her daughter, still wearing her bloodstained clothing, on what was left of the mattress. The doctors had given her "something for the pain" and she was moaning rhythmically, almost musically. She was asleep before her mother left the room.

Outside, the tall black preacher took stock of the situation, shaking his head sadly. Finally, he turned to Moodrow and said, "You should have gotten him before this." He hesitated a moment before repeating it, as if the cops hadn't understood. "You should have gotten him before this." Then he turned back to his parishioner. "We'll have the auxiliary up here early tomorrow, Sister. Get the place cleaned up and some furniture in here. You sure you don't want to stay with Christina and me tonight?" She shook her head and he took a final look around the room. "Tell me, why did he destroy the dishes? Your clothing? What did he want?"

She didn't respond for a few moments, then said softly, "I've got to talk to these gentlemen, Reverend. After that I need to sleep. Hopefully, by the time the ladies get here tomorrow, I'll be ready for them. And I thank you for lending me your strength."

"Praise the Lord," he said, but he got no response. Still, he took her hand and held it briefly before he left.

Louise Greenwood closed the door on his back and, without speaking a word, Moodrow, Jim Tilley and Louise Greenwood began to clean up the apartment. They took the pieces of wood, the torn curtains, and began to pile them against one wall. They arranged the pieces of broken furniture as if the apartment could be made whole again, going at it room by room. Each piece of clothing was examined and most of it discarded. Even the contents of the medicine chest had been scattered on the floor, the small glass bottles ground into powder by the heels of Levander's shoes.

It took the better part of two hours until the last pile of glass had been swept into a corner, until the refrigerator had been stood upright, pieces of the stove fitted together. They worked in silence, almost preoccupied, but when the apartment was finally as good as it was going to get, they had to go over it, to hear the story as if it might somehow get them closer to Greenwood. Louise began without coaxing.

"I worked a doubleshift last night at the hospital, so when I got home from work, it was two o'clock in the afternoon. I should have been home by noon, but I was late because the A Train got stuck in the station at 86th Street. The doors stayed open. I thought it was the kids again, you know, holding them open for a joke, but then the conductor came through and told us the doors wouldn't close and we should think about walking over to Broadway, to the 1 Train, or taking a bus, if we lived in Manhattan. Well, you have to be a fool to take a bus through midtown at that time of day, so I walked to Broadway even though I knew the train would be packed and I might have to wait before I found one I could squeeze into.

"But, of course, I finally made it. I even managed to stop into the Baskin-Robbins on East Broadway for a pint of ice cream. I felt I deserved some kind of a treat after a long day and a longer trip home." She stopped abruptly and looked at each of them, as if they might have some objection to her eating the ice cream. "So, as I said, it was after two o'clock when I got home. Marlee had told me that morning that she would be late and I was surprised to hear noise from the bedrooms. I suppose I knew it was Levander right away. Who else could it be? I recalled the buzzer that the sergeant from the housing police installed and I thought that I should press it right now, before Levander discovered that I was home. But I couldn't do it. I said to myself, 'Louise, if they kill your child in front of you, you won't be able to live with it.'

"Then he came down the hallway. 'Levander,' I said, 'look at yourself.' He was dirty and his hair was very long. It was gray and dusty and knotted. When I heard of all the things he'd been doing, I thought he'd have lots of money. I didn't think he would look like an animal too long in its hole.

" 'Mama,' he said, 'I need money. And I want my Rose and my babies.'

"I said, 'Levander, you know I never did keep money in this house. There's too many robberies in the projects.'

"He took my purse, then, and commenced to go through it. He didn't even ask. Just snatched it off my shoulder and fished out the twenty dollars from my wallet. 'This is it? This little shit. Why are you bitches always doin' bad to me? You and Rose and Marlee. All talkin' against me.'

"I said, 'I'm your mother, Levander. Don't you call me a bitch in my own house.'

"He squinted at me. As if he couldn't quite make me out. Then he slapped me. His hand came forward, quick, like a snake after a mouse. It wasn't a hard blow, but I fell back on the couch. It was the first time he ever hit me.

" 'Listen, bitch.' It wasn't Levander's voice anymore. It was deeper and empty somehow, like there wasn't anybody inside. 'I know you got money here and I know you got Rose hid someplace where I can't find her. You and that fat cop, Moodrow. You in on it together.' He held up the twenty dollar bill. 'How long you think this shit gonna last? Ten minutes? I want the money and I want Rose.'

"I told him that I didn't know where Rose was hiding. Which I don't, even though she calls me nearly everyday. I have never even asked for her phone number, because I guess I had a fear that this situation might come up. Levander sat down on the green chair and took a glass pipe and a small vial filled with little, white pebbles from the pocket of his coat. That's what they call crack. He was wearing a coat, even though it was very hot and he was sweating. First he filled the pipe, then he lit it with some kind of a lighter that sort of sprayed the flame into the pipe. After that he didn't look so frightened. He put the drugs away and took out a knife and began to slice the fabric on my couch. Not crazy, but making sure he got everything and sticking his hand inside. He said, 'I know you got it here, somewhere, Mama, and I'm gonna find it. Yessir, I am gonna find it.'

"He went all around the living room, until he came to the buzzer on the wall. 'What's this? Where does this go?' I kept to myself. What could I say? Levander just grinned, like he had known about it all along. 'You shoulda pressed it when you had the chance, Mama.

Marlee would have pressed it.' Then he pulled it out of the wall and went on with his search.

"It was seven o'clock when Marlee got home. I didn't hear the key in the lock even though I'd been listening, trying to find a way to warn her. Instead, she surprised both of us. The door opened and there she was, staring at what was left of our living room.

"Marlee was always quick. She turned and tried to run, but Levander was on her before she got to the stairs. He dragged her back into the apartment, beating her with his fists. I guess I should have screamed. Or one of us should have screamed and then our neighbors might have called the police, but I didn't do it and she didn't do it and I still don't know why. Maybe I was afraid that he'd kill her if I screamed. Or somebody would come and kill *him*.

"He kept Marlee next to him the whole time he was in the apartment. He wouldn't stop hitting her, wouldn't stop tearing our home apart. I said, 'It was your home too, Levander. You grew up in here. You are destroying everything in your own life.'

"He stopped for a minute then and he smoked his pipe again. Marlee was lying on the floor and she was crying. We were both crying. Levander said, 'I don't have no home, Mama. Not no more. Not ever again. The pig is gonna kill me soon and I don't mind. I don't mind about gettin' killed. I took out my share of pigs and they can't kill me more than once.' He threw back his head and began to laugh. 'Looks like I got over, Mama. I got over on all them pigs. They can't kill me no more than one time.' Then he smoked his pipe again, which seemed to calm him down and he went on searching.

" 'Where's Rose, Mama?' When there was nothing left to destroy, he dragged Marlee into the living room, then let her fall to the floor. I had been expecting this question all along, but I had not come up with an answer that would satisfy Levander. I said, 'Levander, I don't know where Rose is hiding. She's afraid that you'll hurt the children and I don't believe she'll come out of hiding until . . .'

"I didn't have the courage to finish my thought, but Levander knew what I was going to say. 'Till I'm dead. That what you gonna say, Mama?' He grinned at me. That little smile he had when he was a baby and up to some mischief. Then he drew back his leg and kicked Marlee. He kicked her hard again and again. 'Maybe I take this bitch with me, Mama. How you feel about that? Huh? Then you got nobody.'

"I begged him, Sergeant. I cried and I begged him not to hurt her anymore. Marlee is all I have. She is my family and I could see in his eyes that he would take her away from me and I felt my heart turning cold. That turning hurt more than if it was me he was beating. When love goes out of you, there is nothing left but pain. I said, 'Levander, I can get you some money. I can get you five hundred dollars, but you got to stop hurting Marlee. Please, Levander, you can't hurt her anymore.'

" 'What you talkin' about, Mama? Ain't no money here.'

" 'I got a savings account and one of those cards that let you in the bank even when it's closed. I could go there and get the money.'

"He looked at me for a long time, then he took out his pipe and smoked it again. 'You know I'll kill Marlee if you don't come back alone.'

" 'I know that. I know you will.'

"Somehow I got to the bank and returned without giving away what was in my heart, even though I met neighbors and had to greet them and talk about the projects and the heat. Considering what I was carrying, it seemed nearly impossible, but no one noticed anything wrong. People don't seem to see things they don't want to see and I got back to Marlee in about fifteen minutes. Levander was smoking his pipe when I came in. He took the money from me, counted it and said, 'I know that pig cop's got my Rose and my kids. You tell the pig, if I don't get my old lady, I'm gonna take him instead. You hear?'

   " 'Yes, I hear.'

   "Then he got up and walked to the door, but instead of opening it, he stood there for a long time with his back to me. I thought he was going to become violent again, but when he finally turned to me, he was crying hard. 'Goodbye, Mama,' he said. 'Goodbye, Mama.' "

22

When Moodrow and Tilley left the Greenwoods'
wrecked apartment, they were no closer to Levander
Greenwood than when they'd entered. In spite of his
evident madness—an insanity which had put an old
woman face to face with her own death—he'd not revealed a hint of his present whereabouts. His condition, though, was both a revelation and a new source
of fear to Moodrow and Tilley. Crack junkies deterio-
rate quickly, much more quickly than, for instance,
heroin addicts, who often maintain their habits for decades. This is because the most powerful and immediate effect of cocaine in any form—powder, freebase
or rock—is to make the user want more. It's the sim-
plest and most honest way for the layman to understand the drug: as soon as you do a line, you want
another.

In the days when Tilley was a white hope, he'd at-
tended a number of parties where the coke was laid
out on a huge mirror, an ounce or more, and there
were always a group of people who sat around the mirror all night. Just staring into the pile until someone
offered the straw. No matter how much they did, no
matter how pure the cocaine, they wanted more and
more and more and more.

It's worse with crack. Smoking rock cocaine in-
creases this effect, this desire for more and more and
more by a factor of ten. No joke, here. Not even ex-
aggeration. Some people can do cocaine and walk away

from it. That was Tilley's own experience. He did it once or twice, but he was lucky enough to come along after the first wave of cocaine use had destroyed some of the best fighters in the world. He knew what it could do, even that first time when he shared a gram with several close friends. Their plan was to save a small piece for the following day's trip to the beach, but at two in the morning, when they did the last lines, Tilley knew there would be no trip to the beach. What he didn't know was that about an hour later, lying naked on the bed, he would suddenly panic. That he'd be shaken by an awful fear that he believed could only be satisfied by cocaine.

That was the first time and the panic passed in about fifteen minutes. For terminal crack junkies like Levander Greenwood, the panic would last for days and would do more than shake his bones. Levander could easily pass through delusions (if not outright hallucinations) as complex and realistic as those of a paranoid schizophrenic. In the years since Tilley had quit the boxing business, he had three old ring buddies come to him with coke habits, begging him to help them get into treatment programs. They'd been using the drug for days at a time. Literally. One hit after another until exhaustion allowed them enough freedom for a few hours' sleep. Tilley couldn't get them into programs. The waiting lists held hundreds of names. Instead, he talked them through the first couple of days, only to see them fall back into the drug. What they experienced, as their bodies threw off the coke, can only be described as terror.

Both Moodrow and Tilley's thoughts revolved around Levander and his mental and physical condition as they came down the stairs. Marlee and Louise Greenwood were already behind them; the hunt lay in front. What they didn't anticipate was the fat cop huffing up the stairs to meet them. It was Sergeant Handelsman, the desk sergeant from PSU headquarters in building F, the man Tilley had met the first time they visited the Vladek Houses.

"Moodrow," he called, stopping and waiting for the two cops to reach him. "I thought you might still be up here. You better come out quick. Levander got another one, by the laundry room. He must have been waiting." He stopped to catch his breath. "It's Rose Carillo."

Curiously, Tilley and Moodrow had the same initial reaction, though for different reasons. They stopped in their tracks and tried to collect the rapid fire thoughts exploding in their brains.

"Is she dead?" Tilley finally asked. His voice was barely a whisper. For an instant, he flashed back to his mother describing his fireman father's death in an arsonist's fire in the Bronx. He could clearly see the tears pouring down her face as she explained what a hero Daddy had been.

"No, one of ours scared him off," Handelsman said easily. He had no idea of Tilley's relationship with Rose. For him it was just another complication. Another pain in the ass that would require a mountain of paperwork and an apartment-by-apartment search of the Vladek Houses. "She's beat up and she's been stabbed deep, but she's breathing all right and her heart's strong. He stabbed her in the gut, so she's probably bleeding inside. And there's some broken bones."

Tilley took off at a dead run, leaving Moodrow to explain it to Handelsman. His pulse was racing wildly and he was more frightened than he had ever been in his life. She must have followed them? Why? What did she hope to do for Louise and Marlee? What about the children? He pushed through the outer lobby door into the seeming chaos of a crime scene. The housing cops were controlling this one, but the sergeant in charge, O'Malley, was willing to give way to an NYPD detective, even a kid like Tilley.

"Where's the bus?" Tilley asked first. He was referring to an Emergency Services ambulance. "You got an ETA?"

"They're backed up about forty minutes. Even that's a guess."

"How bad is she?"

"She's unconscious."

"Can we take her in a car?"

"She's got head injuries. She's got to be immobilized."

"Gimme your portable."

Without questioning, O'Malley turned his portable over to the detective. Tilley wanted to scream into it, but he knew it would do no good. "Task Force Green. Green Five to Central. K."

"Go ahead Green Five."

"We need a bus at the Vladek Houses. Right now."

"Hold on, Green Five." There was a brief pause and the dispatcher came back on. Her calm voice was maddening. "No ETA possible at this time."

"This task force has priority, Central. I want the first available bus. K."

"I'll try once more. Standby."

Tilley desperately wanted to go to Rose's side. She was lying on her back, a blanket under her head, about thirty feet away, and he could hear her moaning softly.

"Green Five, K."

"Green Five," Tilley returned.

"No earlier ETA possible on that bus. Emergency Services is backed up with elderly aided cases because of the heat. I will advise as soon as we have a definite."

Tilley sighed. "10-4." He looked up to find Moodrow standing behind him. "She followed me here," Tilley explained. "He must have been waiting. I should have known she'd come. I should have figured it."

By way of an answer, Moodrow put his arm around Tilley's shoulders and led him over to Rose. A young man, an Asian, knelt beside her, a pressure pack in his hand. He looked up at Moodrow, then handed the big cop a business card: HOUSE CALLS, INC. Dr. Muhammad Bhutto.

"You're a doctor?" Tilley asked. The man's presence in the Vladek Houses was as miraculous to him as the appearance of the Virgin at Lourdes.

"I am a doctor." His accent was pure British, clipped and upper class.

"This is personal, Doctor." Moodrow stepped in, his arm still supporting his partner's shoulders. "We have to know how she is. The truth. Not what you think I want to hear."

"Your name, sir?" the doctor asked calmly.

Moodrow flipped his shield. "Detective Moodrow. This is my partner, Detective Tilley."

Doctor Bhutto nodded. "Please realize that I am only able to view the external aspect of the woman's wounds. However, as I am Pakistani and have worked in the Afghan refugee camps on the border of our countries, I am quite familiar with trauma. I am certain that she has not sustained a skull fracture in which bone has been displaced and that she has no severe spinal injuries because she is able to move her extremities freely. She is, of course, in shock and losing blood internally from a single stab wound. While the position of the entry wound is in the lower abdomen and her heart is untouched, we cannot rule out damage to any number of organs. It is also possible that a major artery has been cut, but as her color remains quite pink, I must consider that unlikely."

"If her back and her head are all right, why can't we take her to the hospital in a car?"

"She has severe rib injuries. Cracked or broken. I do not believe she should try to sit upright. I think we can wait for the ambulance. It's an acceptable risk."

"Bullshit," Moodrow said. He walked away from Rose and searched the faces of the crowd standing outside the police barricades. "Hey Henry," he said, suddenly striding toward a small, middle-aged man with a thin beard.

"I didn't have nothing to do with this, Moodrow," the man said as the big cop walked over to him.

"I need a favor." Moodrow didn't even bother replying to the ritual denial. "I need a van with no backseat. Maybe with a mattress. Like you sometimes use to carry television sets to your fence."

Henry, to his credit, neither laughed nor denied the charge. "For Rosey?" he asked.

"Yeah. The fucking ambulance is gonna be late. We gotta get her to a hospital."

"All right. Five minutes, but I have to drive it. It doesn't go anywhere without me behind the wheel."

"No problem."

Henry hesitated for a moment, just long enough to ask, "When are you gonna kill this dude, Moodrow? He's been around too long. You shoulda chilled him a long time ago."

Fifteen minutes later, Rose was lying on a thin mattress in the back of a half-ton Dodge van. Doctor Bhutto was beside her and a patrol car was set to escort her to the hospital. It would run the lights and siren. While Tilley stood behind the van, Moodrow instructed the driver of the patrol car.

"No Bellevue," he told the driver. "Take her to St. Vincent's."

"Bellevue is the best for trauma," the cop said automatically. The theory was that emergency room physicians at Bellevue handled so many stabbings and gunshot wounds, they would be the best at treating Rose's injuries.

"If Levander decides to go looking for her, Bellevue's the first place he'll try. I don't want her anywhere he can find her." The cop in the patrol car nodded his agreement and Moodrow walked to the side of the van. "Henry," he whispered, "you're going to St. Vincent's on Seventh Avenue. Just follow the cop in front of you.

By the way, if you don't tell everyone where she is, there's no way Levander can find her at St. Vincent's. I owe you one." Without waiting for a reply, he walked to the back of the van and stood beside an immobile James Tilley. "What do you want to do, Jimmy? You wanna go with Rose?"

Tilley looked at his partner in surprise. "No way, Moodrow. I can't do anything for Rose but take Greenwood off the street. And that's what I'm gonna do. We're too close for me to spend the night in a hospital corridor."

"Take off," Moodrow yelled to the cop in the first patrol car and the two vehicles, the RMP and the van, moved toward Montgomery Street and FDR Drive. Moodrow and Tilley watched it for a moment, then turned to the housing cops still surrounding the crime scene. "Who caught the squeal?" Moodrow asked loudly.

A young cop, a black woman in uniform, stepped forward. "Patrolman Gorman," she said calmly.

"Can you run it down for us?" Moodrow asked.

"I was in the house when we got a call from apartment 3C, Building G. A domestic dispute. Woman screaming between G and F Buildings. I came over to eyeball the situation and also heard screaming. I could see a man striking a woman and I drew my service revolver and called for him to stop. He turned to me and fired twice. A pistol. I ducked behind the corner of Building G, but was unable to return fire due to the close proximity of the victim. When I looked out, the perpetrator was gone. I then ascertained that the victim was badly injured and called for backup and a bus."

"And you didn't see him run into a building? Or have any idea where he went except that it was away from you?"

"That's correct."

For the first time, Tilley seemed to come out of his lethargy. "We're just wasting time, Moodrow. The whole task force is here now. Let them do that shit work. Let's get out of here."

Moodrow looked around in surprise, noting the dozens of detectives and uniforms flooding the scene. As Handelsman had predicted, there would be a search, not only of the projects, but of the entire surrounding neighborhood. If Greenwood was out on the street, he would be snatched up within two hours. Even as Moodrow watched, the task force was setting up a mobile command post and dividing the neighborhood into sectors. Greenwood's status as a cop killer was attracting off-duty cops from every borough. There was no sense in the two of them getting involved in the scut work. Let the pencil pushers plot the logistics. Without another word, Moodrow led his partner to their waiting Plymouth and they began to drive uptown.

23

They drove directly to the Lip Cafe, a small, trendy restaurant fronting Tompkins Square Park. The owner, Frank Parisi, an uptown entrepreneur, had become friendly with Moodrow when he'd been attempting to establish his business. Continuous vandalism had nearly driven him back uptown, but Moodrow had acted as an arbitrator with the local street gangs and negotiated a peace which, surprisingly, had held up. The destruction had ended as soon as the owner stopped calling the precinct and complaining about menacing characters hanging around his establishment.

"Frank," Moodrow said, without even a preliminary hello, "I need your office and your phone for a couple hours. And some dinner."

"Hey," Frankie smiled his most hospitable smile. "You don't even gotta ask. Take as long as ya like. I'll send you a waitress."

"Send Gretchen."

"You like Gretchen?" Frankie asked.

"I like to bust her balls," Moodrow replied.

Each of the cops made a phone call while they waited for the waitress to arrive. Moodrow called Epstein and made arrangements for Rose's protection. It would be impossible to keep the task force ignorant of her whereabouts, but Moodrow could make sure that cops assigned to watch her were good and he pushed Epstein to call in some favors from another precinct, to get a squad of anti-crime street cops from uptown assigned to protect her. If there was enough firepower around her door, even Levander couldn't blast his way inside.

Tilley called his mother, Susanna, and ran down the attack on Rose, assuring her (and himself) that Rose would be all right. In the meantime, she would have to take care of the children, to explain what had happened as best she could. There was no chance he would get home for hours and at least a possibility that he would not get home at all.

Susanna Tilley took it in without asking a single question. She, too, recalled a scene that had taken place long before; of trying to tell a little boy that his father would not be coming home; of trying to make death real to a small child while she held back her own grief. "Don't worry about it, Jimmy. We'll be all right. But, for God's sake, get this man off the street."

After the phone calls were made, they began to discuss drugs in general and Greenwood's condition in particular. Moodrow wasn't surprised when Tilley told of his experiments with cocaine: Moodrow was a long time advocate of the legalization of drugs. ("If some asshole wants to shoot dope and become a zombie, what do I give a fuck? As long as he don't steal my television, let 'im do what he wants.") He was, however, just as glad to know that Tilley wasn't presently doing anything heavier than a Schaefer and an occasional joint. And he agreed with him about Levander's condition.

"The street's already canonized the mighty Kubla Khan. They're making him a cop-killing superhero. Fucking mutt's probably living in a basement hole in some abandoned tenement. Well, I promise you one thing, Jimmy. He ain't got another week. I'm so close I can smell him. I can feel myself settling up for Marlee and Rose and all the rest of them."

They were interrupted by the waitress, a heavy-set

young woman in a frumpy, black dress that looked as
if it came down secondhand from a Ukrainian widow.
Her hair was also black, jet black—except for three
silver spikes, sprinkled with glitter, that stood straight
up in the air.

To say the two cops were out of place in the Lip
Cafe is to put it as mildly as possible, but Moodrow
was wild about the *chimichangas* and they placed their
orders without considering the ambiance. Cops are not
nearly as callous as the media likes to paint them, but
they *know* they cannot carry that pain with them, so
they bury it. And become alcoholics. Or swallow the
gun. Or clown it up at inappropriate moments.

Thus, fifteen minutes later, even as Moodrow ana-
lyzed Levander Greenwood and the investigation, two
things happened, right on cue. His beeper went off and
the waitress arrived with several steaming plates of
food. The beeper was the signal to go to the apartment
on 11th Street and wait for Cecil, which only made
the food seem more appetizing, and Moodrow asked
the waitress to wrap it up.

For a moment, she didn't react, just stood there with
her hands on her hips, staring at them. Finally, she
said, "Ya know somethin', Moodrow? You're really a
pain in the ass."

"Is that what you like?" he asked.

"What the fuck are you talkin' about?"

"A pain in the ass. Is that what you like?"

She wasn't stupid enough to reply, but as she picked
up the plates, Moodrow fired a final shot. "Because if
that's what you like, you should come to my place
tonight and we'll play a little game with my .38."

Without bothering to turn around, she shrugged her
shoulders and said, "I'll take you up on that, fatso. The
day you learn to lick your eyebrows."

Fifteen minutes later, they were in the apartment
on 11th Street. Lucille had taken her seat and was busy

doing the panty bit with her legs. This time she added a special treat. She was wearing a plain white cotton t-shirt with two circular targets, one over each breast. The bull's-eyes were right on her nipples. She excused herself immediately upon entering the room, complaining of the heat, and splashed her face with cold water from the sink in the toilet. In the process, she also soaked the shirt so that her breasts jumped up like two trout from the surface of a pond. All through this performance (and all through her partner's conversation, which she never interrupted), her features remained frozen. Except for her lower jaw, which slowly worked the wad of gum in her mouth.

"You were right, Moodrow. About Blue Thunder. It didn't come back on with Greenwood." Cecil opened the negotiations with a flat statement, then stopped dead, but Moodrow waved his arm wearily.

"No play, tonight, Cecil. Just tell me."

"This is very important to you. This should be worth something," Cecil insisted. "We've been talking to each other three fucking years already. You gotta do better than 'just tell me who.'"

Moodrow's face turned to stone. His features seemed to shrink back into his skull and Cecil found herself staring at a white rock with two black dots about a third of the way down. "Listen," the rock said, "If you don't tell me who's holding that dope, you ain't walking out of this apartment. If you think I'm kidding, just keep fucking me around."

Cecil stamped her foot in amazement. Even Tilley, who was so excited he could barely remain seated, read in her eyes a clear desire to drive that same foot into Moodrow's face, perhaps to see if it was as hard as it looked. But Moodrow towered over her like the giants in Jeanette's nightmares and Cecil had to content herself with complaining. "This is bullshit. You never been like this. I never woulda started up with you, if you were like this. What the fuck is the matter with you?"

"I'm in a hurry, Cecil." He hesitated for a moment, then his face opened up, as if he'd made a decision. "Look, I'm passing on all that shit about Chelsea and Elio. I'm *trying* to take care of that. Correction. I think I *will* take care of that. But I don't have time to talk about it tonight. I want you to tell me who it is and then take off. You understand what I'm saying?"

The carrot and the stick. Threaten, then offer a bone. Tilley recalled a piece of advice Moodrow had given him regarding informants. He'd advised his partner to run them the way a pimp runs a stable of whores. Watching Lucille's tits rise and fall with each breath, Tilley was suddenly completely relaxed, indifferent, really, to the conversation, because he *knew* his partner would, in fact, break their legs before he would allow them to walk out without giving him what he wanted. To Moodrow, Cecil was not a female. She wasn't even a criminal or a businesswoman. She was a stepping stone on the path to Levander Greenwood and he was prepared to "step" as hard as necessary.

"You know a boy named Johnny Mitchell? They call him 'pinky,' because he's white."

"I heard of him, but I don't know what he looks like."

"He's a runt. A dead-end junkie dealing out of the men's shelter on Lexington Avenue. Dealing Blue Thunder. I know someone who copped last night."

"You sure? The person told you this is reliable?"

"Ninety-nine percent. The story goes that Pinky Mitchell suddenly has more dope than ever before in his life. And his regular spot is inside the armory on Lex."

"I know where it is," Moodrow replied. Tilley could almost hear his partner's mind racing away with the information.

Suddenly Cecil broke the tension. She put her hands

on her hips and smiled thinly. "Can we leave now? Did we give you enough, Sergeant? Or should I call you sir? Sir Moodrow."

By way of an answer, Moodrow took her hand and kissed the backs of her fingers. "Thanks, Cecil."

As soon as she'd gone, Moodrow filled his partner in. Pinky Mitchell was a white kid from Alabama who'd gone the whole New York route: from promising kid-exec in midtown; to hip art dealer in SoHo; to cocaine dealer in the West Village; to heroin addict; to small-time, homeless pusher.

"Why would he live in the shelter if he's a dealer?" The question was naive, even by Tilley's standards.

"The kid's a terminal junkie. *Whatever* he makes from dealing or boosting from the stores, he shoots up. Little items, like food and shelter that you and me gotta work for, he gets courtesy of the city. The dirtball's been living in the fucking shelter so long, it's like his office. Other junkies know to look for him there. And that makes all kinds of problems for us."

"How so?"

"In the first place, it's not in our fucking precinct. It's in the One Three. Second, shelters are guarded by private security. The shelter Pinky's dealing from has metal detectors where you come in the main entrance. Maybe five or six security guards."

"I still don't see why we can't put fifty uniforms inside and just take him. He's not expecting us. He wouldn't even know what we're after."

"Fine. But what are we gonna take him for? What cause do we have to stop and frisk him? Much less arrest him." He paused for effect, then went on like he was training a hamster. "Besides which, if Mitchell gets arrested, the suits at the One Three are gonna take the collar. Plus, if you bust a junkie, you gotta take him to the hospital if he asks for it. After which comes a Legal Aid lawyer and you lose two weeks before you get to the bastard. Fuck that. There's a dirty cop here and he's stinking up the whole fucking precinct. I don't know where that cop is or when he'll find out that we took Mitchell. Don't forget, the cop has gotta be running Greenwood *and* Pinky Mitchell. Greenwood rips it off, passes it to the cop who passes it to Mitchell."

"I hear what you're saying. You know how many junkies I saw walking a beat in Brooklyn? The life expectancy of a car radio in Fort Greene is about twenty minutes. The neighborhood's infested."

"Fine. Then you know fucking Pinky Mitchell cannot be running with Levander Greenwood. It'd be like the rabbit running with the wolf."

There was nothing more to say on that point. Of course, they'd expected a buffer all along, a middleman between the rip-off and the resale and this only confirmed their suspicions. "So, tell me what you wanna do," Tilley said, and felt the roller coaster take a sudden twist before dropping almost straight down.

"There's no fucking trick to it," he explained. "It ain't subtle. We take Mitchell out of the shelter and bring him back here. Junkies will sell their mothers' assholes for a fix. We let Pinky Mitchell get sick, he's gonna tell us who's running him."

Tilley couldn't help smiling. He said, "You know what, Moodrow? All those things you just said are right? We sneak in the shelter without anyone knowing. We smuggle one junkie out of the building. We get this junkie down in this basement. The junkie gives us what we want. A very tight chain of logic. Real detective-like. The only problem is that we have to commit a number of crimes in the process. Not the least of which is kidnapping."

"Does that bother you?" Moodrow looked surprised, then anxious, then innocent.

"Fuck, no. But later on it leads to more problems. Like when we take the cop, who's gonna testify against him? Are we supposed to admit that we kidnapped and tortured a witness? If we can't make an arrest on the cop, how do we get him to give up Greenwood?"

Moodrow stopped him with a wave of his hand. "I don't give a shit. And I'm not buying that crap says you can't let a guilty man go free. The first thing is to get Levander Greenwood off the street, before he kills anyone else. Lemme get that done before I worry about the lawyers." He stopped again and fixed Tilley with his hardest stare. It was almost as hard as that of a Latvian middleweight who'd knocked Tilley out one summer night when he was still an amateur.

"Look, Jimmy, I'm gonna make you a promise. You give me the junkie and I'll get the cop. You give me the cop, I'll get you Levander Greenwood. I guarantee it."

Whoooooooooooooooooooooooooosh. Like stepping off a cliff. Judge, jury and . . . What would Tilley say later on? "Moodrow made me do it, your Honor. I'm just a kid and I didn't know any better." Moodrow had thirty-five years in. Thirty-five years of playing on the edge. Now it was Jim Tilley's turn and his career was the last thing on his mind. He thought of Rose, limp and moaning, being hoisted into a van. It was all personal. Every bit of it. To play it according to the Patrol Guide would mean long delays and delays were no longer even thinkable to James Patrick Tilley.

"We won't go in tonight," Moodrow explained. "I can get a floor plan of the shelter and some more exact information on Mitchell's operation. I know a security guard there who owes me a favor. Probably take the rest of the night."

"What about me?"

"You get to go back uptown. Try to do something for the kids. We'll meet tomorrow afternoon and take Mitchell sometime tomorrow night."

"I'm not coming with you now?"

"I want you should be the one to go inside. So nobody should see you with me." He laughed. "Tomorrow night, around six o'clock, you're gonna become homeless."

"You want me to go inside the men's shelter by myself?"

"Yeah. You go in the front door like any other dirtball. But you go out one of the back doors. I don't know exactly how, but I'll have it worked out by tomorrow."

"I suppose I have to go in clean? No gun? No badge?"

"Of course. I told you already. They got metal detectors in the front entrance."

"And if someone recognizes me?"

"Run like hell."

Jim Tilley stopped at St. Vincent's before he headed back uptown. Stubbornly refusing to take the nurse's evaluation of Rose's condition as "serious," he ran down the resident, Doctor Samuel Morris, who'd admitted her. The man was asleep in a private room. He'd been on call for thirty-six hours, but he showed no annoyance when Tilley woke him, not even surprise.

"She'll be all right," he announced firmly. Tilley could not read any doubt in his tone.

"How much damage is there?"

"The stab wound went deep enough, but except for nicking her liver, managed to avoid anything really damaging. Her biggest problem right now is potential infection from the blade. We're anticipating that by feeding her intravenous antibiotics. And, of course, she has a hairline fracture of the skull. Just above the right ear. I think he must have hit her with a brick. There was red dust in the wound. Head injuries sometimes go bad, no doubt about it. There's also two broken ribs on the right side, but no damage to the lung."

Tilley hesitated for a second, before asking the question, but, he knew, if he didn't ask it this way, he couldn't be sure of her condition. "Is there any chance that she'll die?"

The doctor looked surprised, then fed it to the cop without flinching. "The most dangerous time for her was when she was on the table. Under anesthesia. She came through that without complications. Right now, in a woman her age, I'd say the chances of her going so bad we can't save her are one in five hundred. That doesn't mean, by the way, that she won't be in pain for a long time." He waited for the cop to take it in, then continued. "Look, I'm not so stupid or so tired that I can't see she means a lot to you. I'll watch out for her. If you want some real information, call the hospital, ask for the paging operator and have her find me. I'll give you whatever time I can, but, for now, it's 'goodnight and please call me in the morning.' I've been up for a long time."

Susanna was holding a sleeping Jeanette on her lap when Tilley walked into the apartment. She smiled and got up to carry the child into her bedroom. Lee, on the other hand, was wide awake. He was watching an HBO special, a boxing match between the cruiser-weight champion, Richard Hartfield, and a pretty good light-heavy, Matthew Johnson. Tilley'd made a mental note to watch the fight a few weeks before, then had forgotten all about it.

"Tilley, come here," Lee ordered, indicating the seat next to him. It was the first time he'd asked Tilley for anything and Tilley didn't waste the opportunity by resenting Lee's tone of voice. He walked over and sat next to him.

"Who's winning?" Tilley asked.

Lee pointed to the tall man with the sharp features, and Tilley said, "That's Richard Hartfield. He's the champion. The other guy is Matthew Johnson."

Without looking at him, Lee said, "The champion is kicking the shit out of Matthew Johnson." He was

seven years old. "Could you kick the shit out of him?"
He pointed to Hartfield again.

Tilley didn't say anything for a moment. Just sat
there watching the champion as he twisted his body
away from the looping punches of a smaller, slower
opponent. Hartfield had a way of bending backward at
the waist, allowing left hooks to pass harmlessly in
front of his face. Then he'd come back over the top
with devastating rights. It was a very unusual move
and Tilley drifted back to his days in training. At first
glance, Richard Hartfield was the perfect opponent for
him. He stood ramrod straight, his chin in the air. It
looked like an easy target, that chin, but it was almost
never there when other fighters tried to hit it.

"No, I don't think so. I'm not in training anymore."
His explanation left out the conviction that on his best
day, he wouldn't have made a decent sparring partner
for the likes of Mr. Hartfield.

"I could," Lee said quietly.

"Could what?"

"I could kick his ass."

"And how would you do that?"

Lee reached into the crevice between the armrest
and his cushion, withdrawing a black-handled carving
knife. It was thick, sharp and almost as long as his
forearm. His face was earnest and very serious as he
met Tilley's eyes. "I could kick the shit out of him."

Tilley didn't argue the point, or try to take the knife
away. They sat in silence as Hartfield slowly beat his
man into submission. The process took another four
rounds and by the time it was completed, Susanna had
returned from the kitchen and was talking with Lee
about computers.

Exhausted, Tilley excused himself and went to bed.
It was still early, but he drifted off almost as soon as
his head hit the pillow. He saw one last image before
he passed into oblivion. He saw Moodrow and Green-

wood as enormous sumo wrestlers charging from opposite ends of a wrestling mat.

Then he dreamed of the odor of his lover's throat. It
filled each breath. They were wrapped in each other's
arms and she was already maneuvering her body to
receive him. Afterward, they both began to cry. The
intensity was beyond pleasure. It was devouring, and
when Rose said, "I love you, Jim Tilley," he was so
frightened, he almost screamed.

24

Tilley woke up early the next morning and went for what he now thought of as a "cleansing" run. It was hot and rainy, a perfect combination for a jogger—the steady drizzle cooled without chilling and he ran his usual three miles in twenty-two minutes. He didn't think very much about what he would have to do that night. His mind kept returning to Rose in her hospital bed, to Levander beating her, stabbing her. There's a reality to being a cop that parallels the feelings of any hunter after his prey. That the prey consists entirely of criminals, which *obliges* them to undertake the hunt, only serves to heighten the pleasures of the stalk, especially as the end approaches. That end was as far as Jim Tilley's imagination could stretch and when he arrived home, he was mentally prepared for whatever the night would bring.

Moodrow wanted Tilley to go into the men's shelter on Lexington Avenue, an enormous armory that takes up an entire square block between 24th and 25th Streets. Once inside, he would locate and remove a small-time pusher without showing a badge or a gun.

To say that New York's shelters are places of violence is to oversimplify the case by plenty. But it is a fact that on freezing cold nights many of the city's homeless have to be dragged into the shelters against their will, because the Mayor decided, some time ago, that force is preferable to grainy photos of frozen bodies in the tabloids. The homeless, for their part, usually explain their reluctance to accept a warm bed by insisting the dangers inside the shelter are more real than the weather outside; even when the temperature outside is ten degrees; even when the wind is blowing.

Tilley should have been afraid, like any fighter (or soldier, for that matter) going into combat. New York City's system of projects, welfare hotels and shelters is predicated on the belief that *everyone* is entitled to a bed. Literally. Every single person who does not have a place to sleep, must be given a bed.

An apartment is the desired end, of course, and the low income housing projects stand at the top of the ladder, but the housing shortage precludes the possibility of quick placement in a project. Next come the city-owned tenements, abandoned by their owners and seized by the city for back taxes. They are usually in far worse condition than project apartments, but they are, at least, homes: permanent, located in residential neighborhoods and close to schools and shopping. The hotels are the next step down. Although some Single Room Occupancy (SRO) hotels still exist to serve homeless adults, most of the welfare hotels are reserved for families with dependent children. By political definition, they are temporary. But only if you define "temporary" as including stays of eighteen months and longer.

Still, the hotels, with their allocation of one family to one room, are far better than the shelters which, at best, have dormitory-style living conditions. The system was originally designed so that families wouldn't have to spend more than a few nights in shelters, but just as there's a shortage of apartments, there are not enough hotel rooms to go around either, and many families are put up at special "family" shelters for weeks at a time.

But family shelters are still not the bottom. Not even close to it. In family shelters, despite the degradation, there still remains a sense of something to protect, even if it's only the children. At the absolute *bottom* of the system are all-male and all-female shelters for adults who have no place to sleep. Typically, they consist of a single, large room, often with a concrete floor, in which hundreds of numbered beds have been arranged in neat rows, like vegetables in a farmer's field. Into these beds are sent New York's poorest; its most crazy; its most violent; its most addicted. No one can be turned away. Mumblers, drooling over foul, unwashed clothing, sleep next to ex-convicts with less tolerance for odor than a hawk for a rat. Radios blare. Drugs are smoked, snorted and shot. Humans shower and eat. Sex is given and taken. All under the careful scrutiny of a security staff paid so little as to guarantee corruption as surely as the wages of the Tijuana cop sanctify the giving and taking of bribes.

This is why many homeless people prefer the comfort of concrete to the clean sheets of the shelters. But, just as there are people in our society who thrive in jail, there are people, men and women, who have come to accept life in the shelters, who live there as if in extended families, separating into factions and competing for the crumbs—dope, food, a particular bed next to a particular lover—like convicts struggling over prison pleasures.

That's where Tilley was going to go. In with those people. The cliché is that all prizefighters are scared, at one time or another. But the only thing that ever scared Jim Tilley was losing. At that moment, coming up 88th Street, he couldn't wait to get started and he went up the steps to his apartment like Rocky on that monument in Philadelphia. Fuck you, Pinky Mitchell. Here I come. Rose loves me, you bastard, and I'm gonna kick your fuckin' ass.

Susanna was making breakfast when he entered his apartment. The kids were sitting together on the couch in the living room, watching cartoons.

"How are they doing?" Tilley asked his mother.

"They sit together whenever they're awake. I don't think they believe us. About Rose being all right."

Tilley went to the phone in his bedroom, called St. Vincent's, asked for the paging operator and identified himself as a NYPD detective. Then he asked for Doctor Samuel Morris. The operator, apparently unimpressed, put him on hold for fifteen minutes before Samuel Morris came on the line, his voice dripping exhaustion.

"This is Detective Tilley," Tilley said, "calling about Rose Carillo. You said I should call you." He could feel his breath catch in his throat as he waited for the doctor to speak.

"I saw her not more than ten minutes ago. She's okay. Running a little fever, but we expected that."

"Listen, Doctor, I have a problem with her children. I can't really convince them she's all right. I don't know the kids real well and they don't trust me. Is there any way they could see her?"

"I think you should let that go for a few days. Her face is very swollen and she'd probably frighten them. But, if she's awake, I could have her call them. Give me the number and I'll go to work on it."

"You know something, Morris?" Tilley said. "You're a goddamn miracle."

"Fuck you, too, pal."

Ten minutes later the phone rang and a groggy Rose Carillo managed to speak to her children. Though she meant to reassure them, her advice was very practical. "I did a very dumb thing," she told each in turn. "I was safe with Jim and Susanna and I left anyway. Don't make the same mistake. Stay where you are no matter what. Now I'm safe again and I won't leave until I can come back to you. But I'll call you everyday to let you know that I'm all right."

The children listened in silence, only Jeanette asking a simple question: "Did Daddy do this to you?"

Rose answered, "Yes," then began to drift away. Finally a nurse came on and explained to the children about sleep helping their mother to get better.

Susanna took the phone and, very gently, hung it up. The children looked at each other, then went back to the couch and their cartoon, still sitting next to each other, still obedient to the only hope in their lives— Rose Carillo.

By three o'clock, too excited to stay away, Tilley was walking up to Moodrow's door. He knocked loudly (the bell didn't work) and waited a few minutes. Nothing. This didn't mean, of course, that no one was home. Moodrow, who, when awake, appeared to watch everything, fell into utter oblivion when he slept. That was one of the reasons he'd given Tilley a set of keys. And also the reason why Tilley worked the keys quietly and gently in the lock. He was early and he didn't see any reason to wake up his partner.

But he was just as glad to hear the shower running in the bathroom down the hall. He wasn't off the roller coaster, by any means, but he was growing more used to its sudden twists and turns. Studying Moodrow's information would give him an outlet for his excess energy and he started to call to his partner when the bathroom door opened and a woman walked out. She was nude and only partially dry and she didn't notice Tilley at the end of the hall. In an instant, he understood the pleasures of the voyeur. Despite the sense of himself as a peeping Tom (and despite his feelings about Rose) he experienced that sudden flush in the crotch which precludes taking any steps to turn the situation off.

She was short and heavy-set, though not actually fat, with strong, heavy thighs, a thick triangle of jet-black pubic hair and large, sloping breasts. That his attention did not, at first, go to her face and her features indicates, perhaps, a lack of social consciousness. That he spent almost a full minute trying to see the top of her pussy through that black forest, convicts him of the charge. She was young, no more than twenty-five, and for the life of him, he couldn't see how Moodrow managed to get her into his apartment. He even considered the possibility that she was some sort of relative, in which case he was going to look awful bad if Moodrow came out and found him staring at her. Nevertheless, he was too fascinated (and too excited) to step away. He did, however, finally manage to raise his eyes far enough to get a good look at her features. It was the waitress from the Lip Cafe. Her inky hair and the wet platinum spikes, which now lay flat against the sides of her head, left no doubt.

"Jesus Christ," Tilley said involuntarily.

She drew a quick breath, then recognized him. Letting the towel casually fall to cover her body, she stared at him without blinking. "You see anything you like?"

"I saw everything I like," he answered truthfully.

"Everything?" She cocked an eyebrow, turned her back and began to walk toward the bedroom. "Moodrow'll be back in a few minutes." Her large, round ass rose and fell with each step. Tilley could almost feel its warmth on his fingertips. At the doorway, she turned back to him and giggled. "I love guns," she said. "I love them. How come your partner has so many guns?"

Before Tilley could move, she was inside and he heard the door close, firmly. He wandered into the kitchen to make himself a cup of coffee. On the table, on a large piece of white oaktag paper, was a detailed floor plan of the Lexington Avenue armory. And a note which read: "Out bagel hunting. Be back in fifteen minutes. Say hello to Gretchen."

Ten seconds later he was lost in the floorplan. The Lexington Avenue armory, now used entirely as a men's emergency shelter, is really one large (4,000 + square feet) room, holding six hundred beds on its concrete floor with small areas on each side of the building partitioned off for special use. Moodrow's drawing indicated a large security force in a twenty-foot, north-south corridor by the main entrance. On the south, a stairway led to a second floor of offices, the headquarters for Social Services. On the north was a dayroom, separated from the sleeping area by a wall, with a dozen long tables and benches. In the back, on the western wall, were the toilets, showers and sinks. The center, the heart of the building, was the real home for the homeless. A concrete-floored room with a curved, black ceiling hanging forty feet above. It held an ocean of beds with six security desks scattered against the outer walls.

"So what's ya name?"

She came upon him so suddenly, he answered without thinking: "Tilley." Not Detective Tilley, or Jim Tilley. He had never, to his knowledge, identified himself with his last name before.

"I'm Gretchen," she said, extending a hand. Her spikes, he noticed, now stood straight and sparkled with glitter. "Pleased to meet you."

He took her hand and shook it, then asked, as casually as he could manage, "Have you known Moodrow long?" Moodrow never talked about himself. Tilley didn't know, for instance, if Moodrow had any family in the neighborhood or what he did with his time off.

"Everybody knows Moodrow," she replied, somewhat ambiguously. "He's like Mr. Purple. You know that guy who used to get horseshit from the park and bring it to his garden? Then they took down his garden and built a building." She peered intently into Tilley's eyes. "Mr. Purple. You know who I'm talking about?"

"I don't think so. I haven't been on the Lower East Side long. Anyway, that's not what I meant about Moodrow."

"So what'd you mean?"

Tilley looked at her for a moment. There was a nasty edge to her voice, despite a naive midwestern twang. He thought of Rose and the comparison had him instantly annoyed. "What are you gonna do, Gretchen, bust my balls? This ain't the right time."

She gave him a "who cares" shrug and turned away. "If you wanted to know how long I've been fucking him, you should have asked me."

Two minutes later, she and her attitude were both gone. Five minutes later, Moodrow walked in. He was whistling.

"Hey, Jimmy. How's Rose feeling today?"

"She's all right. You don't seem too concerned, though."

"That's because I called St. Vincent's about an hour ago. I talked to the cop in charge of her security. He says she's okay. He's seen much worse."

"Well, I just wanna know if it hurt."

"What hurt?" Moodrow's perplexed look pleased his partner immensely.

"When you played that game with your .38."

He sat in the chair and giggled. "Yeah, it hurt."

"How come you're so sure?"

"Cause we took turns. You want a bagel?"

Tilley was hungrier than he thought and went through two hot onion bagels, spread with lox and cream cheese, while Moodrow outlined the campaign.

"You checked out this floorplan?" He swept his hand across the oaktag, scattering bagel crumbs and specks of dried onion on the floor. Tilley nodded, mouth full, and Moodrow went on. "The only thing you don't know is that the area under the officers on the second floor is for storage. Blankets, linen, mattresses, tables, chairs. My understanding is that the area's big enough to hide in, but crammed full of supplies.

"This front desk, here, is where security operates. What they try to do is control the situation by keeping out weapons and people who don't belong. They do maintain a presence inside the big room, but they try to keep out of the way of the ... fuck, I don't know what to call them. My man says they're all criminals, but he can't treat them like criminals. He only intervenes in cases of violence. As far as drugs and sex goes, he don't wanna know about it. His name's Spender Crawford and he spent eight out of the last eleven years in the joint. He stays at an SRO hotel in Brownsville that he says makes the shelters look like nursery school.

"Anyways, whether security's on the take or not, all the drugs and sometimes sex are done in the back, by the toilets and showers, and security don't go in there. Deliberately don't go in there so's the ..." He stopped for a second time, then chose the word ordinarily used to describe the mass of humans caged in a prison. "So the 'population' can have a place to get off. The day room, on the north wall, is used for meals and card games, a place for the men to hang out before they go to sleep."

Moodrow went on for a few moments, describing details of the day room and the social services floor, and it struck Tilley, his mouth stuffed with food, that Moodrow was proceeding as if Tilley's cooperation was understood. This was the plan—Stanley Moodrow's plan—and Tilley was the hired gun who'd carry it out. Then Jim Tilley realized he didn't give a shit about Moodrow's presumptions and, impatient, interrupted him. "Can it be done?" he asked.

"Anything can be done," he said, evenly.

"By who?"

Moodrow looked shocked, but Tilley only smiled and stuffed even more of the bagel into his face. He said, "Tell me the meat of it. Tell me *how* it can be done." It came out sounding like a fart underwater. Tilley actually sprayed him with bits of cream cheese, but Moodrow, who knew exactly what he wanted, went on eagerly.

"Jimmy, it's gonna be so fucking simple, you're not gonna believe it. You're gonna wish it was harder. You remember what I said about security? Mostly all their force is up front, by the main entrance. That's because all the other doors, except for the fire doors, are locked. There's a security guard assigned to the fire doors in the day room, but there's no security on the western end, by the showers and toilets. Still, the population almost never fucks with those doors because they set off an alarm when you open them and that pisses off security enough so they put a man by the showers for two or three days. Which is bad for business, right?

"So what're we talking about? A corridor, maybe twenty feet wide, with toilets, showers and sinks running from one end of the building to the other. This is where Pinky Mitchell works. He's there every night, selling ten dollar bags of junk for which he pays nine dollars. And right down in this corner, by the showers, is a fire door that leads to an alleyway running along the western edge of the armory. You're gonna go inside around six. Fake it so they give you a bed, which shouldn't be hard because it's summer and there's always extra beds in the summer. Ten o'clock, I'll be out in that alleyway. You take little Pinky Mitchell and push him through the door. The junkie weighs maybe a hundred twenty pounds and on top of that I got it from Spender that the corner by that fire door is very quiet. Very secluded. The reason being that anyone stupid enough to wander that far away from the population is subject to being raped by aggressive bisexuals who like to hurt as much as they like to fuck."

"Sounds like jail," Tilley said. "Sounds like prison."

Moodrow stopped for a moment. He went to the stove and put up water for coffee. "Well, they got metal detectors at the front entrance. That ain't to keep out the pacifists."

"What if Mitchell don't show?"

"Once you're registered, you can come and go as you please. There's a coffee shop on 28th and Lex. If it's a no-go, come up there and meet me. I'll hang around until a quarter of ten. Even if you think it's a go and it don't work out, I'll come back at eleven. After that, it's lights out. Now I got a mug shot of Pinky Mitchell and a walking description. Study it good. You go in at six."

25

Moodrow dropped Tilley at 32nd and Park, leaving him to walk the six blocks to the armory. Tilley was wearing a gray, gymrat t-shirt, dirty khaki trousers, Adidas sneakers and a lightweight, olive-green fatigue jacket. His hair was mussed and he hadn't shaved, but they'd made no real attempt to create a disguise. He didn't, for instance, look desperate or crazy or stoned, because *everyone* is entitled to a bed. Nobody can be turned away unless their behavior is violent or psychotic, and even then only by calling in the cops. If Tilley could walk up to the doors, he would get a place to sleep, even if the armory was full and they had to ship him by van to another shelter.

The rain had slackened into a warm mist that settled on his shoulders like tepid soup as he walked slowly down Park Avenue South. There were officially homeless people on every block, though virtually all of them in this part of Manhattan had places to sleep. There are a dozen welfare hotels within walking distance of the armory, The Prince George and the Martinique being the most famous and the largest. In hot weather, naturally, the residents come outside to look for relief, just like poor people everywhere. But there are no parks here, no benches or trees to sit under. This is the heart of Manhattan, a mainly commercial district that includes both the Empire State Building and the million dollar brownstones east of Lexington Avenue. Out here, the action is on the streets. If you don't believe it, just ask the army of prostitutes who will invade these streets about ten o'clock.

No surprise, then, that knots of people, attached to the outer walls of the armory like barnacles on the bottom of a ship, crowded the sidewalks. They would not give way and longtime residents of the neighborhood were forced to walk around them. In one case, a group of men passing a quart bottle of something wrapped in a brown paper bag were at that stage of intoxication where loud voices and waving arms are taken for granted. As they told their stories, gesticulating wildly, the men and women who rented or owned the wildly expensive brownstones on the other side of Lex, had to step across pools of water by the curb to get to their homes.

None of this bothered Tilley, of course. He had good reason to be there and, according to Moodrow, should not interact with the other men in the shelter. Moodrow had instructed his partner to "play it close to your chest" and "keep your head down until the moment comes, then take him out fast." Unfortunately, he hadn't provided Tilley with a contingency plan. In case he was put in a position where he *had* to "interact."

Tilley was on 26th Street, walking from Park toward Lex and the only entrance to the armory, when a tall white man, about forty, sporting tattooed twin dragons on his bare arms and a string of gold earrings that ran to the top of his ear, greeted him with a loud whistle. He was standing with a small circle of men, casually passing a joint, and his companions all laughed appreciatively.

"Hey, sweetie," he shouted at Tilley's back. "You wanna be my honey tonight? Hey, sweetie, I axed, 'Do you wanna be my honey tonight?' Don't be stuck up. I'll use my Brylcream so it won't hurt but a little bit."

Tilley kept walking, mortified beyond belief, but still walking. He had never been in jail, because when he was fourteen, his amateur coach, Joe Johnson, told him that if he fucked up, he, the coach, would walk away. Before that, despite good grades, he ran with the craziest kids in the neighborhood. Yorkville may not be Harlem, but if your playground is *anywhere* in Manhattan, the lure of the street comes with the territory. The alternative, taken by many parents, is to keep the kids confined to apartments and play groups until they reach high school.

So Tilley stayed out of jail, but he did learn the lessons of jail from friends who went the wrong way, one of which is how to react when another man calls you a punk. Tilley's first emotion was one of wounded vanity. How dare anyone challenge Superman? Couldn't they see what they were dealing with? As he continued down the sidewalk, he suddenly became aware of the eyes staring at him. He felt as if every one of those desperate faces, especially the dark ones, was singling him out for attack, even the droolers and the mumblers, who huddled in doorways across the street.

What he was feeling was (and is) the paranoia of the middle and upper-class residents of Murray Hill and Kips Bay, the neighborhoods closest to the shelter. Tilley didn't understand the process at the time, but, just as the residents do, he quickly replaced his fear with anger. And realized, just as quickly, that even though he felt like one of *us*, he would surely have to become one of *them* if he had any hope of completing his job in the shelter.

At the front of the armory, the large, wooden doors, complete with metal detectors, were wide open and led directly to the front security desk. There were two blue-uniformed rent-a-cops, both black, standing behind the desk. One wore a nametag bearing the name Crawford, the other, the name Foster. Crawford, who sported sergeant's stripes on his sleeve, was the heavier of the two, with a flat, square face and large features. He stared directly into Tilley's eyes until their gazes locked, telling the cop, without words, that he was Moodrow's connection inside the shelter. The other man, Foster, was thinner, especially his face, which was nearly gaunt. A long, raised scar, a bottle scar, ran along the side of his throat, from his chin to his right ear.

"What you want, homeboy?" Foster asked, grinning up at Crawford.

Tilley lowered his gaze, as instructed, and replied, "I need a bed. Someone told me I could get a bed here."

"Well, you in the wrong place, homeboy. The Waldorf-Astoria is uptown." Foster's own wit so amused him, he nearly fell out of his chair.

"I don't have no money for a hotel." Tilley played it straight. Homeless and hopeless. "I don't have no money at all."

"What you say?" Foster's voice rose into a squeal, matching the movement of his eyebrows toward the ceiling. "No money? I heard all you whiteboys is rich. How come . . ."

His monologue was interrupted by the weight of Crawford's hand on his shoulder. "That's enough, Alley. Best let it slide."

Foster looked up in disbelief. "Shit, Sarge," he said, "I'm jus' playin' with the boy. What's your problem with that?"

"Listen, asshole," Crawford said, his grip tightening on his subordinate's shoulder, "how do you know who this whiteboy is? How do you know he ain't from some TV station? How do you know the motherfucker ain't wearin' a tape recorder right this minute? You send this man up to the social worker and stay the fuck off his case. Hear me?"

Reluctantly, Foster pointed to a stairway on the southern end of the building. "See the social worker upstairs," he said. "Her name is Ms. Winters. When you get signed in, she'll give you a paper. Bring it back down and I'll put you in a bed. That suit you, whiteboy?"

"Thank you," Tilley mumbled, turning away.

"The pleasure was all mine." Foster threw one last shot as Tilley disappeared up the stairs in search of Ms. Winters. Moodrow and he had prepared a long story, a "past" in a Detroit factory with closed plants and a trip to New York in search of a job. Their scenario had Tilley staying with friends initially, then tossed out when no job was forthcoming. Lacking the money to get back into the housing market, he was, by all standards, homeless.

But Ms. Winters hadn't the slightest interest in Tilley's history. She asked him if he had ID and when he started to explain that his wallet had been stolen at the Port Authority Bus Terminal, she waved him off. "No ID?" she asked. "Fine, no ID. No address? Fine, no address. No social security number? Fine. You're makin' my life easier." She looked up and smiled, "We don't worry about people using these facilities illegally. Anybody with an apartment who comes here to sleep is crazy enough to rate a hospital bed. By definition."

She handed him a slip of paper, instructing him to return it to the security desk. "If you're still here three days from now, you'll be called back for a formal interview. We serve three meals per day: at eight, twelve and five. That's it, enjoy the facilities."

Foster's mood had turned around when Tilley confronted him again at the front desk. Except for the two of them, the security corridor was empty. "Say, homeboy," he whispered. "Ms. Winters give you some? She clean your pipes? Shit, you finished too fast. Come that fast, y'all won't get invited back up." He began to laugh loudly, perhaps at Tilley's puzzled face. Ms. Winters was tall, fat and fifty years old. She was also warm and friendly. Was his embarrassment the whole point? He could feel his blood starting to rise and he looked at the security guard more closely. He was taller than Tilley by three inches or so, but thin, so that Tilley estimated their weights as pretty near the same. Perhaps he would fake him with a shoulder, then commit to the left hook. Maybe he'd drive a round-house kick into Foster's lower ribs. That'd wake him up in a hurry.

Somehow, Foster caught the change in Tilley's attitude and began to look him over more closely. Tilley could almost hear the gears turning. Finally, Foster reached across the desk and gave Tilley's hand a little slap. "Hey, man, don't take it the wrong way. I'm just playin' with ya. You know what I'm sayin'? We really in the same boat. Got ta keep our spirits up, right? Check it out. I'm givin' you bed number 255. That's a special lucky number. It's right near the security desk which means nobody gon' bother yo raggedy ass."

Having gotten the last word, he pointed toward a door in the back wall of the corridor. Tilley walked to it, pulled it toward him and stepped into his new home. The humidity hit him first. It was nearly seven o'clock and the temperature outside was eighty degrees. The day's rain, light as it had been, seemed to be oozing from the concrete floors and he instinctively flinched as he felt the droplets of sweat collecting in his hair and under his arms. Then he saw the room for the first time. It was enormous, not as long as a football field, but much wider, like four basketball courts arranged in a square, and contained row after row of beds, each with its starched, scratchy sheet and gray blanket.

He must have stood there for several moments, the door held open, too intimidated by the immensity to enter. Then he heard Foster's voice behind him: "What's the matter, homeboy. Y'all don't care for our facilities?" He pronounced the last word syllable by syllable: "fa-ci-li-teeeeees."

Bed number 255, as promised, was in the last row by the southern wall, next to the security desk. The guard, whose nametag read Diaz, looked Tilley over, then nodded. "What's happenin', man. You feelin' okay?" He was short and very broad, with small, serious features. Tilley's first reaction, that Diaz was being kind, was quickly replaced by the realization that the guard had a reason for probing. He was puzzled over what Tilley was doing inside this sweaty room when he could be outside where it was more comfortable. Diaz, himself, was sweating profusely.

"I'm fine," Tilley said. "I'm trying to get the feel of this place. I've never been in a place like this before."

"Well, you can stay wherever you want. I'm jus' tryin' to see if ya feelin' all right." He turned back to his book, indifferent.

Tilley sat at the edge of the bed, a cot really, and noted the number on a small metal tag riveted to the iron headrail. Bed number 255. Now he had a home, a space that was his space alone, which did not belong, by right, to everyone on the street. He looked around, automatically sizing up the "population." There weren't many people in the room, maybe thirty or forty. They were scattered and anything but threatening. These were the mumblers, the droolers, the screamers, the drunks. Too far gone to notice the weather or too tired from staying awake all night, from being chased from doorway to doorway, always looking for a space where they wouldn't be asked to move on, or attacked for sport by sadists masquerading as children.

It was not a place for the mentally alert, however, which is why Tilley stood out and why Diaz had questioned him. Tilley's bed being only fifteen feet from his body, the guard had surely felt that it would pay him to find out how crazy Tilley was. If, for instance, he might suddenly become violent. Once reassured, though, Diaz's book became far more interesting than Tilley's existence.

So Tilley got off the bed and took a little tour. He went, first, into the showers and toilet area. There were no towels or soap in sight, but rolls of toilet paper hung from a chain which was padlocked to the wall on either end. A bearded man, soiled clothes hanging on a shiny, metal hook, showered in the nearest stall. Another man shaved at a sink. From the far stall, at the southern end of the building next to a fire door topped with a red light, Tilley could hear the grunting, slapping sounds of humans in lust. A sign on the fire door, which someone had underlined with a magic marker, announced: FIRE EXIT. FOR EMERGENCY USE ONLY. CAUTION. UNAUTHORIZED USE WILL SOUND AN ALARM. A smaller, handmade sign hung below: If You Get Caught Using This Door, You Will Be EXPELLED From This Shelter. Moodrow was right. If Pinky Mitchell was anything like the burnt-out junkie he was supposed to be, the whole thing would be easier than a stroll down Fifth Avenue.

Tilley left the shower room and continued to reconnoiter. He peeked into the day room, found a small group of men playing poker with matchsticks and another security guard, a bearded Sikh, surprisingly enough, bearing the nametag Singh.

Five more minutes in the armory and he had seen everything but Pinky Mitchell, so he decided to leave and circle the building. Perhaps Mr. Mitchell was outside, with his clientele. Crawford had told Moodrow that Mitchell's usual pattern was to wait until 9:30, when everyone came inside, before setting up in the shower room, but it wouldn't hurt to check. Then too, it was only 7:30 and Tilley couldn't stand the idea of waiting in that steambath for two more hours. He'd come early, to make sure he got a bed, but that didn't mean he had to lie in it until it turned into a salt lick.

It was still overcast outside, still oppressively humid, but the evening seemed positively balmy compared to the fog inside the main body of the armory. Tilley walked south on Lex to 25th Street, then turned west to circle the block. There were a lot more people out now, gathering for the night's bed. A fair number

were "media" homeless, elderly derelicts pushing grocery carts stuffed with a life's possessions, but the majority, by far, were young, in their twenties or early
thirties, and they were just as obviously stoned: on
crack or dope or juice. What difference did it make?

A few of the spectre-thin, hollow-eyed junkies were
sick and some of the drunks were asleep. Most of the
"population," however, was quietly waiting for the call
to go inside. In this heat, they would stay out until
security was ready to lock the doors, or until the cops
came by and moved them on. As Tilley walked slowly
down the block (as befits a man taking a stroll alongside his own home), he searched each face for the
quarry, Pinky Mitchell. Nobody greeted him, but nobody seemed anxious to harm him, either. They were
just looking for a place to sleep, maybe a meal, before
they took off in the morning to pursue whatever pleasure or pain the streets had to offer.

The cliché about prison is that ninety-nine percent
of the convicts just want to do their time and get out,
but the other one percent are so utterly, viciously
crazy, they keep the joint in constant turmoil. This is
because, sooner or later, every convict will come into
contact with the crazy one percent. For Tilley, circling
the building while staring into every face, that principle was raised to the level of self-fulfilling prophecy.
He met his one percenter on 26th Street, standing in
the same place, surrounded by his boys. But this time
he wasn't after Tilley's ass.

"I want them sneakers," he said as Tilley came
abreast of him. "Gimme them sneakers."

The sneakers in question were well-worn Adidas
basketball shoes. The theft here was to be purely sym-
bolic, the humiliation part of the ritual of dominance.

"Boy, you must be hard of hearin'. I said I want ya
sneakers." He pitched his voice high, in homage to his
mostly black audience. He was taller than Tilley, but
slender. And stupid.

Tilley stopped about eight feet away, but kept his eyes off the man's face. The asshole was leaning against the wall of the armory, standing on one leg with the other drawn up against the brick. Very tough. Very bold. But with all his weight against that wall, there was only one way he could move, if he had time to move at all, and that was right at Tilley.

But he wouldn't do that. Tilley's guess, as he took the first step toward the man, was that he was too stupid even to consider that Tilley might fight back. In his surprise, he'd probably try to move backwards, into the wall, and thus become a frozen target.

Maybe Tilley had been Nostradamus in another lifetime, because that's exactly the way it went down. As Tilley took the man's throat in his left hand, the only thing that moved were the man's eyes, which opened wide and gleamed with sudden understanding, but just for the second or so it took Tilley to drive four straight right hands into his face. The slap of his knuckles against the left side of that face and the echoing chunk of the man's skull against the brick were among the most satisfying sounds Tilley had ever heard. Pure, sweet music.

But Tilley didn't stop to admire his work. He stepped away immediately, turning to see how many friends the man had, but the "bros" had moved back, not closer. A short, black man smiled and put up a hand, palm out. "Easy, brother," he said. Then repeated it. "Easy, brother."

"Anybody else want my shoes?" Tilley looked each man full in the face until, one by one, they made the ritual denial by breaking eye contact. Then he turned to check the sneaker thief. The man was sitting on the sidewalk, holding his face in his hands, moaning softly. Tilley squatted beside him and said it plainly: "Don't sleep here tonight. Walk over to the emergency at Bellevue. Spend the night." He hesitated, but got only a groan for an answer.

"Why don't you take off right now?" Tilley had a job to do and he didn't need to be watching his back. He had no illusions about the metal detectors actually keeping weapons out of the shelter. If necessary, he would beat this man until he took the trip to Bellevue by ambulance and the man sensed it. Without looking at Tilley, his hands still cupped over his eye, he struggled to his feet and walked east, toward the hospital.

"The man is nothing but a lowlife fool." A tall bearded man, his accent unmistakably southern, passed Tilley a lit joint, which he accepted, though he didn't draw the smoke into his lungs. Tilley didn't have anything against good weed, but he was already stoned out of his mind. The adrenaline had begun to flow the minute he left Moodrow and the safety of the Plymouth. Now it was gushing.

The rest of the men were as friendly as the southerner and Tilley stayed close to this knot. He let them anoint him as one of their own as they bullshitted about life on the street. About a mission on East 45th Street where the food was deteriorating. Another in the West Village, just opening up. Tilley was questioned, but when his short answers made it clear that he wasn't ready to part with his life's story, they let him alone.

Finally, as Tilley was almost certain it would, the talk turned to drugs. They had broken into smaller groups and Tilley was standing with two men, passing a bottle of wine, when the smaller of the two, Smitty, said, "The vultures be here soon. Uh-huh. Vultures comin'. I can smell 'em." He actually turned his nose into the wind and sniffed. "Uh-huh. Smell 'em."

"What the fuck is he talking about?" Tilley asked the other man, Angel Lopez, a Mexican from Los Angeles.

"He's talkin' about the dealers, man. Now it's almost time to go inside, they come around and set up."

"What kinda drugs?"

"There they be." Smitty gestured with his chin at the three blacks walking on the opposite side of the street. "Uh-huh. Them's the crack boys. Sell crack inside. Bad people. Uh-huh. Vulture people."

Tilley leaned over and whispered into Angel's ear. "Any smack, man? Anybody doin' smack inside?"

"I knew that shit, man. I jus' know you dig dope, man." Angel laughed, delighted with his prediction.

"I ain't no junkie," Tilley protested, "but sometimes it helps take the pain away. Check it out."

"Thass chill, man." The Mexican had a round, chubby face and when he smiled, which he did often, he looked like an animated Cabbage Patch doll. "I'm jus' fooling with you, man. So happens the Lexington shelter got the best dope of any shelter in the city. Little Pinky, man, dealin' Blue Thunder so pure it'll rush you for ten minutes, man. Thass if you boot it. You got works, man?"

The "works" he referred to was the one-piece, disposable syringe addicts used to inject their dope. The plural was a carryover from when junkies used an eyedropper and a disposable needle, fastened together with the edge of a dollar bill for a collar. "Booting" was a technique used by junkies to prolong the initial rush. That rush being the only reason for injecting the drug in the first place. Instead of shooting the whole hit at once, the addict allowed the blood to come back up into the syringe, then pushed it back into the arm, then allowed it to come up again.

"No, man. I was afraid to carry them in there. I didn't know if they'd search me or something."

"Don't worry," he answered, "you can share mine."

Tilley nodded, agreeable, just as if sharing needles in the age of AIDS wasn't equal to walking blindfolded along the edge of the World Trade Center's roof, and they talked for maybe another ten minutes. Until Angel spotted a familiar face walking toward Lexington Avenue.

As advertised, Pinky Mitchell was frail and unsteady, a gray ghost of a junkie in a dirty suede jacket and greasy jeans. Nobody spoke to him as he made his way down the block, though heads jerked up like fans doing the wave at a football game. The look in the eyes of the junkies was intensely greedy, a zombie's imitation of lust.

"Uh-huh," Smitty said, "Las' vulture settlin' down. Come to his perch. Uh-huh."

Angel laughed. "Look at that motherfucker strut. Now that Pinky got the bad dope, he thinkin' he's the king of the shelter."

"I don't see how he keeps it," Tilley said. "Little faggot like that. I'm surprised someone don't take it off him."

"He's in with the security," Angel responded evenly. "They hold most of his shit for him. He probly don't have nothin' on him now."

"Uh-huh," Smitty agreed. "Thass why the boy don't do nothin' on the block. Everything inside where the security protects his ass. Uh-huh. Pinky spend all day boostin' from the stores. Uh-huh. From the black mall on Sixth Avenue. Thass the boy's main income. Uh-huh."

Moodrow's information had Pinky Mitchell paying nine dollars for a bag of dope that sold for ten, which didn't leave much room for security's piece of the action. More than likely, there were two things that kept Pinky Mitchell's ass safe: he never kept more than a few bags on his person and his clientele's understanding that if they took him off, they would lose the connection forever; a junkie's worst nightmare.

It was 9:15 by then and Smitty announced that it was time to begin drifting toward home. Fifteen minutes later, the big room, temperature raised to roasting by the addition of six hundred bodies, was full. Pinky Mitchell had set up, on schedule, in the shower room, dealing bags of dope to the tune of flushing toilets.

There was nothing to do, but wait and hope that Mitchell didn't decide to leave.

Angel Lopez was sitting on the end of Tilley's cot, shouting something Tilley couldn't really hear. The noise level inside that room was unbearable, like standing in front of a practicing rock band. Every kind of music, from Lite FM to the hottest salsa, blared from portable radios scattered throughout the room. Alcoholics, locked in sleep, snored heavily while mumblers stood on their beds, ignoring the pleas of the security guards, and shouted their paranoid complaints to whatever demons haunted their nights.

Add to this the cheers and curses of the regular evening craps game and the hundreds of cot-to-cot conversations and you have some idea of the insanity in that room. There were four fights in the next half hour. They were the only relief from the noise and the heat. Two were unprovoked hitter attacks on mumblers. Two were attacks by victims on criminals after their property. All were broken up by security before Tilley could get over to check them out.

At 10:10, he went into the shower area and found Pinky Mitchell swaying on stoned, rubber legs. He was just to the south of the center of the building, along with a half dozen fellow dopers, about fifty feet from the fire door. The coke dealers were on the north side of the building, gathered about the magic powder. They were considerably more vigorous than either Pinky Mitchell and his junkie pals or the circle of juicers who guzzled wine against the north wall.

In the end, the timing was perfect. Tilley stood in the shower room, close to the circle of junkies, trying to look like a doper with no money, while he watched the action. Pinky was doing bang-up business and thoroughly enjoying the attention. Each time a customer approached him, he solemnly dipped his left hand into his shirt pocket, extended his closed fist, then accepted payment with his right hand.

The situation defied belief, even by a cop who's supposed to know better. The drugs were right out in the open and there was an overwhelming sense that this last bit of pleasure must not be taken away. Thus the swaying junkies, voices slurred; the cocaine freaks chattering away like teenagers on the telephone; the drunks, loud and threatening; the mumblers and droolers; the paranoids and the depressed who sat with their heads in their hands, unmoving, for hours at a time. The whole shelter reeked of hopelessness.

There was a clock on the wall over the sink, with a sweep second hand. Tilley actually watched it, willing himself to remain in place until it stood perfectly upright. Then he took two steps toward Pinky Mitchell and grabbed the junkie's shirt with his left hand, pulling him close.

"Evening, Pinky," he said, reaching into Mitchell's pocket for the small bags of dope. "You're a bad boy, Pinky, but I'm your guardian angel. I've come to save you from a life of sin. See, you shouldn't use this shit. It's bad for ya." He flipped the bags over his shoulder, back toward the contingent of junkies.

The room remained frozen for a moment, stunned by the unexpected violence. Then the boys began to dive, like kids after coins in the Bay of Naples, for the junk on the floor. Pinky struggled feebly, too stoned and too small to do anything, but protest: "What're you doin'? Tell me what are you doin'?"

"I'm taking my dog for a walk," Tilley replied, dragging Mitchell across the room. Nobody tried to interfere, though the dope vanished long before they got to the door. Pinky made one last attempt to pull away just as they reached the fire exit. He managed to twist his body so he was facing his former pals. Tilley shook him like a terrier shakes a rat. "Say g'night to the people, Pinky."

Moodrow was waiting on the other side of the door. He pulled it tight as soon as the two men came through it, then grabbed Mitchell's free arm. Together, they picked him off the ground and hustled him over to the parked Plymouth.

"Any trouble?" Moodrow asked, ducking down to get into the backseat alongside Mitchell.

"Piece of cake, Stanley. Piece of cake."

26

The first thing Pinky Mitchell did, upon finding himself imprisoned in the backseat of an NYPD Plymouth, was vomit all over Stanley Moodrow's shoes. Heroin junkies are prone to vomit anyway, the drug basically being a poison and the amount used as close to a lethal dose as the junkie dares get. Many junkies, when they first begin to use heroin, vomit regularly, fifteen or twenty times whenever they shoot up. Rumor has it they find this experience pleasurable. It certainly doesn't discourage up-and-coming heroin addicts and the nausea gradually subsides as the addiction grows; subsides, but never disappears.

Moodrow knew all about this tendency, of course, so he *should* have made allowances. That's probably why he didn't kill Pinky Mitchell on the spot. True, his small, black eyes grew into saucers and his mouth twitched, but he held himself in check. Tilley, behind the wheel, pressed the Max-Air button and tried not to laugh.

"Sorry, man," Pinky Mitchell said, watching Moodrow clean his own shoes with a handkerchief. "Like I couldn't help it, man. I just hada do it." He leaned back against the seat, unconcerned, and allowed his left wrist to be cuffed to Moodrow's right. Heroin, as a drug, seems to wipe out even the possibility of anxiety and Pinky Mitchell was very, very stoned.

"You know who I am?" Moodrow demanded. He was obviously pissed, but Mitchell didn't pick it up.

"Cop," Pinky said flatly.

"Right. Cop. Then what?"

Mitchell shrugged. He looked like he was about to nod out. "You bustin' me?" he managed to ask.

"Nah," Moodrow said as Tilley turned off Third Avenue onto 10th Street, half a block from Moodrow's basement apartment. "You wouldn't wanna get busted. If you got busted, you'd have to kick in your cell or go in the hospital. You don't wanna kick, do you?"

"Fuck no, man, I really don't. I wanna go back in the shelter. I gotta sleep, man." He shut up then, twisting away from Moodrow to stare out the window. Both cops thought he was out of it, but Pinky turned back a few seconds later. "How come that guy threw all the dope away?" He jerked his chin forward to indicate Tilley.

"He do that?" Moodrow asked.

"Yeah, he threw it all away, man. All the evidence. So what I can't figure, man, is what you guys are arrestin' me *for*. Ya know what I mean, man? Like what *for?*"

"But I already told you, Pinky. We're not arresting you."

He thought about that, letting his head drop to his chest for a moment before he continued. "So where are you taking me, man? What the fuck do you want?"

When he said that last bit about "what the fuck," Tilley expected Moodrow to smack him, but Moodrow was as calm as could be, despite the acrid stench of vomit permeating the car's interior. "We're going someplace we can talk private," he explained.

It was the perfect moment to pull into the curb, for Moodrow to open the door, for Pinky Mitchell to be dragged down the steps into Moodrow's lair. Unfortunately, there were no parking spaces, not even illegal parking spaces. It was after ten and all restrictions had been lifted. Only the fire hydrants were open, but the hydrants are a no-no, even for a cop.

So they circled the block. Slowly. Mitchell's chin remained on his chest. He appeared to be asleep, but he was actually in that stoned out, zombie state which is at the core of the drug's appeal. Moodrow looked almost as sleepy and as unconcerned with the future as his captive, but when they came around in front of the building again, he curtly ordered his partner to double-park.

"How long we gonna be here?" Tilley asked.

"I don't know. Depends on how talkative he is." He looked puzzled.

"What about the guys we're blocking in?"

"Fuck 'em," Moodrow said, then reconsidered. "If one of them needs his car, I guess we're gonna end up with four flat tires. There's nothing we can do about it. We could circle the fucking block for the next six hours and still not get a space."

That last had the ring of truth to it. Tilley stopped right by the front door and Moodrow dragged an unresisting Pinky Mitchell out of the car. "Do me a favor," he tossed back over his shoulder, "leave one of the windows open. The car stinks."

Inside, Moodrow wasted no time on preliminaries. He uncuffed his own wrist, then recuffed Mitchell's wrists and his ankles around a vertical water pipe in the bathroom. The pipe was made of thick cast iron, it came up through the floor and ran to the apartment above them.

"Why're ya doin' this, man?" Pinky asked. There was just a touch of fear in his voice, as if the reality of his situation was finally cutting through the dope.

Moodrow looked at Tilley questioningly, then closed the bathroom door on Pinky Mitchell and walked his partner across the room. "What's this about you threw away the evidence?" Moodrow grinned. "Now we can't even threaten him with arrest."

"I had to create a diversion."

"Did it work?"

"They went nuts, Stanley. All these junkies beating on each other in slow motion. Very ugly, but nobody lifted a finger to help Pinky."

He shrugged. "Big surprise, right? But I never expected to use arrest as a threat. I got something better, even if it's a little slower. Let's go talk to him."

Tilley stopped him with a hand. "You're gonna leave him 'till he gets sick, right?"

"It's a guaranteed strategy. You know that."

"You gonna gag him? Because if you gag him, he's gonna vomit right into the gag. And if he does that, there's an excellent chance he'll suck some of that shit back in his lungs and die. Before he tells us what we need to know. Unless you wanna stay here all night and make sure he doesn't scream for help."

"Nobody's gonna hear him and it ain't gonna take all fucking night." Moodrow gestured to the small basement windows and Tilley saw, for the first time, that they were boarded up and covered with blankets. The place was a tomb. "The old man upstairs can't hear and he wouldn't give a shit if he could."

They marched back across the room and Tilley opened the bathroom door. Moodrow said, "Pinky, could we speak to you for a few minutes?"

Mitchell was sitting on the closed toilet, his arms and legs extended out to the pipe. He was leaning forward with his cheek resting against the wall; he seemed very comfortable. "Okay," he said.

"What we need to know is how you happened to get that dope. That's what we can't figure out."

Pinky raised his head, sniffing trouble in the wind. "Whatta ya mean, man? There's dope everywhere, man. The whole fuckin' Lower East Side is dope."

"I mean Blue Thunder," Moodrow explained patiently. "How'd you happen to get Blue Thunder?"

For the first time, Pinky Mitchell's eyes opened fully. "Eldridge Street, man. That's where that shit comes from. Blue Thunder, man. Like from Eldridge Street."

"It don't wash, Pinky. There's no smack on Eldridge Street this week." Moodrow waited until the message sank down through the heroin swamp and rooted itself in Mitchell's brain. "I spoke to a friend of mine. An Italian man. He promised me there wouldn't be no fucking dope on Eldridge Street. In fact, he told me the only dope would be the asshole who turned up dealing what Levander Greenwood stole from him. This Italian guy is really mad, Pinky. He made me promise I'd tell him who it was if I found out."

It was a nice speech, but Mitchell didn't respond. As predicted, he could not be moved by threats of violence, especially future violence. The best they could do was wake him up enough so he'd remember what they were after.

"We want you to tell us where you got it, Pinky," Moodrow persisted.

"Eldridge Street," he insisted. "That's where that shit comes from, man. Besides, like I ain't got nothin'. He threw it all away."

"Actually," Moodrow responded quickly, "he didn't throw away *all* of it. I got some right here." He took out eight tiny envelopes and waved them in front of Pinky Mitchell's face. They bore the inscription Red Dragon instead of Blue Thunder and Mitchell, though his eyes shone with desire, wasn't blind to the fact.

"That ain't Blue Thunder, man. That's Red Dragon."

Moodrow looked perplexed for a minute, then his face brightened. "You're too fucking smart for me, Pinky. It isn't Blue Thunder. But it's good dope. I mean at least I hear it's good. I don't use smack myself."

Mitchell considered Moodrow's statement, then nodded his head. "Yeah, man, you're right. It's okay dope."

"Great, Pinky. That's great. I'm just gonna leave it here on the sink so you can remember how good it is."

He dropped the bags next to a rusty can of shaving cream. From where he was cuffed, Mitchell would have no hope of reaching it. "We gotta go now. My partner needs his beauty rest. But we'll be back tomorrow and talk this whole thing over. Maybe you'll be in a better mood by then."

Mitchell finally figured it out. His head came up sharply. "You ain't gonna leave me here, man. You gotta be crazy. Like I didn't do nothin', man. You even said Levander Greenwood ripped that shit off. Man, this ain't right."

"You wanna walk out, you tell me who gave you this dope. You don't, you kick."

Moodrow thought they had him, for a second, then he saw the fire go out and Pinky's eyes began to close. Maybe he thought they wouldn't go through with it. Maybe he was too stoned to care. Maybe he was more frightened of Levander Greenwood than of Moodrow and Tilley. It didn't matter and both cops knew it. Time would bring its own motivation.

Just before they left, Moodrow grabbed a limp Pinky Mitchell and jerked him to his feet. "See this?" Moodrow lifted the toilet seat, opened Pinky's belt and pulled his pants to his ankles. "Use it. You fucked up my car. If you shit in my apartment, I'm gonna break your ankles."

27

Moodrow led Jim Tilley to their double-parked (and unmolested) Plymouth without making a comment on Pinky Mitchell's condition. He opened the trunk, took out a roll of paper towels and a bottle of Windex and began to clean up the backseat. He was perfectly content to allow his junior partner to stand around doing nothing. Moodrow had one more appointment to keep before he began his final run on Levander Greenwood and the more on edge his partner became, the better for his own purposes.

Moodrow knew he could have gotten Pinky Mitchell to open up. There's a drug called *Narcan* used by doctors and paramedics to bring addicts out of an overdose. It reverses the effects of opiates and the small vial Moodrow carried in his inside jacket pocket would have thrust Pinky Mitchell into instant withdrawal. And, thus, presumably, into instant cooperation. But there was one more detail to be taken care of.

"Let's go up and see Rose," Moodrow suggested. "I got a feeling Pinky'll be a little looser by the time we get back."

"It's getting pretty late. You think they'll let her have visitors?"

Moodrow laughed. "Just drive, Jimmy. We're not gonna ask permission."

St. Vincent's Hospital, one of the city's older institutions, had been expanding over the last decade and now sprawls across both sides of Seventh Avenue.

Moodrow had Tilley drive up to the main entrance on 12th Street, where they dropped the car in a spot marked M.D. PLATES ONLY and walked straight up the steps to the security desk. The sergeant behind the desk made them for cops before they passed through the front door.

"Gentlemen," he said, "what can I do for you?"

Moodrow flipped his badge, but the sergeant didn't bother to look. "Like I said," he repeated, "what can I do for you?"

"We're supervising the Carillo security. You know about that?"

"Sure."

"What room?"

"Take the elevator to the third floor and turn left to the end of the corridor. They got four cops watchin' the door, so you shouldn't have no problems findin' it."

The two cops turned to go, but the guard called them back. "Better take these," he said, offering plastic identity cards. "It's after hours and you don't wanna get stopped every two minutes. Drop 'em back here when you come out. And tell them asshole cops to clean up their crap. They're throwin' fuckin' coffee cups all over the hall and maintenance is havin' a fit."

"I'll see to it," Moodrow agreed. "A lotta cops figure this kind of detail is like having a day off."

They made their way to the elevator, Moodrow chattering as if they were about to take in a movie. The hospital was fairly quiet and the few nurses hustling along the corridors glanced at the cops' identity badges and passed without comment. At the end of the corridor on the third floor, as advertised, four cops sat in blue, plastic hospital chairs and tried to pass the time with small talk.

"Everything quiet, boys?" Moodrow asked. He showed his badge and identified himself as a member of the Greenwood task force.

"Nothing happening here."

"You got somebody in the room, right?"

"Two cops in the room. Four in the corridor. It'd take an army to get past us."

"Do me a favor. Call the boys outside. We want to talk to Carillo alone."

Moodrow watched Tilley closely as the cops complied with his orders. This was the clincher. He wanted his partner to take a good look at the results of ordinary human beings trying to protect the people they loved. His reward was Jim Tilley's sudden, indrawn breath and the tears that followed. Rose Carillo lay asleep on a hospital bed. A narrow tube ran up into her nose, another to a vein in her arm where it was securely taped. The right side of her face was so grotesquely swollen that one eye had disappeared altogether and the skin had split in several places. The doctors had been very careful when they drew the edges of flesh together, but the scars would never disappear and the two cops, having intervened in hundreds of beatings, knew it.

They watched her in silence for a few minutes. She was lying on her right side, trying to keep her weight off her damaged ribs. Then, suddenly, she jerked in her sleep, and her arm went to the blanket covering her side.

"Rose." Tilley's cry was automatic, a reflex, as was his movement to the side of her bed. He took her hand as Moodrow backed out the door.

"Jimmy?" Rose groaned as she tried to turn her head far enough to see him with her good eye. She turned very slowly, as if any sudden movement would set off the pain. Though Tilley didn't know it, small amounts of morphine dripped continually through the intravenous tube. It was enough to control the pain. If she moved slowly.

"I'm so sorry, Rose." He wanted to say something more, to make some kind of a speech, to take her in his arms, to take responsibility for Greenwood's continued freedom. But suddenly he knew there was nothing to be said, that it never happens in a vacuum. There are thousands of Levander Greenwoods in New York. And thousands of Rose Carillos. Only the politicians invent cures. For the fighters, it's one punch, one opponent, at a time. He knelt beside the bed and took her hand, afraid to touch any other part of her body.

"He came on me out of no place, Jimmy." Her voice, through swollen lips, was nearly inaudible and Tilley bent forward, his ear almost to her mouth. "He didn't even say my name. He had a brick and he hit me with it in the face. When I fell, he started kicking me." She stopped for a moment and Tilley thought she'd gone back to sleep. "Is Marlee all right?"

"Marlee's okay. She's home."

"The children?"

Tilley shrugged helplessly. "The phone call helped. But they're frightened."

"It goes on and on," Rose said. As she became more awake, the pain crept back in. "Jimmy, send Moodrow in for a minute. The nurse gave me a sleeping pill and I can't stay awake very long."

Tilley stiffened. "Whatever you want him to do for you, I can do it. You don't need Moodrow anymore. You can come to me. If you want Levander dead, I'll take care of it."

At first when she began to cry, Tilley thought it was from relief, but she insisted again that Moodrow be brought into the room. By the time Tilley finally located his partner, talking to a nurse at the central desk, and brought him back into the room, Rose was nearly asleep.

"Rose," Moodrow said quietly, "it's Moodrow." He touched her side. "You want to see me?"

Suddenly she reached up and took hold of his shirt, her dark eye riveted to his. "You bring Jim Tilley back, you cocksucker. Or don't come back yourself. If it's gotta be one or the other, you go first."

Fifteen minutes later, they were standing in the shadows of a basement apartment on 11th Street and Moodrow was turning the key in the door. Inside, he displayed the small vial, packed in its own emergency syringe. "Know what this is, Jimmy?"

Jimmy looked at Moodrow uncomprehendingly. The roller coaster was spinning faster and faster. Rose's speech to Moodrow both thrilled and stunned Tilley. He hated the idea of himself as Moodrow's pawn, but if Rose wanted him to come back . . . "Just tell me, Stanley. I'm not in the mood for guessing games."

"This here chemical is called Narcan. I got it courtesy of a nurse at St. Vincent's. What it does . . ."

"I know what it does," Tilley said. "I've seen it used a thousand times on junkies with an o.d. It takes the dope right out of their bodies."

Moodrow grinned. "Whatta ya think's gonna happen if we shoot it up into Pinky Mitchell?"

Pinky Mitchell was sound asleep in the bathroom, but his wrists were bloody from attempts to pull them through the cuffs. Tilley took him by the hair and pulled him erect. "Wake up, Pinky. We got a little surprise for you." He ripped the shirt off Mitchell's back, exposing scarred arms, the veins raised and leathery or invisible altogether. Two pus-filled abscesses leaked clear fluid from below his left bicep to the blood on his wrists.

"What you gonna do to me?" Pinky groaned, obviously still stoned.

"We're gonna bring you down, motherfucker," Tilley said, taking the vial from Moodrow and pushing it into Mitchell's face.

Pinky's eyes flicked from the vial in Tilley's hand to the white packets lying on the sink. "Why you wanna put that shit up in me?" he asked. "That's med-

icine, man. You ain't no doctor. You can't put no medicine in me."

"That means you know what it is?"

"Sure. I overdosed about ten times. I seen it plenty,
man."

"Listen, Pinky," Moodrow interrupted, his voice
gentle. "We don't want you. We want the man who
gave you the Blue Thunder. You tell us and you just
walk away."

"Levander Greenwood, man. He gave it to me. Everybody knows he took that shit, man. On Eldridge
Street. He ripped it off and I bought it to sell."

"You bought it?" Tilley's voice crackled with rage.
"You haven't had two cents in the last five years and
you tell me you bought it? I hate fucking liars. I hate
'em."

"Say, Pinky," Moodrow interrupted, his voice still
calm, "is the reason you won't tell us where you got
the dope because the man who gave you the dope is a
policeman?" Pinky's eyes opened wide and Moodrow
continued. "Because we already know it's a policeman, but we don't know which one. That's our only
problem. Which one."

They waited, the two cops, for Pinky to make a decision, but when the junkie held his silence, Moodrow
and Tilley silently went to work. Moodrow held
Mitchell's right arm immobile, while Tilley searched
for a vein. Being neither medic nor junkie, it took
nearly five minutes before Mitchell's blood rose into
the bottom of the vial and Tilley forced the Narcan
into the junkie's bloodstream.

The effect was virtually instantaneous. Mitchell began to shiver and to scratch his face against the bathroom wall. The sweat was already pouring from his
hair down into his face and over his chest. Then he
threw up. Again and again and again. Finally, his head
swiveled to the dope on the sink. "How do I know

you'll let me shoot up? How do I know you won't just
bust me?"

Moodrow reached into his jacket pocket and removed a syringe, still in the wrapper, a candle and a
spoon. He laid all three on the sink. "We don't want
to arrest you, Pinky. I swear to God we don't want you
at all. I know you probably don't believe me. Maybe
cops have lied to you before. So why don't we do this.
You give me the name, then we'll let you inject the
heroin while we go over the details."

Even as he considered the deal, Mitchell's body was
wracked by another cramp. When he'd pulled himself
together, he turned back to Moodrow. There was no
remorse on his face. The pain was overwhelming. "It's
a big, fat detective from the 7th Precinct. Kirkpatrick's
his name. A fat mick with a red face. That's as much
as I'm gonna say until I get well."

Moodrow rocked back in his chair, then turned and
looked down at the floor as if considering something
utterly private. Tilley thought back to their meetings
with Kirkpatrick. Neither of them had had a clue and
Tilley was sure Moodrow must be seeing it as a personal betrayal.

"Sure, Pinky, you don't have to say no more." Moodrow sat up, pulling himself together. His eyes were
black marbles set in white granite. "And thanks. Enjoy
the dope, but don't get so stoned you can't talk, because if you're lying to me, I'm gonna walk out of here
and this time I won't come back for a week."

Mitchell didn't bother to listen. The moment his
wrists and ankles were free, he stepped to the sink and
knelt before it like a nun taking Holy Communion.
Slowly and very carefully (his hands were still shaking), he filled the syringe with water, then squirted the
water into the spoon. The dope followed, all of it, and
without being asked, Moodrow lit the candle. Mitchell
cooked the mixture until it began to bubble, then left
the soup to cool while he removed his belt and twisted

it into a tourniquet. His veins had long ago retreated to the bone and, even though he was better than Tilley, he had to probe again and again before he finally drew blood into the syringe, until he could push the load home.

The transformation was miraculous. The sickness simply vanished and he began cleaning himself as if nothing out of the ordinary had happened to him. It was a snake oil salesman's dream; a powder that cures sickness, instantaneously and completely. That the powder causes the illness in the first place is not, of course, the salesman's problem. Moodrow waited patiently until Mitchell was finished, then all went into the main room for a talk.

The interrogation didn't take long. Pinky Mitchell had begun his informing career after Kirkpatrick accidentally caught him boosting shirts in Macy's. That had been six years ago and at first their relationship had followed the normal cop-informant pattern. Then, more than a year ago, Kirkpatrick had occasionally begun to supply him with heroin for sale. The split was seventy–thirty, in Kirkpatrick's favor. Considerably better than the dollar-a-bag profit Pinky ordinarily made on his merchandise.

Mitchell sat in a chair while he told his story. His chin lay on his chest and he seemed unconcerned, though he made no effort to hold back. When he was done, Moodrow delivered the bad news.

"You gotta go back inside now, Pinky," he said quietly. "Back in the toilet. You're gonna stay with us for another day or two."

The junkie's eyes darted around the room as he weighed the possibility of escape. As if his doped-up body had any chance of getting to that door before Jim Tilley got to him. Gently, Moodrow took his wrist and tugged him to his feet, leading him back across the room.

"This ain't fair," Pinky whined. "I did what you wanted, didn't I? Please let me go."

"I can't take a chance you're lying or that you might run. Here, I'll leave this with you so you don't get sick." He showed Pinky the small bags he held in his hand, then pushed them into the junkie's pocket. Inside the bathroom, he cuffed one of Mitchell's wrists to the pipe. With his legs and the other arm free, Pinky would be able to reach the sink. And the dope.

"Before I go, there's something I want you to think about," Moodrow said. "You remember that Italian I mentioned before? I'm gonna have to tell him about you, so if you go back on the street, he's gonna kill you. What do you think about that?"

Apparently, Pinky Mitchell didn't think too much of it. He shrugged his shoulders and when he spoke his voice was slurred. He was beginning to nod. "What am I supposed to do? Go back to Ol' Virginny?"

"Look, if you want, I can get you into a program. There's a place in Staten Island. De-tox for the first two weeks, then talk for a month. I'll give you a name to ask for and they'll take you right in. Six weeks from now, you can go wherever you want. No more dope chains. That's all I could do for you, Pinky. That's it."

The junkie stared at Moodrow for a long time. He was as surprised as Tilley was by Moodrow's offer. Finally, he smiled. "It don't matter, anyway, man. It don't matter worth a shit."

"Why's that, Pinky?" Moodrow asked.

"I got the virus, man. I'm just killin' time."

28

Moodrow left the building at a dead trot. He cursed his way to a pharmacy across Second Avenue where he bought a bottle of rubbing alcohol. Outside, by the gutter, he poured the contents of the bottle, first over one hand and then over the other. Tilley wanted to ask him about Gretchen, if he'd used a rubber. If he'd been careful. The club scene on the Lower East Side is notoriously promiscuous. Proudly promiscuous. And riddled with part-time dopers who may or may not be above the sharing of needles. Tilley flashed back to Gretchen's butt as she walked matter-of-factly into Moodrow's bedroom. How could he know where she'd been? Or what she'd done? Or who she'd done it with? Then he thought of Rose and Levander and kept his mouth shut.

The alcohol evaporated readily in the heat and Moodrow's hands were dry even before he stopped rubbing them together.

"Remind me to throw that cup away," he said. "As soon as we get back. And buy rubber gloves, too."

"You can't get AIDS from saliva," Tilley reminded him.

"Then remind me to shove it up your ass where you *can* get AIDS." He wiped his face, then stared at his hands for a moment. "I don't like this shit, Jimmy. I don't like when little things you can't see get inside you and kill you. It's not a right way to die. I mean that syringe is as deadly as my .38. How can that be?

282

What about the blood on his hands? How do I know I didn't touch it?''

Finally, Tilley couldn't resist. "What about Gretchen? No risk there?''

"Are you kidding?'' He stared at his partner in disbelief. "Okay, so it took me thirty-five years to learn how to do it right. I still cover my tongue with Saran Wrap. I don't wanna die like that.'' He turned and walked to the corner, to the wire trash can, and threw the bottle and cap into it. Tilley followed slowly, as befits a smartass put in his place.

"It's done now,'' Tilley said. "But if you want, I'll clean up the apartment after we come back for Pinky.''

The relief on Moodrow's face was almost comical, like he was a puppy about to lick his mama's nose. Not that Tilley wanted Moodrow's saliva on his flesh—you can't be too careful. He thought of Rose, of her legs pulled back against her chest, of running his tongue along the inside of her thigh. Then he saw her in a hospital bed, heard her shallow breathing.

"You're right,'' Moodrow said, his voice a little steadier. "Look, I'm gonna call Higgins. I think we should get her in on this.''

"I thought you didn't want anybody there?''

Moodrow smiled suddenly, his eyes turning inward for a second, then declared, "Don't worry about Higgins. She's as safe as me. I'm not saying we should take her along, but you don't have to worry that she'll snitch. Plus she'll advise us how to cover our asses. There's a big potential to fuck it up here, Jimmy. In ways that could end your career, at the least.''

The pay phone on 10th and 2nd was being used by a short dumpy woman in a white polka dot dress that spread out across her rump like a tablecloth on a picnic table. Behind her, a Spanish guy sporting tattooed forearms was already muttering about the wait. There was a second phone there, but someone had torn the receiver off.

There was no chance that Moodrow would hang around until the phone was free, but it was too hot to be trotting off to the next one, only to find the same problem. He gave the stores a quick look, then led Tilley to Ben's Hardware, about a third of the way down the block. It was only 7:30 and the Manhattan traffic was just starting to build, but inside the store, a tiny old man with a yarmulke pinned to the fringe of hair above his ears fussed with his merchandise. The fixtures in the store were ancient. Old barrels filled with odd boiler parts, bits of pipe, assorted valves, nails, stove bolts, cotter pins ran along the south wall. Tools and electrical supplies—plugs, wire, extension cords, fuses, switches—lay in boxes along the north wall. In the back, sheets of glass were stacked against each other, ready to be cut to the size of whatever window the junkies had broken this time. Ben's Hardware was one of the last of a dying breed in New York. Sooner or later, Ben's lease would run out and he would retire in the face of an astronomical rent increase. The new owners, if they stayed in the same business, would replace the barrels with small appliances, the cans of white paint with textured wallpaper.

"Good morning, Sergeant," the old man said politely. "How are you today?"

"I'm fine," Moodrow responded. "I wanna introduce you to my new partner, Detective Tilley. Jimmy, this is Ben Karpman. When I was a kid, my father used to send me here for nails and lightbulbs. Ben, you think I could use your phone?"

"Certainly, Sergeant. It would be my pleasure. And while you're in the back, there's seltzer in the ice box next to the telephone, for an egg cream. Also, sweet sodas. Help yourself. You too, Detective Tilley. Please, take whatever you want. Cool yourself."

Moodrow settled for the telephone, only to find out that Higgins was on her way to the Criminal Courts building on Centre Street, to file a motion in a homicide case. She offered to meet them there, in Part 16, but Moodrow declined. "See us later," he said. "Around noon. At my apartment." He listened for a few seconds, then added, "One o'clock? I guess it'll wait till then. It'll have to."

The phone back in its place, Moodrow helped himself to a couple of Orange Crush sodas, thanked Ben Karpman and led Tilley out of the store. Without discussing it, they understood that the precinct house (which Moodrow called "the station house") was their next stop. While Tilley drove down Second Avenue toward Delancey, Moodrow kept up a running stream of commentary. At first, he confined his talk to tactics. They could probably locate Kirkpatrick by checking his paper trail. His address would be on his 10-Card, his working status on the Duty Roster. Even his love life would be captured on the "vulva file," an informal (and voluntary) list of addresses where detectives can be located in an emergency.

No, Paul Kirkpatrick would not be hard to find. The problem would be to isolate him, to talk to him alone. That might take time and there was no way to predict when Levander would go off again. Of course, they could have taken Pinky Mitchell straight to Internal Affairs and let them fry Kirkpatrick until he gave up Levander Greenwood. Internal Affairs would be glad to accept responsibility for the butchering of the 7th. It would be no problem if Moodrow wanted to sidestep the issue.

But there was no real chance of that. Tilley was convinced that Moodrow would shoot them both before he'd go to the headhunters. He was committed to the "blue wall of silence" in a way that post-Vietnam recruits will never understand. He would sacrifice his children before he'd betray another cop. Of course, not having any children, there was no way Tilley could be sure that he, Tilley, wouldn't make a suitable substitute and he considered this flash of insight while

Moodrow shifted the talk to his memories of a young
Irish cop who'd followed him onto the job.

"Kirkpatrick wasn't a bad cop. Just mean, which was
all right in 1958, when you could bang heads together
until somebody said, 'I did it,' and the confession
would stand up. Kirkpatrick's problem was he couldn't
handle the Knapp Commission and the bullshit paperwork that came in afterwards. The brass got so crazy
about image, they dreamed they could protect the department with paper. Mountains of fucking paper. Until half of every tour was triplicate forms or waiting
around for some assistant D.A. to check the forms or
drinking coffee in the Police Room at the courts while
the lawyers jerked each other off.

"Kirkpatrick never got behind it. He made detective
early, but, after Knapp, he became a hairbag overnight.
Just do the least and take it on home. I was sure he'd
retire when he finished his twenty, but his wife got
sick about fifteen years ago. She went senile when she
was only forty years old and he sunk down even lower.
The job is like family after a while, especially to an
Irish who didn't make any kids. There's no way he
could leave without being thrown out. I got fifty bucks
says Kirkpatrick ain't been laid in five years. And that
he kicks ass on every piece of shit he brings into the
house. And another fifty that his partner helps him.
And a thousand says he's got medical bills piled to the
fucking ceiling."

"You think he's in it with O'Neill?" The question
had been rattling around, waiting for a place to surface.

"Maybe. But Mitchell told us he never saw anyone
but Kirkpatrick. If Mitchell became Kirkpatrick's
snitch because Kirkpatrick just happened onto him in
Macy's, there's a good chance O'Neill's clear. By the
way, O'Neill's a bigshot in the Holy Name Society.
Novenas. First Fridays. Communion Breakfasts. You
know about that, right?"

"Yeah, I know." As a rookie, he'd been heavily recruited by the Emerald Society, an association of Irish-American cops, and by the Holy Name Society. He'd joined the first, declined the latter.

"It doesn't mean he couldn't be turned, but I have a feeling that O'Neill confines his felonies to assaulting dark-skinned criminals. Probably figures they deserve it anyway. But O'Neill is not our problem. And neither is Kirkpatrick. Levander Greenwood is the game. Kirkpatrick's only the map. If we can get him alone and keep him away from the lawyers and talk real, real sweet."

Higgins didn't arrive until nearly two, waking Moodrow and Tilley who'd jumped for the covers and their last chance at a few hours sleep as soon as they'd come into Moodrow's apartment. Higgins had been delayed by the arrest of a middle-level coke dealer with a penchant for violence and a string of dead bodies trailing back to his arrival in Miami. A *marielito*, a Cuban criminal released by Castro and carried across the Atlantic by a yachtsmen-smuggler eager for the bucks and the contacts, he had been recruited into the life before he'd reached the two mile limit. His arrest was quite a feather in the department's cap. It guaranteed a thirty second clip on the eleven o'clock news and a page three headline, with photo, in the tabloids. Higgins had stayed to make sure there was no fuckup at the arraignment and that the chain of evidence was intact.

"They had cartons of paper, Stanley," she complained, accepting a cup of coffee (a signal, really, that they were there to work). "Literally. The complaint follow-ups were insane. 'May 15. Called registered informant 5D461. No result.' What're they after, fame and glory? What's the point?"

"The point is not to get screwed by the department," Moodrow said.

"Really? I thought the point was to make the paperwork so complicated, no one ever got convicted."

"Not true," Moodrow said. "Every cop has to account for all his time. Or her time. On patrol, you have your memo book. Which the patrol sergeant signs everyday. For a gold shield, it's the DD-5, the complaint follow-up. If there's no Five in the file, then what'd you do all day?"

"Don't forget the Dailies," Higgins said slyly. "They give a pretty good idea of what you do with your time."

Moodrow turned red for a moment, then launched himself into the business at hand, explaining every move they'd made since their last meeting with her and Epstein. Higgins received it all calmly, asking Tilley a question or two about his adventure in the armory, then frowning when Moodrow described their subsequent treatment of Pinky Mitchell. After Moodrow finished, she thought for a few minutes while the name Paul Kirkpatrick continued to float in the air.

"Do you have a copy of your Patrol Guide?" she asked, her voice soft and protective.

Moodrow sat back in his chair, looking annoyed. "My Patrol Guide? I haven't seen it in ten years."

"After we met last week," Higgins continued in the same soft voice, "I went over the statutes to see if *my* ass was covered. It is. Then I checked on *your* position. According to the Patrol Guide, you're supposed to report corruption or allegations of corruption directly to the Action Desk at Internal Affairs. Not to me or even to Epstein. Which means that you're already in violation of department procedure."

"If Levander goes down," Moodrow insisted, "it won't matter. The papers'll pick it up and the brass'll go along with the hero bit. I've seen it a hundred times."

"And Kirkpatrick? When does he get it? If you don't arrest Kirkpatrick, then you can't allow Greenwood to surrender. Have you thought about that?" As she piled up the reasons, her voice rose. "Now you're considering murder. Nothing new about that, right?"

"You know what'll happen if we turn Kirkpatrick over?" Moodrow changed the subject. "The headhunters will invade the precinct. Literally. They'll go through every file. Put men on the street to observe the behavior of patrol officers at 'known drug locations.' Follow rookies into coffee shops to make sure they pay for their donuts. And most of all they'll lean on Paul Kirkpatrick until he gives up names. Even if he has no names to give up. You think they'll believe O'Neill didn't know about it? Leonora, when those assholes come into a precinct, the first thing that stops is police work. And the first ones to get fucked are the citizens we're supposed to protect."

"And what about Jim Tilley?" Higgins asked. "If something goes wrong, he'll fall with you. Do I get the pleasure of preparing an indictment against him?"

"He gets to make the decision," Moodrow said flatly. "If he says I should give it over to I.A.D., I'll make the phone call while you're in the room."

Both heads swiveled toward the young cop. He was standing at the stove, pouring hot water onto instant coffee. His face was composed, relaxed . . . and in no way revealed the rage boiling inside. "Is someone here suggesting that Kirkpatrick gets off without paying for his part in the murders of three cops?" That was the other side of Moodrow's "blue wall of silence." The part that read "cop killers *must* pay."

"I thought about that," Moodrow replied.

"And?"

"I don't know. I don't fucking know." He spread his arms wearily. "But I won't let him walk away clean. I can't."

"If you can't bust him and you can't cut him loose, what do you do? You can't kill him. He's a cop, not a black man with a history of extreme violence." Tilley left the dilemma hanging and tossed the next question to Higgins. "How bad are we right now? Legally."

"Legally, you've got yourself covered by keeping the district attorney's office up to date. I've got a file started with appropriate dates. The biker associated Greenwood with a cop, but we can say we got the actual name of the cop from an anonymous tip and that'll get Pinky Mitchell out of it. In my opinion, you don't have any legal problems, because without Mitchell, you don't have probable cause to arrest Kirkpatrick. And, of course, you don't have probable cause for Mitchell unless you give up the snitch who gave you his name. No, Moodrow, it's not that you've committed a criminal act. You're outside the law altogether. What you've got is NYPD problems."

"I agree with Moodrow," Tilley said. "If we take Greenwood, they'll buy all the bullshit about anonymous tips. We don't hurt ourselves any worse by talking to Paul Kirkpatrick."

"And what if he doesn't roll over?" Higgins asked. "What if he wants a lawyer?"

"He'll turn," Moodrow said flatly and Tilley echoed the conviction. There was no doubt in either cop's voice.

"What about you, Leonora?" Moodrow asked. "You wanna come along with us?"

Leonora shuddered. "Thanks for the invitation, but considering what you undoubtedly have in mind for Detective Kirkpatrick, I'll settle for the role of 'liaison.' It's sexier."

Higgins cocked her head and gave Moodrow her best "dead-eye" stare, but Moodrow was up to it. His return grimace held nothing but anticipation. It was the smile of a wolf when the shepherd abandons the flock.

Then Higgins threw in the clincher. "There's no reason why you can't claim that you found Greenwood through an informant's tip. Who's to say otherwise? Kirkpatrick? You didn't feel the tip had enough credibility to bother informing the task force. An error in judgment. So, sorry. Then let Greenwood give up Kirkpatrick and you're out of it."

"And if Greenwood decides not to give up Kirkpatrick? If Greenwood decides to go down with the ship?"

"*Insh Allah*, Stanley," she returned. "As Allah wills."

29

According to the duty roster, Paul Kirkpatrick's tour had two hours to run, but when Moodrow made a call to the 7th Precinct, headquarters for the Greenwood task force, he found only Steve Marisso, who was manning the twenty-four-hour hotline. It was a Friday afternoon and with all the evidence sifted through a dozen times, O'Neill and Kirkpatrick had given their men a weekend off. They tried Kirkpatrick's home next, but there was no answer at his house on Staten Island or at three other addresses listed in the emergency file, which left them with nothing to do except call back every twenty minutes until he showed up somewhere. Higgins made the calls, pitching her voice up an octave while tossing in a thick Spanish accent. They wanted to *find* Kirkpatrick, not speak to him on the telephone and they were afraid that a man's voice, followed by a hang-up or a "sorry, wrong number" would spook him into running.

With nothing else to do, Moodrow and Higgins began to argue over the death penalty; she was for it and he didn't give a shit. Tilley wandered around the kitchen. Heated water for coffee; cut an onion roll in half, smeared both sides with butter.

"There is no way," Higgins repeated for the fourth time, "that you can justify letting a man like Levander Greenwood continue on. His whole life is violence. Pain to others."

Tilley tuned them out; only vaguely heard Moodrow

preach about the money involved in drugs. Money that allows twelve-year-olds to walk into school with 9mm automatics. He compared this phenomenon with the rush of oil wealth to the gulf states in the 70s, much of which flowed back to the West through arms deals. That sudden influx in wealth was supporting the arms industry, had shaped, if not actually created it.

They went on and on and on. And Tilley knew it was all bullshit. Moodrow wanted to make every street dealer into a millionaire, but the most dangerous junkies are the strung-out, destitute addicts who do virtually anything for a fix, especially rob and kill each other.

But, Tilley supposed, there are worse ways to entertain yourself then playing devil's advocate with an assistant D.A. twenty years your junior. The progress of an investigation is full of starts and stops. The closer you get to the quarry, the worse your nerves in the dead spaces. And the longer each step seems to take. Kirkpatrick didn't show himself until nearly eight o'clock, when he finally picked up the phone at a First Avenue address. Higgins whispered something in Spanish, then hung up.

"A man?" Moodrow asked.

"Yeah," Higgins responded. "Probably Kirkpatrick."

"Call again. See if you got the right number."

The man on the other end of the line must have asked what number Higgins wanted, because she began to rattle it off. "Tres, tres, quatro . . ." she stopped abruptly, then hung up. "He said I should shove the phone up my greaseball ass."

"That's gotta be Kirkpatrick." There was no humor in Moodrow's voice. His eyes narrowed slightly and his hands clenched. Without another word to Leonora Higgins, he stood up and pulled on his jacket, instructing Tilley as he went. "I want *you* to handle him physically, Jimmy. Like we did with Pinky Mitchell. Remember, he's got a piece on his hip. If he makes a

move for it, you gotta stop him without killing him or
fucking him up so bad, he can't talk to us. Keep your
eyes open. Stand close to him. Figure he's smarter than
he looks. And more desperate."

"Hey!" Higgins stopped them just as they got to the
door. "You gonna say goodbye to me? And thank you?"
She waited a second, then added, "Be careful, old man.
I know you'll run after Greenwood the minute Kirkpatrick gives you his location. Do me a favor, watch
your ass."

"Goodbye, lady," Moodrow said. Smiling for a
change. "You sure you don't wanna play cop for a little
while?"

"Not tonight. Call me when you need someone to
pick up the pieces."

"You'll be the first. Now do me one favor. After we
leave, contact Epstein. Tell him what's going on. If I
tell him, he'll take Kirkpatrick to I.A.D., but if we're
already into it, he'll figure a way he can protect us if
something goes wrong."

The address Kirkpatrick had left in the emergency
file, on First Avenue, between 23rd and 24th Streets,
sat directly across from the men's shelter at Bellevue
Hospital. The sooty brick building, a six story walk-
up originally designed to attract the middle-class, had
seen better days. Nevertheless, it was jealously guarded
and Moodrow, armed with knife and screwdriver,
could not get past the lock on the outer door. The two
cops had to wait fifteen minutes for someone who
lived there to arrive so they could follow him in. The
old man who finally showed up looked at them dubiously, but couldn't make either of them for muggers.
He went to his first floor apartment with a half-smile
on his face, grateful, probably, to see Moodrow and
Tilley attack the stairs instead of him.

Apartment 3A was a black door in a white plaster
hallway. There was no rug on the wooden floor, nor

any decoration on the walls, but everything was clean. A definite improvement for Tilley, considering the slums he'd been in recently. Neither one of them expected violence at this point, but they instinctively took positions on either side of the door before Moodrow gave it three sharp raps.

"Who is it?" Kirkpatrick's voice was strong, a cop asking questions. He slid the peephole cover aside, then repeated, "Who is it?"

Moodrow stepped out where he could be seen. "It's me, Paulie. Moodrow. Open up."

There was no place for Kirkpatrick to go. Nevertheless, he took the time to consider his position and when he opened the door, he tried to present the same confident cop who'd sat at Moodrow's table discussing strategy. Unfortunately, his ashen face, a far departure from his usual florid complexion, gave his fear away.

"Moodrow. What're you doing here?" He glanced at Tilley out of the corner of his eye. The simple fact that they'd arrived on his doorstep without calling first, had to mean trouble.

Moodrow pushed into the apartment and Kirkpatrick gave way as if he'd offered the invitation. Except for a tiny bedroom and an even smaller kitchen, the place, with its ancient furniture and gray threadbare rug, was almost identical to Moodrow's on 11th Street. And must have been used for the same purpose.

"What do you do here, Paulie?" Moodrow asked innocently. Kirkpatrick and Tilley were standing next to each other, Kirkpatrick with his jacket off, while Moodrow strolled into the bedroom.

"It's my girlfriend's apartment." He looked at Tilley and raised his hand apologetically. "My wife is sick. You know how it is. I gotta get it someplace."

The key to any interrogation is the first lie. It doesn't matter how irrelevant the lie. Even if it has no bearing on the crime, it makes everything else a lie. Kirkpatrick should have known better, but lying comes by habit with criminals. That's the whole point.

"So where is she?" Moodrow asked. "I'd like to meet your girlfriend."

"She went to her mother's for the weekend."

"Uh-oh." Tilley could see and hear Moodrow opening the dresser drawers. "I don't see no panties, Paulie."

"What?" Kirkpatrick was still looking at Tilley, but he turned at Moodrow's question.

"There's no panties," Moodrow repeated patiently. He held up an empty drawer for Kirkpatrick's inspection, then put it back in the dresser. "There's nothing in these drawers at all. You're lying, Paulie. That ain't right. Gimme your gun."

"Huh?"

Suddenly Tilley realized that Kirkpatrick was nearly drunk. He hadn't smelled it on the detective's breath, but he picked up the odor of beer floating in from a box of garbage in the kitchen. Kirkpatrick's piece, an ancient Smith & Wesson, was completely exposed on his left hip and Tilley kept himself close to it. Drunks are unpredictable. Sometimes they don't give a shit.

"Maybe she moved out on you." Moodrow changed the subject without changing his deadpan expression. "Maybe that's why the drawers are empty." He sat on the bed, which nearly sagged to the floor. "Jesus," he said, but stayed put, nonetheless. "No wonder your girlfriend took off, Paulie. You can't fuck on a bed like this. It's bad for your back."

"Hey, screw you, Moodrow," Kirkpatrick growled. "I don't need no hairbag busting my balls."

"Lemme have the gun, Paulie. For a little while. Then I'll give it back."

"You want my gun, you scumbag?"

His hand moved up to his waist and Tilley took the opportunity to make his presence felt. He drove his left hand into that basketball gut and Kirkpatrick stopped moving altogether. Just grunted, "Ugh, ugh, ugh, ugh," as his lungs released air in little gasps. Tilley slid the .38 out of the rig on Kirkpatrick's hip and passed it over to Moodrow, then gave the cop a thorough frisk.

He was clean, but that didn't mean his apartment was clean. While Moodrow waited patiently, Tilley sat Kirkpatrick down in a straight-back chair in the center of the living room, far from any potential weapon. By the time Tilley was finished, Kirkpatrick had recovered enough to speak. Surprisingly, he chose to come after Tilley, not Moodrow. "You little fuck," he groaned. "You're gonna pay for this. You assaulted a police officer." He made no move to get off the chair, however, apparently satisfied to express his defiance verbally.

Tilley ignored him, taking a second chair, a low stool, actually, and placing it to Kirkpatrick's left and slightly behind him, while Moodrow set a rickety table and a greasy, blue armchair between himself and Kirkpatrick. Then Moodrow sat in the chair, displaying Kirkpatrick's .38. "This is a wonderful piece," he began. "You have it since the Academy?"

Kirkpatrick didn't answer, just stared back sullenly. Tilley let Moodrow ask the question again, but when Kirkpatrick still didn't respond, he kicked the chair out from under him. Kirkpatrick wasn't used to being on that side of it. The rumor in the house was that he was brutal, that interrogation was his strong point and that O'Neill deliberately made himself absent so his partner could work.

"You want more?" Tilley asked. "You wanna give me that look? I don't like that look." Kirkpatrick was on his knees, rising like a whale from the greasy carpet and Tilley slapped him with the back of his hand. A very quick, not very hard shot that let him know the young cop was so confident, he didn't need to hurt him. He could humiliate him.

"You're crazy," Kirkpatrick shouted, which is the highest compliment you can pay an opponent in a fight.

Moodrow held the gun up again. It was a Smith & Wesson Police Special. At any given moment in New York, there are 26,000 men who own guns that are almost identical. The grip was worn smooth, but it looked clean. It looked ready to go.

"So, did you get it when you were at the Academy? You drag it along all these years?"

"Yeah." Kirkpatrick, back in his seat, was trying to watch Moodrow and Tilley at the same time.

"You musta changed barrels when you made detective, right?"

"Yeah."

"Then it's not the same gun you had in the Academy." Moodrow paused as if waiting for an answer, then launched into it again before his partner could move. "See, the same gun would have to have the same barrel. If you change the barrel, it's not the same gun. That's why you gotta change the info on your 10-Card. Don't you agree?"

Kirkpatrick didn't wait to be prodded. "Whatever you say, Moodrow. You and your goon are in charge. Right now."

Moodrow ignored the last part. "Good. I'm glad we agree on something. Because it's important that you should answer each question truthfully. So's we don't waste a lot of time." Carefully, respectfully, he released the cylinder of the .38 and let it fall into his palm, then reversed it to let the bullets drop onto the table. It always works great in the movies, but this time two of the cartridges stuck in their chambers and Moodrow had to pull them out with a thumbnail. It was comic, but nobody laughed.

"When I first made detective, I had to have the barrel changed, too. I hated it, then. It didn't go with my image. I wanted a Bulldog .44, like Son of Sam used, but with a shorter barrel. You know what I'm saying? A real stubby, fat .44 that makes the perps think they're peering into the tunnel of death. So it's like a shotgun." He let his monologue stop dead; held the silence for a few seconds longer than necessary, then started up again. "But then, about ten years ago, everything changed. I fell in love with my piece again. It seems right that California cops should use ammunition that shoots through walls. Here it's different. It's more civilized, even if it's more violent. You agree with that?"

"Why don't you get to the goddamn point?" Kirkpatrick said it to Moodrow, but he couldn't keep his eyes from flicking over at Tilley, who caught them, holding them prisoner for a second before Kirkpatrick could jerk them away. Tilley was looking forward to action and Kirkpatrick read it. "You think I'm afraid to get my ass kicked? You think muscle-brain over here is gonna make me shit my pants?"

"I just asked you if you agree with what I said about the weapons?"

Suddenly Kirkpatrick turned to face Tilley, his face red with anger, and Tilley instinctively kicked out before he completed the turn. Kirkpatrick hit the carpet face first and flashed Tilley a look of pure hatred.

"Don't hit him in the face," Moodrow said, his voice tight. "Don't mark him."

Tilley was considering the request when Kirkpatrick decided to make one last stand. He drove a fist in Tilley's unyielding gut while he made a grab for the young cop's balls. Somehow, without making any decision to do so, Tilley managed to close his legs and Kirkpatrick came up with a hunk of his thigh. Then Tilley drew his own piece and placed it against the top of Kirkpatrick's head.

"Don't do it," Moodrow shouted. "Don't do it."

"Why not? He don't deserve to live. He don't answer no questions. He goes after people's balls. Nobody seen us come up here. Let's do him." Actually, Tilley had no intention of shooting Kirkpatrick, neither before nor after he gave them Greenwood. On the other hand, Rose would have been very disappointed if Tilley came back without his balls. Fortunately, Kirkpatrick froze as soon as he felt the steel on the top of his head and by the time he was shoved back in his chair, he understood, for the first time, how strong their intentions were. His physical defiance dropped away and he began to stare at the floor and to answer questions in a monotone.

"So what do you use the place for, Paulie?" Moodrow started over, his voice patient, soothing.

"What does any cop use a splash pad for? I meet people here. Snitches. Sometimes I bring a broad up. Sometimes I just come up here for a few beers. I got a houseful of bad memories in Staten Island."

"You mean about your old lady? About Maryann?"

"Yeah. Mostly."

"She went senile, your old lady. Right? About fifteen years ago."

The words went through Kirkpatrick like an electric current. His whole body shivered. "It's not called senile anymore," he said quietly. "Now it's got a name. Alzheimer's Disease."

"Yeah, I heard about that. It's incurable, right, Paulie? You can't do nothin' about it."

Kirkpatrick was whispering by this time. "No, there's no treatment."

"That's rough, Paulie. It's hard on a cop. We need support. So where is she? In a nursing home?"

"Yeah, in New Jersey."

"She still recognize you? You still go see her?"

"I go."

"She recognize you?"

"No. She don't know who I am." Slowly, Kirkpatrick's head came up until he was looking Moodrow in the eye.

"You could live a long time with Alzheimer's Disease?" Moodrow persisted.

"What's the point?"

"I'm just asking, Paulie. Don't get so upset."

"Yeah, she could live another fifteen years. Maybe more."

"Must cost a fortune, right?"

"It's very expensive."

"Tell me something, Paulie. Where would they put her if you couldn't pay no more?"

"They'd put her in some kind of public place. The ones the city pays for."

"Like they used to do for the retarded kids at Willowbrook?"

"Like that." Kirkpatrick looked beaten, but wary, like he didn't know what Moodrow was getting at. Tilley was having trouble with the same thing, but all he had to do was make sure Kirkpatrick kept answering.

"You got anything to drink in here?" Moodrow asked. "You look like you could use a drink."

"In the cabinet on the left."

Moodrow went for the drinks, leaving his partner to guard the goods. He came back a minute later with two plastic tumblers, both covered with greasy fingerprints, and a half-filled quart of Jim Beam. "I couldn't find any mixers," he said. "The refrigerator's broken, too. No ice. You want a drink?"

He poured a couple of inches into the bottom of each tumbler, then pushed one toward Kirkpatrick. Though he must have known better, Kirkpatrick drained the glass at a gulp, then held it out for Moodrow to fill again. One more proof that he was ready to fall. Moodrow waited for him to settle down, then asked, "Did you know little Bennie Goldstein personally?"

Bennie was the first cop Levander Greenwood had killed, the undercover cop working by the Williamsburg Bridge. When Kirkpatrick heard the name, he let out a long, soft groan that hung in the air, high and full of pain.

"Answer him," Tilley said, on cue. "Answer Moodrow when he talks to you."

Kirkpatrick looked at both of them, head swiveling slowly and mechanically from one to the other. Finally he swallowed hard and said, "No, I didn't know him. I don't know many of the younger guys."

"Then you probably didn't know the two kids, Franklyn Peters and Orlando Cruz. The ones who got it in that tenement?"

Tilley was fascinated, but not so lost as to forget his job. Kirkpatrick didn't have much hair left, but Tilley grabbed as much as he could get and yanked him upright. "You set them up, you scumbag. You wanted to get rid of Greenwood and you set up three cops. You killed them. You murdered them the same as if you pulled the trigger."

Once again, Moodrow pulled his partner away, helping Kirkpatrick, who was crying, back into his seat. He let Kirkpatrick sob, reloading the detective's gun, spinning the cylinder, closing it up. He eyed the .38 speculatively for a while, then laid it gently on the table. "You ever shoot anybody with this?" he asked.

Kirkpatrick sniffed it up, his eyes riveted to the piece. "Once," he answered, probably glad for a neutral subject.

"Did he die?"

There was a hesitation, then, "No. He was okay. Out of the hospital the next day."

"Did you know Franklyn Peters and Orlando Cruz?"

A groan. Again. A high, keening sound announcing utter loss. A wail of sorrow. "I didn't know them, Moodrow."

"Did you go to Bennie Goldstein's funeral?"

"Please, Moodrow. What's the point?"

"I knew him," Moodrow announced. "We worked together on a narc operation near Henry Street. I liked him a lot. Short, feisty guys always get to me. They should have the good sense to keep their mouths shut, but Bennie was always at war with someone. If there weren't any skells handy, he'd attack the job. He was anti-crime, not a gold shield, and he hated the Patrol Guide. It's up to six hundred pages now, and, if you take his word for it, set up with contradictions so if the headhunters or the brass want your balls, they can have them. I met his wife at the funeral. She told me he was gonna run for P.B.A. delegate. Get off the street."

Kirkpatrick stopped him by thrusting his glass across the table. Something in him had hardened again. Moodrow filled the glass, as calm as ever. His speech about Bennie Goldstein had been matter-of-fact, as was his next comment. He reminded Tilley of a good boxer matched with a very weak opponent. He was circling, slipping in the jab, waiting for the right moment.

"Don't pass out, Paulie," he said. "Don't get too drunk for decent conversation."

Kirkpatrick laughed bitterly. "Those days are long gone. I don't hardly get high anymore. Just even."

"Did you ever use this apartment to meet Levander Greenwood?" The question finally asked, Moodrow sat back to admire his timing.

"You ain't read me my rights or nothin'," Kirkpatrick accused. "No matter what I say, you can't use it."

Tilley pushed his face within an inch of Kirkpatrick's. "Cop killers don't have rights," he reminded him. "Not to another cop. You think we don't know you set up those two cops? You think we don't know you phoned in that tip on Greenwood's location? You probably hoped they'd blow Greenwood away. Them or the cops that backed them up. Only thing, someone made a mistake and Levander wasn't where he belonged."

"How many more funerals?" Moodrow asked, without waiting for Tilley to back off. "How many?"

"You ain't read me my rights," Kirkpatrick insisted.

He was settling down into a pattern. Hardening himself. Which is probably why Moodrow threw in the dynamite. "We got Pinky Mitchell, Paulie. Took him out of the shelter."

"Where is he?" Kirkpatrick's fear came off him in waves. It stunk of beer and bourbon.

"I got him in an apartment like this one. Over on 11th Street."

"Did he make a statement yet?"

"Only to us," Moodrow replied. "He told me about meeting you in Macy's. About your business relationship. You know how it is. When junkies get sick, they tell you whatever you need to know."

"You still ain't read me my rights."

"I don't wanna arrest you. If I can help it. I wanna try to find some other way, but first you gotta tell me about Greenwood. He's gotta come off the streets, Paulie."

"If I tell you, what happens? You gonna let me off the hook? I got a sick wife, Moodrow. There won't be nobody to help her out if I'm gone."

"You shoulda thought about that before you started in with Levander Greenwood." Moodrow picked up Kirkpatrick's piece and began to play with it, unloading it again, then dry-firing it. "I can't let you go for killing a cop."

"It wasn't supposed to be that way." It came out in a rush, the dam finally broken. "When we started it was just business. How was I supposed to know he'd start using crack? That's when he lost control. After he started in with crack, he needed money every second and he got crazier and crazier. I couldn't control him no more and he kept coming back to me."

"Why didn't you give him up?"

"For shit sake, Moodrow, they'd take away everything. I wouldn't even get a pension. I been on the job more than thirty years. Maryann wouldn't get a dime.

What would she do if I wasn't there to protect her? I wanted to let nature take its course. That's why I dropped the dime to Carerro. I never thought that stupid wop'd send three cops when he should've sent a hundred." He hesitated for a moment. "I never thought Greenwood'd go down two flights to buy crack. I thought he'd stay holed up with his girlfriend on the fourth floor."

Moodrow put the gun back on the table. He poured another drink for Kirkpatrick and one for himself. The bottle was nearly empty. Time for the end game. "Why didn't you kill him yourself?"

Kirkpatrick took his time answering. "It ain't that easy. He's armed all the time."

"So you sacrificed two cops, instead?"

"I didn't mean for them to get hurt. I thought they'd send an army after Greenwood." He turned then and looked directly at Tilley. "I didn't give *you* up," he said. "Levander knows you and Moodrow had his old lady stashed somewhere. He wanted your address and I told him, 'No.'"

"He took that?" Tilley asked quickly.

"Well, he didn't *know* she was there. Besides, he still needs me to sell what he steals. Every thief needs a fence. Plus he thinks I can find out where his kids are."

Moodrow reached out and took Kirkpatrick's hand. "Look at me, Paulie. I wanna ask you one more question." He waited until Kirkpatrick turned back to him. "Do you got the death benefits in your pension plan?"

Absolute silence as Kirkpatrick and Tilley took it in. Death benefits are cash payments made instead of a pension to cops who die in the line of duty. They are also paid to the heirs in cases of suicide. Every cop knows about suicide. Especially the old ones and the drunks.

"Yeah, I took 'em when they first come out. I wanted to have Maryann protected in case something happened to me. I did a stupid thing when I went over the twenty year mark and became eligible. I dropped all my insurance. That's why I took the death benefits."

"How much your wife get if something happens to you?" Moodrow's voice had just the slightest edge and when Kirkpatrick didn't answer, he went on quickly. "Cause if we give you up, Paulie, you don't got nothin'. They strip away your gun and your shield and your pension first. After that comes jail. You're a cop killer. Even the P.B.A. won't give you a lawyer." He picked up the gun, emptied it again, then put it in Kirkpatrick's hand. "You ever think what it would feel like? You ever put it in your mouth?" Kirkpatrick's eyes were riveted to Moodrow's and Tilley knew, at that minute, Moodrow was taking Kirkpatrick over familiar ground. "You know what them places are like? Where they put senile people who don't have money? They treat 'em like meat, Paulie. I seen it with my own eyes. I been in those places. The attendants fuck the young ones and beat the old ones. I'm serious. There's no government money anymore, so the asylums hire the cheapest attendants they can get. Pay 'em like security guards in the shelters. For crowd control." He stopped abruptly, as if expecting a response, but Kirkpatrick had nothing to say. His eyes were frozen, unblinking, reaching into Moodrow's. "So tell me, Paulie, how much you got in the death benefits. Thirty years on the job, it oughta be a nice piece."

"About three hundred thousand." Kirkpatrick swallowed hard.

"You got someone to handle it for Maryann? Someone to pay it out if you're not there?"

"Maryann's sister lives on Staten Island. Right near me. We talked about it already."

"She in the will?"

"She's the executor and the trustee. She controls the money."

"You trust her?"

"Yeah. She's got enough for herself. She don't need mine."

"You mean, she don't need Maryann's."

"Yeah." Kirkpatrick's eyes dropped to the table again. "I got no loose ends. I thought ahead." He laughed for a second, then choked on it. "Can't you let me off the hook. For Maryann? You knew her."

"No way, Paulie. What you done, you gotta pay for. You understand that? 'Don't do the crime, if you can't do the time.' Isn't that what the skells say?" Kirkpatrick didn't bother to respond. "I want you to tell me where Greenwood is. Then we're gonna leave you to think about what you have to do."

"You're gonna take Greenwood alone?" Kirkpatrick's voice rose, reflecting the hope that suddenly jumped in his eyes.

"Forget it, Paulie. Other people know what you did. There's only one way you could beat it. Take it for Maryann and for yourself. If you go to trial, they'll put you away for thirty years. Long enough to die. If you go into the population, the cons'll kill you for sure. If you take protective custody, you'll be wishing for the electric chair before you do a year. Tell us where Greenwood's hiding, Paulie. Let us take him out."

Kirkpatrick spilled it. His voice was flat, without apology, as he gave up each detail of Levander Greenwood's lair. There was nothing more to protect and he knew it. Moodrow and Tilley didn't bother to say goodbye, just got up and walked out the door, unconsciously tapping their weapons, and wishing for hand grenades, rockets and helicopters.

The air on the street was warm and muggy, but somehow cleaner than the air inside that apartment. Their minds were on the coming confrontation, consumed with it, because Kirkpatrick's voice, quiet yet audible, from the window above, jolted both of them.

"Moodrow, I can't do it. I can't. I tried a hundred times, but I can't do it. Let me come with you. I'll set him up. I'll call him out. He knows I know where he's holed up. He won't be afraid if he sees it's me."

"I told you already, Paulie. There's other people who know about you. If you're trying to set us up, it won't help you."

By way of an answer, Kirkpatrick held his .38 aloft, then placed it against his temple, then into his mouth. He drew back the hammer, but wouldn't (or couldn't) pull the trigger. "I can't make it, Moodrow. I want to, but I can't. Let me go with you. I know what to do."

Moodrow didn't hesitate, though his voice was tired. "All right, Paulie. Come down. Do what you gotta do."

30

There are two popular conceptions of the New York City subway system. The first is of trains running between smooth rock walls with stations every eight or nine blocks. The other involves a maze of abandoned or half-used tunnels, a system as dark and murky as the sewers of Paris in a nineteenth century French novel. In fact, neither is true. With the exception of a very short tunnel in lower Manhattan, cut as an experiment years before the present system was begun, the track is in constant use. Still, the image of trains tearing along between featureless black walls is also false. For example, there are dozens of short spurs, called layover tracks, where trains are parked at night, as well as thousands of unused equipment storage rooms, built according to no discernible plan and stuck at odd points throughout the system. These storage rooms have come to play an unexpected role in the New York City housing scheme. In every part of the city where the M.T.A. provides service, they have become an alternative to the doorways, park benches and terminals for New York's homeless—private accommodations for those insiders smart enough to find them and strong enough to keep them. This lifestyle has become so entrenched that transit workers, performing routine maintenance on the hundreds of miles of subway track, accept and ignore the men who rest on newspaper mattresses or scribble desperately in old notebooks, preaching their truths accompanied by the echoing thunder of the trains.

Even the transit cops make no attempt to sweep these people out. What would be the point of it? Their residency harms no one. It can, however, provide cover to a man on the run; to a man who cannot let himself be seen on the streets, who has gone so far down he can accept the grease and the steel dust and company of the desperate.

Thus, Levander Greenwood came to rest, and an explanation for the failure of a hundred cops and their informants. In the first ten days following the massacre on Delancey Street, the task force had received and investigated a dozen tips, sometimes arriving within hours of Greenwood's departure. The scenario had followed the typical pattern of the fugitive with no place to lay his head and everyone had expected a quick arrest. Then Levander simply disappeared and new tips were either entirely false or led to addresses where he hadn't been seen in weeks. The baffled detectives had jumped on the hypothesis that he had come to bay in one of the Lower East Side's abandoned tenements, but surprise sweeps by the black-uniformed SWAT team had turned up only the usual assortment of junkies and squatters. The situation had driven everyone involved with the investigation crazy. Except, of course, Paul Kirkpatrick.

As they drove, Moodrow, Kirkpatrick and Tilley, straight down Second Avenue toward Houston Street, Kirkpatrick recounted his failures at length, searching for an excuse. After the deaths of the two young cops, he'd been afraid to set Greenwood up again. Of course, he had wanted to kill Levander, but he couldn't find a way to accomplish the deed without involving himself and he was unprepared to explain how he'd come by his knowledge of Levander's whereabouts. Besides, Greenwood didn't expect to be taken

alive and the continual use of crack had made him as
paranoid as a cockroach at a polka festival.

"I admit I did it for money, all right?" He spoke very
quickly, his words partially slurred, yet coherent. "But
I ain't the only one. It's been going on for a long time.
Right here, Moodrow, and you fucking know it." He
paused for a response, but Moodrow ignored him. "After Bennie Goldstein was killed, I got sick. Levander
was so crazy with the cocaine, he wouldn't even wait
for me to sell the dope he ripped off. He wanted cash
up front, as soon as he made delivery. If it wasn't for
the goddamn cash machines in the banks I woulda had
to carry a thousand dollars with me all the time.
Whenever I tried to walk away, he'd threaten to make
a phone call to Internal Affairs. The cocksucker knows
more about the job than I do. I kept hoping he'd get
blown away trying to take some dealer off, but it went
the other way. He came to me twice a week with some
kinda dope. Speed, smack, hits—whatever he could
grab. He told me he was filling the Lower East Side
with 'fertilizer.' "

Kirkpatrick went on and on. Like any other criminal, once started on his confession, he couldn't shut it
off. That's why cops say, "Just tell us about it and
you'll *feel better*." Every detective has had the experience of listening to a suspect relate details of crimes
that have never been reported. And that's also why
Moodrow and Tilley didn't bother to respond. Just let
him make his Act of Contrition. The roller coaster
was all downhill from here to the final stop.

After a ten minute ride that seemed to take an hour,
they parked on Houston Street by First Avenue. Moodrow carefully locked the door, then opened the trunk
of the Plymouth and removed two bulletproof vests.
He handed one to his partner and put on the other.
Though a third vest lay in clear view at the bottom of
the trunk, Moodrow didn't offer it and Kirkpatrick
didn't ask. He shut his mouth, accepted a black, six-

cell flashlight and they went down into the station like three androids in a science fiction movie.

The Second Avenue stop on the F Train is only one block from Houston Street and the Bowery, an intersection with a century-long tradition as headquarters for New York's alcoholic derelicts. The entrances are located at First and Second Avenues with the station running along Houston Street. A flight of stairs leads to a token booth and a set of turnstiles, then a second flight to the train level. There are two platforms here, with a single track on the outside of each platform and two tracks between them. This is a common arrangement at stations served by express and local trains, but only one train stops at Second Avenue, the F, and the center tracks lead to a dead end in a closed tunnel several hundred yards down the line, a layover track with its length characterized by a widening of the tunnel and a series of storage rooms, each now a private apartment. In the opposite direction, back toward Broadway and Lafayette, the next stop, the layover tracks disappear and the living space shrinks to nothing. It was here that Levander Greenwood had found his cave, in a neighborhood that was completely private, a space that didn't exist.

It was eleven o'clock when the trio walked past the Second Avenue token booth and the station was fairly busy, as it usually is on weekends. The clerk, locked in her booth for protection, looked up momentarily as they pulled open an exit door, then back down at her newspaper. She couldn't give a shit if they paid or not. It wasn't her job to make them pay.

There were men sleeping on every bench. Men lying or sitting with their backs against the stone walls. Men passed out in the center of the platform. Passengers stood in knots as far away from these men as possible, yet moved for the cops. They marched past tattered posters advertising the joys of wine and cigarettes and a movie, *Over The Top*, which had bombed several

years before. Above it all, the acrid smell of urine, of
men too stoned to find or care about a toilet, cut
through the humidity, as it does in every slum on the
Lower East Side.

At the end of the platform, a set of iron steps led to
the track level. They walked, Kirkpatrick in the lead,
directly to them, then waited as a train shrieked into
the station. Tilley had seen it coming down the tunnel, its single red eye announcing F to the straphangers
leaning over the edge of the platform, but when it hit
the open space of the station, the metallic screech of
the brake pads echoing back and forth between stone
walls awakened him to the possibility of crouching in
a narrow tunnel with a train bearing down on him and
an electrified third rail at his feet. There are depressions in the walls of the tunnel so workers can get out
of the way, but the thought of being pressed back
against the stone, with the wheels of the subway car
passing two feet from the end of his nose, was less
than comforting and he began to be aware of himself
and his surroundings for the first time since his visit
to Rose. It wasn't a movie. It wasn't cops and robbers
with a plastic gun and red caps. He could easily die
here, ambushed by Greenwood or Kirkpatrick or both.
He looked over at Moodrow and found a poker-faced
cop utterly absorbed in the job at hand. Then, with the
train already making its way toward the next stop, they
walked down the stairs and into the tunnel.

Kirkpatrick led them due west, keeping to the
southern side of the four tracks running into the station. A hundred and fifty yards from the platform, well
into the shadows of the tunnel, they found a small,
concrete room just before the junction of the east-
bound and the layover tracks. The room was empty,
though someone had dragged a filthy mattress through
the station to make a home out of it. A steel ladder,
bolted to the concrete on the north wall, led up to a
metal grating and there was just enough light coming

from the single bulb to show another level, an unlit level, above it. Moodrow ran his hand across one of the steel rungs and held it up. It was clean and Tilley looked at the ladder a little more closely. The edges of each rung were covered with greasy soot, but the center, where a foot would press, was spotless.

"What's up there?" Moodrow asked. "Go over it again. And don't make any mistakes, Paulie. If it goes wrong, I'm gonna take you out first."

"You don't think I know it's over?" Kirkpatrick turned to meet Moodrow's gaze. "I'm thanking you, Moodrow. For Maryann. Anybody else woulda turned me over to the headhunters and washed his hands of it. The whole squad thinks you're an asshole, but nobody else woulda given me a chance to make it good."

Moodrow bristled at the word "asshole." "Dump the bullshit," he ordered. "Just go over the rest of it so there's no mistakes."

"That's a continuation of the token level." Kirkpatrick pointed at the grating. "But it's been closed off for years. You can get to it through here or through the ventilation grates that go up to Houston Street. Greenwood's hole is about two hundred yards west and down a small corridor. I'm going first. The signal, in the beginning when I had to bring him money, was to swing the flashlight from side to side, like a windshield wiper. With that light coming at him, he won't be able to see anything past me. You stay close to the walls and he won't have no chance at all."

Tilley wanted to stop the both of them, to ask if either had any intention of accepting a surrender, but it would have been a waste of time, despite Moodrow's promise that he would make the decision. Circumstances were making decisions for all of them. Tilley fully realized that Moodrow had something in mind. That the first movement had been played out with Higgins in his apartment and the second with an old frightened rogue cop named Paul Kirkpatrick. Moodrow had promised it would lead to Levander Greenwood. Then Tilley remembered the men in the task force; their computers and maps. Those men were enjoying a free weekend, no closer to Levander Greenwood than on the day they'd put their task force together.

Kirkpatrick went up the ladder first, easily pushing aside the grating. The opening was small and he struggled for a moment, trying to get through, a perfect target for anyone waiting in the darkness. Moodrow followed, his passage even more difficult. Tilley had no problem, his shoulders being narrower than Moodrow's and his gut flatter than Kirkpatrick's. For a few seconds, they peered down the platform, half-frozen. It was as wide as the first level, called the mezzanine level, with its token booth and turnstiles. Perhaps, at some time in the past, it had housed a command post for the engineers or the cops, but it obviously hadn't been used in years. The walls and the floor were covered with greasy soot. Even Levander Greenwood's footprints were only darker depressions in the filth.

Slowly, calmly, Kirkpatrick flipped on his flashlight and began to swing it back and forth. In the sudden glare, they could see the side corridor, exactly where Kirkpatrick said it would be, about halfway between the cops and a tiled wall at the end of the level. The flashlight, one of the newer ones, had a halogen bulb and threw an incredibly bright beam. Behind it, as Kirkpatrick had insisted, Moodrow and Tilley were invisible.

Despite Kirkpatrick's warnings, Moodrow stayed close behind him as he began to move away. He wasn't about to let Kirkpatrick turn that corner unobserved. Tilley, following the two of them down the corridor, felt a fear as intense as anything he'd ever known. He'd always hated the filth, the closed-in, trapped paranoia of narrow tenement stairways, but they were nothing compared to this. He *knew* there was an insane crack

addict with a sawed-off shotgun waiting somewhere in
that darkness. Though all three of them had drawn
their weapons as soon as they came through the grating, a .38 is no match for an auto-loading shotgun. Neither was there any realistic hope of surprising a cocaine
freak who slept for three or four hours every other day.
In one sense, they were at the mercy of a detective
who was already responsible for the deaths of three
cops.

Tilley thought of Rose living in her apartment on
the Lower East Side, of the permanent fear becoming
terror each time she heard a footstep on the stairs, of
the dread to be inspired by a key turning in a lock.
How does it feel to open up on a crowd with a shotgun? To see the flesh peeling back, the explosion of
red blood? Tilley had never shot anyone in his life, but
the image of Levander Greenwood's fists on his lover's
flesh clouded all perspective. He asked himself for a
reason why such a man should live and found only
rage. And fear.

"Levander. It's me. Kirkpatrick."

Kirkpatrick began to call as soon as he turned the
corner. Moodrow and Tilley were only a few feet behind him, but they stopped at the mouth of the corridor, flattening against opposite walls, peering around
the corner while Kirkpatrick plodded along. He kept
his weapon pointed at the ceiling, but the beam of the
flashlight swept back and forth across a doorless opening thirty feet away, so close they could almost touch
it.

"Hey Levander, it's Kirkpatrick. You in there?" His
voice was cop-strong. Tough and confident.

"What you want, pig? Why you come here?"

"I got a place for ya, Levander. Crack dealer in
Queens. Outta the Lower East Side where you're not
so hot. Guy does about a thousand vials a day. I can
get you in the apartment."

A long pause as Kirkpatrick stopped ten feet from

he doorway and Levander considered the proposition.
The bit about Queens held just enough hope to be en-
icing, like a miniskirt on an old whore. Tilley's
veapon was pointed directly into the doorway, as was
Moodrow's. Within the room, a light flared and the
ucking sound of a flame pulled down into the bowl
f a pipe filtered through the silence. It only took a
ew seconds, then Greenwood, his spirits fortified,
poke out.

"How you wanna do this, pig?"

"I got a guy can get you into the apartment as a
uyer. Once the door is open, you do your thing. Best
art is we know the dude picks up in the morning, so
ou go in when he's holding the bundle. It's a lock."

A shotgun appeared in the doorway, caught in the
lare of Kirkpatrick's flashlight, then the edge of a face.
evander was checking the scene, his caution a matter
f habit though he had met with Kirkpatrick only a
ew days before. "Whyn't you put up that light, moth-
rfucker? Yo blindin' me."

From behind, Moodrow and Tilley could see Kirk-
atrick's shadow against the circle of light at the end
f the corridor. Could see him slowly raise his .38 un-
il the barrel pointed at the ceiling. "I told ya last
ime," he said. "Get a fuckin' lantern down here.
What're you so scared about, anyway? Everybody loves
ou."

Without missing a beat, Kirkpatrick fired a round
nto the ceiling. The crack of his pistol, incredibly loud
n the confined space, was instantly obliterated by the
oar of the shotgun and his body flew backwards even
s it received a second and a third blast.

The silence that followed was louder than the explo-
ions. Kirkpatrick was lying in a pool of blood, his
veapon clutched in his hand. The flashlight had rolled
gainst the far wall, but still pointed directly at the
ow-empty doorway. A miracle for which, right then
nd there, Tilley thanked whatever gods were above

him. Now they could watch that doorway without re
vealing their position. Or even their existence.

Unfortunately, Moodrow erased that tactical advan
tage as soon as the echo of Levander Greenwood's
shotgun died away. "Hey, fuckhead," he screamed. "
heard you're lookin' for me."

"Who's that? Who's that?"

Tilley expected a cloud of buckshot, but the door
way remained empty. Moodrow's face, across the cor
ridor, was a blank shadow, but he could fee
Moodrow's satisfied smile, could hear it in his voice.

"It's Moodrow," he said cheerfully.

"I'm gon' kill you, motherfucker." He may have
meant it as a scream of defiance, but his voice wa
filled with hopelessness.

"There's no way out, Levander. You gotta give it up
Even a fucking moron could figure that out. Even
stoned-out freak like you." He hesitated for a moment
then went on. "Oh, by the way, Rose says to give yo
her best. Likewise from Jeanette and Lee. Rose say
she's sorry she won't be hearin' from you no more, bu
what with all the cops you killed, you won't see day
light 'till you're around ten thousand years old."

"You cocksucker. I'll kill you. I swear I'll kill you."

"So who's stopping you?" Moodrow bellowed th
words and the question hung in the air. "You don'
think you're gonna get another chance, do ya? This i
Custer's Last Stand for Levander Greenwood. Las
stand. Come on out and say goodbye."

Nothing. Not a sound. Tilley expected a suicida
plunge. That "all right, you dirty copper" blaze o
movieland glory. But Levander Greenwood's only re
sponse was to relight his pipe, to take one more sho
at passing ecstasy.

"What if I give myself up?" The question, totall
unexpected, rattled in the empty space. "You gonn
get me a lawyer?"

"Anything you want, Levander. You just come o

out with your hands on your head. After we get the cuffs on, we'll talk about it."

"You gon' kill me, pig. Ah know what you gon' do."

Then silence again. Dead silence. Moodrow, smiling over at his partner, knelt and took a backup gun from an ankle holster, a 9mm automatic with a fifteen shot magazine.

"Let's see if we can't motivate the man," he said cheerfully. He dropped his .38 back into its holster, transferred the automatic to his right hand, then pumped fifteen shots, as fast as he could pull the trigger, into Levander Greenwood's small, concrete hole. The rounds pinged back and forth like the beeps of a berserk computer, flashing back down the corridor. Tilley pressed himself against the wall, but Moodrow kept Levander's doorway in view at all times. Even as he slammed another clip into the 9mm and smiled over at his partner.

"Hey, Levander," he yelled. "You wanna talk about it some more? You wanna open negotiations again?"

Dead silence. The one thing Moodrow didn't expect. At the very least, Greenwood should have returned fire. Should have tried to drive them back.

"What's the matter, Kubla? That's what they call you, right? Kubla Khan? The Emperor?" He paused briefly, then continued to push, praying for a reaction. "The Emperor of Filth. King of the Sewers." Still no response.

"Maybe you hit him," Tilley said. "Maybe you got lucky."

Moodrow's face showed no emotion whatsoever. "I'm going down the corridor." He tossed the automatic to his partner. "Keep it trained on the doorway. You see any movement, open up. Don't let him come out with that shotgun."

Moodrow was gone before Tilley could protest, flattened against the wall, his .38 held straight out before him. Tilley knew, if he'd been in charge, he would have opted to wait for backup. The idea never occurred to Stanley Moodrow.

The stalk went slowly, Moodrow careful not to make any noise by sliding his feet. He was listening intently. Listening for a shell jacked into the firing chamber of a shotgun. A hit on a crack pipe sucked into an addict's lungs. The desperate breathing of a badly wounded man. He heard nothing and he turned into the open doorway with the full expectation of sudden death.

With a sigh, he let his weapon fall to his side and called his partner down the corridor. Tilley walked into the room, expecting to find Levander dead. What he found was a ventilation grating in the ceiling. It led directly to the street and Levander had easily pushed it aside before making his escape.

31

Levander Greenwood emerged into the rank humidity
of a New York August night like an earth dwelling
animal flushed from its den into an alien world beyond
all hope of safety. If he had stopped to think, he might
have asked himself why he had so patiently chiseled
his way through the concrete which had once an-
chored the subway ventilation grate to the sidewalk
on the north side of Houston Street. What point in
creating an escape route for a man whose only hope of
refuge lay within?

But Levander Greenwood did not stop to think.

Levander Greenwood ran across the gray pavement
of a children's playground to 1st Street and then down
an alleyway alongside a tire repair shop to the partitioned strips of land behind the tenements fronting 1st
and 2nd Streets.

New Yorkers like to call these patches of dirt "gardens" and, perhaps, in the money neighborhoods, a
network of vines and shrubs might create that impression in a patch of earth which receives less direct sunlight than the floor of a cave. But in poorer
neighborhoods the backyards become the dumping
grounds for any piece of refuse too big to be carted
away by the Department of Sanitation in the course of
its ordinary rounds. Boxsprings and mattresses; refrig-
erators and stoves; burnt, threadbare rugs; legless
chairs. The smaller stuff follows . . . from tenants too

lazy to carry a plastic bag down a flight of stairs. And the smells follow that, especially on hot nights.

But while the rest of us, sitting behind air conditioners, pull away in disgust, Levander Greenwood smelled only the smell of his own burrow. He sat in a damp puddle on a burnt-out mattress, lost within the shadows, and went to his pipe. The smoke ripped into his throat, tore at inflamed flesh, but the pain was instantly forgotten as Levander Greenwood became "well."

He wasn't high, wasn't anywhere near the astonishing ecstasy that had characterized his first use of crack; he had never known pleasure at that level, hadn't even dreamed that such pleasure could exist. All he knew, fifteen minutes after that first time, when he began to panic, was that he would continue to seek it as long as he remained alive and free.

Sitting in the darkness, oblivious to small lifeforms crawling in the slime of the backyard, to rats and roaches, he tried to concentrate on a single idea—escape.

They would be after him.

They would be after him.

They would be after him.

He had to fix it in his mind so that he could make a plan. So the mighty Kubla Khan, who used to be, would rise and keep Levander Greenwood alive for a little while longer. *They* would be coming.

Then he fixed it more exactly: *Moodrow* would be coming. That was perfect. Moodrow would come. And whoever was with him.

But if Moodrow had the whole precinct out, then Houston Street would have been flooded with cops. And Kirkpatrick would not have fired his pistol until he was sure of his target. They would have announced their overwhelming presence and, secure in their majesty, settled down to wait for him to show enough flesh for a clean shot.

Then Levander remembered the automatic going off and the slugs bouncing from wall to wall and pulling himself up onto the street before he was hit. There was no question now. They would never let him surrender. They were going to kill him.

He reminded himself to say it right. Not to forget. *Moodrow* would be coming to kill him. Just as he'd come all along. Just as he'd taken Rose and hid the babies away. Moodrow liked to come alone. Levander knew Stanley Moodrow. The one who killed Stanley Moodrow would have a rep forever.

Levander began to move east, toward First Avenue, pushing through the garbage as quickly as possible. The high was already beginning to wear away, but he instinctively headed deeper into the Lower East Side with its faceless housing projects, its derelict tenements. He had to think of something. He had to have a plan. *Moodrow* was out to get him. He heard sirens far away, but there were always sirens at night. No reason to believe the sirens were coming for him. No reason. Just keep moving.

And think. Think.

Suddenly Rose, smiling kindly, floated up in front of him, straddling a wooden fence between two "gardens." He stood before her defiantly, hands on his hips.

"Bitch, I done everything for y'all. I took yo white ass off the street when yo was makin' enough money to keep me fresh *every* minute. I took y'all and named you mah woman alone. I din't *never* make you give the pussy to no other man and my homeboys was beggin'. They woulda paid anythin' I axed for the pussy and I turned 'em away. All of 'em." He stared up at her unchanging face. She was wearing a long blue dress and he could see her body through it. There were no bruises. No white bandage covering a deep wound. She was the perfect child-woman he had met in the bus station long ago. She was so beautiful, like that first hit of crack. "Why you fuckin' me so bad, Rose?" He began to cry. He couldn't help it. "Why you hurtin' me, Rosie?"

She turned to him and smiled, shaking her head sympathetically. "But you're a little nigger boy, Levander. Why can't you remember that? It's such a simple thing and you always forget."

He reached up for her and heard a deep continuous rumble from the other side of the fence. A yard dog was banging hard into the lower boards and growling, not trying to frighten him, but like a fighting dog that's been in the pit. Then Rose was gone and he knew Rose was never real. This was so much easier. He caressed the Mossberg .12 gauge which swung from a thong between his right arm and his side. The stock was gone and the barrel protruded a bare three inches. Levander slid down to sit, cross-legged, on the dirt.

"Hey, Fido, you fucker, Ah gots ta warn y'all. Ah bites back." He lit the pipe and sucked deeply. The dog pawed frantically at the soft earth, its nose appearing under the fence. "Ain't you a hard workin' little mutt?" Levander patted the dog on the nose and the infuriated animal strained to open its mouth far enough to bite.

"Thass right, puppie. Les' see? What ah'm gon' call you?" He dropped to his knees and pushed his face to within inches of the dog's. "Ah calls y'all Ol' Yeller. Yeah. Ah be's like that kid and you tryin' ta save me from the bear. You fightin' hard cause you loves me, but the bear too big for y'all." He rocked back on his heels and offered the shotgun barrel to the dog who pushed up through the fence, tearing away a piece of the slat, and took it in his mouth.

The roar of the shotgun filled the night and Levander, the panic rising up in a sudden, unexpected flurry, recalled the central proposition: *Moodrow* is after me. *Moodrow is coming.*

He moved north, up an alleyway and across 2nd Street to a fence of straight steel rods. The sign, above the locked gate, proclaimed *The Marble Cemetery* and another plaque announced this tiny plot as the final resting place of two eighteenth century mayors of New York City. Levander knew only that it was dark in comparison with the streetlights that penetrated the shadows where he stood. The shotgun blast would have them coming soon. There might be hundreds, like after he beat up Marlee. He had waited then, waited for Rose and she had come. Stupidly. Without looking. Even Moodrow had rushed up to the apartment. So stupid. After he killed Moodrow, his rep would be made forever.

When the first grave opened, he thought it was meant for him. He thought he should go down into it, but his father sauntered forth, swaggering, dressed in his motorman's uniform. "How you been, Levander? You been a good boy to your momma?"

Instead of answering, Levander sat on a gravestone and filled his pipe. He had enough crack to last forever if forever didn't outlast the night.

"Poppa, you jus' a jive muthafucka. Go off dyin' and leave us on the welfare. Why I wanna listen to you?"

"Can't help dyin', Levander. Everybody gotta die. Ain't you gonna die tonight?"

Levander squeezed the shotgun under his arm. Didn't matter if his daddy was ten feet tall. Twenty feet tall. Shit, he could probably take an elephant. Why not? They were all afraid of him. When he went into the bars, they stopped talking. When he bought crack, there was never a problem with the count. They were always so happy when he paid them; when he didn't kill them.

He sucked on the pipe, lighting up again and again. He hadn't been asleep in a long time.

"You fucked yourself up with Rose." His poppa's voice was stern. "You was always a stupid boy."

Levander smiled, then broke into laughter. "Ah'm well, now, Daddy." He put the pipe back into his pocket and leaned against the cool stone. "Ah'm real well. Feel nothin' but fine."

"Then where you gonna go, boy? Cause Moodrow's comin' for you. Moodrow's comin' soon and you just gonna be lyin' here like a damn fool."

Levander stood up and held the shotgun. He wanted to tell his father about the power of the weapon. Of the strength it gave him. Of bodies flying through the air like they were hit by the breath of God, like crack breathing down from God into your lungs.

"Ah'm goin' home, Daddy."

"Ain't no home for you, Levander. The man's gonna kill you tonight."

The graves began to open. All of them. They were coming for him. The dead ones. He began to move again. Through the backyards, fighting his away over the heaps of trash. Faster and faster. Panic closing in behind him. He needed to smoke again, but they were too close now. There were sirens everywhere. He could hear sirens piercing the wet night air.

"My mama would let me in." He spoke to no one, not even to the dead; not even aware that he was speaking aloud. "I know my mama would let me in." He tripped and fell heavily, jamming his hip into something hard and sharp. He had to get off the street, but his momma's apartment was far away. Too far. Too many cops. *Moodrow* was after him. The sirens were closer and closer. The sirens were screaming at him.

Think. Think.

He sucked on the pipe, sucked until he was straight, until his thoughts went in a straight line. There was a place to go. He remembered it now. And it was *his* place; his *rightful* place. The bitch had thrown him out. The bitch had gone to judges and lawyers to keep him away. To keep *him* away? He laughed out loud.

"Kubla Khan don't scare so easy. Kubla Khan returns and take what he want." He could see Rose in front of his eyes. Naked. Frightened. That was the place. It was close by and he could get well there. Let Moodrow look for him in the streets. He would be safe in *his* place. Maybe Rose would be there. Maybe Moodrow had brought her back. Maybe Moodrow had brought his babies back. He looked for his father. He wanted to tell his father that he'd be safe now. If Rose wasn't there, he'd wait for her. He had vials and vials of crack. His pockets were stuffed with crack. He'd simply wait until Moodrow sent her home.

He began to go faster. Across to Avenue A and then north through the alleyways and over the fences, running close to the schoolyard walls; finding a fire escape alongside an ancient tenement; pulling himself up into the shadows. He felt his strength returning and he checked the windows as he passed, hoping one of Rose's neighbors would pull the shade aside to see who was climbing past. But none were so stupid and he stepped onto the roof and looked out over the streets.

They were empty. The sirens were gone; not even an ambulance or a fire truck. Where where *they?* The police should be everywhere. He had imagined the final scene again and again as he lay in his subway cave and pulled deeply on his pipe. An army of cops closing off the streets. A hurricane of bullets so loud it closed off your mind, then closed off your life. Where were *they?*

The door to the stairwell hung open. The steps were noisy, broken, littered with junk. Levander felt the Mossberg against his side, as familiar as a third arm. He held it out in front of him, pointed it at the closed, blank doors.

"Come on out, muthafuckas. Ah'm goin' home to see mah lady. Yeah. Thass right, muthafuckas. She gon' do me the way I like it, tonight. Do anything I say."

The doors remained closed and no sounds came from behind them, not even a television or a radio. Levander laughed. They had good reason to be afraid of him. One time he had come to see Rose and some stupid white boy had stopped him on the stairs, telling Kubla Khan, "You have to leave her alone."

"The only thing I got to do is cut up yo white face, honkey asshole."

But the boy had disappeared before the knife came out, running for his telephone, for his locks and bars. And Levander had gone in to see Rose, as he did now, pushing open the unlocked door and stepping into the darkened apartment.

As he closed the door, Levander felt safety overwhelm him despite the black room. Every window shade had been drawn, the curtains pulled closed. Even the streetlight, which hung close to the front windows, was out, vandalized by predators, like Levander Greenwood, who find comfort in darkness.

Carefully, Levander locked the door behind him and stumbled to the couch in the center of the living room. For the first time, he slid the .12 gauge off his shoulder and laid it gently at his feet, remembering, vaguely, that there was a round in the chamber.

"Ready to go, baby," he said aloud. "Ready and waitin'." Now he could smoke to his heart's content. Smoke till he was better than "well." The locked door would give him time. No surprises now. He lit the pipe once, then again, then again, never considering that there might be someone already in the apartment, someone sitting patiently in a chair fifteen feet away, waiting to be recognized.

When he finally noticed the figure, he thought it was Rose. Another hallucination sent to test his resolve, but it stubbornly refused to disappear.

"You must be crazy comin' back here. This the worses place you could go, Rosie."

"I ain't Rosie."

The figure flicked on a lamp and pulled the light

closer until it bathed both her face and the gun she
carried.

"Marlee?" Levander tried to take it in, noting the
swollen face, the bandages. "What you doin' here? This
Rosie's house." He hoped she would disappear, her and
the revolver she held in her hand; disappear like his
father on the grave and Rosie on the fence.

"I come to pick up some clothes for the kids," Marlee said evenly. "You put Rose in the hospital."

"And don't she deserve it?" Levander felt his anger
rising again. "I done *everything* for that bitch. I took
that bitch off the street when she was turnin' more
tricks than any whore in my stable." He stopped suddenly and lit his pipe. Marlee couldn't be real. It didn't
make any sense. "If you gettin' clothes for the babies,
how come you sittin' in the dark? You ain't gon' find
no clothes in the dark."

"Moodrow said you'd be coming. First he called
mama, to warn her that you were loose, and when she
told him where I was, he phoned me. He said you'd
probably be coming here. He gave me the gun, too,
after I came back from the hospital. He told me to kill
you right away. Don't hesitate."

Levander laughed again. "Well, he right about somethin', Marlee. I gotta say the man ain't no total fool."

The gun never wavered. It was compact, with a
thick, black barrel; a hole as big as Levander's pipe, big
enough to kill. "I finally got it right in my mind, Levander. I understand it, now."

Levander went for his pipe, pouring out the small
pellets of crack cocaine, sucking greedily. "What you
figure out, Marlee? You just a nigger bitch sellin' to-
kens down in some hole. What you figure out?"

"I realized that it wasn't anybody's fault, Levander."
Her voice was strong, filled with conviction, but de-
void of triumph. "For a long time, I wanted to blame
it on somebody. Mama tried so hard. She worked at it
everyday until it was ready to eat up her life. I thought

it couldn't be all for nothing. But it was. It was for nothing. Mama's life. My life. Rosie's. All for nothing. There was never a chance for us or for you, Levander. But I'm not gonna let you hurt those children anymore."

Levander put the pipe down. Marlee was floating slightly above the chair and the .12 gauge was resting at his feet. "Mama know you here, don't she? You kill me, she gon' know you done it. Think she forgive you? She be goin' to the church a long time before she forget you killed her baby boy. She be in her grave before she forget."

"Mama don't care about you no more, Levander." Marlee hesitated, but did not look away. "And maybe it don't matter about Mama, anyway. Those babies are the only chance for this family. How can they grow up with you alive? You hurt them so bad they might never get it right in their minds. You tried to kill their mother. There ain't no control for you."

Levander, his mind wide open, felt Marlee's finger tighten on the trigger. He could go for the .12 gauge, but she'd get off one or two shots. If only he hadn't put it down. If he had it there as his third arm it would be so much faster. Suddenly he burst out laughing and the laughter froze Marlee. "Shit, Marlee, you ain't sposed ta kill me. That's Moodrow's job. If he callin' you on the phone, he mus' be on the way over. Les' jus' be waitin' a little bit. See if the man come by. If he do it, then Mama don't have nothin' ta say. Y'understand what ah'm tellin' ya, girl?"

"Finally making sense, Levander?" The voice came from behind him. From the doorway to the bedroom. It was unmistakable. Moodrow had come. Levander felt the steel of Moodrow's pistol against the back of his neck, the shotgun taken away. His strength taken away. He knew, at that moment, that he was going to die, but it didn't bother him, just a passing thought while a greater need overcame him. He took out his pipe and began to smoke.

"How you get here?" he finally asked.

"Through the fire escape. Just like you," Moodrow replied, stepping carefully away. "Say, Marlee, you think you could let my partner in through the front door. Knock three times before you unlock it." Marlee started to move, but Moodrow stretched out one hand. "And give me the gun, Marlee. Let's not have any accidents."

When Tilley stepped through the door, weapon in hand, he stared at Levander unbelievingly. Waiting outside, he had imagined some final combat. Fists. Guns. This was the man who had tried to kill Rose. Who had made her life a hell for years. Who'd terrorized the Lower East Side. But the man reeked of vermin, of lice and weeks away from soap and water. His weight couldn't be more than a hundred and fifty pounds. Under any other circumstances, he would be pitiful. Without asking, Tilley moved in, cuffed Levander's wrists behind his back and tossed him for a backup weapon. He found a gravity knife and threw it across the room.

"Let's just be a little cool," Moodrow said. He quickly retrieved the knife, wiping it free of prints while Tilley watched Greenwood. "You're gonna kill him," Tilley said to Moodrow. It was a statement, not a question.

"I'll let Marlee do it. How 'bout it, Marlee? You want to put him away?"

Marlee spoke very quietly. "If I could have done it, it would already be done. All I could do was hold him for you. Like you asked." She looked him in the eye. "It sounds so easy when you imagine it. But it's not like that. It's not like in the movies. Not when someone's actually there breathing."

"There's people can do it between courses at a wedding," Moodrow said flatly, then turned to his partner.

"And you, Jimmy? You ready to chill him? Walk u₁
and pull the trigger? You can use Marlee's gun. We'l
dump it later."

Tilley stepped closer, his hand reaching for the re
volver Moodrow held out to him. He stared at it; rolled
the cylinder in his palm. It was an ancient .44, a close
range weapon meant to stop anything smaller than
rhinoceros. Coming out, the slug would leave an exi
wound the size of a softball.

Then Levander Greenwood spoke for the first time
since Tilley had come in. "Gimme mah pipe, man,"
he whined. "I need my pipe. I gotta smoke. I gotta ge
well. Please." His voice held a note of terror, of over
whelming fear. He was coming down. "Then shoot me
Ah ain't afraid to die. I took plenty with me. Get m
well or shoot me. That's fair, ain't it?"

Tilley handed the gun back to his partner. He coul
feel his breath whooshing out as he admitted that h
couldn't do it. Couldn't pull the trigger despite the ha
tred. Despite the persistent image of Rose in her hos
pital bed. "I guess it's up to you," he finally said.

Instead of answering, Moodrow went to the phon
and quickly punched out a number.

"Dominick Favara," he said after a minute. Then
"Tell him it's a man with a gift. An old acquaintance.'
He listened intently. "I'll wait. He's gonna want t
hear this, but it's for his ears only. And for whoeve
has the phone tapped."

In the silence that followed, Greenwood began t
beg again. "Please. Please, man. You don't got to be
leavin' me like this. I ain't gon' be no problem for y'all
Yo, please."

All three ignored him until he tried to rise, to figh
the cuffs. Then Tilley stepped forward and hit him in
the face with a straight right hand, driving him dow
to the floor where he continued to babble.

"This man is a slave," Tilley, who'd seen hundred

of heroin addicts, said in wonder. "He's an absolute fucking slave."

"Dominick," Moodrow said, "you know who this is? It's your old friend from Blue Thunder. Don't say the name. I got your man for you. Not the little one. The big one." He listened for a moment, then laughed. "You wanna meet up with him, huh? Well there's two conditions. He's gotta be found when you're through. Dump him somewhere close, but not where you pick him up. Any problems?" He laughed again. "I didn't think so. You ready to go right away? I mean *now*, Dominick. Good. We'll be out of here in ten minutes. We don't know who else is listening. Let's not have anybody beat us to it."

He gave Favara the address, hung up and began to tie Levander, hand and foot, with the cords from the drapes. Levander continued to beg and Moodrow continued to ignore him, removing the cuffs as soon as he was sure Greenwood could not escape. Finally, he turned to Marlee and said, "You understand what's gonna happen?"

"Yes," she answered. Her voice was strong.

"One of those people who kill before breakfast is gonna come over here and take care of your brother. That okay with you?"

"Yes."

"The body's not gonna be found here, so it doesn't matter if anybody saw you come in. I'll get rid of the gun for you."

"I won't need it anymore."

"And you, Jim Tilley? What about you?"

"I wish I had the guts to do it myself."

Suddenly, Moodrow stepped forward and took his partner by the shirt. "This isn't about revenge. This is about the 7th Precinct and Allen Epstein and Internal Affairs and the people who live on the Lower East Side." He pointed to Greenwood. "The man's already paranoid. In an hour he'll be a jibbering idiot. He'll finger the whole precinct just to get ten minutes attention. If he turns up dead in a vacant lot, the brass'll be happy for weeks. They'll be suspicious about Kirkpatrick, but ya know what they'll do? They'll give him a fucking inspector's funeral and bury the whole thing. Only I.A.D. busts for corruption. The big brass never do it and with Kirkpatrick dead, they have that much more reason to forget about it. I was hoping Marlee would take care of the situation, but she didn't. Now it's up to us."

Tilley pulled away abruptly, stepping back and out of Moodrow's grasp. "What's the difference between this and doing it yourself? Why don't you pull the trigger?"

"Because I don't want to explain it. I don't want to explain about Kirkpatrick in that tunnel. I don't wanna try to put a throwaway piece in a dead man's hand. I don't want to explain why I didn't call for backup as soon as Kirkpatrick went down. I don't want two hundred headhunters in my fucking precinct."

"But there's another reason, Stanley. You can't bullshit me anymore." His eyes bore into Moodrow's. "You can't pull the trigger, either. You can't do it. You're not a killer."

Moodrow stared at his partner for a moment, then smiled. "Let's get the fuck out of here. Before the pros arrive."

32

In a way, it went exactly as planned. When Levander Greenwood's body showed up in a vacant lot on 6th Street, a neat hole behind his left ear, it was assumed that person or persons unknown had exacted the ultimate penalty for his past transgressions. True, the task force (and, naturally, Moodrow and Tilley) had failed to find him, to bring him to justice. But he was through menacing the citizens of the Lower East Side. And he would never kill another cop. Levander Greenwood was dead.

Kirkpatrick, on the other hand, wasn't found for nearly a week. A transit worker, sent to investigate the open ventilation grating on Houston Street, had merely kicked it back into place and put it on the welding schedule. It took an anonymous tip from Jim Tilley to bring Kirkpatrick's body to light and, as that tip didn't come into the 7th until a week after the shooting, there was no one to remember seeing him in the company of two other men when he stepped off the platform.

There was, of course, a good deal of speculation about what Kirkpatrick was doing in an abandoned subway corridor. A careful search of the small room had turned up proof that Levander Greenwood had been living there and, for a short time, there was talk of denying Paul Kirkpatrick his death benefits pending a more complete investigation.

But the threat of a civil action by lawyers from the Detective's Benevolent Association put an end to that

kind of talk and Kirkpatrick's death was marked "line
of duty." As per Stanley Moodrow's prediction, he was
given the full inspector's funeral accorded to every
member of the force who dies while performing his
job. He was an official hero.

At almost the same time Kirkpatrick's body was
"discovered" and brought to the surface, Rose Carillo
hobbled out of St. Vincent's Hospital. She gathered her
children together and took them home to her apartment on the Lower East Side. Tilley, on the few nights
he spent uptown, didn't mistake the relieved looks on
his neighbors' faces once the children were gone.
Though no one actually approached him, he found
himself avoiding the people he'd grown up with as if
they were strangers. It was obviously time to move on.
It was all he thought about as he ran along the Drive
in the mornings. He was past this place and these people.

Moodrow kept him busy, introducing him to the
various players on the Lower East Side, players on either side of the law. Along with Moodrow, he took to
volunteering at a small boxing gym in a Boys Club on
Houston Street. He found that if he pulled the head-
gear low enough and kept his left hand close to his
head, the cut wouldn't open. The kids, all black or
Puerto Rican, recognized his ability and accepted him
easily, just as the whites on the Lower East Side accepted Rose and her children.

Then the roof fell in on Moodrow and the 7th Precinct. At some point, the Mayor and his advisors had
made a simple decision. The homeless were messing
up Manhattan below 96th Street. They were much too
visible, much too available to television crews looking
for filler on slow news days and, therefore, the city
would eliminate the welfare hotels, most of them in
midtown Manhattan. Then the Port Authority suddenly decided that the bus terminal, where hundreds
of people slept every night, would close at one in the

morning. Grand Central and Penn Station would follow as soon as there were shelters established to house the homeless who slept there. And the small parks would be subject to a curfew. No more overnight guests.

Thus Tompkins Square Park, occupying two square blocks of a rapidly gentrifying section of the Lower East Side, was to be closed every night and the NYPD was sent out to enforce the edict. They were met by hundreds of people—artists and derelicts; Hare Krishnas; skinheads and punks; even a few liberal junior executives.

Later, the cops claimed they were provoked. They claimed they were pelted with bottles and rocks while the civilians claimed the cops simply went berserk. The bits and pieces captured on videotape tended to support the civilians and established, without a doubt, that a number of cops had covered their nametags and the numbers on their shields. Which, the reporters were quick to point out, proved that the cops intended to violate regulations before the riot began.

Allen Epstein was not in charge of the operation. The mobile command station was set up by a deputy chief, a hairbag named Charles Doyle, who knew nothing of the Lower East Side. He did not set up in a spot that afforded him a clear view of the troops he was expected to command. But he commanded them, anyway, along with an inspector, John McGuire; commanded with a heavy hand, calling in three hundred extra cops (all from other precincts) and ordering them to get the situation under control, which they did by clubbing anyone within five blocks of the park.

There was plenty of blood and the media had a field day. Epstein, who was against a curfew in the park and who *knew* he could have avoided a confrontation, was advised to hand in his retirement papers within the week. He did as he was told, then submitted to an enormous farewell party. Long retired cops showed up, along with cops from other precincts who'd once worked in the 7th. Allen Epstein was a stand-up commander. If you screwed him he would find some way to get you, but he would never throw you to the department wolves. He would never sacrifice his men.

As Moodrow had predicted, Captain Ruiz took over. The department felt that he would have more rapport with the Hispanics (almost none of whom were in Tompkins Square Park on the night of the riot), than the others who coveted the job. Initially, Ruiz and Moodrow ignored one another. Moodrow and Tilley made two decent busts, one for second degree murder which stuck and the other for assault with a deadly weapon (a machete) which was plea bargained down to simple assault on the grounds that the perp, though he'd given it his best effort, had not actually managed to strike his quicker adversary. But the arrests were a sham, anyway. Moodrow was teaching his partner the neighborhood, teaching him to separate the merely tough (a mandatory condition for anyone coming up on the Lower East Side) from the truly predatory. The tough ones would help you, if you could present yourself to them as an equal. They hated the criminals as much as Tilley, though they understood crime better. And they hated the gung-ho cops who, out of ignorance, treated every poor New Yorker as a criminal.

But Captain Ruiz, again as Moodrow had predicted, had no place for an uncontrollable force of nature in his precinct. He called Moodrow into his office a month after taking over and declared him the new community affairs officer for the 7th Precinct. He even wanted to throw a press conference. Now Moodrow would go to the public schools and lecture the students on the evils of drugs. He would also attend meetings of the Rotary Club and the Lions Club and the Elks Club whenever their respective memberships needed reassurance.

Moodrow and Tilley were together when Ruiz called

Moodrow into the house and, with a satisfied smirk, gave him the bad news. Moodrow nodded, his face a blank, and requested, in his softest voice, that Ruiz wipe the smile off his face (which Ruiz did, immediately), then announced his retirement. Moodrow had seen it coming, of course, but still put on twenty years as he passed the already filled-out paperwork across Ruiz's desk.

Afterwards, Moodrow and Tilley had a hell of a drunk. For two days they walked around the Lower East Side, glaring at anyone who appeared even slightly out of place. They must have looked especially fierce, because no one cared to challenge them. But on the third day, when Tilley woke up on Moodrow's couch and heard Gretchen giggling in the bedroom, he knew it was time to go home. Moodrow was clearly able to take care of himself and had already had calls from two New York criminal lawyers who wanted him to look into the affairs of their clients. Now it was Tilley's turn.

He walked the few blocks to Rose Carillo's tenement. The kids were visiting their grandmother and he found her alone, her wounds, after a month, nearly healed. Still a bit drunk and certainly hungover, he begged her to marry him. She was standing at the sink in a pair of loose jeans and a blue halter that scooped to the tops of her breasts. For a moment, she had nothing to say, then she turned back to the dishes.

"I guess I don't have to give you the lecture about the white couple with the black children," she said.

"Fuck the racists. And fuck the goddamn dishes. Turn around and look at me."

"If I do, that's the end of the small talk. We're gonna be in bed before you can say, 'I do.'"

Tilley put his hand on her shoulder and turned her toward him. "I'm serious, Rose. I want to talk about it. To get it out in the open."

But she was right. She slid into his arms and his

hands ran down her back and over the globes of her ass before he could form a coherent sentence. Five minutes later, soaked in sweat, they writhed on her bed. Jim Tilley hasn't left it since.